D0191057

The
HELLION

OTHER TITLES BY CHRISTI CALDWELL

Sinful Brides

The Rogue's Wager
The Scoundrel's Honor
The Lady's Guard
The Heiress's Deception

The Brethren

The Spy Who Seduced Her

The Heart of a Scandal

In Need of a Knight
Schooling the Duke

The Theodosia Sword

Only for His Lady
Only for Her Honor
Only for Their Love

The Heart of a Duke

In Need of a Duke
For Love of the Duke
More Than a Duke
The Love of a Rogue
Loved by a Duke
To Love a Lord
The Heart of a Scoundrel
To Wed His Christmas Lady

To Trust a Rogue
The Lure of a Rake
To Woo a Widow
To Redeem a Rake
One Winter with a Baron
To Enchant a Wicked Duke
Beguiled by a Baron

Lords of Honor

Seduced by a Lady's Heart
Captivated by a Lady's Charm
Rescued by a Lady's Love
Tempted by a Lady's Smile

Scandalous Seasons

Forever Betrothed, Never the Bride
Never Courted, Suddenly Wed
Always Proper, Suddenly Scandalous
Always a Rogue, Forever Her Love
A Marquess for Christmas
Once a Wallflower, at Last His Love

Danby

A Season of Hope
Winning a Lady's Heart

Brethren of the Lords

My Lady of Deception

Nonfiction Works

Uninterrupted Joy: A Memoir

The HELLION

CHRISTI CALDWELL

WITHDRAWN

Montlake Romance

This is a work of fiction. Names, characters, organizations, places, events, and incidents are either products of the author's imagination or are used fictitiously. Any resemblance to actual persons, living or dead, or actual events is purely coincidental.

Text copyright © 2018 by Christi Caldwell
All rights reserved.

No part of this book may be reproduced, or stored in a retrieval system, or transmitted in any form or by any means, electronic, mechanical, photocopying, recording, or otherwise, without express written permission of the publisher.

Published by Montlake Romance, Seattle

www.apub.com

Amazon, the Amazon logo, and Montlake Romance are trademarks of Amazon.com, Inc., or its affiliates.

ISBN-13: 9781503935228
ISBN-10: 1503935221

Cover design by Michael Rehder

Cover illustration by Chris Cocozza

Printed in the United States of America

To Daddy ("Papa"):
Every moment of my life, you encouraged my dreams:
from when I decided at ten years old that I would be
the first female umpire in the MLB to when I began
taking voice lessons for the dreams I had of Broadway.
And when I was all grown up and dreamed of being an
author, you cheered me on then, too.
Thank you for believing in me—and more, encouraging
me—even when there were times I found it impossible
to believe in myself.
Cleopatra's story is for you!

Chapter 1

St. Giles, London
Early Spring 1825

Adair Thorne was destined to be destroyed by fire.

Orphaned more than two decades earlier by a blaze that consumed his father's bakery, his parents, and his sister, Adair now stood at the burned ashes of his own establishment.

Numb. Frozen. Unmoving.

Gone. It was all gone.

The conflagration had only just recently been tamed by the fire brigade; the hiss of those fresh embers still crackled in an eerie stillness of St. Giles. Servants, guards, serving girls, and the men and women who called this place home hovered on the cobblestones, silent but for a soft weeping among the women.

Adair stared blankly ahead at the metal gargoyles, still fiercely proud and intact, at the scorched stone steps of the Hell and Sin Club.

It was gone. The kitchens. The guest suites. The gaming hell floors. All but the private offices and suites kept by the men and women who lived here.

Agony wadded in his throat, choking at him, until a primitive, desperate moan better suited for a wounded animal filtered past his lips. It blurred and blended with the quiet weeping at his back.

". . . several with bad burns . . . a miracle none were killed . . ."

Yes, everyone had safely evacuated. And despite the hell of all they'd lost this night, some of the tension eased in Adair's chest. Human lives had been spared.

It is just everything else you lost—everything.

"They'll never be able to save it . . ."

Those casual utterances from two members of the fire brigade who'd wrestled the blaze under control brought Adair back from the edge of confusion, horror, and despair.

He blinked slowly. Yes. They had been fortunate. Not a soul had perished in that fiery blaze, and yet—Adair curled his soot-stained fingers into tight fists—there was still an ungrateful fury. A longing to toss his head back and rail at the world for all that had been lost this day.

He dimly registered his brother of the street Ryker drawing up beside him. Numb, Adair glanced over.

His cheeks ashen, the street-hardened head proprietor had a haunted glitter in his eyes. "Come," Ryker said. "We can't do anything standing here. We have to find a place for our displaced workers and . . ."

His voice droned on and on in Adair's clogged mind. Of course, that was why Ryker had always been the leader of their gang in St. Giles. He'd commanded and taken control. He'd harnessed his blinding rage and hatred of the world around them and dictated the terms of survival against their foes.

Ryker settled a hand on his shoulder. "Come."

"Oi'm not leaving," Adair snapped, wrenching away. "Ya'd have us walk away? Not me. This club means something to me."

His brother's nostrils flared.

Like the head guard he'd been, rushing to break up fights in the now burning club, Niall sprinted over. His recent marriage to Lady Diana, a duke's daughter, hadn't managed to erase that indelible part of who he'd always been. "Enough," he barked, quickly putting himself between Ryker and Adair.

"Oi'm not leaving," Adair repeated, and resolutely planted himself on the pavement.

Their other brother of the street, Calum—calm by nature, even when presented with fire—abandoned the staff he'd been speaking to and joined them. "What is it?"

How is he so damned calm? "This one"—Adair jerked his chin at Ryker—"wants to leave." While their dreams burned down around them.

"Nothing can come of us watching . . . this," Ryker countered, motioning to the blaze.

Adair lifted frantic eyes up to the cracked and shattered windows. Before any of his siblings could speak, the words rasped from Adair's throat. "This place is our very existence." This was the dream that had sustained them when they'd not allowed themselves that whimsy. "It got us through freezing winters, vicious knife fights, and ruthless beatings by Mac Diggory, and now you'd have us simply walk away?" There was a frantic timbre to his voice that hadn't been there since he was a boy, watching his birth family and their bakery burn down in a similar conflagration.

The fight seemed to go out of the trio . . . just as it always did with mention of their former gang leader.

Mac Diggory. Dead these two years now, he lived on still in their minds and also in the actions of the men and women who'd sworn their fealty to that Devil . . . and who'd taken on the cause of revenge after Adair, Ryker, Calum, and Niall's sister, Helena, had ended the bastard. It hadn't mattered that a place beside Satan in the flames of hell was too good for that ruthless whoreson. He'd beaten, killed, raped, and pillaged, and yet he'd earned the eternal fealty of a few.

"It was Killoran," Adair whispered. Broderick Killoran, the owner of the Devil's Den—their rival club—was to blame. Over the years, the battle for supremacy between them had played out not upon the streets but in the fine clubs resurrected with stolen riches. "He's been trying to ruin us since he inherited from Diggory."

His brothers stopped talking, and their silence stood as their agreement.

"And we trusted him to honor an oath of peace," Adair spat. After Diggory's now dead wife had captured Diana, it had been Killoran's family who'd led Niall back to her. Adair and his brothers had struck a dangerous alliance only now to be proven fools for letting their guard down. "Ya said to trust him." *But I'm just as responsible because I did so, even against my better judgment.*

The hot-tempered one of their group, Niall shed his earlier control. "This ain't my fault," he growled, surging toward Adair.

Calum and Ryker swiftly caught them each by an arm.

"It ain't your fault." Adair spat in the street. "It's all our faults. We all let our guard down." It was one of the most basic rules for survival, and they'd been lax—and it had cost them their club. Bile stung his throat, and he choked it back.

"Enough," Ryker gritted out. He looked pointedly at the ashen employees scattered about. They stared on with fear in their gazes.

The weight of responsibility settled heavily on Adair's shoulders. It was the only thin thread that kept him from giving in to the panic tearing at the corners of his mind. It reestablished purpose. Purpose was good. It kept him from giving in to despair. The men, women, and children behind them depended upon the club for their very existence. They'd been loyal workers and deserved more than this uncertainty and fear.

"We need to see to them," Ryker said in grave tones.

A large, burned corner of the stucco establishment tore away and tumbled to the alley, falling atop a pile of debris. That crumbling ushered in a new flurry of tears and agonized moans from the men, women, and children around them.

"We've survived worse," Calum said somberly, ever the optimist of their core group. "We will survive this." He spoke with the same confidence he'd had when they'd been boys without a roof over their heads in the winter months. Calum flexed his jaw. "And we'll grow stronger."

Yes, they'd survived worse.

Adair briefly closed his eyes. It surely spoke to his brothers' strength and his weakness, but the prospect of rebuilding from the ground up set panic rioting in his chest. Selfishly and cowardly, he wanted to dwell at the top of their kingdom and never again know the beginning. The beginning of everything . . . from drawing one's first breath, to getting on after tragedy, to finding a new family or building a new home was work. It was uncertainty and fear and the unknown.

"Come," Ryker said again. "We need to see everyone off the streets until . . ." Dark glitter sparked in Ryker's eyes, the first evidence of the ever-confident Ryker Black's uncertainty. Ryker strode out into the street, barking out orders and commands for the terror-filled employees.

Adair glanced back over his shoulder at the scorched building, and a feeling of desolation squeezed at his chest. At best, there had been seven years of his life when he'd been capable of innocence and goodness, but that had died with his parents and sister in a different fire. In this instance, grateful though he was that none of the men, women, and children who called this place home had suffered the same fate as his family, he still raged inside. For the club hadn't been just a building or a place of employment . . . it had been a dream and his home and the only thing he'd wanted in his life. And it was gone.

"Adair?" Calum called out. "We need help organizing the staff into hacks and carriages."

Adair nodded and immediately turned his focus over to the task, ordering men, women, and children about, and in that, he found a distraction from the tumult of his mind and spirit.

With his brothers at his side, he worked through the long hours of the night until every servant and guard and serving girl and dealer had boarded a carriage and been ushered off to Ryker's, Niall's, and Calum's townhouses. Until at last, the only ones who lingered in the streets of St. Giles, outside the charred remnants of the Hell and Sin, were Adair, Calum, Niall, and Ryker: the men who'd brought this club into existence.

Adair narrowed his gaze on the facade destroyed by fire. *Truce. What foolishness.*

A truce had been struck between Killoran's people and the proprietors of the Hell and Sin. That peace had died in the fiery embers that had raged the previous evening.

"The deal is off," he said quietly, and his brothers looked over to him. "Killoran wanted Ryker and Penny to introduce his bastard kin to Polite Society. The only person a single one of us will introduce them to is the Devil himself."

His brothers looked around at one another, and then over to Adair. In unison, they nodded.

"The deal is off," Ryker confirmed, his lips hardened into an unyielding line that promised retribution.

Not a single Killoran would ever benefit from any efforts of the Hell and Sin family. Adair would rather gut himself than give over an inch to that vile crew.

Pledges be damned.

Chapter 2

A thick tension, better suited for an impending battle in St. Giles than a Mayfair townhouse, hung heavy in Ryker Black's office.

But then, it was not every day the most ruthless fighters and leaders of the darkest streets of London gathered for a meeting.

Adair, Ryker, Calum, and Niall had assembled more than ten minutes ago with Broderick Killoran, a burly, ugly guard at his side, and Killoran's sister Cleopatra. Since that trio's arrival, not a word had been spoken. Each person stared mutinously back at one another in a silent dare of who would speak first.

Through that strained quiet, Adair passed his stare over the three people before them. Broderick Killoran sat as comfortable as a king in one of Ryker's winged leather chairs. With his palms resting upon that fine leather and a familiar cocksure grin on his face, his ease was only belied by a fierce glitter in his eyes. The guard, a towering bear of a figure who looked more like a mountain than a man, stood behind his lord and master, hands planted on his hips. Adair flicked his gaze dismissively over the brute, nearly three inches taller than Adair's six feet, three inches. He'd learned firsthand from countless street battles that even a child could take down a person three times his size with a well-placed blow, bite, or kick. He moved his focus on to the childlike figure alongside the brute. Not even a hair above five feet, her slender form was draped in fine satin fabric. Bespectacled and in possession of a mop of brown curls, she'd a fire in her eyes that promised death to all who crossed her.

Adair settled a hard stare on her . . . Cleopatra Killoran. Broderick Killoran's sister. The one who'd arranged the truce between their families . . . who'd led them to Niall's wife, Diana, so she might be saved. It had all been orchestrated to knock down their guard. And how easily they'd fallen into the trap. She had the look of a child, but she bore the evil of the street in her ruthless gaze. Only a damned fool would see nothing more than a bespectacled miss with a mop of drab brown curls when they looked at her. He'd marked her as trouble for them the moment she'd revealed herself.

Miss Killoran stiffened and glanced about. Her keen gaze missed nothing, touching on every corner and detail of the room.

Their stares clashed. Any other person would have had the sense to look away.

Cleopatra Killoran curled her lips up in the corners in a derisively mocking smile. Then, with a slight shake of her head, indicating she'd sized him up and found him wanting, she looked back at the front of the room.

A palpable hatred burned in his veins.

The faint groan of leather jerked his attention back to Killoran as he dropped an ankle over his opposite knee. He opened his mouth to speak, but Miss Killoran swiftly placed her right palm on the back of his seat.

The gaming hell owner, in his elegant wool suit better fitted for the fancy end of London than the slums he'd grown up in, glanced at his sister. A look passed between the pair.

A lord or lady of the *ton* would never note the silent exchange. Adair had learned firsthand a lesson in what came with opening one's mouth in the streets. A person either perished, or learned a new language. That's the one that was now being spoken before him. The slight arching of Killoran's blond eyebrows, the tightening at the corners of Miss Killoran's too-full lips.

Then Killoran reclined farther back in his seat and continued on with an intractable silence. The little hellion behind him looked back at Adair and smirked.

Smirked. A muscle jumped at the corner of his eye. He cracked his knuckles. Damn this family and damn this meeting.

In the end, the impasse was broken by the unlikeliest of people. "The deal is off," Ryker announced in his low, gravelly tones.

Abandoning his earlier nonchalance, Broderick sprang forward in his seat. "We have a deal, Black." The rival proprietor slammed his fist on the edge of Ryker's desk. "A damned deal."

And even as he damned his brother for conceding the first word in this war, a thrill of triumph went through Adair at yanking the one thing Killoran craved, that only they could give him. More specifically what Ryker and his wife, Penelope, could orchestrate for the bastard—*respectability*.

Miss Killoran caught her brother's eye and gave a slight shake of her head. Cheeks flushed, Killoran jumped up. Planting his hands on the edge of the immaculate mahogany piece, he leaned forward. "You bloody bastard," he spat. "If it weren't for my family, that one's . . ."—he jerked his chin at Niall, who stood to the left of Ryker—"wife would be dead." The seething man straightened. "I should have left her to her fate."

Niall's primitive shout went up as he launched himself forward. Calum and Ryker quickly scrambled over, grabbing him by the arms. "Ya bloody bastard," he thundered as he struggled to break free. "Oi'll rip your entrails from your throat and feed them back to ya through your gutted belly," he bellowed.

The ugly guard at Killoran's side took a step forward.

Adair quickly yanked his gun out and trained it on the towering brute, halting the man in his tracks.

Most women would have cowered and shook at a gun being brandished at a man a foot away from her. Cleopatra Killoran tipped her chin in Adair's direction and held his gaze squarely as she moved herself between the muzzle of Adair's gun and the guard.

He stitched his eyebrows. The hellion was either mad, fearless, or a lackwit. She'd put herself between a bullet and a man in her brother's employ? Mayhap she was a combination of the three.

"Cleo," Killoran said sharply.

That swift change from unaffected bastard to a man poised for battle marked his weakness. Killoran cared about the girl behind him.

She angled her shoulder, presenting herself full-forward to the room. "Did you truly expect a Black, or anyone inside the Hell and Sin, to honor their word?" She spat on the floor at Adair's feet.

A muscle jumped in the corner of his eye as the tension thickened.

In the street, a man was only as good as his word. It was a currency more valuable than gold.

Killoran shouldered himself before her. Again, like the London thief she no doubt had once been, she ducked out from behind him and took a place at the head of the desk. She stood there, arms akimbo, engaged in a silent battle with Ryker.

Adair rocked back. And by God, for the first time in his life, he doubted his brother's ability to win a particular fight . . . and against a slip of a Killoran, no less.

"Our agreement ended the day a fire was set to the Hell and Sin," Ryker said in steely tones.

"*Pfft*, your patrons were better for it."

At the young woman's brazenness, Adair's mouth fell open and fury stirred to life.

"But we didn't need to burn down your club to destroy it. You all"—she gestured to Adair and his brothers—"managed to do that on your own. Marrying yourselves fancy ladies."

"And isn't that precisely what you want for you and yours?" Adair called over to her. "Pretending ya are different from what ya, in fact, are," he taunted, deliberately using those Cockney tones as a reminder of just what she and her kind were.

The young woman laughed, and the droll, derisive edge to it sent heat climbing up his neck. People, regardless of station, size, or gender, hadn't ever dared laugh in his face. As a boy, he'd beaten another boy for it. There hadn't been a girl brave enough or stupid enough to attempt it. That a bloody insolent Killoran now should grated.

"Men without loyalty, I didn't suspect should have a brain in their heads, either. Polite Society turns an eye to their men marrying our sort. Black was pardoned because he's a duke's bastard. But you"—she jabbed a finger at Niall—"and you"—she pointed to Calum—"marrying duke's daughters?" She chuckled. "The arrogance of you whoresons marrying as you did. It's one thing for a lord to sell himself for a title . . . but you, binding yourselves to their kind? You may as well have struck the torch to your building the day you signed your marriage documents." She paused and looked between them. "That is, I take it, if Black can read?"

Ryker's cheeks went red, and he glanced to Calum. Together longer than any of their brothers, those two had always served as the one and two of their family and club. Calum puzzled his brow and looked helplessly to Niall and Adair. Bloody hell, the chit had confounded them all.

"Am I to take that as a no?" the relentless Cleopatra Killoran posed to Calum.

Niall whistled. "Your sister is mad, Killoran," he said, with a shockingly pitying glance for the other proprietor.

Killoran stiffened. "As one whose mother-in-law landed herself in Bedlam, and you who found yourself in a family given to madness, I expect you've a good grasp on insanity, but I assure you Cleo is far cleverer and stronger than you or the rotters you call brothers."

All earlier commiseration faded as Niall launched himself across the desk at Killoran. The room descended into a flurry of shouts and curses as Adair's brothers gripped Niall by the legs and dragged him back.

And through it all, Miss Killoran stood on with a wide, smug smile. She jerked her hand at her brother. "We're done here, Broderick. I told you they'd renege on their pledge." The young woman marched toward the door. The surly guard instantly sprang into movement.

Broderick Killoran, however, remained resolutely fixed to his spot. "I'm not leaving," he said with a smile. He reclaimed his seat. "They promised me something, and I'd have them honor their word."

A little growl escaped Miss Killoran, and she wheeled back. With jerky movements that would never be considered even a hint ladylike, she stomped back over, jerked out the chair alongside her brother, and sat. She glowered at Killoran, but he gave no indication that he either saw or cared about her displeasure. With his usual casualness, Broderick Killoran drew off his leather gloves and beat them against each other.

Ryker hesitated, and Adair silently willed his brother to turn this trio out on their arses. To have them thrown into the street for what they'd done and for what could never be undone. Ryker, however, sat.

Cleopatra Killoran leaned back in her seat, her small frame lost in those large leather folds. She glanced over, lingering her gaze on his still-extended pistol, and the young woman snorted. "You can lower your pistol, Thorne." She winged a thin eyebrow up. "That is, unless you're afraid? Then I advise you to carry on as you are." Killoran's sister lingered her gaze on the head of his pistol. "Remember, you've just one shot. I'd choose wisely."

He blinked slowly. By God, she'd called out his family's honor, laughed at him, and now questioned his courage. If she weren't a damned Killoran, the woman would have earned his appreciation. As it was, he'd sooner choose the one shot she referred to on himself than admit as much. "You tart-mouthed—"

"Well, get on with it," Niall growled, silencing Adair with a sharp look.

Again, Adair went hot. A person didn't lose control . . . to do so and show that weakness, particularly before one's enemy, had the potential to destroy a man. What was it about this sharp-tongued vixen? It was not only her Killoran blood but also the effortless way in which she wielded her tongue like a sharp blade.

Killoran steepled his fingers and rested his chin atop them. "I didn't set fire to your club."

"You're as responsible as those under your control—"

Cleopatra Killoran sat upright in her chair. "Our family isn't controlled."

"I can see that," Calum muttered under his breath.

The bear of a guard who'd taken up place between the Killorans choked on a laugh. Both Killorans quelled him with a look.

Ryker's mouth tensed. It was the mark he'd finished with the discussion. "Your people . . . your"—he grimaced—"family, answers to you." What an odd concept. These vile foes they'd battled for years were also one another's family. But then, everyone born to the streets ultimately found others to help one survive, and the ones who didn't, perished. "Just as when you were tied to Diggory, you owned that man's crimes."

"And you own what he did to my wife," Niall said tightly, stepping up behind Ryker's left shoulder.

Cleopatra Killoran peeled back her lip in a sneer, answering before her brother. "And what did we do? Save her from being carved up like a Christmastide goose? Next time, we'll not interfere and let your family suffer their fate." She made to rise. "Come on, Broderick—"

"Did you just threaten my family?" Ryker whispered, halting the young woman midmovement.

And it would seem even the stupidly brave Cleopatra Killoran had sense enough to know some fear. The color leeched from her cheeks, and had Adair not been studying her closely, he'd have failed to note the slight tremble to her hands. The hellion did know fear. Of course, everyone did. Even the most vicious fighters in St. Giles.

"My sister was not—"

"I don't make veiled threats," she pronounced, a surprising strength in that retort. "I don't mince words. You'll know when you're threatened, Black," she vowed.

Ryker sized her up for a long moment, then shifted his focus back to her brother. "Someone set the blaze."

Killoran dropped his negligent pose. "I give you my word that not a single one of my kin or myself are to blame."

Adair's body coiled tight. Surely his brother wasn't naive enough to trust a Killoran for a second time. And yet . . . by the way in which he carefully eyed the man across from him, that is precisely what he did. Weighed his words and measured their worth.

Adair looked to Niall and found the same fury and frustration reflected back in his more hardened brother's features.

And Killoran caught that weakening, too, and pounced. "We had an agreement," Killoran pressed. "Why would I sacrifice that?" He chuckled. "I'd at least wait until my sister makes her match."

That misplaced levity earned equal glowers from Adair, his family, and the man's sister.

Ryker captured his chin between his thumb and forefinger and rubbed.

Don't you dare, Ryker, Adair thought. *Don't you dare cede a goddamned inch to these bloody bastards . . .*

"You've already proven you aren't to be trusted," Ryker said at last, and Adair straightened. "Aligning yourself with Diggory marked the value of your pledge and the depth of your honor."

If looks could kill, Miss Killoran would have scorched Ryker with the fire burning in her brown eyes. "Bastards," she hissed, jumping to her feet so quickly she knocked her spectacles askew. "We're done here, Broderick. We need nothing from a Black. Nothing." She directed that to the men assembled. "It's clear they never had any intention of honoring the agreement reached."

"I was not in London last Season," Ryker said tightly.

No, Calum had stepped in and filled the role of head proprietor when Ryker had been at his country estates for the delivery of his first babe.

Broderick Killoran chuckled. "How very convenient? Is it not, Cleo?"

"Indeed."

Brother and sister shared a jaded, humorless laugh.

"My brother said we're done here." Adair took a step forward, tired of this game they played. "We're done. We'll not ask you again. Get—"

The door flew open, and as one, everyone sprang to attention, unsheathing their knives and training weapons at members of the opposing family. Adair briefly contemplated Broderick Killoran but ultimately settled his gun on the man's unpredictable sister: a sister who already had her small silver pistol pointed at his head while brandishing a jewel-encrusted dagger in her other hand.

Ryker's wife sprinted into the room. "What is the meaning of this?" Penelope cried out. It was a testament to Lady Penelope Chatham's courage that she'd not run off, screaming and crying in terror, but rather advanced deeper in the room, past the strangers and family leveling their knives and pistols.

"Penelope," Ryker commanded sharply, "we are in the midst of a discussion."

The lady stopped in the middle of the room, two feet away from Broderick Killoran.

Adair took a step closer toward his sister-in-law, and Cleopatra Killoran waved her weapon in his direction. "Not a step," she commanded.

"This is most certainly not a discussion," Penelope said in beleaguered tones better suited for a governess scolding recalcitrant children than for addressing a room of London's most ruthless kingpins. "Discussions are over tea and biscuits and not . . ."—she motioned to Miss Killoran's hands—"knives and guns."

Everyone eyed one another. No one made the first move.

"Ryker," Penelope said sharply.

He shook his head.

And an unspoken language passed between the married couple. Only this wasn't the language of the street. This was an intimacy of two who loved one another. Even as Adair loved his siblings as if they shared his own blood, this closeness was one he didn't know, or understand.

Ryker entreated her with his eyes.

"Down," she mouthed.

Her husband briefly closed his eyes, then slowly lowered his weapon to his side.

Penelope glanced about, lingering her gaze a long while on Cleopatra Killoran. "All of you, now."

The bespectacled hellion was the last to comply. She dropped her pistol into the pocket sewn along the front of her gown. Then, hiking her skirts up slightly, she sheathed her knife inside a peculiar pair of black boots.

What manner of woman is Killoran's sister? Adair's sister, Helena, had been raised in the streets, but she'd never have gone about lifting her skirts before a room of strangers—and certainly not the enemy. Adair's gaze lingered on Miss Killoran's trim ankle.

The young woman straightened and glared at him through her perfectly rounded spectacles. "Did you want a longer look, Thorne?" she taunted.

And despite his annoyance with the saucy chit, his lips twitched. The women he'd always favored had been curved in all the places a woman should be curved, and yet, if the feisty baggage before him didn't have the name Killoran attached to hers, he might have found in her the exception to his usual preferences. He touched the brim of an imagined hat. "Not at all, Miss Killoran."

She narrowed her eyes.

"They are just leaving," Ryker said in frosty tones as he moved around the desk to meet his wife.

"No, they are not," Penelope said. The stubborn set to her shoulders was one Adair recognized. After all, this was the same woman who'd not only wrapped Ryker around her finger but also transformed the rooms of the Hell and Sin and struck down prostitution in their establishment. "We gave our word to this family."

"They burned our club," Niall gritted out.

"Did they confess as much?" she shot back, then looked around. "Did you?" she posed that to Broderick Killoran. "Destroy my family's club," she clarified.

Surprise marred Cleopatra Killoran's face, but she quickly concealed it behind her mask of drollness.

"Surely you don't expect the truth from these people?" Adair said with a growl, earning another black look from Killoran's sister.

With a charm better suited for a gentleman in a London ballroom, Broderick Killoran swept an elegant bow. "My lady, I assure you, I neither set that fire nor ordered a man, woman, or child to see to it."

"He's a damned liar," Adair called to Penelope, earning a slight frown.

"Do you have proof?" she shot back. Silence descended over the room. Penelope smiled. "Then I daresay it would be wrong to break our word on nothing more than past hatred and resentment."

Adair swiped a hand over his face. His damned trusting sister-in-law. She'd spent all but two years of her life in the fancy streets of London, unscathed by the world's ugliness.

17

"Penelope," Ryker began quietly.

"Do *you* have proof, Ryker?" his wife cut in. "If not, then I expect us to honor our commitment. We offered them a Season. We"—she motioned to the small circle of people that was their family—"all of us. I'm not one who'd have us break our word."

"Everything has changed," Ryker gritted out.

"Has it?" Killoran piped in, wholly unfazed by the glowers trained on him. "Cleopatra promised to lead Marksman to his now wife." He stuck a finger up. "Which she did. And you vowed to sponsor one of my sisters for a Season."

Penelope nodded. "And that is precisely what we'll do, Ryker," she challenged.

A cocksure grin turned Broderick Killoran's lips up, revealing a flawless white smile. "I am grateful to you—"

Ryker's wife swiveled her attention over. "I don't like you, Mr. Killoran."

The proprietor's mouth froze in a strained, befuddled grin. With his crop of golden curls and his rumored ability to charm the peers whose paths he crossed, he was no doubt unaccustomed to disapproval.

Ryker's wife continued speaking. "You infiltrated my family's clubs. When I was first married to Ryker, you provided a vile note to create conflict between my husband and I." With each charge ticked off on her list, she raised a finger. "You sought to sow unrest in my marriage. So, do not mistake my decision for kindness. Are we clear?"

Even a Killoran had the good grace to blush. He bowed his head slightly. "We are, my lady."

Adair stared at the other man humbling himself so with a potent disgust. How different this family, with their love of the nobility, was from Adair and his own brothers who, outside the women who'd married into their gang, despised the *ton*.

Penelope held her hand out. Killoran hesitated a moment, then sealed the agreement with a handshake.

The Hellion

"A Black with honor," Cleopatra Killoran muttered. "Who could have imagined it?"

Killoran gave his sister a quelling look that the spitfire diligently ignored. "I will have one of my sister's belongings readied, and—"

Miss Killoran and Ryker spoke as one. "What?"

"Her belongings?" Ryker barked, his nostrils flaring.

Cleopatra sprang forward on the balls of her feet, a look of horror stamped in her features, and a question in her eyes. The look was gone so quickly, Adair may as well have imagined it. *Interesting.*

Adair whistled. "You are mad, Killoran." He earned another black look from the young woman. Surely the both of them had brains enough not to expect them to take one of their kind in.

"What are you on about?" Ryker demanded. "Surely you don't truly expect I'd allow any of your family to sleep inside my home."

The proprietor of the Devil's Den drew out his gloves and casually pulled them on. "My intentions are an honorable match for one of my sisters."

This time, worry lit the hellion's eyes. So, she had like fears of them.

"I cannot have Gertrude returning each night—"

"No," Adair said tightly.

"—to the same place those gentlemen will invariably end up." There was a faint smirk to that subtle boast, and Adair curled his hands tight, despising the reminder of how far they'd fallen to the rival establishment.

"You're not staying here," Ryker said resolutely. He folded his arms at his chest.

Broderick Killoran chuckled. "Well, not me, of course. I could hardly live here. I've my club to see after. The eldest of my sisters, however, can and will."

The bloody gall of the man. Adair took another step forward and jabbed a finger in his direction. "Those weren't the terms agreed upon."

19

"Sponsoring one of my sisters for a Season were the terms," Killoran shot back. "I know enough to know that young ladies aren't scuttled from one home to another when they have their Season."

And that was even more information than Adair had about anything to do with the damned *ton*.

Penelope tapped a fingertip against her lips. "Very well."

A curse exploded from Adair's lips. "They aren't to be trusted, Penny."

Calum nodded. "He is right in this."

From the corner of Adair's eye, he caught the flash of outrage in Miss Killoran's brown eyes.

"It's not your decision, Penelope," Ryker clipped out, his Cockney sliding back in. "They can't stay here."

"Their sister can and will." Penelope looked curiously back at the younger woman. Miss Killoran eyed her warily in return. "You are?"

She is the Devil's spawn and a demon incarnate.

"Cleopatra Killoran," her brother neatly supplied. "I've two additional sisters."

Two more like this tart-mouthed sprite before him? Adair shuddered.

"One sister," Ryker snapped before his wife could speak. "One Season."

"And then the debt is paid," Niall said solemnly.

"We are done here." Killoran dropped an elegant bow. "Gentlemen, my lady." With that, he proffered his arm for Cleopatra Killoran.

Ignoring that offering, the girl marched wordlessly from the room, setting a path like the queen herself.

Chapter 3

Do not say anything. Do not say anything. Do not say anything.

As Cleopatra Killoran stalked through the pale-pink-carpeted corridors of Ryker Black's townhouse, she focused on the rap of her heels striking the floor. It was a trick she'd mastered as a girl, when her mind had tried to take her to dark places. Mayhap another person would have been awestruck by the lavish wealth on display in the Grosvenor Square residence. Cleopatra, however, was no ordinary person, and she certainly wasn't the manner of woman to walk the halls of a viscount's home.

She was the manner of one who knew the taste of blood in her mouth and the feel of a blade in her hand and the echo of nightmares of long ago.

And so, she allowed herself to hear nothing but the tread of her own footfalls.

Anything to keep from thinking of the bloody brother who walked close behind, who'd all but groveled at the feet of a lady for the chance to mingle with the blue bloods. She gritted her teeth.

Broderick Killoran had come into her family when she was a small girl and he a boy on the cusp of manhood, just orphaned and new to the streets. With his fancy speaking and nourished frame, but with fear showing in his eyes, Cleopatra had hated Broderick on sight. That loathing had lasted all of a month before she saw his worth and benefited from his protection . . . and from that point on, love. Or it had been. Now she was quite back to hating him all over again.

They reached the foyer. Ryker Black's butler and an unsavory lot of servants stood in wait with cloaks in hand. One of Black's guards came forward. He made to drape her cloak over her shoulders, and she yanked the muslin garment from his hands. Cleopatra pulled it into its proper place. She reached for the bonnet in another waiting guard's hands, and he wisely handed it over and backed away.

The butler drew the door open, and she gave silent thanks. The Blacks had accused Cleopatra's family of setting their hell ablaze. It was a crime they bore no guilt for . . . one of the few times they could claim that luxury in truthfulness. In this instance, she would sooner burn this place to tinder, too, than linger in the fancy townhouse any longer. Bonnet in hand, she strode from Black's residence and stomped down the stairs.

"Cleo," her brother said after her.

"Not a word," she gritted out, weaving around a fancy lord and lady out for a stroll.

They flicked cool, condescending stares over her, and she paused, turning her fury briefly toward them, glowering.

That pair hastened their steps.

Bloody nobs. Another woman might be cowed and hurt over that disdain. Cleopatra, however, had hardened herself long ago to the world's opinions. She'd seen those same fancy lords bugger children in the streets and beat whores inside their clubs. As such, she'd hardly credit a single one of them with any moral standing of which she cared about or after.

Cleopatra reached the carriage and, ignoring the hand held out by Finnett, hefted herself up.

"That bad, Miss Cleo?" the older driver asked, glancing back at the townhouse.

"Worse." Her lip peeled back in an involuntary sneer, and she fought the urge to wheel back and plant her brother a facer to break his damned perfect nose. She took up a spot on the plush pale-blue squabs and glared at the doorway.

His damned affable-as-always smile on his face, Broderick climbed inside and settled into the spot across from her. A mutinous battle of silence waged between them as Cleopatra and Broderick locked gazes.

A moment later, their carriage lurched forward and rumbled away from the fancy streets of London to the gutters where the Killorans belonged. Only her brother Broderick was the one who seemed incapable of knowing as much. Or mayhap he was accepting it.

When Mac Diggory, the ugliest, blackest rotter in St. Giles and the Dials combined, had brought Broderick into their gang, he'd become the first person in her then-miserable existence who ever smiled. That smile hadn't been the street-hardened grin that promised death and retribution . . . but rather something . . . genuine. Something that she'd never known or identified with because of the hell that was life.

In time, that smile had shaped and twisted and transformed, and even as he wore that grin in amusement still, sometimes . . . now she recognized it for the practiced expression it was. Damn him for his control just then. Where had that bloody pride been earlier in Black's townhouse? That snapped her patience. She hurled her bonnet on the bench beside him. "What in blazes was that?"

He winked, that slight, silent acknowledgment of her defeat. "What in blazes was what?" he asked with a nonchalance that brought her hands reflexively curling into fists once more. "That victory over the Blacks?" He stretched his legs out, knocking into her knees.

She whistled. "You're nicked in the nob." He was and always had been. "You've become mad with a lust for respectability."

His cheeks flushed red. "There is nothing wrong with wanting a better life for all of us."

She scoffed. "You still haven't accepted that we've been born with the stench of the street on our skin. And it can't ever be scrubbed away, no matter the fine bath oils or fragrances we use."

When he said nothing, Cleopatra kicked him in the shins. He winced, drawing his long limbs back into their proper place. "Furthermore, that back there was not victory. That was you licking the boots of our enemy." The smug, satisfied triumph on Adair Thorne's face as Broderick had all but pleaded for a restoration of the vow struck between their families. She tightened her mouth.

A vein throbbed at the corner of her brother's eye. "I lick no man's boots," he whispered with a steely edge that had sent countless people running in the opposite direction.

"No," Cleopatra conceded, and some of the tension left his shoulders. "This time it was a lady's slippers."

He surged forward. "It is for our family that I do this. We've built a fortune to rival Croesus, and once we secure noble connections, we can ensure the Devil's Den's place in this damned uncertain world."

She'd not humble herself with the truth that she didn't have a jot of an idea who this Croesus fellow was. She'd learned long ago to listen to Broderick's fancy talk and not reveal her own ineptness on those ends.

"Once we have those noble connections, nothing will stop us, Cleo." A glint hardened his blue eyes. "Nothing."

Forcibly concealing her disgust, she lifted her chin and got to the heart of it. "Who?" Who of the Killoran sisters would he sacrifice like a lamb upon the altar of his aspirations?

He set his mouth.

"Who?" she repeated, laying her palms on her knees.

"It should be Gertrude. She's the eldest," he said, tugging off his gloves. "The order of things matters to Polite Society," he explained, stuffing the elegant leather scraps inside his jacket.

"Gertrude," she repeated slowly. The eldest of their siblings, blind in one eye, and the quietest, meekest of their lot, she'd be eaten alive by the lords of London, and worse . . . destroyed by the nob who took her as wife. The carriage hit a bump and knocked an already unsettled Cleopatra back. She shot a hand out, catching the edge of her seat. Except . . . one word gave her pause. *Should.* "You won't send Gertrude."

He shrugged. "A gentleman doesn't want a spinster bride, and she's nearly on the shelf."

Cleopatra growled, those tonnish words he tossed about only highlighting his sick obsession with the nobility. Which could only mean . . .

"Ophelia is the logical one to send." Because with her ethereal beauty, any lord would wed her in an instant.

"You'd sell her to achieve your own gains?" It was a naive question that left her mouth before she could call it back where it belonged. Of course, that was the way of the streets. One did what one must, including selling one's soul—or in this case, one's sister—for their own gains.

Broderick scoffed. "This is as much for me as all of you. Look at the Blacks. Look at what became of them—"

"Because those bastards thought to marry into the nobility." She jabbed her index finger against her gloveless left palm, punctuating her words. "Our place is not among the nobs, Broderick."

"You would not understand it, Cleo."

She growled. It didn't matter that he was correct in that she didn't understand the ways of the *ton*. No one, man or woman of any station, put her own ignorance on display.

"Lords in need of a fortune always welcome a marriage to a lesser—"

"Think before you finish that, Broderick Killoran," she said with the same deathly calm she'd used on the first man she'd slayed in the streets.

Wisely, her brother fell silent. He scrubbed a palm back and forth over his forehead. "Cleopatra," he tried again as she prepared to beat him back with her words, "this will make us stronger."

She froze. There it was . . . the goal they'd always striven for. Power allowed a person not only to survive but to thrive and lead. It kept one from a hungry belly and safe from death. Now Broderick would place that mantle upon the shoulders of one of the Killoran girls.

"Look how quickly Black and his crew fell from power," he pressed. After Diggory's death, Broderick had set the Devil's Den on a path of respectability. Noblemen had become patrons, and the Killorans' wealth had grown . . . and just as he did in every aspect of life, Broderick—and all the Killorans—flourished. They had lured away Black's members, and then his club had been taken down by a fire. "That could very well be our fate," her brother murmured with an uncanny reading of her thoughts.

Noble connections would make the Killorans stronger. They had their club . . . and that was all. What else were they? *He'll not relent until one of us makes a match with a nob . . .*

"Not Ophelia." Hauntingly beautiful, she'd be prey for every desperate, lecherous nobleman.

He made a sound of impatience. "It has to be—"

"Not. Ophelia."

"Gertrude, then," he gritted out. "She's the eldest."

"No." Power grab be damned, the Killorans wouldn't grow their empire at the expense of their weakest member. From the King of England to kingpin of the underworld, there wasn't a man of any station she couldn't control. She might be the youngest, but she'd killed long before Broderick had ever stumbled into their midst, and she'd always looked after her sisters, so she'd be the one who did it now. Cleopatra tipped her chin up. "It's me."

Broderick blinked. "But . . ." There was a world of wealth to that single-syllable utterance.

With her dull brown hair, elfin frame, and tendency to wield her tongue like a knife, she'd never be any gentleman's first choice for a bride. "It doesn't matter what I look like. It matters what they need. They need our wealth," she said with the same pragmatism she'd used when doling out meal rations to Diggory's gang. "It will be me. You'll have your connections to the nobility and then your entry into society."

"Our entry," Broderick murmured, his gaze the same contemplative one as when he had a book in hand, lost in absorption to those pages.

The carriage drew to a stop, and they remained seated on the benches.

"I'm not afraid of a bloody toff."

"Your sisters aren't afraid of anyone, either," he reminded her.

He was wrong. For the bond between them, there had been too many years where Broderick had not been a part of their existence. As he'd pointed out, their siblings might have managed to battle demons and hide their fears. Cleopatra, however, knew the monsters that lived within still . . . for each of her siblings.

Finnett drew the door open.

"Not now," Broderick snapped, and the old servant instantly slammed it closed.

"This isn't a discussion, Broderick," Cleopatra said flatly. "This isn't a debate or a decision *you* are making." She thinned her eyes into narrow slits. "This is one I already decided. For everyone." Gertrude and Ophelia.

He shook his head. "You despise the nobility."

An inelegant snort burst from her lips. "And do you believe our sisters have an affinity for those lords?"

"No." Broderick grinned, his first real expression of amusement that day. "But you're the only one I suspect would stick a blade in a nobleman's belly for even an unintended slight."

She tightened her mouth, content to let him believe her that ruthless. It meant she'd crafted a flawless facade for herself over the years. One where not even her family knew the depth of what she was capable of.

Relentless, Broderick shook his head. "It cannot be you. You're too val—" He cut himself off.

Valuable. She'd been his second as long as he'd had ownership of the club, and guided him long before that. "Gertrude was nearly buggered by one of those ruthless peers you'd now marry her off to," she snapped. That had been the first man Cleopatra had stabbed, and she'd do it all over to help any one of her siblings. "I won't let you send her into a den of those bastards. It will be me," she said in chilled tones.

Her brother opened and closed his mouth several times, and then he cursed. "Oh, bloody hell. Very well. It will be you."

Grinning at that triumph, she shoved open her own door. Cheeks flushed, Finnett jumped back, taking care to avoid either Cleopatra's or Broderick's eyes. "F-forgive m-me. I was waiting, and . . ." He cleared his throat and dropped his guilty gaze to the cobblestones.

This time she let him hand her down with a word of thanks. He'd been listening. As one who'd become adept at reading a person's furtiveness, she knew as much.

Marching ahead of her brother, Cleopatra bounded up the seven steps leading to the impressive establishment. From the corner of her eye, those gaslight sconces in their crystal casing snagged her attention. Those impractical adornments her brother insisted on, which were broken over and over and always promptly replaced, served as a mark of Broderick's love of that noble connection. The ornate oak doors were flung open, and she swept inside.

Since Cleopatra had long moved freely about the gaming hell floors, the gentlemen and guttersnipes who tossed down their coin here had ceased staring whenever she or her sisters wandered around. With focused footsteps, she made her way through the crowded club. Her sister Ophelia, hovering at the hazard table, caught her gaze with a question in her eyes.

Cleopatra shook her head once. She didn't care to speak about the meeting with the Blacks. Not now. And her siblings knew enough to honor that.

Cleopatra exited the gaming floors and continued down a long corridor with an intersecting hall. Pausing at the back wall, she found the clever switch of the hidden door and let herself in. The wise in St. Giles never forgot that danger lurked in every corner. One would be a fool to let one's guard down, and as such, regardless of the wealth or powerful connections one had, danger was always at hand. She reached her rooms and, loosening the fastenings of her cloak, kicked the door closed with the heel of her boot.

Cleopatra dropped the fine garment and stalked over to her armoire. Yanking the doors open, she proceeded to draw out gowns and dresses of satins and silks. Finer garments than any she'd worn while Diggory had been living, which largely hadn't been worn outside the streets of St. Giles until now. For it hadn't been until that bastard had taken a deserved bullet to the belly by Black's crew that she'd known a hint of the fineries he had with the club's success. All the bastards Diggory had whelped and the street thugs who'd taken on employment here had found a roof over their heads and food in their bellies and nothing more. That had been the truest debt they owed Black's family—offing that cruel bastard. Cleopatra gritted her teeth. Not that she'd ever given a rat's arse about the fineries. It had only and always been about security. She tossed a dress on her wide four-poster bed.

But in this—God rot his soul—Broderick was correct.

Their establishment could crumble as easily as Black's club had. The difference between them? That man had a title behind his name and a fortune beyond his gaming hell. *What do we have?*

She stopped and eyed the mound of clothes she'd heaped upon the bed. This would be nothing more than a business transaction struck between Cleopatra and the peerage. It was no different from the contracts they signed with their liquor distributors or wheat suppliers. For the gentleman who sold his title for their fortune would be a partner in a business endeavor and not much more.

A knock sounded at the door.

"Come in," she called.

Regina Spark, affectionately dubbed Reggie by their family, rushed inside. "What happened?" The ethereal woman who swept in had been more like a mama trying in vain to tame her unruly daughters. Concern gleamed bright in Reggie's aquamarine eyes. "Cleopatra?" Reggie demanded impatiently, moving over in a whir of noisy, drab skirts. That sudden movement knocked her chignon loose, and several loose curls fell down her back. "What did he de—" Her gaze alighted on the stack of garments, and her words trailed off. "It's you," she breathed.

"It has to be me," Cleopatra said tightly, and resumed gathering her belongings.

"It does not."

Cleopatra glanced over, and Reggie flattened her lips into a hard line.

"Why need it be any of you?"

Older than Cleopatra, Reggie had been rescued years earlier by Broderick, and she had devoted her loyalties, services, and friendship to him and his siblings ever since.

"You know my brother," she explained matter-of-factly.

"Yes, I do," the woman muttered. The details surrounding that night Broderick rescued Reggie from the streets were ones Cleopatra had never gleaned from either of them, and she'd lived long enough in St. Giles to know not to pry or probe. "I will speak to him."

"I'm not afraid of a man, Reggie." Civilized society might be bound by laws and rules, but Cleopatra and her kin had gotten on without those societal dictates. "I'd kill a man before I let him hurt me." She'd done it before . . . for herself and her sisters.

Reggie's expression darkened. "Sometimes it is beyond your powers, and spending a life forever bound to one is vastly different than what you speak of."

What I speak of. Cleopatra knew not what the other woman's life had been like before she'd joined their gang, but her tendency to skirt descriptive words and truths told of a different rearing than Cleopatra's.

"I am going to speak to him." Reggie spun on her heel and stomped over to the door.

"You'll not speak for me, Reggie," she said in solemn tones, willing the other woman to understand that this was Cleopatra's decision and she'd own it.

"I'll not let him send you there—"

"I volunteered myself." No one made Cleopatra Killoran do anything. Not even the siblings she loved and would sacrifice her very life for.

Reggie opened and closed her mouth several times, and then a sigh slipped out. "Of course you did." She strode over. "Here," she said with her usual mothering, taking the blue satin striped gown from Cleopatra's fingers. She proceeded to organize the piles into day dresses, undergarments, and ball gowns . . . ball gowns that had been useless scraps before, but now served a purpose. "I have it," she muttered, slapping at Cleopatra's fingers. It spoke volumes to the bond between them.

Cleopatra hitched herself to the edge of the bed and allowed Reggie to oversee the task at hand. They all had their distractors. Cleopatra's was the tread of her own steps. Reggie had always been an organizer.

"What happened?" Reggie asked, fetching Cleopatra's trunks. She dragged one back to the bed.

Cleopatra lifted one shoulder in a negligent shrug. "They tried to renege."

Stooped over that massive trunk, Reggie awkwardly lifted her head.

"Black's wife was determined to honor their word," she explained, answering that unasked question. She proceeded to share the details of that meeting.

The door exploded open.

Both women looked as one to the glowering boy. He'd already found out. Another Diggory bastard without a definite birthday, Stephen was likely just nine or ten years old, but he possessed a temper to rival most men.

Reggie released the gown in her hand and wordlessly backed out of the room.

Stephen slammed the door. "I hate you."

Regret suffused her breast. "You don't hate me." One of Diggory's many bastards, Stephen had been a snarling, snappish, beastlike boy until Broderick had taken him under their care. "If you did, you wouldn't be here," Cleopatra said with more gentleness than she'd ever let another person hear from her. She shoved her armoire doors closed.

"Well, then I hate you . . . for now," Stephen snarled. That she believed. Her youngest sibling had a temper to rival a once-beaten dog. "I knew you'd be the one. I knew you'd not let anyone else do it. You're always protecting everyone else." With an angry shout, he pulled his dagger from his boot and hurled it at the opposite wall.

Despite herself, she gasped. A knife in the wall had long been Diggory's unspoken seal. "Stop it," she said tightly. Stephen was spoiling for a fight, and when he was in one of his tempers, one had a better hope of reasoning with Satan himself than the boy.

Cleopatra strode across the room and, bracing one palm against the plaster, wrestled free the buried tip. "You need to control your temper." It would see him ruined, and if they hadn't been provided security at the Devil's Den through Broderick's efforts, he'd have been destroyed long ago for it.

"I'm declaring war."

"On who?" she snapped. "Broderick?"

"On them . . ."

"Do not say it." Cleopatra glowered him into silence. The last thing their family could afford was a heightened feud with Black's family, particularly now that their rivals had links to the nobility.

In a bid to defuse his volatile rage, Cleopatra tossed his blade aside and returned to her bed. "It is done, Stephen." She knelt and withdrew a small valise from under her bed and set it atop her undergarments. Dropping to her knees once more, she peeled back the Aubusson carpet and partially rolled it back. She found the loose floorboard, and lifting it, she reached inside and drew out several daggers. "Put those in my valise."

Stephen stuffed his hands in his pockets. "I ain't your lady's maid."

Cleopatra grabbed her two pistols and shoved them across the smooth floor so they landed at his feet. "Certainly not. After all, which lady's maid would be helping a lady pack an arsenal of weapons?" She followed that with a wink.

Despite the earlier fury that had blazed in his eyes, Stephen's lips twitched. This was how she preferred her youngest brother—with a teasing light in his eyes and a smile dimpling his cheeks. "That's better," she said.

He quickly tamped down his grin. Mirth had so long been a sign of weakness for all of them that it was too foreign to trust oneself over to any emotion. That was something Cleopatra well understood.

"You're mad," he grumbled, then proceeded to help her pack her weapons.

"It is just marriage." They'd all sold their souls more times than even the Devil wanted anymore. Broderick had simply found another part to sell. So why, practical and rational as she was, did that knot her insides? She lowered the floorboard back into its proper place and reached for the corner of the carpet.

"You don't have to go," Stephen said gruffly, looking up from his task.

She froze midmovement. *I don't want to . . . I have to . . .* Not because she gave a rat's arse about a connection to the nobility but because if she didn't succeed in the goal Broderick had for them, then he'd turn to another one of their siblings to oversee his goals. "It has to be me."

"Let Gertie go."

Cleopatra frowned. "No." It wouldn't be Gertrude.

"Because she's weak," her brother muttered.

Blinded in one eye because of a fist Diggory had delivered to her head, and silent as the grave, Gertrude had greater strength than most men. Cleopatra would be damned on Sunday if she let her elder sister sacrifice all for their brood. "Marriage to a lord would shatter Gertie," she said quietly to her brother. Cleopatra, however, could battle any man, woman, or child and emerge triumphant.

"Because she's no spine," he spat again.

And even with the deep bond between Cleopatra and Stephen, and for all his grumbling, he loved Gertrude and Ophelia just as much. Cleopatra quit her spot on the floor and joined her brother at the bed. She took his hands in hers and gave them a squeeze.

"Look at me," she commanded when he directed his focus at the floor.

He slowly lifted his head.

"There are different kinds of strength."

There was a wavering in his blue eyes, and then the steel was back in place. "You marry one of them, you're never coming back."

And despite what she'd resolved to do, and matter-of-factly signed on for, Cleopatra reeled as the weight of her brother's words slammed into her. If she did this—nay, *when* she did this—her sisters would be spared from sacrificing themselves, and yet she'd be bound forever in that fancy end of London . . .

"Send Ophelia, then," Stephen entreated. "Anyone but you."

"I cannot do that." Her throat worked, and she damned her weakness. "I *won't* do that," she corrected. She would not sacrifice any of her siblings.

Stephen wrenched away and, turning on his heel, fled her rooms. Cleopatra stared at the door long after he'd gone, the ormolu clock ticking down her remaining moments here.

I'm never coming back . . .

Chapter 4

The following morning, Adair and his brothers gathered in Ryker's Mayfair office. This meeting was not unlike so many others before it: the Devil's Den and Killoran's people remained at the heart of their conversations.

Hands clasped behind him, Adair stood at the floor-length window of Ryker's office while his brothers discussed the state of the scorched Hell and Sin and the impending arrival of a Killoran into their fold. Adair stared out at the Mayfair streets.

For all the sameness of listening to Ryker, Calum, and Niall discuss Broderick Killoran, a suffocating vise squeezed about Adair's chest in being in this place. The fancy servants and the lords and ladies passing by the Mayfair townhouse served as a reminder of all he'd spent his life hating, and now because Killoran had burned his home down, he'd be forced to dwell among the elite. *Bloody Killoran.* Sharp loathing coursed through him, and he fed that fury and abhorrence, for it kept him from giving in to the madness of calling this place home—even if it was a temporary one.

So, this is what Helena felt when we sent her away to live with the Duke of Wilkinson. At the time, it had seemed the right decision to keep her safe from Diggory . . . and it had proven the right one, as she'd ultimately found happiness here. But Helena had been born to this existence. Adair would rather gut himself with Broderick Killoran's dullest blade than ever remain here.

". . . Adair?"

Calum's visage reflected back in the crystal panes.

Adair's mind raced as he sought to put order to what had just been discussed. "I wanted you all to look at this," his brother elucidated.

Neck heating at having been caught off guard, he turned. Ryker sat behind his desk like the king of this new empire, with Adair, Niall, and Calum awaiting guidance, as always. His brothers studied the sheets of vellum in their hands. Ryker stared expectantly, with one of those sheets extended toward him. Abandoning his place at the window, he strode over and collected that sheet. "What is . . . ?" His words trailed off as he scanned the perfunctory list.

HELL AND SIN

HOTELS

STEAM-POWERED BOATS, SHIPS, AND RAILS

PHILANTHROPY

"What in blazes is this?" Adair breathed, looking up from the page marked sloppily in his brother's hand.

Ryker folded his hands before him and rested them on the desk. "The future."

The future?

"Given the fire and our plans of rebuilding, Penelope and I discussed at length the future." The future. Not the future of the club. "Mayhap some good can come from the blaze," Ryker continued. "We've never thought of a life beyond or outside the Hell and Sin."

Adair recoiled as his brother's meaning hit him. "You want us to *forget* the club." Was his brother addled? "After everything we've dedicated and invested in it, you'd throw it away for"—he looked down at the page—"hotels?" He cringed. And furthermore, what did a single one of them know of anything other than gaming? Those skills they'd learned on the streets. They were the only ones they had.

"It wouldn't be throwing it away," Calum said somberly, bringing Adair's head up again. "Mayhap from the ash of the Hell and Sin, something new can be born."

Adair studied his sheet as his brother's words rooted around his mind, and then a dawning understanding slipped in. Ships and rails. Philanthropy. Hotels. Staggered, he glanced around at his siblings of the streets. "You've already spoken." Of course. Niall had taken to traveling with his wife, Diana; Calum and Eve had taken up work on behalf of the Salvation Foundling Hospital. A discourse that had occurred between husband and wife, not the men who'd built one of the greatest clubs in the whole of England. Adair slammed the damning scrap of their betrayal down on Ryker's desk.

They didn't even have the good grace to deny it or look away.

"We cannot raise our families in the streets of St. Giles," Ryker said in his gravelly tones. No. Calum's wife, now expecting their first child, had moved them out of the club . . . just as Ryker had months earlier. It was a practical move that Adair, even though he had no wife or child of his own, understood and respected. "We spent our lives seeking to escape, and we did."

Adair flexed his jaw. "You're a bloody fool if ya think we're ever truly free of those streets." He gave his head a disgusted shake. "You're no different from Broderick Killoran and his lust for a connection to the nobility."

Niall took a step closer, and Adair braced for the fight the hot-tempered sibling had always been eager to give. He stiffened as the other man laid a hand on his shoulder. "You don't believe that." Niall's mastery of his Cockney, when Adair was wholly unable to control a single bloody thing in this instance, grated on his last nerve. "This is for the good of all of us."

A battle waged inside, born of panic and uncertainty. "And so, we each take on different endeavors and begin from the ground up?" His mouth went dry at the horrifying prospect: the blood, sweat, fears, and silent tears he'd cried through the hell his existence had once been.

Calum rolled his shoulders. "We've done it before, Adair. We did it before when we had nothing but stolen coin to our name." He caught his stare and gave a little nod. "We can certainly do it now with the fortune and connections we've built."

To hide the tremble in his hands, Adair again picked up that hated page. He briefly closed his eyes as he was transported back long ago to the boy he'd been, returning from delivering goods for his father to find his family's business destroyed and his parents and sister lost to the flames. Just like that, the past came flooding in. The acrid sting of smoke burned his nostrils. *Nooooo . . . Papa . . . Mama . . .* His own desperate cries churned around his mind. He fought the need to clamp his hands over his ears in a bid to dull the distant sounds of his own misery.

"I will see to the Hell and Sin Club, then," he said at last, when he trusted himself to speak through the damned, unwanted emotion there.

"Is that what you want?" Ryker asked cautiously.

Adair chuckled. "Does it truly matter what I want?"

"It is a new beginning." Calum motioned between them. "For all of us. If we wish the club to remain as it is or build it again, the options are both there."

"Leave it as it is?" Adair was unable to keep the incredulity from his question. The clink of coins being thrown on the table and the laughter of their patrons on crowded nights pealed around his mind, familiar and fresh as the first night they'd opened their doors to the lords of London. "You would do that?" he challenged.

"Calum is only laying forth all the options," Niall supplied for the silent trio before Adair.

"This," Adair hissed, "is not an option. That club is everything of who we are." Without it . . . who were they? Nay . . . who was Adair? He was the scared, cowering orphan in the streets wading through the uncertainty of an even more uncertain existence. "What of all the men and women dependent upon us?" Children, too. "All people like us, born to St. Giles and the Dials who'd finally found security. We'd just yank that away?"

"There's more good we can do, the more ventures we have," Calum said quietly. "Expanding our business—and taking on philanthropic pursuits, as we should have done long ago—only allows us the power to help others."

Damn Calum for always being the calm, logical one of their group. And damn him for being correct.

Adair dusted a hand over his face, searching his mind for reasons to counter a plan he'd not truly had a say in.

"It is settled, then?" There was a question there as Ryker settled back in his chair. "The restoration of the hell falls to you."

That was it. Just like that, after a lifetime of honoring a hierarchy where Ryker ruled inside the Hell and Sin, they'd all turn the decisions and responsibilities over to Adair. "It falls to me?" he asked slowly.

"We are partial owners in all endeavors and investments," Ryker said, explaining the plan he'd hatched, "but with each of us overseeing one joint venture."

It was a clever scheme. What his brothers spoke of was a way they might diversify their ownings and investments. It would cut them free of that dependency they'd had for so long on the nobility. If executed with the same success as they had with the Hell and Sin, they'd grow in ways they never could have with only the club to their names.

"This is the future," Calum quietly urged, misinterpreting the reason for Adair's silence.

And through the panic and despair at beginning again, Adair found something vital—purpose. He nodded slowly.

Ryker laid his hand out, palm down. Adair eyed it a moment and then, dropping the list back on his brother's desk, covered his hand. Calum and Niall stacked theirs atop his, sealing the empire-building they'd agreed to undertake.

An unexpected excitement stirred in the embers of resentment. By the earnings he'd amassed in his days as a thief, Adair had found himself behind the other stakeholders. They'd all had an equal contribution to decisions, but Ryker had always had the final word . . . and that had gone for everything—from the location in St. Giles to the gargoyles that lined the steps of the Hell and Sin.

Agreement reached, Ryker stalked over to his sideboard. He lined up four glasses, and dragging a crystal decanter of brandy back and forth over that horizontal line of snifters, he poured drinks. "There still remains the matter of the Killorans."

Adair glanced over at the longcase clock. "They are not to be trusted," he insisted, taking the drink Niall carried over to him. He clenched his jaw as the bespectacled, spritelike warrior sprang behind his mind's eye. "And certainly not Cleopatra Killoran."

"I don't disagree on either score," Ryker confirmed, cradling his drink.

"You didn't believe their earlier claims of innocence?" Adair pressed, setting his drink down next to that list.

"I don't know either way," his brother said. "And in the absence of evidence, I choose cautiousness."

Some tension went out of Adair's shoulders. For all the changes that had faced them since the club had burned down, and all that had been tossed at him yesterday with the Killorans and now the proposed changes over their roles and dealings, there was a familiarity to this side of Ryker. It brought reassurance that for all that had been altered, the street remained alive and strong. "What are you thinking?"

"We'll honor our vow until they give us reason not to, and the moment they do . . ." Ryker downed his drink and set the empty glass down beside Adair's.

Calum cracked his knuckles. "Then we'll destroy their name and, with it, Killoran's hopes for the only thing he craves." Respectability.

Niall gave an approving nod. "And our debt to them for saving Diana is paid."

Adair opened his mouth to speak, but Calum held up a silencing finger and nodded toward the front of the room.

A knock sounded at the door.

"Enter," Ryker boomed.

The tall, graying guard, West, who'd been made head butler, shoved the door open. "They're 'ere, my lord . . . Black, sir. Just arrived. Sitting out in the carriage they are."

Adair's brother nodded. "I'll be there shortly." After the servant rushed off, Ryker turned back. "While you're here, I'd ask you to watch her closely."

Before this instance, living in this temporary residence, Adair had felt like an interloper in an unfamiliar world . . . as unsettled as the former guards, dealers, and serving girls who'd taken up work and residence within Ryker's, Niall's, and Calum's London residences.

The quick patter of footsteps sounded on the other side of the door. A moment later the door flew open, and Penelope and Diana stormed inside. "She's here," Penelope announced with far more of her usual cheer than the circumstances merited.

When Ryker, Calum, and Niall started forward, Niall's wife, Diana, tossed her arms wide, blocking the entrance. "Wait! I'll have you remember that no matter what blood runs in her veins and what name is attached to hers, Cleopatra Killoran is no more responsible for her brother's crimes than I'm responsible for my mother's," she said somberly. It had been, after all, Diana's mother who'd not only sold

Ryker and Helena over to Diggory but who'd then tried to orchestrate Helena's murder.

"This is different," Niall growled.

"No, Niall, it isn't." His wife gave him a sad little smile. "No matter how much you might wish it to be. Those acts carried out by Broderick Killoran against Ryker were his actions. Not his sister's. Not any of his sisters'."

"You don't know that," Adair said quietly. "You don't know what she is capable of or what crimes she's committed. None of us do. And until we do, we'll treat her with the proper cautiousness."

Penelope tightened her mouth. "She saved Diana's life. That is all we know of her thus far. As Diana said, we owe the young lady our kindness."

Young lady. Adair snorted. A Killoran was no more a lady than he was a fancy gent. No matter how much the young woman's brother wished it to be. "Come," Penelope urged. "Let us go greet our guest."

As his siblings and their spouses filed from the room to greet Killoran's sister, Adair took up his previous spot at the window. He stared down at the elegant, black-lacquered carriage that no doubt contained Cleopatra Killoran along with whichever sibling would take up residence here.

The garish pink curtain parted ever so slightly, and Adair narrowed his eyes as he shoved open his jacket, deliberately revealing the pistol tucked at his waist.

"A guest," he muttered.

The day a Killoran was anything but an enemy of the Hell and Sin family was the day the world ceased spinning.

Chapter 5

After nearly twenty years spent on this miserable, cold earth, Cleopatra was capable of hating far more than she loved.

In fact, she could count on her two hands, and not even all the way up to the ten digits, what she loved. Or rather, who—the people whom she loved.

It was the same people who now sat in the spacious conveyance. Cleopatra looked from her unusually stoic eldest brother to a downcast Gertrude, and then to a seething Ophelia. With Reggie perched atop the carriage, there was but one missing from their ragtag bunch. Stephen had refused to accompany them to *a bloody Black's*, as he'd always referred to that rival family.

"You're a bloody bastard, you know that, Broderick?" Ophelia spat.

"It's for the good of the group," he said tightly, his icy tones the ones he used when doling out tasks and assignments inside the Devil's Den. "You know that." He looked pointedly about. "You all knew long ago what my intentions were. Why . . . Cleopatra even struck the terms with Black and his men," he correctly reminded them.

"Because of you," Ophelia snarled. "*You* insisted on introductions to Polite Society."

Their brother tossed up his hands in exasperation. "What in blazes did you think the damned introductions were for?"

As brother and sister launched into an all-out attack, Cleopatra welcomed the focus to remain there and not on her. For the palpable tension in their exchange, it also offered a balm to Cleopatra's restlessness. For all the fights and challenges that arose among their group, in the end, it had never resulted in a fist or slap or hateful words that oftentimes could be more painful than an actual physical blow. *And I'm leaving it behind . . .*

Because Broderick would not rest until his goals had been achieved. She'd known that the moment she'd gone to Niall Marksman and struck the agreement between them. Why, it was something she'd learned the moment the terror-filled boy, on the cusp of manhood, had entered their midst and challenged Mac Diggory on their behalf. When Broderick committed himself to something, nothing could alter him from that course. It had been that steely determination that had enabled them to rise to the level of greatness they had.

Where was the greatness in this? A ball of regret stuck in her throat, and she struggled to choke it back. It was a bloody goodbye from the only place she belonged, for a place she could never truly be part of.

". . . I don't care whether we have noble connections," Ophelia screeched, making another appeal to their obstinate brother.

Cleopatra winced at that shrill cry. Ophelia still hadn't truly discovered the depth of Broderick's resolve in binding their family to the *ton*. She still hadn't accepted what Cleopatra had long ago—Broderick's single-mindedness in this endeavor.

Restless, Cleopatra cracked the curtains ever so slightly and stared out at her new home. She ran her gaze over the white stucco front of the Grosvenor Square residence.

"Home," she mouthed, and a palpable loathing coated her tongue. This place would never be home. She'd but one, and as Stephen had accurately pointed out yesterday morn, it was one Cleopatra would never return to. Instead, she'd trade off all that and trust herself over to the Blacks. They'd been raised first as gang members on opposite ends of London, and then as hated rivals. Now her brother would trust those people to honor Marksman's pledge? *This is not forever . . .* Only—the only thing to get her out of this prison would be shackles to a fancy toff. Her pulse pounded in her ears in a beat of panic. She lifted her gaze upward and caught the belligerent figure glaring at her.

Adair Thorne. At three inches past six feet, his gold-tinged brown hair pulled back in a queue at the base of his neck, he'd the look of a street tough, as out of place at that window as Cleopatra herself was in these streets. He propped his hands on his hips, emphasizing the gun on his person.

The sight of it brought her eyes closed and ushered in a deeper peace and calm.

"It should be me," Gertrude said softly, and Cleopatra snapped her eyes open.

Dropping the curtain, Cleopatra faced her sister. "Don't be silly."

Her sister's mouth was drawn so tight it drained the blood from a scar at the corner of her lips. "Why is it silly?" she demanded in uncharacteristically firm tones. "I'm the eldest."

"Because . . ." What answer could Cleopatra give without insulting Gertrude? Even valuing truth and straightforwardness, as each of the Killorans did, in this instance Cleopatra's mind shied away from the truth. She'd sooner cut herself than hurt her siblings. It was why she was here now. "I need to be here."

"I should be protecting you," Gertrude pressed. "And Fie and Stephen," she added.

"You're needed at home," she finally said.

"I—"

"It is done," Cleopatra swiftly interrupted, and before her sister could argue any further, she shot a hand up. That firm rap instantly cut across Broderick and Ophelia's heated argument. The door was immediately opened, and ignoring the guard's hand, Cleopatra hopped out. Her boots settled with a quiet thump on cobblestones cleaner than most beds and floors she'd known for the first years of her life.

At her back, she dimly registered her siblings joining her on the pavement and Reggie scrambling down from atop the carriage. Elegantly clad lords and ladies strolling down the street stared back at the Killorans like circus oddities had just been deposited outside Ryker Black's residence. But then, that is precisely what they were to these people. People good enough to lose their fortunes to, but shameful enough to avoid for anything more than that. Cleopatra set her jaw, and when Lord Sanderson, a miserably clad dandy, took an extended look, she growled, "Ya've got a problem?"

Swallowing hard, the young man spun on his heel and sprinted off in the opposite direction.

"Bloody hell, Cleo," her brother griped at her side. "The point is to catch a husband, not scare every lord out of London."

She'd gladly scare them all the way to the Devil to be spared a future with one of those fops—if the end result would be different for her sisters.

"Come," he murmured, holding out his elbow. "Let me—"

"Lead me into the enemy's lair?" she snapped. These same people he'd taught her to hate, and now expected her to live with? "I don't require an escort. I will do this." And disapprove until she drew her last breath. "But I'll be damned if you or any of my sisters are the one to usher me through that doorway."

For the devil-may-care attitude he'd adopted and worn like a second skin through the years, the column of Broderick's throat moved. He had some regret in asking Cleopatra to do this—nay—in expecting *any* of his sisters to. Good, the blighter could chew on the Devil's trident for it.

More than half fearing all her confidence and strength would crack if she stole another look at her siblings, Cleopatra started forward. She kept her gaze trained on the open doorway, then stopped. Wheeling around, she marched back to her brother. She spoke in a low voice reserved for him. "When we met you, and you gave us names, I loved you for that." At that time, she would have sooner slit her own throat than admit as much. Cleopatra searched her gaze over his unreadable face. "You gave us the names of queens." A wad of emotion stuck in her throat, and she despised herself for that weakness. It had seen her beat by Mac Diggory too many times as a child until she'd learned to conceal that weakness. "Now I know it's not because you saw girls of strength and power, as you said . . . but because you wanted to make us into something we're not."

"Cleo," he said gruffly.

Cleopatra glowered him into silence. "Shut your bloody mouth," she said, her voice raspy. "I'll have this done in several months, and you'll not expect my sisters to . . ." Marry. *My God, I cannot even bring myself to spit that word out.* ". . . do the same. Are we clear?"

"It is for the good of the group," he repeated somberly, with a resolve that made her believe she'd merely imagined the flash of remorse she'd spied earlier. "If we have noble connections, we will *never* have to worry about losing all and living in the squalor we did." He took her hands, squeezing. "Think of it, Cleo. We will be dependent upon *no* man." As they'd been with Diggory.

Adair Thorne's sister killing that blighter was one favor she'd be forever grateful to their rival gang for, but she would sooner slice her own throat than breathe that thanks aloud.

Cleopatra briefly squeezed her eyes shut. She didn't want her siblings to be racked with the fear they'd once known, beholden to a bastard like Diggory. Didn't want to suffer through the cold nights, with nothing but tattered garments to drive back the winter's chill. As much as it pained her and she despised it, she knew Broderick was right. She had thought his plan was logical from the moment he'd laid it out years earlier. That did little to ease the panic and pain in her leaving her life behind, now.

Turning on her heel, she stalked forward, bag in hand, toward Black's residence and his butler. By the glower on the graying, scarred stranger's face, he was just another one of Black's guards.

"Thank you," Broderick called after her.

"Go to hell, Broderick," she shot back, not breaking stride.

"Cleo?" Gertrude called out, her voice quavering.

Cleopatra damned her heart for wrenching and quickened her steps to enter the enemy's lair. Grateful for the muslin cloak that shielded her actions from the army of waiting Blacks, Cleopatra burrowed inside the folds. Warily, she passed her gaze around the eclectic gathering: Black and his scarred, battle-marked brothers . . . and the smiling, innocent-eyed misses who stared warmly back.

Warmth. It was something Cleopatra had only ever known and been shown by her siblings.

"What are you doing here?" Adair Thorne snapped.

Cleopatra's face went hot. Stiffening, she shot a go-to-hell glance over her shoulder to where the surly bastard stood.

"Do hush, Adair." Favoring her brother-in-law with a glower, Black's wife came over to greet Cleopatra, a question in her eyes.

"I came instead," she said lamely, not offering details as to why she'd taken Gertrude's place.

Lady Chatham smiled. "How lovely to have you back among us, Miss Killoran—"

Niall Marksman's wife, the same woman Cleopatra had helped to freedom nearly a year earlier, interrupted. "Given you'll be living among our family, I expect we should dispense with formalities? You may call me Diana, and this is my sister-in-law Penelope." Black's wife lifted her fingers in a cheerful little wave.

Mad. They are utterly mad, this lot. Cleopatra stole a glance about to Black's gang and found her own pained consternation reflected back in their ruthless eyes. She tamped down a sigh. Who in blazes would have ventured that she, Cleopatra Killoran, member of the Devil's Den, would ever have a moment of commiseration with Black and his men?

A footman came forward to help her with her cloak, and Cleopatra automatically shot a hand out, slapping his fingers for daring to touch any part of her—garments included. "Cleopatra," she clipped out. "You may call me Cleopatra." For whether she wished to be here or not, these were the people she'd be spending the remainder of her unwed days with.

"Splendid," Penelope Black piped in. *What reason did the woman have to be cheerful?* "And I believe you know my husband. Please, you may call him Ryker—"

"No," Cleopatra said sharply, glancing to the man her own family had called enemy for too many years to overcome.

An awkward pall descended. "Mr. Black, then," Penelope suggested with the relentlessness of a starved dog with a bone.

And the staggering reality of being here . . . among Black and his kin . . . with the purpose of making a match among a world she would never belong to, cinched the airflow to her lungs. But the horror of horrors continued.

Penelope slipped her arm into Cleopatra's. "We shall see that your time in London is good fun."

Good fun? She'd rather pull her toenails out one by one. And as Black's wife prattled on, Cleopatra was again that small girl with Diggory's meaty hand wrapped about her throat as he choked off her breath and gleefully threatened her with death.

"We've a number of events already planned to introduce you to the *ton*, with your first formal introduction, a ball being held here—"

"Next week," Diana supplied, widening her smile.

Penelope nodded. "It shall be a small, intimate affair."

An event attended by nobles . . . all men she'd spent countless years of her life either stealing from or seeing inside her family's club. Only now, she'd step into their world as an outsider.

". . . quite lovely . . . not all of them . . . but the ones who've been invited are . . ."

The viscountess's voice drifted in and out of focus as Cleopatra fought through the panic.

"If—"

"My rooms?" she blurted, her voice hoarse to her own ears. Her incoherent request was met with perplexity among Black's kin. "I'd like to be shown to my rooms." Before she crumpled into a ball of panic and despair before them.

For a long moment where hope was born, she believed Black and his family would exact the ultimate torture and force her to remain here through a cataloging of the hellish polite events to come so that Cleopatra's only recourse would be a swift flight through that appealing front door.

The young ladies exchanged concerned looks, and that sent Cleopatra's hackles up. "Of course. Of course," Penelope Black murmured. "I expect you would like to see your new rooms."

I'd rather burn those rooms to the same ash that the Hell and Sin now finds itself than take up place here.

"We'll have your belongings brought up. Allow me to accompany you—"

Cleopatra and Mr. Black spoke in unison: "No."

The last thing Cleopatra wanted in this instance was company. She wanted to shut a panel between herself and all these strangers and allow herself a moment of weakness to rail at her brother for the horror of it all. "I do not require your escort."

Black's wife gave her husband a long look.

The stony-faced proprietor shot a hand up, and Cleopatra automatically reached down toward her boot when Black's next words stayed her.

"Adair, see to Miss Killoran's belongings," he said in a steely voice, his deliberate use of her surname a pointed testament that he saw her as an enemy.

She hesitated, casting a wary glance back at that miserable blighter.

"Miss Killoran," Thorne taunted with an edge that dared her to take the first step.

Angling her chin, she returned her attention to the woman who'd opened her home, regardless of the bad blood between their families. "I am . . ." She struggled to get the words out. ". . . grateful to you for . . ." *I can't.*

"There is no need to thank us, Cleopatra," Penelope said, reaching for Cleopatra's hands.

She recoiled from that gesture. Time had taught her enough to never trust one of the men and women connected to the Hell and Sin. Shoulders back, she backed away and fell into step alongside Adair Thorne.

She didn't want their kindness. Feeling the two young ladies' stares on her every movement, Cleopatra clutched her valise close.

"After you," Thorne said, gesturing ahead.

She gave her head a slight shake.

"I'm not asking you," he said tersely.

They locked gazes in a silent battle. So, she was to be escorted to her new rooms, not as a guest within their household, but as a person who bore watching. Black and his men were far cleverer than she'd credited, then.

The back of her neck prickled at the vulnerability of presenting herself so before these men she'd been raised to loathe. As she climbed the steps, she strained to hear the discussion that ensued in her wake. Alas, the streets had no doubt conditioned Black and his men with the same wariness Cleopatra herself had learned. They reached the top landing. "I understand you're afraid of me, Thorne. Rightly so." She watched as he knitted his tawny eyebrows into a single line. "But I cannot very well lead the way if I don't know where to go," she taunted, taking pleasure in baiting the man. Since she'd known Adair Thorne, he'd proven himself to be an arrogant rotter who didn't have the sense to see a woman's worth. It did, however, appear he had sense to be cautious of her.

"Straight, Killoran. End of the hall and left. Four doors down." How very different those guardlike commands were from the deferential respect and fear shown her by the men at the Devil's Den. The lords who visited her hell, along with the dregs of society and the staff there, feigned a respect for the Queen of the Dials, as she'd been nicknamed. She wanted to despise Thorne for his boldness but found she rather preferred this realness.

When she made no move to leave, he tipped his chin. "I said move."

All her brief appreciation turned to dust at his order. She might respect his genuineness, but she didn't take to being bossed about by anyone.

Gritting her teeth, Cleopatra resumed walking. As they moved down the plush carpeted halls, from the corner of her eyes, she took in the doors they passed. She'd learned early on to always measure the layout of her surroundings. One always had to be prepared to escape. Time to explore Black's home would come later when she wasn't under Thorne's suspicious gaze.

At last they reached the far recesses of the townhouse: one of the last doors in the long hallway. Thorne shot a hand out, and she stiffened. He merely pressed the handle. She hesitated. It would be unwise for Thorne, Black, or any other of their men to inflict harm upon her. That act would result in an all-out war of the streets. Nonetheless, she bore the scar upon her hand from having entered a room with far less caution than she should. Cleopatra ducked her head inside.

Sunlight streamed through the windows, bathing the spacious, pale-pink chambers in a soft light. Pink. She curled her fingers tighter around her valise handle as a memory whispered forward: Cleopatra as she'd been in her youth, prowling the streets of London in search of unsuspecting lords, and seeing a fancy toff alongside a small girl in pink ruffles. The two had laughed and spoken with such a tenderness that, from that point forward, Cleopatra had come to abhor that soft shade of innocence because it reminded her of what she'd truly gone without—a loving parent.

"Not to your liking, Cleopatra?"

She started, grateful to Adair for pulling her back from the humiliating melancholy that struck. It was the first time he'd laid claim to her given name. Hearing him wrap it in his low baritone roused . . . something peculiar inside. A damned, unwanted fluttering that didn't have anything to do with hatred or danger, and was all the more unnerving for it. She forced herself to look back at him. "That'll be all," Cleopatra said, dismissing him like a servant.

Splotches of color suffused his cheeks.

It was entirely too easy getting under this one's skin. And for the first time in the whole of that miserable day, she felt the stirrings of amusement.

"Turn around," he said gruffly.

"Wha—" Cleopatra gasped as he laid his hands to her waist. Her valise tumbled from her fingers, and God help her, the weight of his powerful hand upon her person brought her eyes briefly closed. She fought to draw in a steady breath, but it emerged ragged.

"Wh-what are you doing?" She managed to complete her earlier question, reaching belatedly for her weapon.

Adair gripped her two hands in a firm hold that also had a shocking gentleness to it. He lowered his lips close to her ear; the hint of coffee and cheroots stirred the sensitive skin of her nape. "Surely you don't think we'll not search you," he muttered, wholly unaffected, as he patted her through her gown.

She tried to squeeze out an inventive curse—and came up empty.

Through the fabric of her satin skirts, the heat of his bold touch continued to burn her, holding her immobile. It had been years since a man had dared to touch her . . . in any way. That man had lost two fingers for that affront by Cleopatra's hand herself. Adair's touch, however, was nothing like that grasping, clumsy one of a toff trying to take a girl against an alleyway wall. His hand lingered on her belly, and her mouth went dry. In a bid for both nonchalance and control, she peeled her lip back in a sneer. "What good would a weapon tucked inside my gown do me?"

Ignoring her, he dropped to a knee and tugged her skirts up. The slap of cool air on her exposed legs effectively doused whatever maddening pull his touch had inflicted on her senses. "Bastard," she hissed, shooting her boot out.

With his unencumbered hand, he caught her ankle. "No armed Killoran will sleep under our roof." In quick order, he divested her of the sapphire-studded dagger and tossed it at the opposite side of the wall.

She silently screamed at the loss of that weapon and struggled against his hold. "Give me my damned knife," she railed, yanking her foot left and right. Propelling her body sideways, she made a futile grab for the blade. Adair tightened his hold and glanced over at the weapon they battled for. His gaze lingered on that piece she'd retained of Diggory's. "Don't even think of it, ya lousy bugger," she seethed. It was the only material item of any value to her.

When he'd joined Diggory's gang, Broderick had convinced that hated leader of uniform blades to mark their connection. However, with the Celtic symbol of inner strength formed with the gems upon it, the blade was a reminder of her strength and ability to survive in the face of ugliness and evil. She'd be damned if Adair Thorne or any other claimed it for their own. She opened her mouth to bring his ears down but registered his stillness.

A flash of hatred flared in Adair's green eyes. Did he recognize the blade for what it was? Then, how many who'd crossed unfortunate paths with Mac Diggory or his men had had a similar weapon touched to their throat at one time or another? Or in Cleopatra's case, countless ones.

Taking advantage of Adair's distraction, she shot her boot out and caught him between the legs.

The air left him on a swift exhale, and he immediately freed her to clutch at himself. Cleopatra dealt him another kick to his lower belly. She gasped as her toes collided with a hard wall of muscle better suited to a stone statue than a man. Nonetheless, her efforts had the intended effect, and another sharp breath left him. Cleopatra sprang into action and lunged for her dagger. She cried out as that firm, unyielding grip collected her ankle once more, upending her.

Cleopatra pitched forward. She put her palms out to catch herself. Adair swiftly brought her atop him, breaking her fall.

"Hellion," he whispered, rolling her under him.

Their chests moved in like rhythm as her panting gasps for air blended with his noisy inhalations. The heat and power of him doused her logic and drove back her fear. Unbidden, her gaze went to his lips. Only one man had managed to place his lips this close to her own. She'd been a girl, and he'd been a blighter who'd liked to bugger children. At Broderick's hand, that bastard had paid the price with his life. Yet, the hint of cheroots and coffee lingering on Adair Thorne's breath was so very different. Intoxicating. His gaze lingered on her mouth. Did she imagine the way his throat worked? "Do not ever put your hands on me, hellion," he whispered, and that slight movement nearly brought their lips into contact.

Her heart thudded as he slid a hand about her, cupping her at the nape. *He's going to kiss me. He's going to kiss me, and I want it . . .*

She recoiled. What in blazes was wrong with her? *Get control of yourself. You are Cleopatra Killoran. One of the Queens of St. Giles.*

"It wasn't my hand that brought you down," she whispered. She wrestled her knee back, but this time he caught her before she connected. Only, instead of wrestling it back into place, he caressed that portion of her leg.

Cleopatra gulped.

"Adair."

They looked as one to that sharp exclamation. Ryker Black, Niall Marksman, and Calum Dabney stood at the end of the hall, pistols trained on them. Burning with humiliation at her own body's reaction, Cleopatra had never been more grateful in the whole of her rotten existence for both having a gun pointed at her person and the intrusion of a Black.

"Wot in blazes are ya doing?" Marksman growled, eyeing his brother as though he'd sprung a second head.

A ruddy flush marred Adair's chiseled cheeks. "The girl was armed."

"That wasn't a weapon you were grabbing," she taunted, relishing the deepening color in his cheeks. "And I'm not a girl." She bucked against him.

"You no doubt sprang from Satan's side," he muttered. "You're barely—"

The tread of footfalls cut across whatever other insult he intended to toss out.

"Adair," Ryker Black said sharply.

Using that distraction, Cleopatra jerked her knee between his legs.

With a groan befitting a wounded beast, Adair rolled off her and collapsed onto his back. She scrambled out from under him and crawled over to her knife. Cleopatra grabbed the serpent handle and got herself into a fighting stance. "Get the 'ell away from me," she warned, breathless. My God, she'd been lusting after Adair Thorne.

She jabbed the dagger in the direction of each Black. This was never going to work. The mistrust was too great on each of their parts. One simply couldn't overcome a lifetime's worth of hatred, not even to achieve a goal that Broderick felt was for the greater good.

The proprietor of the Hell and Sin lowered his weapon to his side, and his brothers followed suit.

Guarded, she pressed her back against the wall.

"We have no intention of hurting you," he said in gravelly tones. He looked over to Adair, who shoved himself into a standing position. "You were asked to escort her to her rooms, not to wrestle her in my damned corridors."

Most other men, even the fearless Killoran lot, would have backed down when presented with Black's palpable fury. Adair dug his heels in. "She is armed." Not taking his gaze from Cleopatra, he grabbed her valise and unlatched it. He dumped the pistols and knives contained within on the hall floor. The cache clattered to the floor with a noisy thump.

"I'd be mad to enter your home weaponless," she spat into the silence.

Tucking his pistol inside his waistband, Ryker Black dragged a hand over his face. "You cannot remain here, armed as you are."

Then I'll leave . . .

The words hovered on her lips and hung there. For if she marched out with her head up and her weapons in hand, where would they be? Broderick would merely send Ophelia—or worse—a too-compliant Gertrude back in her place. Only—giving over her ability to defend herself went against every lesson she'd learned on the streets of St. Giles.

"What will it be, Miss Killoran?" Mr. Dabney pressed. Had that emerged as a barking command, it would be easier than his calm matter-of-factness.

"Leave," Adair said in hushed tones out of the corner of his mouth. His demand barely reached her ears. He wanted her here no more than she wanted to be here . . . and yet—she slid her eyes closed. There was a challenge there, and she heard it. And the world could say any number of things about Cleopatra Killoran—most of which would be true—but none would ever find her one to back down from a threat or challenge.

She forced her eyes open. Bending slowly, she held Ryker Black's gaze as she purposefully resheathed her dagger. "You can have my guns and other knives. But this one I keep."

He was already shaking his head. "No one here means you harm, but I have people here dependent upon me." And he didn't trust that she wouldn't bring harm to his kin. Then, that was the way of their world.

"What about this guard you've set on me?" she nodded toward Adair.

"Given what we've witnessed, you're quite capable of protecting yourself against Adair," Niall Marksman drawled, earning a round of guffaws.

Adair shot his middle finger up in a crude gesture that merely resulted in another bevy of laughter.

She started. Those expressions of amusement and mirth were unexpected and unfamiliar. She'd seen the men before her as blank souls with blackness inside. To now know they shared her own family's sense of loyalty, and managed to find amusement in life, stirred a restlessness. She preferred them cold and unfeeling to . . . *human.*

"What will it be, Miss Killoran?" Ryker Black repeated, his amusement fading so quickly that she might have well imagined that crack in his icy veneer.

She hesitated, at war with herself. *Think of your sisters. Think of Gertie and Fie* . . . "God rot all your souls," she muttered, and removed her knife once more.

Black nodded and glanced over her shoulder. Adair came forward, hand extended. "When you are done here, it will be returned to you."

Triumph glittered in his green eyes, and if she were as ruthless as the late Diggory himself, she'd have plunged the tip of her dagger into Adair Thorne for that gloating victory. Tamping down a curse, she tossed it at his feet. Her palms went moist as he bent and retrieved her most cherished weapon. "If anything happens to that, I'll end you, Adair Thorne."

His eyes flashed fire. "Did you just threaten me?"

"I gave you a vow." She glanced over at his brothers. "All of you."

Bereft at the loss of her family and now her dagger, her heart wrenched viciously while all these strangers stared on. And before she did something like crumple before them, she stormed into her new rooms, slammed the door hard behind her, and turned the lock.

Cleopatra leaned against the wood panel and, borrowing support, slid herself down to the floor. She squeezed her eyes shut, and a single tear slipped free, rolling a path down her cheek.

Chapter 6

The house quiet since night descended, Adair climbed the stairs to the main living quarters in this, his new temporary home.

It had been one day.

One day had passed since Cleopatra Killoran had made herself at home in Ryker and Penelope's home.

In that time, her belongings—after being searched and rid of additional hidden weapons—were delivered to her rooms. Meals had come and gone. Trays were delivered and taken away.

And there wasn't a single thing Adair trusted about her actions.

Calum and Niall had since gone off to their own residences, ensuring their respective wives remained free from any harm a Killoran might inflict. However, Penelope, Ryker, and their babe resided under this roof with their enemy still. And not a single Black would ever know even a displaced hair on their head by the Killorans.

He reached the main landing and stopped alongside a crimson-clad servant. "Anything?" he asked from the corner of his mouth.

At first glance, one would only take the tall young man as a proper servant. "Nothin', Mr. Thorne. Not even a hint of sound in 'er room."

When he spoke, however, Finch revealed the hardened tones of a London street tough. One who'd gone from guard inside the Hell and Sin to temporary servant.

Adair's muscles went taut. "Someone's had eyes on her?"

"Maid went in, went out with the dinner tray about an hour ago."

Some of the tension left him. One could never be too careful where a Killoran was concerned.

"Adair!"

They looked toward Ryker's wife, who came racing down the hall.

Finch immediately sprang to alert, but quickly took in her carefree smile and flushed cheeks as she skidded to a stop beside him.

"Hello, Mr. Finch."

"Your Ladyship," the footman greeted, and dropped a belated bow.

"You are dismissed for the evening." The guard hesitated, and then beat a quick retreat. The ever-cheerful viscountess turned her focus to Adair. "If I might speak to you? There is a matter of import I'd discuss."

With him? He eyed her warily, and with a nod at the other man, sent him back to the shadows he'd occupied at the end of the hall. Adair looked to Ryker's wife. "Is everything all—"

"Fine, just fine," she hurried to assure him. His sister-in-law looped her arm through his. "Walk with me for a bit."

Adair hesitated, lingering his gaze on that suspicious doorway.

"I trust that given Cleopatra hasn't left her rooms in a day now, our halls are quite safe," she said wryly.

"I'm not afraid of the girl," he said curtly.

Penelope winked at him. "I was jesting, Adair," she said on an exaggerated whisper. "Come," she urged, and it was spoken with the same persuasiveness that had managed to convert Ryker Black from ruthless, unbending gaming hell owner to one who sought his wife's opinions and . . . took in Killorans.

He fell into step beside her as they walked away from Cleopatra's chambers. "I'm worried about our guest," she said when they'd stepped around the corner.

This is what she'd come to him about? "Our guest?" he echoed. Surely that isn't how they'd refer to the termagant who'd brought him down not once, but twice, in the span of a few minutes—with all his siblings staring on as witnesses, no less.

"Cleopatra," Penelope clarified. As though there was another person residing with them now.

"What has she done—"

"Nothing," Penelope said on a beleaguered sigh. "You and your brothers are seeing monsters in even scared young women."

He snorted. "Cleopatra Killoran was born with less fear than Lucifer him—*oomph*." Adair rubbed his stomach, where he'd taken his sister-in-law's sharp elbow.

"That young woman is *afraid*," she insisted, glaring at him.

"She's a Killoran," he said in a bid to talk sense into her.

Penelope abruptly stopped, forcing him to halt beside her. She settled her hands on her hips. "Are you suggesting they're incapable of being hurt simply because of their *name*?"

"Yes," he said bluntly. Anyone who could take up with Diggory, destroyer of innocence and scourge of the streets, was incapable of it. "That is precisely what I'm saying."

Regardless of Cleopatra Killoran's gender, she was the same rotted, ruthless bastard as her brother. After all, her selling her soul and moving into Ryker Black's residence on the hope of acquiring a title was testament to that.

Penelope gave her head a sad shake. "You and your brothers," she said softly. "You're still so consumed by your past . . ."

He stiffened. "I suggest ya speak to your husband about the treatment of your guest."

Sister-in-law or no, other than his siblings, Adair hadn't shared a single part of his existence with another soul. And even his brothers and Helena had made it a point to studiously avoid all talk of what they'd each endured. One didn't speak of one's suffering—not even with family.

"Ah, yes," Penelope said, waggling her eyebrows. "But you see, my husband wasn't the one who wrestled the young lady to the floor and divested her of her weapon."

His neck went hot. Of course she had heard of the scuffle he'd gotten into with Cleopatra yesterday afternoon. *I'll not feel guilty. I'll not feel guilty.* Searching a person, man or woman, who'd come to live with them—particularly a Killoran—was the height of wise. "She was armed," he groused, shifting back and forth on his feet. He'd not be made out to be a man who went about assaulting women.

"You are all armed. We all are," she corrected.

It was a mark of how Ryker's wife, a lady of the *ton*, had been transformed that she, too, should carry a dagger about.

"But none of us would harm one another. Cleopatra Killoran . . ." Could gut them all in their sleep if they let their guards down. He'd spare Ryker's wife those gruesome details.

"I was her," Penelope pressed, like a dog with a bone where the Killoran woman was concerned.

Incredulity swept over him. "You were never Cleopatra Killoran." That hellion had likely ended as many men and women as Adair himself.

His sister-in-law gripped his shoulder and gave a slight squeeze. "I was alone in a world away from my family . . . just like her. For what you think you might know about the lady, she is scared, and I'd have you at least treat her with kindness as long as she's living with us." Penelope sent another long, sad look to Cleopatra's borrowed chambers. "I would wager she's alone in there, worrying after her future, and hating every moment of being here." Her lips twisted. "And who could blame the young lady? After all, you and your brothers have treated her as more prisoner than guest."

"We haven't treated her as a prisoner," he said defensively.

They'd had countless patrons who'd harmed members of their club or hurt the girls employed by the Hell and Sin. Those men had been dealt with as the criminals they were. "I hardly believe opening your arms, allowing the hell . . ." At his sister's look, he swiftly amended his word choice. "Allowing the *girl* rooms, food, and an entry to society merits the comparison to a prison." Having himself entered Newgate to free his brother Calum years earlier, he could testify that rat-infested, dank hell bore no hint of a resemblance or comparison to a Grosvenor Square residence.

Adair tamped down a sigh. There would be no reasoning with Ryker's innocent wife. "Unless she gives me reason, I'll treat her with . . ." He grimaced. He couldn't bring himself to say it.

"Kindness," Penelope supplied.

"Kindness," he gritted out. Kindness for a woman who was, with her connections to Killoran and Diggory, an enemy in every way. The same woman who'd drawn a knife and, by the glitter in her eyes, would have gladly gutted him yesterday afternoon. And now his sister-in-law painted her as a wounded, scared young woman. It was laughable. It was inconceivable. It was . . .

Adair's gaze involuntarily slid to that doorway down the hall. It was damned possible. How many times had he marched down these corridors and put questions to the guards stationed at the end of the hall? Not once did Cleopatra exit her chambers. In fact, if it weren't for the meals she consistently ordered and the bath she'd called for, he'd have doubted the hellion was even in those rooms. But she was. And damn if he didn't feel the unwanted sting of remorse. For Adair and his brothers *had* treated Cleopatra Killoran precisely as Penelope said—as more prisoner than guest.

With a frustrated sigh, he dragged his hands up and down over his face.

"I understand the need for caution," Penelope said, speaking the way she might to a fractious mare. "But we needn't treat the lady as though she is a criminal." Cleopatra Killoran was undoubtedly a criminal. A person couldn't survive in the streets without breaking society's laws. "It is late. You needn't stalk her chambers and dog her footsteps."

"I can hardly dog her footsteps when she's shut herself away," he muttered.

A twinkle lit Penelope's eyes. "That is because she is sleeping," she said on an exaggerated whisper.

Life had given him too many reasons to be suspicious . . . particularly of the men and women who were part of Diggory's crew. "But what if—"

"Adair," his sister-in-law cut in, her earlier teasing gone and replaced with a military-like command. "It is late. Find your chambers, and we can try again with Cleopatra tomorrow."

Did Penelope think this was truly about forging a relationship with the young woman? The only thing he'd try to do with Killoran's sister was determine how to coordinate her exit out of this household.

"As you wish," he said tightly. Feeling his sister-in-law's eyes on him, he started down the hall to the rooms he'd been assigned—next to Cleopatra's. For Penelope's defense of Cleopatra, Adair well knew the lady's husband was not of a like opinion where Killoran's sister was concerned. Adair being placed in the guest suites next to hers had been no matter of coincidence but rather a strategic plan designed so he could keep a close watch on the unpredictable hellion's movements.

Entering his rooms, Adair pushed the door closed behind him. As he walked, he loosened his cravat and tossed it aside. He claimed a spot at the edge of his bed.

Shadows cast by the handful of lamps danced off the walls; the only sound of the room was the groan of the floorboard as he removed his boot. Setting it aside, he tugged free the next and laid it beside the other. And then he registered the absolute still.

He frowned. Life in the streets had taught him proper wariness of those stretches of silence.

"Nothin', Mr. Thorne. Not even a hint of sound in 'er room."

There were plenty of reasons why there wouldn't be a sound in those chambers. The young woman was friendless, in a strange household. The hour was late. And yet . . . With a curse, Adair stood. Barefoot, he stalked over to the shared wall, and much the way he had as a boy raiding the local bakeries after they'd closed for the night, he put his ear to the wall . . . and listened. The moment stretched on, with no answering sound. Only silence reigned. Some of the tension went out of him.

She slept. Grateful to be at last resolved of his responsibilities where the hellion was concerned, he quit his post at the wall and sought out his own bed for the night.

At last, silence filled the hallway outside Cleopatra's chambers as Penelope Black and Adair Thorne ceased their yammering.

For a boy born of the streets, he'd certainly shown remarkably weak moments where Cleopatra was concerned. She'd knocked him on his arse—twice. And by the click of the door closing, he'd dismissed her room outright and found his chambers—for a second time.

Cleopatra slipped down Black's halls, inspecting her surroundings. One who cared about surviving always had to have a familiarity with one's surroundings. It would be perilous to share a roof with the Black family and not have a grasp on the layout of the setting she was to call home.

As she strode along the carpeted corridors, she mentally counted the doors—as well as the lit sconces. The number of lit candles in a given corridor provided an unwitting indication of just how many people occupied a certain hall. She glanced to the shadows flickering off the silk wallpaper. By the dearth of lit ones here, the Blacks had kept her largely isolated inside their townhouse. Which proved they were far cleverer than she'd credited.

Cleopatra reached the end of the wide corridor and stopped. Hands on hips, she swept the area in a small circle. Her plaited hair fell over her shoulder, and she pushed it back. There were ten doorways on one side and—she wrinkled her nose—eleven on the other. It was an incongruity that didn't fit with lords and ladies who preferred everything neat and orderly. All in all, one and twenty doors total, on this floor. She did another glance about, then stretched her arms out on either side of her to measure the distance between doorways. With her eyes, Cleopatra took in every detail, from the types of door handles, to the slightly faded portions of carpeting indicating which areas were most heavily traveled.

She owed her twenty years' existence to having never missed a detail, and she was certainly not so naive that she'd miss one inside this household. Making the return trek, Cleopatra counted her footsteps across the length of the hall, then stopped abruptly.

A faint glow penetrated through the crack at the room two doors down from Adair's. Frowning, she eyed that oak panel. For all the pride she took in noting the details of her surroundings, she'd failed to register the faint light coming from under that door. She automatically reached for her knife.

Her fingers curled into reflexive fists. For the first time in her entire life, she was without her weapon. She'd been stripped of control and placed in a hall where careless maids forgot to douse all the candles at night.

Fire . . . Run, just go. Leave me . . .

Cleopatra gulped several times as those dark memories trickled in. Mayhap it was the vulnerability of being away from her siblings. Or mayhap being forced to remember the power wielded in shattering lives, as it recently had Adair's club, that brought forth thoughts of a night she'd not recalled in more years than she could remember.

I'm simply tired, is all. "Bloody careless maids," she mouthed into the quiet. With renewed purpose, she closed the space between her and that door. Mindful of the danger in entering unfamiliar rooms, she quietly pressed the handle and let herself in the dimly lit room. She blinked several times to adjust to the dark. Cleopatra inventoried the space—the empty space. Of what had apparently once been a bedroom and had since been converted into some haphazard, thrown-together . . . office-like space. The mahogany desk littered with papers called to her . . . beckoned when everything said to get herself gone. But then, Cleopatra had never been one to do as she was expected or ought. Closing the door at her back, she quickly located the nearest sconce. Drifting over, she blew, snuffing the candle. A trail of dark smoke wafted a path up.

The pungent odor burning in her nose briefly held her frozen. That acrid scent sent her belly churning, as it always did. *Ye show any more of that weakness, and I'll end ye, girl . . .* Sucking in a slow breath, she sought out the other flame, making her way over to it. She might despise Diggory and would gladly spear him with the Devil's trident when they met in hell, but he'd left her invaluable lessons on survival.

Except . . .

Cleopatra paused, leaving that candle lit, and adjusted her path.

She crossed to the cluttered pedestal desk. The green-leather top peeked out from under stacks of papers and ledgers, bringing her to another stop. Only this time it was not fear that compelled her . . . but rather, intrigue.

She wetted her lips and took another swift glance about. The shadows serving as her only company, she wandered closer. Sifting through the pile, she took in drawing after drawing. Some copies had been marked with an *X*, and others, a question mark. Her earlier reservations gone, Cleopatra dropped her palms on the available space on the desk and evaluated the numbered sheets. Then it hit her what she was looking at. "They're plans for their club," she breathed into the quiet.

It was the kind of information Diggory or Killoran would have used to their advantage to destroy their competition—decisions she once would have wholeheartedly supported. Never, however, would she have urged ruination by fire. There was too much that could go wrong from the flicker of a flame: lives lost, excruciating suffering, expansive damage. No, what held her rooted to her examination was a genuine intrigue.

It was a glimpse into the gaming hell world that she so loved, and in this instance, it didn't matter that this was Adair Thorne's club, a rival establishment whose failure she should be more fixed on. Instead, it was an essential thread connecting her to the familiar. Now damning the fact that she'd snuffed one of those candles, Cleopatra leaned over the sheet, squinting at the meticulous drawings.

She trailed her fingertip over the charcoal markings where the faro and hazard tables were arranged. Wrinkling her brow, she compared the plans drafted here to another, laying them side by side. Why in blazes would—

The faint click of a pistol screeched across the quiet.

"Drop the page."

Adair's low baritone emerged coated in ice. She swallowed hard, damning herself for making a faulty misstep. Her fascination with the Hell and Sin's building plans had compromised her focus. Her fingers trembled slightly, and she now gave thanks for the cover of dark that hopefully concealed that faint quavering.

"I said, drop the—"

"I heard you clearly, Adair," she said in forced bored tones, laying possession to his name in a bid to assert herself in the precarious situation.

"If you heard me, hellion, then do as I said," he commanded on a steely whisper.

Cleopatra released those plans, as instructed.

"Now turn and face me, Cleopatra."

Not Cleo . . . *Cleopatra*. She'd always adored the name chosen by Broderick for her, for the power it implied. And yet, she hated that her brother and those in their employ insisted on shortening it as they did, lessening its relevance. Not Adair. His whispered mastery of those four syllables was heady stuff, indeed.

She quirked her lips in a smile and faced him.

He narrowed his eyes. "Is there something amusing about this?"

"Actually, yes." In a bid to stir his ire, she drew herself up onto the edge of his desk.

"Y—" He faltered in his reply, moving his gaze up and down her person, before settling once more on her face.

Her skirts rucked about her ankles in a way that would have earned embarrassment from a proper lady. She did not, nor would she ever, fit into that category—no matter how much her brother sought to stuff her into that mold. "Am I expected to believe you'll shoot me here in Ryker Black's home?"

Adair eyed her carefully for a long moment, and then, not taking his gaze from her, he tucked his pistol inside his waistband. "Is that why Killoran chose to send you? To learn our plans and bring them back?"

She was torn between flattery that he thought her capable enough to be the one sent as a go-between, and . . . frustratingly hurt that he saw the inherent silliness in her being the sister to make a match. It didn't matter that she was in complete agreement on the matter of her form and face. Knowing his disdain, however, rankled.

"They're rubbish," she countered.

He stitched his eyebrows into a single warning line.

"Your plans," she clarified.

His jaw worked, and she braced for him to order her on to hell. "There's four of them there," he said gruffly, unexpectedly engaging in a discussion on his club. And they were drawn up by several builders and quickly. He'd not mention that point.

"All right, then. I've looked through two of them, and *these* ones"— she indicated the pages in question—"are rot."

"You had no more than six minutes to study them," he challenged.

Cleopatra widened her eyes. He'd been there the entire time?

The hint of a smile curved his lips. "I heard you in the hall."

"Impossible." Her fingers made contact with the thick sheets, and they wrinkled noisily in the room.

"Do you make it a habit of wandering the halls of another man's home and snuffing out candles?"

Shame at having been discovered, and against her knowing, brought her toes curling so tight her arches ached. "I thought the room had been left vacant and the flame was left lit," she groused.

There was a mocking edge to his grin, belied by the hardness in his eyes.

"And you were worried because you know the danger posed by an errant flame?"

A memory slid in of a beloved figure she'd made herself forget.

Joan. The closest Cleopatra had ever come to a true mother. Another fire. One set by the Devil himself.

Leave me . . . you need to leave . . . And coward that she'd been, she'd not hesitated before gathering her sisters and abandoning the decrepit building. Unable to meet his gaze, she briefly contemplated that sconce in question. "I know about it," she gruffly admitted. Just not for the reasons he believed—the ones having to do with his burned club. Hopping down from her perch, she wandered several steps, presenting him her back. Cleopatra drew in several slow, quiet breaths.

"Is that a concession of guilt?" Adair's whipcord body went taut, bringing her attention to the previously escaped detail about the towering figure. Having discarded his jacket at some point, he stood in his bare feet, with his cravat gone, and only his shirtsleeves and breeches. It was a familiar state of undress she'd witnessed countless men in before. Only the tufts of dark curls peeking out from the opening at his neck and the olive hue of his muscled chest were so very different from the gents caught in dishabille at her family's hell. Her pulse kicked up.

He moved fast, like a tiger she'd once witnessed pounce in the royal menagerie. "I asked you a question."

Cleopatra retreated until the backs of her legs collided with the desk. Her heart hammered a wild beat that had nothing to do with fear and everything to do with the heat pouring off his chiseled frame. "My family didn't torch your hell," she got out, her voice far too faint to merit any respect or authority. Nonetheless, she surged on the balls of her feet, going toe-to-toe with him. "Ya were destroying it enough without any of ours bringing you to ashes."

His nostrils flared. "Yet you spoke about the power of a blaze—"

"Because I do," she snapped out, annoyance making her careless in all she revealed. "Not everything is about you and your ruined club." Cleopatra pressed her palms against his chest to shove . . . but the heat of his skin pierced his shirt, the feel of his muscled physique burning her as sure as any of the blazes they now fought over. She curled her palms into the lawn fabric.

"You know about it, then," his melodic voice washed over her.

She nodded slowly. "Oi do."

Run . . . you need to take your sisters and . . .

Cleopatra pressed her eyes briefly shut. More than a foot shorter than he was, she'd have cursed and lamented the staggering difference that weakened her. Now she fixed her gaze on his chest, giving thanks that he could not see her.

Adair brushed his knuckles over her jaw, forcing her neck back to meet his gaze. His quixotic touch muddled her senses as his intense, piercing green eyes sought hers. "Your parents?" he ventured.

Her parents? What was he . . . ?

Why, he assumed she was just another whelp taken in by Diggory. Numbly, Cleopatra dropped her arms to her side.

"My parents and sister were also claimed by a fire," he said gruffly, a surprising confession that let her into his world.

Then the significance of that loss, coupled with the one he'd recently suffered, penetrated her shock. He'd lost not only his family but his club. Cleopatra dipped her eyes once more. Despite the horrors that gripped her nightmares still of that long-ago day, she'd not allowed herself to think of Adair's club being consumed in a similar way. Of the terror he and the men, women, and children inside would have known. The smell of burning flesh—

"Oi'm sorry about your club," she said hoarsely.

Chapter 7

Cleopatra hadn't probed and pried about the admission he'd made about his past: the parents and sister he never spoke of. Instead, she'd fixed on just one . . .

Oi'm sorry about your club.

There were five words there he'd never imagined a Killoran could or would ever string together.

Everything about that apology stank of a street trick. A bid to deceive one's enemy, all to gain an upper hand. After all, she'd been discovered sneaking about Black's home. Her emotional response was likely nothing more than a bid to distract from the fact he'd caught her red-handed.

Only—

She spoke about fires as one who knew. It had been there in the flash of horror and the emotion thickening her tone as she'd simply stated an understanding for what he'd lived through . . . not only recently at the Hell and Sin . . . but as a boy.

The young woman lifted her gaze to his, those luminous depths impossibly big behind the round rims of her spectacles. And something far more dangerous than a weakness for a Killoran consumed him—desire.

Dismayed, he stepped around her, brushing her out of the way. "Don't you ever come in here again," he ordered, swiftly stacking the numerous building plans Phippen had designed. "Don't wander the halls at night, and don't let yourself into rooms that don't belong to you," he gruffly ordered.

Cleopatra pulled herself up onto the edge of his desk, and from behind those silly, large wire-frames, rolled her eyes. "*All* the rooms here are unfamiliar."

His lips twitched. "Fair point."

"As much as you'd prefer to keep it that way, I'll not let you make me a prisoner here," she said.

Adair gathered the finalized design plan for the Hell and Sin and purposefully tucked it in the middle of the pile. For as sneaky as this one had proven herself to be on countless scores, he'd be wise to lock up his paperwork and any room he wanted this one to keep out of.

"That's the one, then?"

He paused, midmovement, and looked over.

She nudged her chin. "It's just you placed all the other pages on top, but you stuck that last one in the middle. So, I take it, you were attempting to . . . *hide* it." By the amusement in that slightly overemphasized word, Cleopatra found that to be of extreme hilarity.

"You're observant." It was a good reminder that he should trust this imp as far as he could throw her, but having lived the life he had, there was also an admiration for her cleverness.

"No choice but to be," she said simply, lifting her shoulders in a little shrug. She gave him a half smile that dimpled her cheek. "Learned quick that to not be watchful will ruin a person."

"I didn't see that one," she said, contentedly filling the void of his unresponsiveness.

"And you won't," he muttered.

A cynical snort escaped the young woman. "Afraid of even a Killoran seeing your club? I didn't take you as smart, Thorne."

Thorne. Cleopatra used his surname to make her annoyance known . . . or to bait him.

"Why would I show you my plans?" he retorted. Relinquishing his pile, he folded his arms and met her gaze. "Isn't one wise to keep one's enemy close?" One also didn't engage in casual discourse or make mention of one's past . . . but he'd done—and continued to do—both this night. *It's boredom. Nothing else to account for it, but the tedium of living inside the fancy end of Mayfair.*

"You've seen my club."

My club. Not my brother's. Not Killoran's. Nor even Diggory's. *My* club. Even in her boldest, most confident day, his own sister, Helena, had never laid claim to the gaming hell. This boldness and strength in Cleopatra only sent that blasted admiration swirling.

"Only fair you show me yours," she continued over his tumult, giving a little shrug of her shoulders.

"Show me yours?" He chuckled. "Using a child's argument."

"It is the only way I seem able to reason with you."

Adair stilled. Wait. By God, had she just . . . ? Why, did she call him . . . ?

Cleopatra winked and stretched her palm out.

He was going mad. There was no other accounting for the fact that even now he considered turning his plans over to a damned Killoran. Adair shot a glance over his shoulder at the closed door. His brothers would have his head for such foolishness. Returning his focus back to the persuasive minx, he dropped his gaze to her hand—and stopped.

A jagged *D* stood stark upon her palm. That possessive tattoo that marked her connections to the beast who'd tortured Adair and his brothers. Cleopatra balled her hand and yanked it back to her lap. It also served as a reminder of the folly in lowering his defenses where this one was concerned. He opened his mouth to deliver a jeering taunt.

It was her lips, however, that halted that flow of words. Or rather . . . the corners of her lips. White, tense lines that revealed that for her brave show and grand displays, she wasn't the unaffected, deadened person Diggory had been.

"Never mind," she mumbled. "Keep your damned plans. If they're as rubbish as the other ones I looked through, then you needn't even worry about competition in the first place." She jumped to her feet, and any grand exit she surely intended to make was ruined as her spectacles slipped from the bridge of her nose and clattered noisily upon the floor.

Cursing, Cleopatra sank to her knees and stretched her fingers about. Why . . . why . . . she really had a need for those frames.

Swiftly joining her on the floor, Adair rescued the slightly bent pair. "Here," he murmured.

"What are you—?"

He tucked the curved wires around her delicate, shell-like ears and perched them on the bridge of her freckled nose.

Freckles. She had freckles. A faint dusting upon her nose and upon her cheeks. It . . . *softened* this woman he'd thought could never be taken for delicate.

Adjusting her glasses, Cleopatra glowered at him through the smudged frames, shattering his foolish musings. "What are you staring at?" she demanded.

He frowned. Ignoring her cursing and questioning, Adair plucked them from her face and stood.

"Thorne," she gritted, jumping up.

Yanking the tails of his shirt free of his waistband, he proceeded to scrub the frames with the soft material. "For someone who requires glasses, Cleopatra Killoran, you're certainly one who doesn't take proper damned care of them." Ignoring her grasping hands, he held the spectacles higher, out of her reach, and continued cleaning them. "Here," he muttered, replacing them again.

She blinked wildly like an owl startled from its perch, and in this instance, she may as well have been any innocent lady of Polite Society and not a ruthless member of Diggory's—and now Killoran's—gang.

He cleared his throat. "You need to clean your glasses."

Just like that, the charged moment was shattered. "Don't tell me wot Oi need," she barked. "You with your presumptuous hands and . . . Where do you think you're going?" she demanded as he returned to his desk. "Oi was . . ."

Shuffling through the stack, he withdrew the most recently agreed-upon plans for the club. "You wanted to see it," he pointed out. "Here's your chance to glimpse inside the greatest club in England."

A half laugh, half snort filtered from her lips. Without hesitation, she joined him at the cluttered desk. He'd been so damned busy overseeing the construction and this one here that he'd really neglected his makeshift office.

"You really should tidy your space, Adair," Cleopatra said, unerringly following his very thoughts.

"Shut it, Killoran," he said without inflection. "Or don't you want to see my hell?"

She wrinkled her pert nose. "I want to see it," she conceded.

He stretched out the plans before them, laying the long sheet out for her viewing. Adair cast a sideways glance over and found her squinting hard. Quitting the place beside her, he crossed over to the nearest sconce. Carefully lifting the candle, he carried it about the room, setting the other candles alight, until the room was doused in light. Feeling Cleopatra's eyes on him, he looked over.

The glowing candles played off the surprise in her eyes. "Do you think me so much a bastard that I'd have you squint to see the damned plans?" he asked gruffly.

"Yes," she said softly. "I did believe that."

Blowing out the one in his hand, he rejoined Cleopatra. "My family is not evil." Unlike hers, who'd been loyal to the Devil. Just like that, he shattered the easy camaraderie, and a formal relationship between them was restored.

Angling her body away from his, Cleopatra examined the finalized plans for the renovated Hell and Sin. As she leaned forward, scraping her gaze over every portion of the page, the implications of what he'd given her access to registered. His brothers would kill him—and with good reason—were they to see him with Cleopatra even now. It didn't matter that when the hell opened, there would be men of Killoran who infiltrated and reported back. His stomach queasy, he made to grab the page.

"This is all wrong," she said, moving her finger up and down the hazard and faro tables stationed along the right portion of the club.

"Beg pardon?" he blurted, her observation instantly staying his hand on the sheet.

"You have your private tables set up here." She drifted the tip of her index finger to the area in question.

Do not engage her . . . you've already shared enough with a Killoran. "And?" The question came as though pulled from him. For the truth was, he'd made enough sacrifices in his life that he wasn't too proud to take advice proffered.

"Pfft." The bold minx lifted her gaze from the designs and arched an eyebrow over the rim of her spectacles. *"And?"* she asked, and had her tones been mocking, it would have been far more palatable than the painful emphasis there. "You have your gaming tables separate. That means they have to walk"—she jabbed the page as she spoke—"one, two, three, four, five, six . . . twenty paces before they get from their private tables here"—Cleopatra swiveled her judgmental finger to each point in question—"to here."

As they had for years. "Noblemen prefer to have a place to converse with peers over drinks, separate than where they play."

"Of course they prefer it. A fancy toff doesn't know what he wants by way of seedy lifestyles." Cleopatra gave another skyward point of her eyes. "It doesn't matter what they want or prefer. It matters what *you* get out of *them*. They're too accustomed to their fancy clubs." She paused and searched about, muttering incoherently to herself. "Ah." Killoran's sister grabbed a charcoal pencil. Over his sounds of protest, she etched small *X*s upon the plans, marking the sheets. Adair lowered his hands on the table and leaned closer to assess her work. The scent of her—a hint of apple and strawberries—filled his senses, and he took it in, breathing deep.

"You paying attention, Thorne?" she snapped, glancing up.

Heat slapped his cheeks, and for the first time in the whole of his damned life . . . he was . . . blushing. "I am." *A liar.*

"Look here." She refocused all her attention upon the desk.

All the while I stand here sniffing her like a damned rose pushed into my hand by a London peddler, he thought, disgusted with himself.

"You place drinking tables here. One here, and here," she continued, writing on the page. "All through it, interspersed with your gaming tables. This way your patrons are drinking all evening, and the wagering is always a step away." Her spectacles slipped, and she paused to push them back into place.

Adair dusted a hand over his jaw, contemplating both her opinion and the markings she'd made. "Many lords come to discuss business."

"Then you give them a place for that," she said before he'd even finished. "Apart from your main floors. You don't let the handful of ones there for nondrinking, whoring, and wagering drive the whole club." She wrinkled her nose. "I forgot. You don't have whores."

Since Ryker Black had wedded a lady and had ultimately made the decision that they'd no longer offer the services of prostitutes for their clients, their profits had taken a blow. For Adair's appeals to his brothers, they'd been adamant to continue on without those services offered. "You think it's foolish," he predicted.

"My brother does," she automatically answered.

Interesting. "And you?"

The young woman paused. He shot her a side glance. Cleopatra chewed at the tip of her finger, and indecision raged in her eyes. Again, it occurred to him . . . for Cleopatra Killoran's bold displays and unwavering confidence, there was still a vulnerability to her. It was far too easy to forget that the snarling, hissing hellion was, in fact, a young woman. Perhaps that was why he even now spoke in depth and at length with Killoran's sister about the Hell and Sin. What else accounted for trusting her in this way?

"I . . . I don't know," she finally said, revealing an unanticipated hesitation. "My brother would certainly say so."

"I don't care what Killoran thinks," he said bluntly. "I'm not asking his opinion. I'm asking yours." A marvel, in and of itself. He must be going mad. There was nothing else for it.

She gave her head a frenetic shake. "I can't answer that." She looked about, and then she settled her stare upon his ledgers. "Not without knowing your profits."

So, she was of a similar mind frame as Ryker, Calum, and Niall, that some profit could be sacrificed for philanthropic good. Who would have ever expected it of this woman?

"It's enough I've shown you my plans." A far too dangerous allowance he'd made. "I've no intention of discussing my profits—"

"Or lack thereof," she mumbled.

"—with you," he said loudly over her tart reply.

"I'm not interested in your books, Adair." By God, she was fearless. "What your numbers are or are not hardly indicate how successful your club is or will be. Your plans, however, reveal more than enough about the vitality of the Hell and Sin."

His hackles went up. "You'd challenge the might of my club," he said on a silken whisper, facing her squarely so that she had to crane her head all the way back to meet his gaze. "Our hell is different than yours." The Hell and Sin and Devil's Den had begun the same, but ultimately, they'd evolved, becoming places that powerful peers visited and lost fortunes at. The Devil's Den, however, had surpassed them in growth through its offering of prostitution.

"No truer words were ever spoken than those," she said with her usual arrogance. "Do you know what your problem is, Adair?"

"That your brother burned my club to a pile of ashes?" he retorted, longing for a fight that would restore them to their proper places as hated rivals.

To the lady's credit, she didn't rise to that bait. "Your problem is that you and your family don't know what type of club you want to be." She turned up one hand, and with their bodies positioned as close as they were, that action brought her palm brushing against his chest. His pulse leapt at the unwitting touch. "Is it a fancy place like White's and Brooke's where only fancy lords come to play?" Cleopatra lifted her other palm, the one marked with a *D*. "Or do you want to be precisely what you are . . . men of the streets who offer those vices we know about to lords who wanted a taste."

By nothing more than the sheer nature of enmity that had forever existed between their gangs, he wanted to throw counter-protestations in her face . . . to point out that they were nothing alike—in any way. In this, however, Cleopatra Killoran had surely spoken the truest words to ever emerge from her plump red lips. "Our clientele is not your clientele," he said finally. That decision they'd undertaken long ago when they'd first purchased the Hell and Sin, before his brothers had married ladies of the *ton*.

"We know precisely what we are and the clients we serve. You are the ones who don't." She touched her gaze on the fine furnishings belonging to Ryker and Penelope. "The Devil's Den caters to men who come to sin and are comfortable in doing so. You"—she gesticulated wildly as she spoke—"don't know if you want to cater to the nobs or be part of the streets."

Her words flummoxed him. Given her next diatribe, with Cleopatra's quickness and rapier tongue, he wouldn't ever want to be caught in a knife battle with this one.

"You design your fancy club . . . in St. Giles." With irreverent fingers, she scooped up the stack of plans. "If the lords want a White's, they'll go to White's. They want Brooke's, they'll go there. That's not what the Hell and Sin is, and it isn't what the Devil's Den is, either. The names alone say as much. If you're looking to give them a fancy club, then you'd be better off designing an altogether different plan for a different club, in an altogether different part of London."

Damned if the young woman's logic didn't make sense, too.

"Not that I believe this is necessarily the club you've got in mind for your patrons," she said, casually waving that sheet. "But even if it's got a hint of the layout here, you're in trouble of your own making, Thorne." She slapped the page down decisively.

His mouth fell open, and he quickly forced it closed. By God, she'd realized that. "Are you always this astute, Cleopatra?"

She hung her head slightly, that telling gesture a mark of Diggory's response to faulty missteps. "Not astute enough if I failed to realize you were in the room I'd entered."

For the first time, he wondered what her life had been like as one of Diggory's whelps. He'd not considered . . . until now—until seeing that *D* upon her hand and her dropped shoulders—that she also might have known suffering.

His gut clenched. Or she could be as deceptive as the man who'd become Diggory's second-in-command—a man so much like him that he'd inherited all as though he were a firstborn son.

Don't be fooled by her downcast appearance and seeming innocence. The fact he'd caught her snooping in this room, and just fielded too many questions from her, was proof that he'd be wise to watch her far more closely than he had this day.

Adair took her by the lower arm, encircling it in his palm. She gasped and made to wrench free. "Why did you tell me this?" he demanded gruffly, tightening his hold.

The young woman puzzled her brow.

He drew her closer so the walls of their chests brushed and she was forced to tilt the long column of her neck back to meet his gaze. "Pointing out errors, making suggestions." Adair dropped his head down, shrinking the space between them. "Why should I believe there's a thing real in that offering?" It was a question he asked as much for himself.

Did he imagine the hurt that sparked in her revealing eyes? If so, it was gone as soon as it had flickered to life. Through the glass lenses he'd cleaned a short while ago, Cleopatra glowered at him.

"Un'and me, ya jackanapes," she hissed, giving her wrist another tug.

He gave another light squeeze, and that instantly quelled her. Detecting her faint wince, he gentled his touch. "Despite my brothers' and their wives' trusting nature in letting you share a roof with us, I'd be a fool to trust your motives, Cleopatra."

She jutted her chin up mutinously, and that slight angling brought their foreheads colliding. "Then go ahead an' build yar sure-to-fail hell. 'elp yarself along to your demise." For Cleopatra's remarkable composure, her greatest tell was the lack of mastery over her practiced, cultured tones.

"I've offended you," he wondered aloud.

Cleopatra slammed the heel of her boot on his bare foot, and a hiss exploded through his teeth. The spitfire pounced, shoving her spare elbow against his rib cage. He grunted, and his grip slackened at the well-placed blow. She slipped around him.

"Hellion," he gritted out, reaching for her.

A furious cry climbed to the rafters as he wrapped an arm about her waist and brought her back against him. She kicked and flailed with the same desperation of a person fighting for their freedom from the constable. "Ya bloody bully," she spat, breathless as she wrestled against him. "Ya brainless, witless—"

He brought his mouth close to her ear, relishing far too much her spirited show. "Rather uninventive of you, love," he taunted.

She stilled, and then with another shriek, she renewed her struggles. Bucking and writhing against him, she fought for her freedom, and just like that, all his mirth fled as a wave of desire slammed into him. The surge of lust was momentarily crippling.

". . . useless, cock-less . . ."

Except . . . blood surged through his shaft, and he sprang hard against her lower back.

He swallowed hard; his breath came hard and fast.

Cleopatra ceased her struggles, and he gave thanks for small favors. Then—

"Let. Me. Go," she spat, bucking against him.

I am lost.

With a groan, he spun her around and covered her mouth with his, swallowing the tide of inventive curses escaping her. He slanted his lips over hers, devouring the satiny-soft flesh.

Cleopatra went taut against him, her lithe frame so stiff she could splinter in his embrace. A half moan, half whimper left her. Reaching up, she twined her arms about his neck and, pressing herself against him, met his kiss.

And he, who'd always feared and despised fire, embraced this conflagration between them. Adair filled his hands with her buttocks, anchoring her close. He kneaded the perfect contours and, not breaking contact with her mouth, continued his search. Adair worked his hands over her: down her trim waist, the narrow curve of her hip. Then parting her lips, he searched his tongue around the moist, hot cavern.

Their raspy groans melded as one. He reached between them and found the modest swell of her left breast. Through the fabric of her gown, he molded it against this palm. How perfectly she fit within his hand. His tongue mated with hers in a battle for supremacy he was content to lose. Hungry to know all of her, he sprang her breasts free of her modest dress and cupped her without the hindrance of the garment.

She tossed her head back. "Adair," she cried out breathlessly.

The sound of his name on her lips fueled him. Gathering her right leg, he brought it up about his waist, twining that sinewy limb around him. He guided her back against his desk and, reclaiming her lips, swallowed the breathy sounds of her desire.

Cleopatra twined both her hands about his neck and dragged him down closer, a woman in command who knew what she wanted, and his ardor burned all the greater that she'd been transformed into a gasping, pleading temptress in his arms.

She is a siren and I am ensnared . . .

Through the thick fog of lust consuming him, that truth registered, and he pulled back. He ripped away from her as horror penetrated the madness that had driven back his judgment.

Cleopatra sagged back on her elbows. Glasses askew, hair mussed, cheeks flushed, she had the look of a well-ravished woman.

My God, I kissed Cleopatra Killoran.

She blinked slowly; the cloud in her eyes slowly lifted as she met his gaze. All hint of desire receded under the full weight of her ire. "Ya needn't look so horrified," she retorted. "It . . . it was just a kiss." That mocking rejoinder was countered by the tremble there, and the unsteady way she got herself back to her feet.

Unable to form a suitable mocking retort, he retreated several steps. "You aren't to come here again," he said, needing distance from her. Frustration with himself, and this inexplicable hold she had over him, made his words come out more sharply than he intended.

For a long minute, he believed she'd strike him. Little gold specks of fury glittered brightly in her eyes. And for an even longer moment, he wanted her to. He deserved a facer. Then she marched off, brushing violently past him.

"Cleopatra," he called out as her fingers found the handle.

She stalled, but she made no move to turn around.

"I don't want you wandering these halls at night," he ordered. "Are we clear?"

"Go to hell," she spat.

She'd taken his orders as an insult. Guilt knotted in his chest. She didn't know he wanted her gone for his own sanity. Regardless, it was safer not engaging her, letting her form whatever erroneous opinion she had.

Letting herself out, she pulled the door shut behind her with a barely discernible click.

What in blazes had overcome him? He slammed a fist on the desk so hard, the ledgers leapt from the force of that movement. It only brought his attention to the design plans he'd pored over with Cleopatra. She'd raised valid points in terms of the layout of the hell, and her questioning seemed innocuous. Only she was a Killoran. Since Adair and his siblings had freed themselves of Mac Diggory's clutches and established a fortune and future of their own, they'd earned eternal enemies in that gang. Through countless criminal acts carried out against Adair's family and his gaming hell, he knew better than to trust her. Knew better than to desire her . . .

A knock infiltrated his tumultuous thoughts—a hard, strong, powerful one that marked it different from the waiflike Cleopatra. "Enter," he called, swiftly straightening.

Ryker entered. His keen gaze did a sweep of the room, taking in everything. "I observed Killoran in the halls."

Killoran. It was, of course, the young woman's surname . . . but there was a detached coldness that no longer fit with the spirited minx he'd held in his arms. "I sent her to her rooms," he said as his brother entered the room and shut the door behind him. Ryker had been watching after the newest houseguest. After his exchange with Cleopatra Killoran, Adair had no right to any annoyance at having his responsibilities questioned. Adair concentrated his efforts on righting his piles.

"You sent her to her rooms? And you didn't see fit to personally escort her there?" Ryker asked.

Adair briefly stopped in his tidying.

He'd been tasked with looking after Killoran's sister, and yet here he'd stood instead, sharing the building plans for the Hell and Sin, letting her inside that world, and then nearly taking her on his desk. "It won't happen again," he finally said, that reassurance laced with a double meaning. His brother could never know. It didn't matter that Cleopatra's kiss had said she was no virgin. It mattered the gang she belonged to, and the spell that had blotted out all logical hatred for her.

"Carelessness—"

"Kills," he cut in brusquely. "I know the damned rules." He, Ryker, Niall, and Calum had established the very guidelines for survival as boys. "I won't forget."

"See that you don't," Ryker commanded in gravelly tones. "My family lives here." Recently a father, Ryker, who'd always been over-protective of his kin, had developed a singular intent to look after his loved ones.

"I will not make the same mistake," he assured.

With a nod, Ryker let himself out. Abandoning any hopes of sleep for the night, Adair, in a bid to set Cleopatra from his thoughts, claimed a spot at his desk and evaluated the most recent design plans for the Hell and Sin.

His family and his club were everything . . . he'd do well to not, as Ryker said, let a Killoran threaten either.

Chapter 8

The following day, Cleopatra didn't leave her temporary chambers. She rose, dressed, and took her meals—or at least accepted the trays—and remained closeted away.

But her exile was not a result of that frosty warning issued by Adair the evening prior.

Seated cross-legged on her bed, she stared at the doorway.

"I kissed him," she whispered, and the horror of that admission being spoken aloud for now the twenty-sixth time did not blunt the shame of it.

She, Cleopatra Killoran of the Devil's Den, had kissed Adair Thorne, proprietor of the Hell and Sin Club. Not only had she kissed him, she'd panted and pleaded like a bitch in heat. And despite her scorn and disgust for the women she'd witnessed who made fools of themselves for a man's touch, Cleopatra had wanted more of his embrace.

Groaning, Cleopatra dropped her head into her hands. She'd vowed to never give herself the way the whores in her club did. Those embraces were, at best, lust-crazed responses from women without any self-control; at worst, they were acts of desperation. And Cleopatra had tired of desperation long, long ago.

Yes, she was a woman of logic, reason, and sense who'd never part her thighs for any man.

But how very close you came last evening . . .

Cleopatra cringed. On a desk no less, like one of the fancily dressed whores employed at the Devil's Den. Yet, it wasn't her body's response to him that curdled in her belly like spoiled milk. She'd actually enjoyed being with him. For the first time since she'd learned that she would be moving out of the Devil's Den and giving up the only life she'd ever known, she'd been at ease.

Adair Thorne wasn't a fancy lord, or even like the rough-talking guttersnipes turned guards inside her brother's hell. He'd spoken freely to her and requested her opinion on business matters.

It was surely those reasons that she'd forgotten herself and returned his embrace.

Of all the wonders of the world, it had been bloody Adair Thorne to break the haze of desire and restore order to her upended world. And she was grateful for it. "It was just a kiss," she muttered. She wasn't a delicate lady. Why, it was simply by the grace of a God she didn't truly believe in that she'd not been divested of her virginity long ago. Nor would she ever be one of those wilting misses.

In the world she'd been born to, a person assuaged one's wants where they could. If one was hungry and there was food at hand, one ate. If one was thirsty—be it whiskey, ale, or water—one drank. If one had an *itch between one's legs*, as the prostitutes had often referred to it, then one had it scratched.

Cleopatra, however, hadn't had an itch or wanted anything scratched. Judging by the whispers and giggling she'd overheard through the years, the whole business of bedding a man had seemed onerous and uncomfortable. Then Adair had put his large, callused hands all over her, and the ache between her legs had proven why a woman took a man to her rooms: reasons that didn't solely have to do with coin . . . but rather, a wicked yearning.

Cleopatra dragged her knees to her chest and dropped her chin atop them, as she'd been wont to do since she was a girl, taking shelter in hovels during storms. She'd made a bloody fool of herself, lusting after Adair, and he'd been wholly unaffected. Oh, she'd felt his manhood pressed against her and, from it, had felt his desire. But his hatred had proven far greater.

With his coolly aloof warnings and dismissals last evening, she'd been reminded that they were enemies. He'd cut off her ability to freely roam this fancy townhouse or familiarize herself with the layout. Now she was a prisoner, stripped of her weapons and freedom of movement.

She firmed her jaw.

Alas, if Adair thought a curt command would stifle her, he was even more a fool than his club design plans had revealed him to be.

Squinting in the dark, she sought to bring the numbers on the porcelain clock into focus.

Thirty minutes past twelve . . .

The last of the shuffling footsteps from the other side of the shared wall had come twenty-three minutes ago, indicating Adair, her guard, now slept.

Nonetheless, she'd made mistakes last night. Too many of them. And after a day spent alone, in silent contemplation, she didn't intend to make the same missteps.

After scooting to the edge of the bed, she silently stood. He'd advised her to not roam the floors. Ordering her about like the prisoner Broderick had made her into. Well, she was no weak ninny. Be it a St. Giles gutter or a Grosvenor mansion, she'd be prepared.

After having spent the day measuring the weak, protesting floorboards, she carefully sidestepped them and started for the window. Reaching it, she stopped and cast a glance over at the plaster divide between her and Adair.

Did he truly believe she'd be contained and quelled by him or anyone?

This wasn't the first time Cleopatra had been underestimated. Not even by Adair Thorne—a man who'd challenged her more than a year earlier when she'd first proposed a truce between their families.

It had simply proven the most convenient. She grinned wryly. Hitching herself on to the ledge of her opened window, Cleopatra glanced briefly down. At least one hundred feet to the street; she'd certainly scaled far higher buildings. As one who'd been locked away in a closet as punishment by Diggory and his loyal minions, Cleopatra found even being suspended above the ground preferable to any make-shift or imposed prison.

She braced her palms on the edge and pulled herself upright. Standing on tiptoe, she grabbed the ledge of the window above hers. The distant rumble of carriage wheels echoed loudly, and she focused, driving back all hint of sound or distraction. One slight slip or miscalculation had seen too many pickpockets tossed to the cobbles. *And I have far grander hopes than dying outside Black's posh Grosvenor Square townhouse.* Pushing back thoughts of the Blacks or her family or fear of falling, she drew herself up.

Even though she had scaled countless townhouses and establishments without ever a broken limb, her pulse still raced at a maddening beat inside her ears. Using all the muscles in her forearms, she slowly lifted herself up. Concentrating all her efforts on her climb, she angled a knee to brace herself on her precarious perch and then brought herself upright.

Cleopatra pressed herself against the crystal windowpane and peered into the darkened space. An entire day spent inside her own chambers and the dearth of movement from the room above had marked it as some extraneous space in Black's home. She squinted, making out the empty chamber. The spring breeze whipped at her white skirts. With slow, measured movements, she brought her palms to rest on the opposite corners of the panes, slowly applying pressure. Satisfaction coursed through her when the window instantly gave way. The servants who cleaned these lofty homes were all responsible for the same mistake . . . believing those top windows could never be penetrated. That Black's own staff should also demonstrate that carelessness spoke of a man who'd been removed from the streets too long. He'd gone soft. Then, her presence here was proof of that.

Cleopatra braced herself on the edges of the windowsill. The heavy, solid wood grounded her, driving her heartbeat back into a normal cadence. She lowered herself and then swung inside the room. The leather soles of her boots hit with a soft *thud*. She shot her arms out to keep her balance. Breath frozen in her lungs, she glanced about, more than half expecting a rush of Black's men to storm the room. The only company, however, proved to be the ornate mahogany bedroom furniture. Adjusting her spectacles, she picked up a porcelain shepherdess and turned it over in her hands.

"So, this is what has become of you, Black," she mouthed into the quiet. He'd gone from gaming hell proprietor to . . . fancy viscount with delicate porcelain and open windows.

And that was the path Broderick was headed down, if he continued on with his lifelong fascination with respectability.

Over her dead body.

She returned the ruffled shepherdess to its proper position and brought the window back down. She'd lay down her life for Broderick. He was as much her sibling as Gertrude, Ophelia, and Stephen were, but he didn't have the blood of the streets coursing through his veins. Oh, when he'd come into their fold, able to read and write and speaking so fancy, she'd wanted to clobber him on the head and jumble all those damned words up. For he'd made her feel—for the first time in the whole of her then short existence—inadequate. But he'd saved her life more times than she deserved, and what was more, he'd cared after her sisters and younger brother. She'd never allow them to become weak, as the Blacks had.

Her purpose that night reinvigorated, she firmed her mouth and made her way to the door. Whenever one entered a new territory, one needed to identify how the land lay. One needed to know all the doorways and windows and halls that could lead one to escape, just as much as one had to be prepared for the walls that would block a hasty retreat. She'd monitored one floor last evening; she'd add another this night. Having been divested of all her weaponry, she'd need not only a new knife but also a map of Black's house.

A memory flitted forward of Adair as he'd cupped her breast, all the while feasting on her mouth like a man starving for her. Any other man of St. Giles, particularly one she'd been in the midst of battling, would have gladly let her fall flat on her face. In fact, he'd have given the final push or kick and sent her sprawling—especially after the way she'd assaulted Adair Thorne's manhood with her knee. But he hadn't. Even as curses had dripped from his lips and fire had lit his eyes, he'd rolled her atop him, breaking her fall.

And he stole your damned knife . . . don't forget that much . . .

Prodded back into movement, she pressed the handle and opened the door a fraction. The hum of silence spilled into the darkened chambers. She hesitated, counting several seconds, and opened it farther. Where the whores at the Devil's Den were always lauding the benefit of their plump, curved frames, Cleopatra had long given thanks that she'd been born with a child's form and maintained that narrow waist and smallish stature. It had allowed her a furtiveness to rival the fleetest London pickpocket. It also enabled her to sneak about Ryker Black's home.

Letting herself out, she drew the door closed behind her with a silent click. Cleopatra glanced up and down the hallway, silently estimating the distance in each direction. Then with measured steps, she started forward. She ran her gaze over each doorway, mentally calculating the number and size of those wood panels. By the stillness on these floors, Black and his family didn't inhabit this portion of their sprawling townhouse. What a waste of bloody rooms. How many years had she spent in one-bedroom apartments with her sisters, brother, and other bastard issue of Diggory's men? Cleopatra reached an intersecting hallway. A faint whine pierced the quiet, and she stopped abruptly. Only silence met her ears.

Except—narrowing her eyes, she started in the direction of that previous sound. As she drifted farther down the hall, that keening cry suited to a hungry kitten grew louder. Cleopatra stared at the door handle a long moment. When none of Black's servants or men came rushing forward, she pressed the handle and stepped inside.

Cleopatra blinked into the inky darkness and tried to bring the room into focus through her wire-rimmed spectacles. She stilled, her eyes quickly taking in a child's armchair, the matching mahogany waterfall bookcase, and the floral curtains and upholsteries.

Pink. "More pink," she muttered under her breath.

What in blazes was it with the nobility and that color? Given she stood in a nursery belonging to her family's mortal enemy, it was a nonsensical wondering that could see her killed. One that Diggory, had he been alive still, would have said *should* see her killed. And yet, since she'd spied a lady years earlier with a girl clad in pink, she'd been riveted by that color of childlike innocence. It was a shade of lightness that stood in direct contrast to the dark hues and dirt-stained garments Cleopatra and her sisters had been forced to don.

Another sharp cry echoed around the room and slashed across her nonsensical musings. Cleopatra furrowed her brow. Surely there was a nursemaid about? A loud snore punctuated that thought, and Cleopatra instantly found the doorway. Cracking it open, she glanced inside. A young woman lay sprawled on a small bed, with a brass cylindrical flask just beside her pillow. With a sound of disgust, she closed the door, then wandered back to the small cradle and looked down.

A plump babe with thick black curls rooted around, making suckling noises with her mouth.

And for all the hardness of the exterior she'd built up, warmth suffused Cleopatra's heart as it invariably did when presented with a small baby. *I should leave.* Standing at the bedside of Black's babe was the kind of act that would see them slay her first and ask questions later. The girl emitted a sharp cry, and Cleopatra closed her eyes and instantly scooped up the small girl. Her weight settled slight and yet reassuring against Cleopatra's chest.

"*Shh.*" She whispered nonsensical soothing sounds and gently rocked the girl back and forth. Since she'd been a child, she'd taken on the role of caring for Diggory's and his men's bastard babes. It hadn't been any sense of loyalty that had led him to look after his enormous brood, but rather his kin had served a utilitarian purpose—to run the streets on behalf of his empire. Cleopatra, however, had imagined in each child who'd fallen to her care a different life. In them, she'd dreamed of her own escape—wanting more, hoping for more, for each of those children.

She went cold and ceased her distracted rocking. In the end, the only ones who'd made it free had been the ones who'd died.

The ominous click of a pistol held her frozen.

"Put the child down. Now, Killoran. Or I will end you."

Adair's steely whisper filled the quiet nursery and sent gooseflesh racing along her arms.

For a second time in Black's household, Cleopatra had let her guard down and been caught by Adair Thorne . . . only this time with his family's cherished babe in her arms. That, on the heel of his warnings last evening, sent fear twisting in her chest.

Bloody hell.

"I said put her down," he demanded, taking a step closer.

The child wailed.

Fighting the instinct to protect the child, Cleopatra hesitated before returning her to her cradle. "Thorne," she drawled, in a bid for calm. *This is the same man you teased and kissed last evening.* That reminder didn't help. Inside, her emotions ran amok. Not because Adair had a gun pointed at her head but because she'd rather he fire that pistol than realize her inherent weakness for those tiny, helpless creatures. "If you'd wished to speak to me again, you need only have—"

"Walk away from her cradle. Now." He took a step closer, briefly silencing her attempted bravado. She didn't want it to hurt that his doubt of her was so strong he'd point a gun at her chest. And yet . . . it did.

The child continued to cry at their backs, babbling incoherently. Cleopatra tightened her mouth. "I wouldn't hurt a babe. Not even one of yours," she said coolly.

"Quiet."

Cleopatra continued over that sharp demand. "Your family would do well to find a reliable nursemaid and not one who is nipping at too much brandy and sleeps through the child's tears."

"How do you . . . ?" Adair blinked slowly, then gave his head a firm shake. "I said quiet, and move away from her." Stuffing his gun back in his waistband, he grabbed Cleopatra about the waist.

She gasped as he spun her around and proceeded to pat her. The thin fabric of her nightskirts provided little barrier against his heated touch. This touch, however, was so very different from the hungry searching of last night. Even so, her body didn't care either way for any distinction. A dangerous fluttering started low in her belly, and she hated herself for her body's damned awareness when it should be so distantly removed. "Damn you." That curse tore from her lips—for him as much as for herself. "Oi wouldn't 'urt a babe."

He snorted.

"Oi wouldn't." It shouldn't matter whether or not he believed her, and yet that he thought her capable of the same evil Mac Diggory himself had mastered grated on her nerve—and worse, sent a pang to her heart. "A-and you already stole my weapons." The bloody bastard had taken the only material item of value to her.

"I didn't steal them," he muttered, spinning her back to face him. Dragging her by the shoulders, he brought her up on her tiptoes and bent his head down so their noses nearly touched. "Nor did you need a weapon. You needed nothing more than a pillow to snuff out her life."

She recoiled. That allegation leveled her far more than any other insult or accusation he might hurl. "You're a monster if ya even *thought* of that."

"And this from a woman who gave her loyalty to a Devil like Mac Diggory."

Cleopatra shot her palm out, catching Adair hard on his right cheek with such force it brought his head snapping back. The suddenness of her attack and that movement knocked loose his hold on her. Adair brought his palm up and rubbed the wounded flesh.

She stumbled away. How dare he? He'd paint her as one devoted to Diggory. The choices for young girls on the street were far different from the ones permitted boys. Suffering through her earlier life with Diggory had still been far safer than navigating through London without that distinction, and two sisters—one of them partially blind—to care for. "You know nothing of it," she spat into the silence.

Her handprint stood out in stark contrast to his olive-hued cheeks. And despite her hurt, outrage, and fury, uneasiness stirred low in her belly. How many times had Diggory's men knocked her around for daring to strike them? She backed slowly away.

"I said get away from the cradle." With a growl, he lunged for her—

The bedroom door flew open, knocking against the wall so hard it snapped back and nearly hit the menacing, scarred figure there.

Black and a handful of guards surged forward. The explosion of sound and activity at the front of the room roused the baby to another round of noisy tears.

"Keep it silent or Oi'll silence it forever."

Diggory's threats echoed around the chambers of her mind. Panicked, Cleopatra looked to the baby.

"Get away from my child, Miss Killoran," Black ordered in death-promising tones.

The babe's crying reached a fever pitch, and Cleopatra shook her head in befuddlement. "Oi don't . . ."

"I said—"

Penelope Black sailed into the room. With her skirts whipping about her and a knife in her hand, she very much had the look of a London street warrior. "What is it?" she rasped, settling her hard stare on Cleopatra.

Feeling as cornered as when Mac Diggory's number two had pressed her against the wall and threatened to split her belly open for failing to obey his orders, Cleopatra clutched at her throat. "Oi wasn't. Oi wouldn't—" *Why should they believe you? Why should any of this enemy family believe you?* She searched frantically about for escape. "She was crying," she said hoarsely, as Black's wife stormed over and rescued the babe from imagined harm.

"You expect us to believe you were just here to calm Ryker's babe?" Adair asked with incredulity.

He thought her mad, then. That realization drove back her panic and confusion, replacing it instead with righteous indignation. She jutted her chin up. "Oi don't care wot ya believe, Thorne."

"Where is the nursemaid?" Black commanded.

"You're all a bunch of bloody fools," Cleopatra snarled to the room at large. "Ya, too," she said to Black's wife, who was hugging her child close. How quickly all that pretend warmth and kindness from a day earlier had faded. It only proved what she really thought of Cleopatra. Not that Cleopatra blamed the woman . . . she'd simply, however, reinforced the truth that they were enemies. And would always be so, deal or not. "Your nursemaid is in her bed, drunk enough to sleep three nights straight."

That charge was met with a heavy silence.

Penelope glanced between Cleopatra and Ryker Black. "I don't—"

"Know anything?" Cleopatra supplied insolently for her. "Ya certainly don't."

A muscle ticked in the corner of Black's right eye, and then he stalked wordlessly across the room and shoved the door open. A bleating snore met that sudden movement.

The roomful of Blacks stared on at Cleopatra with varying degrees of mistrust. She studiously avoided Adair's probing green eyes.

Black reemerged with that brass flask in hand; top removed, he held it up in silent confirmation.

Shoulders back, Cleopatra started over to the door.

"Cleo," Penelope said quietly, regret filling those two syllables.

"Oi'll be gone tomorrow," Cleopatra returned. This had all been a mistake. Broderick would have to find some other way to have his respectability . . . but using the Blacks' connections was not, nor would ever be, the way.

"Miss Killoran?" Ryker Black barked after her, staying Cleopatra's steps. She stiffened, and her hands curled into reflexive fists.

"Thank you," he said gruffly.

Ignoring his useless words, Cleopatra stalked past his guards and returned to her rooms for her final night.

Chapter 9

She left the next day.

Or to be precise, Cleopatra Killoran left somehow, somewhere, in the early-morn hours, after the house had finally rested. With the stealth with which she'd moved about Ryker's home and then escaped unseen, she could rival the greatest London pickpocket. Which, given Adair's own prowess and familiarity with nicking from the *ton* years earlier, was saying something indeed.

Now the hellion was gone. Seated at the breakfast table, sipping his coffee, Adair confronted the quiet in this stuffy—and temporary—residence. With the tumult that had dogged his life since the Hell and Sin burned to the ground, he'd now be able to rest, knowing he didn't have to safeguard his family from an enemy within. There should be peace . . . and at the very least, calm. There *should* be. Instead, Adair sat restless.

Oi wouldn't 'urt a babe . . .

Cleopatra Killoran's indignation rang in his head as clear as it had in the dead of night. Adair stared into the dark contents of his glass. Nay, she'd not hurt Paisley. Rather, she'd seen what Paisley's own parents had been unable to about their drunken nursemaid.

And for her efforts, Adair had pointed a pistol at her breast.

Grimacing, Adair took a sip of his coffee. *I'll be damned if I feel guilty.* He'd reacted as any sane, rational guard would to finding a Killoran with Penelope and Ryker's babe in her arms. The Killorans were the manner of people who dwelled with the Diggorys of the world. Anyone—man, woman, or child—who chose to live with the Devil was capable of the same evil. Whereas Adair and his siblings? They'd plotted and planned their escape from Diggory's hold and dreamed of a life apart from him. They'd sold their souls to survive, but they'd not made a deal with the Devil to do it.

If he were being honest with himself now, in the light of a new day, he accepted that which he'd not been able to see in the moment of immediate danger: Cleopatra had been cradling Paisley and humming a discordant tune. Hardly the actions of one about to snuff the life out of a child. Rather, there had been a maternal warmth that, had Adair been asked up to that moment, he'd have wagered every earning he'd made on the Hell and Sin Club the termagant was incapable of.

Even so, it was a risk he'd not have taken with his brother's precious babe . . . or any of the family and staff dependent upon them.

Yet, sitting here with his plate full, damned if he did not feel the unwanted strains of guilt plucking at his conscience still. Guilt that came not only from the fact that he'd succeeded in driving off Cleopatra Killoran, but that she'd sneaked out into the streets of London, unarmed, and had no doubt found her way back to the Dials, where her family's club was located. His gaze went to the serpent-headed dagger that rested alongside his silverware.

Diggory's knife . . . but still also, Cleopatra's. She'd a right to it, and she'd certainly had a need for it hours earlier when she'd slunk off. "Enough," he muttered under his breath. Searching for a distraction, he set aside his glass and picked up the leather folio that rested alongside

Cleopatra's knife. Adair popped the folder open and proceeded to read the first page that enumerated the damages incurred at the Hell and Sin.

And just like that . . . his fury at Cleopatra Killoran and her rotted family surged to life. God rot them all.

Footsteps sounded in the hallway, and he glanced up as Ryker and Penelope, baby in arms, entered the breakfast room. Instead of making for the well-stocked buffet, they claimed their respective spots and stared pointedly back at him.

He frowned.

It was his loquacious sister-in-law who broke the quiet. "We have to bring her back." She stared pointedly at Adair. "*You* have to bring her back," she amended.

Him? After nearly taking her on his desk and then following that effrontery with a pistol pointed at her chest, he was the last person she'd care to receive an escort from. "Killoran's sister would rather see me in hell," he said with more confidence than anything he'd felt since the bold spitfire had entered this household.

"With good reason," Penelope agreed. "And that is for all of us. We've been nothing but accusatory since the club burned down."

Since they burned *his* hell down. That reminder of all he'd lost rekindled the hatred he'd long carried for the Killoran gang. It was familiar and safe. Far safer than the burning longing to know the taste of her mouth—he growled. "Let it be, Penelope."

His sister-in-law set her jaw at a pugnacious angle. "She's coming back."

Adair groaned and cast a hopeful look at his brother. Ryker met his gaze with a stony determination. So, there would be no help there. They were determined to bring Cleopatra Killoran back. The tart-mouthed hellion with too-full lips and a skillfully dangerous ability to wield her limbs like weapons. "No," he said curtly, closing his folder.

"It is the right thing to do," Ryker said somberly, weighing in at last.

"It is not going to work." Adair set the leather folio aside. "The girl . . ."

I'm not a girl . . .

Nor did she feel at all girl-like when you ran your hands over her lithe frame. He choked on his swallow. Lusting after a Killoran. What in blazes had become of him? "The young woman left because she had the sense enough to know that. Whether or not she was going to hurt Paisley—"

"She wasn't."

"You're certain of that?" Adair paused to look at his sister-in-law. "Because you were far less so last night, Penelope."

"Yes." She flattened her mouth. "But I am now."

He lifted his shoulders in a shrug. "It doesn't matter either way. There is far too much mistrust between our families for this arrangement to ever work." They'd been foolish to believe it could ever . . . even if it was to honor an agreement made.

"Regardless," Ryker said, motioning over a servant. A young footman instantly sprang forward with a cup of coffee. What had his brother become? A man comfortable calling over servants like a titled lord born to the station . . . and conceding a point to a Killoran? "It wasn't our place to break the terms of the contract." There was a resolute edge that hinted that Ryker's decision had been made.

He, however, had never been afraid to go toe-to-toe with anyone . . . including his brother. "She broke the terms when she left," Adair insisted.

"She was wronged," Penelope said tersely. Worry clouded her eyes. "*We* wronged her. And we need to make it right."

Adair launched a full-out protest, with Penelope raising her voice over his.

Ryker held a silencing hand up. "Enough." That gravelly, two-syllable utterance cut across the din. "The girl made the decision to leave—"

"Because—"

"Because of our . . . inhospitality," Ryker said over his wife's interruption. She stared angrily back. "We cannot force her to return if she doesn't wish to be here. We can, however, make our apologies and extend an olive branch."

Adair choked on his coffee. He sputtered as tears filled his eyes. A branch extended to a Killoran. The world had been flipped upside down, indeed.

"It is settled, Adair," his brother said quietly. "We'll leave now." Shoving back his chair, Ryker came to his feet.

"Bring her back, Ryker," his wife called out.

With all the enthusiasm of being marched to Diggory's to account for a bumbled theft, Adair stood and followed reluctantly behind his brother.

"Adair?"

He glanced back to his sister-in-law.

She gave him a stern look. "Be nice to her."

With a sigh, he inclined his head, and then he marched after Ryker. What his sister-in-law failed to realize in her innocence was that simply being nice would never erase the resentment. That the anger between their family and the Killorans was ingrained into the fabric of who they were.

A short while later, Ryker's carriage rumbled along the noisy, dirty, familiar streets of East London. Having long been a man unwilling or unable to share many words—even with his siblings—Ryker stared forward, as silent as he'd been before his marriage to Penelope.

Adair took advantage of the quiet. Staring out the crystal window, he took in the passing cobblestones. Unlike the clean, even ones of Mayfair, these roads were covered in grime and dirt. They were the same streets that as a boy he'd thieved upon and raced along, in a bid to escape constables and Diggory or his men's punishing fists. And for the danger that had, and would always, lurk here, there was also a familiarity that calmed him.

They rolled to a stop outside the Devil's Den. Velvet curtain still drawn back, Adair fixed his gaze on Killoran's establishment. The cracked redbrick facade showed its age. Only the gleaming black double doorway with two brass knockers hinted at the rising prosperity of this place. Bitterness soured his tongue, making it difficult to swallow. Killoran's club was standing and thriving, while his own had been reduced to nothing more than largely ashes and upstairs apartments.

"Come," Ryker murmured.

Giving his head a shake, he followed his brother outside.

The thick scent of rot and horse shite clogged the air.

He belonged here far more than he did Mayfair. They *all* did: he, Ryker, Calum, and Niall. They spoke of moving their club to the fancier ends of London, but this is where they all belonged—no matter whom they each might wed. Being immersed here, once again, roused a restiveness inside, a hungering to return to this world, no matter how violent it was. Instead, he'd march up to the steps belonging to the man no doubt responsible for Adair's loss and extend a branch to the bastard's sister.

Growling, he and Ryker walked side by side to the front doors. Not bothering with so much as a knock, Adair reached past and let them in.

The raucous laughter and discourse spilled out into the streets, near deafening. That cacophony of sounds served as a greater sign of Killoran's success than the gleaming black itself.

The tall, heavily muscled guard stationed at the front glanced over and stiffened. He reached for a weapon.

Adair drew a blade from his boot. "We're here to speak with Killoran." Killoran's head guard instantly stopped. The color leeched from his cheeks as he eyed that jewel-encrusted dagger. So, the man recognized it as belonging to Cleopatra Killoran.

"Bastards," the guard spat. His muscles strained the fabric of his jacket, and he cast a look about.

Adair and Ryker followed his stare to where Killoran stood conversing with a flame-haired woman. Modestly clad, heavily freckled,
and hair drawn back tight at her nape, she stood apart from the other
whores about this hell. Those two spoke, heads bent, with a closeness
that moved beyond lovers.

Another uniform-clad guard approached the pair, saying something
to the proprietor.

Killoran went taut. He whipped his head in Adair and Ryker's
direction. His eyes narrowed. His lips barely moved as he spoke to that
guard.

With a nod, that man came sprinting through the club. "Killoran
will see you in his office." Then, jerking his chin, he motioned Adair
and his brother forward.

Adair, gaze trained forward, braced for his meeting with the enemy.

Chapter 10

"You did what?"

One might have otherwise suspected that Gertrude had failure with her hearing, instead of her vision, for the number of times she'd repeated that very question since she'd rapped twice on the adjoining door in that age-old code between them.

Having sneaked back in her family's home, her private rooms, she'd expected something more than this thick, tense silence from the two sisters who occupied a place at the edge of her bed.

"I escaped," she muttered, staring at the naughty mural painted overhead. Any lady, and most women, would have been scandalized by the couple cavorting among a sea of voyeurs. Cleopatra, however, had witnessed men, women, and oftentimes a variation of the two engaged in far worse in the streets of St. Giles. And now, she'd partaken in a taste of those forbidden acts with Adair Thorne.

"Why?" Ophelia asked, suspicion heavy in her tone.

At last a query different from the perpetual one Gertrude had taken to asking.

Because I'm a coward . . . because I briefly entertained the idea of a friendship with our enemy and then begged for his kiss . . .

Only to be proven so wholly foolish for thinking there could ever be anything but antipathy between them. With a sigh, Cleopatra flipped onto her side. "Because . . ." She froze midspeech, staring at Ophelia. "Why are you wearing breeches?"

As if seeing her for the first time, Gertrude glanced to Ophelia, momentarily distracted by the peculiar sight.

Ophelia hurled her hands up. "I daresay your fight with the Blacks is of far more interest and pertinence than the fact that I've shed skirts for the day," she mumbled.

Cleopatra sighed. Yes, in this, the most spirited of her sisters was, in fact, correct. "They're buggers. The Blacks," she clarified. As if there could be any doubt.

Her eldest sister's lips twitched. "Though I do not disagree with your opinion, I hardly expect Broderick will take *that* as reason to return."

No, he wouldn't. He was too blinded by his need for respectability. If he knew the true reason, however, he'd put a bullet between Adair's eyes and end the truce struck. He'd always demanded respect where she and her sisters were concerned. Adair, however, hadn't acted falsely where she was concerned. He'd only given her raw honesty. Restless, she swung her legs over to the edge of the bed and propelled herself to a sitting position alongside Ophelia.

"He won't accept it," Gertrude said needlessly. "You'll need a far better reason than—"

"Very well. They took my weapons."

"That is wise," Ophelia said so matter-of-factly. "Or was wise. Given that—*oomph.*" Cleopatra elbowed her in the side. "What? I'm merely pointing out that were the situations reversed, Broderick would have never even let them through the front door with a weapon in hand."

Ophelia propped her hands on her hips and gave her a censorious stare. "Nor would you."

Cleopatra bit her tongue to keep from pointing out that despite Ophelia's confidence, their brother had done precisely that last year when he'd let Niall Marksman through their doors. And that bloody family had been intertwined with her own ever since.

"I . . . read about the debut ball Lady Chatham has planned for you," Gertrude ventured.

"Is there a question there?" Cleopatra gritted out. As much as many had questioned Gertrude's capabilities, the fact remained, she'd always been more tenacious than ever credited.

Her eldest sister coughed into her hand. "I merely wondered whether your sudden defection and return had to do with"—she paused slightly under the weight of Cleopatra's glower—"your presentation to society."

There it was.

"Neither of us would blame you," Ophelia said quickly.

Doubts cast upon Cleopatra's confidence and conviction. It was far safer to let her sisters believe Cleopatra's fears of entering Polite Society were the reason for her defection. Nonetheless, Cleopatra hated the sting of betrayal at their questions and their lack of enthusiasm over her return. She hopped up. "Is that what you think this is about? About me being afraid . . . of the *ton*?" she demanded, spoiling for a fight. Where in blazes was their loyalty? "You'd defend the Blacks and question my reason for returning?" Cleopatra punched her fist into her open palm. "They"—*he*, she thought to herself—"took my weapons." *After I offered wise advice to help his damned club . . . and let him kiss me . . .*

Her sisters exchanged a look. "We're not defending them," Gertrude murmured in her usual placating manner.

"Good," she said bluntly. "Don't."

"We're—"

"Merely pointing out that Broderick will not simply allow you to return for . . . that," Ophelia concluded for their eldest sister. A harsh glint lit Ophelia's crystalline eyes. "He is determined to have his *match* with a bloody nob," she spat.

A bevy of curses stung Cleopatra's lips, and she let them freely fly. For the truth remained . . . in this, they were correct. Broderick would not be content with that flimsy excuse as the reason for her return. When he'd set his mind upon a goal, nothing could steer him from that course. *And if you don't return, he'll just send one of your sisters . . .*

"What really happened?" Gertrude's quiet question sounded from over her shoulder.

Shoulders sinking, Cleopatra stalked over to the window and stared down into the streets below. She ached to share the truth, wanted someone to help her sort through the new, inexplicable feelings she'd had these past few days for Adair Thorne. But she could not. To tell her sisters about that embrace would certainly see them pay a visit to Broderick, who'd then battle Adair, and—she pressed her fingertips against her temples and dug. "Oi was discovered in the nursery," she muttered, cringing as soon as the damning admission left her mouth. For all her indignation and fury this morn, she, Cleopatra Killoran, best roof climber in the Dials and St. Giles combined, had been caught.

"The nursery," Gertrude repeated.

She gave a jerky nod, grateful that she couldn't see their expressions . . . and the likely shock or disappointment.

"I was doing a sweep of my surroundings, and I heard the babe," she muttered. Why had she always had this blasted inherent weakness for those defenseless ones? It was what had led her to take on the care of those babes Diggory took in, when one knew that any attachment in their world was dangerous for the temerity of it. She proceeded to tell her sisters all: from her nighttime climb and then exploration throughout Black's home, to her inevitable discovery at Adair's hands.

Ophelia cleared her throat. "Ahem."

Cleopatra took deliberate care to avoid mention of the rugged proprietor's heated search of her body . . . how he'd run his hands all over her and roused a dangerous fluttering.

Ophelia cleared her throat. "I said . . . *ahem* . . ."

"I heard you," she mumbled, reluctantly facing the pair.

"It's just simply that if I or Gertie"—she gestured to their eldest sister—"or Broderick or Reggie—"

"Be done with your point," she gritted out.

Her sister wrinkled her nose. "Very well . . . if a Black was hovering over one of our babes—"

"We don't have any babes," she muttered under her breath.

"Then we would have responded in a like way."

Damn Ophelia for being right. Damn her for being logical.

Cleopatra stared unblinkingly at the window. *Blast* . . . She was always the logical one. It had been that way since they'd lived on the streets. She was the one who'd not faltered in the face of Diggory's evil, but instead sorted through ways in which they could survive it—and thrive. So, what was it that had so upended her? Turned her into one of those easily hurt misses who'd storm from Black's residence and slink off, like a pickpocket in the night.

It is him . . . bloody Adair Thorne, with his overly familiar hands and total lack of reverence for Cleopatra Killoran for simply being a Killoran. When all the Dials respected her because of her connection to Broderick, Adair despised her for it and warily waited for her to make a dangerous move. It was, however, as Ophelia had said . . . precisely how Adair Thorne should behave. It was how Cleopatra or Gertrude or Ophelia or Broderick or Stephen would be. So why did his damned ill opinion matter so much?

Unnerved, she tugged back the curtain and looked out.

She stiffened when a hand fell to her shoulder. Dropping the velvet fabric, Cleopatra glanced back.

"I'll go," Gertrude said quietly. She spoke over Cleopatra's protestations. "It should have always been me."

Ophelia and Cleopatra spoke as one.

"Do not be foolish."

"You are not going," Cleopatra said tightly, shrugging free of Gertrude's touch. She'd spent a lifetime protecting her eldest sister, and she'd not abandon that responsibility now. She silently cursed her rashness that had sent her here.

Her sister gave her a sad smile. "Because you believe I cannot make a match with a fancy lord."

Cleopatra frowned. "Don't be silly," she snapped. "It doesn't matter that you are blind."

"Fine, then. Because you believe me weak."

Cleopatra hesitated—too long. A flash of hurt sparked in the older woman's eyes, and Cleopatra unleashed a stream of curses. She'd bungled all of this. "Do not make this into anything more than it is," she snapped, angry at herself for altogether different reasons—for hurting her sister. "This isn't about you, in any way. This is about me . . ." She faltered.

"Looking after others," Ophelia somberly interrupted. "As you always did and as you always do." Her sister moved into position alongside Gertrude, and they formed a formidable pair, flanking one another's side. "This was never a responsibility you should have undertaken." She steeled her jaw. "It was never a demand Broderick should have put to you." She passed a hard glance around their small group. "It was never something he should have put to any of us."

When had her sisters become this resolute? It was uncharacteristic for her sisters to join forces and question decisions and judgments Cleopatra had reached for their clan. As such, she sought to navigate the unfamiliar terrain. "What are you saying?" she demanded gruffly, hating the defensive edge there.

"We're saying that one of us should go," Gertrude said bluntly, not dancing around what she meant, as she so often did.

Ophelia was already shaking her head. "Nay. We're saying one of us is going," she amended, and Cleopatra's sisters exchanged a look and nod of solidarity. Ophelia sucked in a breath. "It will be me. I will do it."

Her?

"You?" Gertrude echoed Cleopatra's unspoken utterance.

"Do you doubt that I'm capable?" she shot back, fire dancing in her eyes.

"Never that," Cleopatra said quietly.

And yet, over the years, Ophelia had made little attempt to conceal her loathing for the nobility. Her offer spoke to the ultimate sacrifice.

Cleopatra dug her fingertips into her temples and rubbed. What in blazes had she done? One of them would go and live under Black's roof, but beyond that . . . make a match with a nob and forever be crushed by that lord's spirit? Over her dead and bloodied body. "No," she said tersely. Putting distance between her and her sisters, Cleopatra marched past them. They'd already gained too much of a foothold in the discussion, and she needed to change the proverbial landscape in some way. "I'll return and . . ." She forced herself to say the hated words. ". . . marry one of them."

"And live forever amid Polite Society?"

Did Gertrude sense Cleopatra's weakness in that instance? If so, she'd far greater insight and instinct than Cleopatra had ever credited.

"It is not a challenge," Ophelia said gently.

Gertrude flared her eyes into wide circles. She shook her head, befuddled. "No. I didn't mean . . . I didn't intend it as . . ."

Cleopatra held her hand up, quelling the stammering explanation. And that precisely there was why Gertrude could never go. For the flashes of strength she sometimes showed, ultimately, she doubted herself. A fancy toff would crush her spirit the moment Gertrude failed to fall in line with his plans for her.

Ophelia had opened her mouth to speak when a knock sounded at the doorway.

Broderick. He'd of course have discovered her arrival already. Cleopatra might be stealthier than every thief in London, but ultimately her brother always had people reporting back. Who had it been this time?

Another sharp rap struck the wood panel. Her two sisters looked to her.

Bringing her shoulders back, Cleopatra stalked across the room and drew the door open.

Broderick entered, his expression veiled, saying nothing.

Wordlessly, Gertrude and Ophelia filed past him. As soon as they'd gone, he turned the lock and leaned against the panel. "Did they hurt you?" he asked suddenly, unexpectedly. The frosty edge to that question belied his casual repose.

She furrowed her brow.

"Black or his brothers or his men, their wives, or so much as a dog inside their residence?" he put to her on a steely whisper.

His tone promised death, with questions coming later should she answer in the affirmative.

"You know a Black could never hurt me." And yet, if that were, in fact, true, why did she stand before Broderick even now? Why had she fled? *Because your honor was called into question.* Nay, it was more than that. She'd revealed her greatest weakness to Adair Thorne.

"What do you want to do, Cleopatra?" he asked.

I want to stay here. I want to stay here where I have a place and a purpose . . . one that moved beyond the match her brother would have her make.

And then the truth slammed into her.

She had fled out of cowardice.

She'd spent but a handful of days as an outsider, away from her family, and had been on the cusp of being presented to Polite Society.

Since she was at last being honest with herself, she accepted the truth: any slight, perceived or otherwise, she would have made into something more—just so she could have returned . . . here. For in the end, the fruition of Broderick's goals entailed not only Cleopatra humbling herself before a world of people whom she'd spent her life hating, but worse, severing Cleopatra from this life—the only life she'd known. She caught the inside of her cheek hard. *I am leaving. I am leaving, and avoiding, delaying, or running from my entrance before Society would change nothing.* If she intended to make this sacrifice for Ophelia and Gertrude, then there was no other suitable end except her marrying. "Return," she said softly. "I want to return." She flexed her jaw. "I don't want a Black . . ."—Thorne's suspicion-laden eyes flashed to mind— "questioning my trustworthiness."

Her brother snorted and pushed away from the door. "Trustworthiness is earned . . . as is respect."

Cleopatra scrunched her brow up.

"A clever girl told me that once." He followed that with a wink.

Yes, when he was new to the gang, she had hurled those words at him like a curse. To her, Broderick had been just another street boy who'd garnered Diggory's respect and been afforded power because of his gender, and Cleopatra had hated him on sight. Only to be proven so wholly wrong where he was concerned.

You'll not touch her, Diggory. Not her, nor her sisters. Not if you want your books kept and your letters written and missives read. Are we clear . . . ?

From the moment he'd challenged Diggory and asserted his role in their underworld kingdom, Broderick had ensured Cleopatra and her sisters something she'd desperately striven for and failed to find— safety. And even as proud as she was, she had never resented him for so effortlessly conquering Diggory. Rather, she'd loved him and called him brother from then on.

"Black and Thorne are in my offices," he said somberly.

She went still. So that is how he'd discovered her presence here. "Oh?" she asked with feigned casualness. They'd followed her here? To what end? Why should they care whether she'd left? Nay, they should only be happy to have her gone, and be done with all the Killorans.

Her brother propped his hip on her vanity. "They mentioned you'd saved Black's babe from a drunken nursemaid." Pride filled his voice.

She shifted. "I'd hardly call it saving her. I merely brought it to their attention that she was a drunk." She'd always been as uncomfortable with praise as she was a compliment. Disquieted, she reached for the ornate Prometheus porcelain clock resting on the desk in front of her.

"Thorne asked to speak with you."

The Meissen timepiece slipped from her fingers, and she hurried to catch it. Given that Black was master of his household and the one who'd reached the agreement with Broderick, he should be the one wishing to speak to Cleopatra. What did Adair want with her? Setting it to rights with unsteady fingers, Cleopatra felt her cheeks burning. "Th-Thorne?" she squeaked. The man who'd passed searching hands over her in a possessive manner that left her breathless still wanted to speak to her, but for what purpose?

Feeling her brother's gaze boring a hole into her person, she forced her gaze up.

Suspicion darkened his eyes. She damned her blushing and stammering and faltering. What hold did Adair Thorne have over her that he could turn her into a cake before her brother of all people?

"Something happen with Thorne?" he asked with his usual practiced casualness.

Her mind stalled. Yes and no, all at the same time, it did. For his hostility toward her bespoke a man who despised her, and yet his tender touch, even through his fury, hinted at a man who felt desire for her. It had been there in the hardening she'd felt thrust against her lower belly.

"Cleopatra?" her brother snapped.

"Nothing," she lied, her voice steady once more. "Nothing happened outside of him taking my weapons, doubting my word, and finding me in the nursery." She finished that enumeration as much for her benefit as Broderick's. It was crazy to hunger after a man who'd treated her with such disdain.

And yet, how many times had women roughed up by Diggory craved his attentions and affections? She cringed. *I will not be that woman.*

"What will you do?"

There was a double meaning there that asked as much about her plans for Thorne as her intentions to see through the plans for connecting the Killorans to the peerage. *I'll do what I'm supposed to . . .* Just as she'd always done with the betterment of her siblings in mind. Cleopatra squared her shoulders. "Where is he?"

"My office."

She started forward. Most men, regardless of station, would have never granted the use of those private spaces to a sister, wife, or any woman. Broderick, however, had always respected her role inside the family and the club, and for it, he'd forever have her love and fealty. The floorboards groaned behind her, indicating her brother followed along at a slight distance.

Cleopatra smiled wryly. Broderick might trust her judgment and capabilities to hold a meeting with any rival of their establishment, but he'd also not be far should she require intervention—which she rarely did.

Marching past the guards stationed around the private quarters, Cleopatra found her way deeper into the bowels of the establishment, close to the wine cellars and kitchens. One would never expect a proprietor to keep one's quarters there. She'd heard that Black and his arrogant brothers all held offices above the rental suites, but Broderick, just like Cleopatra, knew one was best posted where one least expected to find you.

While she made the long trek to her brother's office, she considered her impending meeting. What could Adair Thorne have to say to her? He'd been abundantly clear in their every exchange that he saw her as a vile Killoran. What would he say if he knew she was, in fact, not just another whelp taken in to Diggory's gang? If he, Black, or any of their kin knew that, they'd have never even agreed to a peace offering in the first place.

She reached the end of the corridor leading to Broderick's office and slowed her steps. She'd faced countless street fights with girls, lads, and fully grown men. None of those exchanges had ever kicked her heart-beat into this frantic rhythm. *It's because he's a miserable blighter . . . an enemy of your family's, and you despise him . . .*

And yet, being in Black's company hadn't roused this peculiar sensation inside—a sentiment she could neither explain nor understand.

"Cleo?"

Startling, she glanced over her shoulder.

Broderick held a knife toward her.

She blinked slowly, eyeing that gleaming metal as it glinted in the dark corridors.

"Never arrive unarmed to any meeting," he said, reminding her of another lesson she'd handed a then-naive *him*. Had there been more suspicion in her brother's eyes, it would have been easier than the veiled nothingness there. For that hinted at a man who'd seen too much and knew more than she cared him to. Taking that offering in one hand, she continued her march.

Ryker Black stood outside Broderick's office. One of their tallest, widest, strongest guards, Cullen, stood sentry beside him . . . and yet for all the world, Black may as well have owned the office.

Black briefly lingered his gaze on the blade in her hand, and she braced for his challenge. Instead, he inclined his head in a silent greeting, an apology in his eyes. With her spare hand, Cleopatra pressed the door handle and entered.

Adair stood in the center of the room, his arms folded at his chest. He stared at her through hooded dark lashes.

"A moment, Brewster," she murmured to her brother's second-in-command. The guard, lingering in the shadows, quit his spot and let himself out.

Alone with Adair, Cleopatra matched his pose and arched an eyebrow. Broderick's dagger dangled awkwardly over her arm.

"I'd expect a quality guard would know better than to leave a Killoran alone with one of Black's kin." His was a casual observation.

She snorted. "The guards in our establishment know me and my sisters enough to know we don't need protecting from one of yours."

The ghost of a smile hovered on Adair's fine-cut lips, and her stomach did a little somersault. In this, she could almost pretend they were the pair poring over his gaming hell plans. Reality intruded . . . and along with it, his cold orders and heartless suspicions about her. *He believes me capable of harming a babe . . .*

Cleopatra let her arms fall to her side. "Surely you've not come to speak about the differences between our staff and yours?" she asked, unnerved and desperate to regain her footing.

His half grin withered. He reached inside his boot, and she instantly stiffened. But he only withdrew a blade.

Her breath caught. A familiar blade.

Adair held it out.

She took an immediate, lurching step toward it, then caught herself. Even as her fingers, toes, and every muscle strained toward that one valuable possession, she restrained herself. She'd already shown too much. The keen glint in his eyes indicated as much.

"Go on," he said gruffly.

Still, Cleopatra took slow, careful steps. Carefully training her weapon on him, she inched closer. He'd given her too many reasons to not trust him, when she'd entered the household with enough to never allow him that honor in the first place. Any of the men the Devil's Den called patrons would have balked at having a weapon pointed at them by Cleopatra Killoran. Adair Thorne was as coolly immobile as the stone statues her brother had recently set outside the hell.

She stopped when they were a handsbreadth apart. They eyed each other a long moment, silently assessing. One arm held protectively at her chest, she opened her other palm.

Instantly, he turned it over. The heat of his callused palm burned her, dangerous in the delicious shivers he sent radiating up her arm. Cleopatra swallowed hard. What accounted for her body's awareness of him, as a man? He was her enemy. She hated him. And yet, just then it was all jumbled. She quickly folded her fingers around the jewel-encrusted dagger and backed away.

"You think I'd kill you here in your brother's office, Cleopatra Killoran?" he asked drolly, and yet there was also a tautness to his tone. She'd offended him, and selfishly she gave thanks that he'd misinterpreted the reason for her actions.

"Not his office. Mayhap his hallways." Her attempt at humor was met with another frown. Cleopatra fought back a sigh. They two were destined to butt heads like angry dogs in the street. Their birthrights and rivalries demanded as much. Knowing that as she did still didn't erase the peculiar regret that thought stirred. The first to look away, Cleopatra tugged her skirts up and deposited Broderick's weapon inside her other boot.

She glanced up.

Adair remained with his hooded gaze locked on her leg. Horror mingled with shock, and the bald emotions sent heat slapping at her cheeks. "Oi didn't mean ta offend your delicate sensibilities," she snarled. It didn't matter that he'd been repelled by her too-slender limbs. *Like chicken bones made to be snapped,* Diggory had often taunted, and threatened.

"I was wrong."

At that abrupt shift, she furrowed her brow in befuddlement.

"You attempted to . . ." He grimaced. "You *did* tell me about Ryker's nursemaid, and I doubted you." He lowered his voice. "At the expense of my niece's safety," he said solemnly, more to himself.

It was a familiar sentiment to those in the streets, an emotion greater known and experienced than love, warmth, or affection—guilt.

"Oi'm a Killoran," she said gruffly, in a concession meant to assuage some of that sentiment. It shouldn't matter what Adair Thorne's opinion of her was—and yet it did.

He nodded once. "But our families also reached a truce. The Blacks will give one of Killoran's sisters one Season, and then the terms are met." How coolly unaffected he was. As he should be when speaking of the hated arrangement she'd gotten this family to agree to. "Listen, Cleopatra. We don't like one another."

Yet, nor did she hate him. She understood his way of life, and that made him . . . comfortable.

"Nor will our families ever be friendly or friends. But when deals are made, my family is not one to renege on the conditions."

This is why he'd not only come, but handed her back her knife. To strike a new accord. Not one of friendship or peace between them, but rather to meet the terms of the concession she'd gotten them to agree to. "Ya asking me to come back with ya?" she taunted, anyway.

Had she not been studying him as close as she was, she'd have failed to see the muscle jumping at the corner of his eye.

She resisted the urge to wrinkle her nose. Where her own brother had been given to displays of temper too many times, and emotion . . . Adair remained remarkably in control, and damned if she did not find herself appreciating him for it. "I want my weapons back."

"I just gave—"

"All of them," she interrupted.

He was already shaking his head. "I'm not allowing a bag of arms inside the house where Black's wife and child sleep."

She steeled her jaw. Because for his earlier apologies and concessions, he still didn't trust her.

"Because your weapons could find themselves in the hands of those who might have less honorable intentions."

Cleopatra started. How had he followed the unspoken path her thoughts had taken? Quickly masking her features, she met his gaze. "You don't trust the people on your staff?"

Another muscle leapt at his eye. "I made the mistake of trusting implicitly once. I'll not do it again."

Her intrigue piqued at not only Adair revealing that weakness but with questions about the man or woman who'd betrayed him and his family. Slowly nodding, she lifted her skirts and placed her dagger in its proper sheath along the inside of her calf. Feeling Adair's piercing stare on her every movement, she snapped the fabric back into place and straightened. "Who was it?" she asked, curiosity pulling the question from her.

Adair swiftly lifted his gaze back to her face. "Do not mistake my honoring the terms of our peace for an offer of friendship," he said tightly.

That curt dismissal shattered the seeming accord they'd struck. "Of course," she said tersely. She forced an icy grin. "We both know anything but hatred between our families"—*us*—"is an impossibility." And with the sting of shame sharp, she stalked off to make her goodbyes once more to her family, before she rejoined the frosty Adair Thorne and his family.

Chapter 11

First, he'd kissed her.

Now he'd been caught eyeing the hellion's leg.

Twice, if he was being honest with at least himself. There had been the instance she'd entered Ryker's household, that he'd put his hands upon her lithe frame and longed to explore her.

Living on the streets for most of his life and then owning a hell that offered prostitution, Adair had come upon whores being taken against a wall or fondled inside his club.

None of those flagrant shows, however, had borne even a hint of eroticism compared to the sight of Cleopatra lifting her skirts and working her long fingers down her calves and inside her boots. Dark boots. Clever ones—made of leather, higher than fashion dictated, and gleaming as they did—that had him conjuring wicked musings of the lithe miss in nothing but those boots and—

He groaned, grateful for the loud banging that drowned out that pathetic sound.

What's worse was that afterward, in a bid to erect the safe wall between him and the enticing Killoran, he'd rejected an offer of friendship she'd never even extended. In that, he'd turned himself into what he'd always hated—a damned bully.

For despite the fire flashing in her eyes, there had been no doubt that Cleopatra had been hurt by his brusque dismissal. Such a fact wouldn't have bothered him a week ago. But in a handful of days, she'd ceased to be the amorphous hellion who called Killoran kin. She'd proven herself to be a fearless, spirited woman who'd given him valuable advice regarding the renovations to his club, and who'd looked after Ryker's daughter.

Then there was also the matter of Cleopatra happening to have enticing ankles.

"Mr. Thorne? You wanted to see me regarding the design plans?"

Startling, Adair looked to the head builder overseeing the reconstruction of the Hell and Sin. Large sheets open in his hands, the builder, Phippen, stared expectantly back at Adair. He silently cursed. "I did." Withdrawing the pages from inside his jacket front, he unfolded the designs. "I wanted to make changes to the earlier agreed-upon plans." Holding them out, he guided the builder toward the back of the hell. "We'd originally had private tables set along the back. I'd have that area moved."

Then you give them a place for that. Apart from your main floors.

He glanced over to see if Phippen followed his requests. Brow wrinkled, the young builder blotted his forehead with the back of his forearm. "And the hazard and faro tables?"

"They'll remain, as we'd originally discussed. The deviation will be that private tables are now scattered between, along both sides of the club."

"Hmph." That single-syllable utterance conveyed his disapproval, and also an inability to challenge Adair. Unlike Cleopatra . . . who was part of Adair's world, more than the businessman before him. Regardless of her age, gender, or connection to Killoran, the woman was right. He swallowed a groan. He'd come here with the purpose of setting

Cleopatra from his thoughts. Instead, since he'd arrived more than ten hours ago, she'd maintained a manaclelike grip over his thoughts.

"Do you have the space to add private rooms with tables?" he asked Phippen impatiently.

Studying the page in Adair's hands, he stared a long while. "It will be difficult."

Difficult but not impossible. "We own the adjoining building," he reminded him. There should be space aplenty for the requested changes.

"There is a problem with that."

Of course there was. Nothing had gone right since his club had burned down. "What is it?" he asked. Folding up the revised plans he'd made, he tucked them back inside his jacket.

Near Adair in height, the architect, who'd not hesitated to take part in the building when it was called for, gave no hint of unease at Adair's sharp tone.

Holding up the plans in his own grip, the other man directed Adair's focus to the area in question. "This wall here." Phippen adjusted the page in his hand, attempting to point at the same time. Muttering to himself, the builder again shifted the sheets in his hand. "That is . . . here." He gave another awkward jab.

Wordlessly, Adair took the page and stalked up the cracked steps. The din of the construction grew deafening in volume as he walked over to a hazard table now covered with an enormous white sheet. Adair laid the building plans down, spreading them open to the previously indicated page.

As in command of his employees as Adair was those in his hell, with a single lift of his hand, Phippen brought the men working to a jarring halt. "As I was saying, Mr. Thorne, there is a problem . . . here . . . with this wall." Pointing first to the sheet, the head builder then gestured to the area in question. "The fire burned through the plaster and penetrated even the stone wall between your establishment and the adjoining one."

Adair frowned, eyeing that spot. Since they owned that property, it should hardly be a problem to merit Phippen's catastrophic response.

"It's more complicated than that."

"Of course it is," he mumbled. Because nothing since the fire had gone even remotely to plan where the rebuilding of the club was concerned.

"If you'll look here." Not waiting to see if Adair followed, he strode to the wall. Several builders hurried out of his way, clearing a path. Those same men hastily averted their eyes, just as they did every time Phippen revealed another flaw in the old structure. "The burned plaster revealed cracks and holes inside the adjoining brick wall."

Joining the builder, he assessed the flawed stones. "Can't you have a bricklayer replace the ones that were damaged?"

Phippen gave his head a negating shake. "This damage, I suspect, is unrelated to the blaze. Upon peeling additional plaster away, it's shown a consistent pattern." He doffed his hat and mopped at his sweaty brow. "If I had to make a venture, it expands all through the entire building."

Moving closer, Adair inspected the ruined stones. He touched the damp portions.

"Lime near the surface destroyed them," the builder said with a frustrating matter-of-factness.

"What does that mean for the timetable?" he asked, already knowing before Phippen even spoke.

"All the plaster needs to come down, and new bricks need to be laid."

Bloody hell. His mind raced. The damned timetable of one month to completion had originally been given with a rigorous, nearly day-and-night long building plan . . . that had not taken into consideration warped stones and faulty beams throughout the club. "How much longer?"

Phippen jammed his hat back atop his head. "If I'd to hazard a guess?"

He bit his tongue to keep from saying he'd already demanded a *guess* from the man.

"At least another month."

At least, which indicated a possibility of more errors. A sure possibility.

A large crash echoed around the barren-but-for-workers hell. Phippen immediately cursed and went rushing off, calling out orders to his men.

Adair jabbed his fingertips against his temples and pressed furiously. This had certainly not been the diversion he'd sought from Cleopatra Killoran. Sidestepping the workers scurrying back and forth with pieces of plaster overflowing in their arms, Adair made his way back outside. The sun had begun its descent in the early evening sky.

He briefly consulted his timepiece and then glanced over to his carriage. *I should return.* There was the ball introducing Killoran's sister to the lords of London, and Adair was expected there. According to Ryker, he was to be there to keep a wary eye on her at all times during the event. And to Penelope, his presence was necessary to show a solidarity built on friendship.

It spoke to Penelope's naïveté but also hinted at Ryker's inability to shed his suspicious nature. It gave a man hope . . .

"Oi was told Oi could find you here."

Niall's coarse Cockney broke through the din of carpenters' banging hammers and the clank of wood beams going back into place.

Turning about, he faced the other man. Usually there would be jeers and jests at having been caught unawares. It was a fault that could not be forgiven in St. Giles. However, since the destruction of their club and the uncertainty of the new futures his brothers—nay, they—had agreed to embark upon, there had been less goading and grins. He redirected his attention to two workers laboring to bring a sizable beam inside the hell. "I had to speak with Phippen about some changes," he muttered.

"All day?"

"They're important changes," he groused.

"At the end of the day?" Niall persisted, relentless.

It was telling that his brother didn't first present questions about the design plans for the Hell and Sin.

Then—

"What kind of changes?" he asked gruffly.

Adair tamped down a grin. Regardless of how Calum and Ryker had moved away from their devotion to the Hell and Sin for more respectable ventures, Niall would always have a connection to this place. Niall had been born to the streets, and it would forever be in his blood. "I'm moving the private tables to the gaming floors."

Niall frowned. "What about the areas set apart for gents to conduct their business?"

Cleopatra's advice rolling around his head, Adair proceeded to share the new plans and his rationale—her rationale. When he'd finished, Niall was contemplatively rubbing his chin.

"All good ideas."

"Cleopatra," he said automatically.

His brother's expression instantly darkened. "What was that?"

Cursing under his breath, Adair shuttered his gaze. Niall might have admitted to being indebted to Cleopatra for helping save his wife, but he was not so forgiving or trusting that he'd want her holding the plans to the club in her small hands. Not when those plans revealed every chamber, secret, and hideaway.

"Cleopatra Killoran," he amended, carefully picking through his words, "made mention of the Devil's Den and their table configuration."

Niall scoffed. "And you altered our plans based on *that*?"

"I altered our plans because it made sense to do so, and made less not to do so simply because Killoran runs his a certain way," he said evenly.

They locked stares. Anyone else would have been petrified by that frosty challenge. Niall was a man who bore every element of his days of crime and the filth of the street on his person. Adair, however, had saved his arse enough times to know that no man was infallible—including his brother. Niall was the first to look away. He glanced about the streets. "You intending to stay here all day *and* night?"

"And where should I be?" Not allowing Niall to speak, he indicated with his hand four workers guiding a long beam through the gaping entryway. "There's rotten bricks and four bearing walls that need to be replaced. And those are just two of the issues I'm dealing with."

Two boys scurrying by with buckets stepped a wide berth around them as they climbed the steps inside.

After they'd passed, Adair continued, "If we . . ." He paused. *They don't want to really call these streets home anymore. Only you do.* His brothers and sister all had homes that would never again be the Hell and Sin. "If I," he somberly corrected, "ever expect to return home, I have to oversee the work here."

With his gaze, Niall scoured his face. Carefully schooling his features, Adair met his stare. "That's what all this is about?"

"All this?" he retorted. Of course his brother didn't, nor couldn't, know that Adair stood here lusting after Broderick Killoran's sister. "Why don't you say whatever it is that's brought you here." And be done with it.

"You've been avoiding Ryker's townhouse," Niall said without preamble. For a horrifying instant, Adair believed his family had gathered that this dangerous fascination with Cleopatra Killoran had driven him out.

"I haven't been avoiding it," he offered in a belated declination. *Her. I've been avoiding her.*

"It wasn't your fault that she was discovered alone with Paisley."

So that was the erroneous conclusion that had been drawn. That Adair had fled because of some sense of guilt at having neglected his responsibilities. What would they say if they knew the truth? All of it. Content to let them to their opinions, Adair scrutinized the builders bustling about.

"Ya can't stay here forever," Niall snapped. "Overseeing Killoran's hellion of a sister is your other task," Niall needlessly reminded him.

Adair frowned. He'd thought of Cleopatra as a hellion on countless scores. Something in hearing Niall utter it in those frosty, lethal tones was altogether . . . different. "She discovered Paisley's nursemaid was a drunk," he said, feeling the need to point out that fact. Another round of banging commenced. "When Ryker and Penny trusted the young woman implicitly," he added.

His brother scratched at his brow. "Are ya all right?"

He stared back, unblinking. What was his brother on about?

"You're defending the girl."

I'm not a girl.

Again, those damned words conjured forth the memories of her under him, bucking, twisting, begging for his kiss. Tamping down a groan along with an unwanted burgeoning of desire, he focused all his efforts on the two builders bringing a shorter but wider beam inside. "I've got more responsibilities than just seeing to Cleopatra Killoran." He'd once scoffed at the pomposity of her name. Now, having been battled by the spirited minx on several scores, he conceded there wasn't a more apt one for her.

"The ball is in two hours."

His gut clenched. Another one of those infernal affairs. He'd been forced to suffer through too many polite events since his sister, Helena, had married a duke. Those bloody despised obligations had only increased with Ryker's and Calum's marriages to proper ladies.

"Ryker wants to know if you'll be back."

Adair snorted. "Wants to know? Or demands?"

"The latter," Niall said with a grin. He'd been tasked with bringing Adair back.

"I'm overseeing the work, and then I'll return." *Coward. You're avoiding seeing Cleopatra, again.* Stalking forward, Adair climbed the handful of broken steps, but the carved demons outside froze him in his steps. The horn of one gargoyle was broken, and a jagged crack ran through the entire winged body. Even the first adornments they'd ever affixed to the club had been ruined.

And Killoran's club still stands and thrives . . .

Energized by his hatred and the need to end Niall's pestering, Adair entered the Hell and Sin. Floors once carpeted and filled with guests were now littered with a sea of workers: men and small children, bustling about. Periodically they'd lift their heads from their tasks and lift a hand or call out a greeting.

Adair masked his features, attempting to hide the shock and pain that came from what his club had become.

"We'll make it into something better," Niall said quietly at his side. "We always do."

Adair flexed his jaw.

Niall settled a hand on his shoulder. "I know you hate the girl for what she's done."

"What her family did," he corrected. A woman who'd look after Black's babe and offer accurate input on his design plans would never start a blaze. Knowing her even the short time he did, he knew she was too proud to assume victory that way.

"Same difference," Niall incorrectly argued. "But you still need to be there tonight . . . not solely to watch her, but because all of London is going to see how she's received by our family."

Adair opened and closed his mouth several times, but no words came out. When he managed to speak, he was unable to keep the disgust from his question. "And you suddenly care for those details?"

"I care for how it reflects upon my wife, and someday you'll understand that, too." A steely glint hardened his eyes until he was effortlessly transformed once more into the ruthless head guard at the Hell and Sin. "It's time to leave. We all need to be there."

Feeling like one being marched to the gallows, Adair reluctantly fell into step beside his brother, making his way toward Ryker's carriage. Fortunately, Niall was the one sibling who'd always been driven by purpose, and he never needed to fill quiet or prattle on.

Steeling his resolve, Adair climbed inside the black conveyance and started the long journey back to his mission for the night.

Chapter 12

She looked like a bloody fool. Nay, to be precise, Cleopatra looked like a plate of lemon meringue without the benefit of the marshmallow top.

Focusing on the horrid state of her dress was far safer than focusing on the quixotic hold Adair Thorne had on her thoughts as she sat trapped in Black's guest chambers. Willingly trapped, but trapped nonetheless.

Now, however, there was no escaping it. Cleopatra would have to venture out. She flinched. For a bloody ball—that formal introduction of a guttersnipe to Polite Society.

She exhaled slowly, dispelling that impending horror and Adair from her mind.

Doing a small circle, she eyed her frame in the mirror.

To be fair, no matter what she donned, she always looked rather silly. Her brother had erroneously believed through the years that in putting her in fine fabrics and gowns he could somehow set her worth among Polite Society as something greater than it ever was. Greater than it ever could be. Broderick hadn't seen the inherent contradiction in their fine garments being worn at one of the wickedest clubs in London.

But Cleopatra knew enough . . . knew what her brother hadn't yet accepted—the *ton* was going to cut their teeth on her . . . and quite happily, too.

Staring at her reflection in the bevel, Cleopatra took in the canary-yellow satin against her pale skin. For all intents and purposes, she may as well have been a child playing at dress-up. She gulped.

All along she'd believed the last place she cared to be was in this household, only to have it clearer that it was, in fact, Ryker Black's ballroom that she'd rather set afire.

And what was worse, she'd enter that ballroom with the sole intent of capturing some gentleman's notice, so she might become a lord's wife, and then live forever among the *ton* and—

Her stomach lurched. Of its own volition, her gaze crept over to the window, and she contemplated escape. A swift one. One that the lady's maid, Dorinda, bustling about the room and humming to herself, would never see coming, and would see Cleopatra free.

Singing to herself, Dorinda carried over a diamond-studded crown, a small tiara her brother had commissioned for all of his sisters. "Now for your crown, miss."

Crown. She angled out of Dorinda's reach. *I'll be damned if I put that piece on.* The laughs Polite Society would have with her, a girl born of the gutters rubbing elbows with them and presenting herself as some kind of royalty. Damn Broderick. Damn him to hell. "Oi don't need that," she said gruffly, angling back.

Nonetheless, the maid persisted. "Lovely piece it is, Miss Killoran."

Cleopatra would certainly credit the girl for having more gumption than she'd previously believed. "Oi said that won't be necessary," she snarled as Dorinda made another grab.

"It would be a shame for such a piece to go unworn."

Cleopatra made a futile lunge left, but Dorinda settled her hands on her shoulders. With a resolute set to her mouth, she guided her back to the vanity and proceeded to arrange the tiara upon her head. All the while, the girl sang in a discordant soprano.

> Farewell to the Highlands, farewell to the North,
> The birth-place of Valour, the country of Worth;
> Wherever I wander, wherever I rove,
> The hills of the Highlands for ever I love.

> My heart's in the Highlands, my heart is not here,
> My heart's in the Highlands, a-chasing the deer;
> Chasing the wild-deer, and following the roe,
> My heart's in the Highlands, wherever I go.

Cleopatra's fingers twitched with the need to clamp her hands over her ears and drown out the cheerful servant's song.

Artfully arranging two curls—two limp curls—over Cleopatra's shoulder, Dorinda eyed her work with far too much pride. With a pleased nod, she reached for the velvet case. "Now the necklace."

Garish diamonds her brother had insisted she don at the *ton* events. The diamond-and-ruby necklace in her hold, Dorinda came at her again, with determination in her every movement.

"No." She might have donned the meringue gown and allowed Dorinda to put the bloody crown on her head, but she drew the line at gaudy necklaces.

The younger woman furrowed her brow. "But—"

"I said no." The *ton* would see the extravagant display as precisely what it was: an interloper, in the market to snare a titled husband, in exchange for some coin. *In short, a whore . . . my brother made me a bloody whore.*

But you're the one who volunteered for the role . . . you've agreed to this to spare Gertrude and Ophelia . . . and help your family . . .

"You really must wear it."

137

She snapped. "I said no." What was it to the maid whether or not she wore the damned necklace?

Dorinda paled but did not back down. She offered a coaxing smile. "Come," she gave the necklace a slight shake, and the heavy piece jangled noisily. "It will complete your ensemble, miss."

Why in blazes was she so tenacious? And this time as the girl came closer, Cleopatra—who'd gone toe-to-toe with thugs from the street—knew she was going to lose this blasted battle. That Dorinda would see her dripping in diamonds, as Broderick intended. She skittered her gaze about. "Oi said Oi ain't going to wear the bloody—"

The door opened with a faint click, and she and the maid looked as one as Lady Chatham let herself inside. Saved by a Black. Both she and Dorinda. Who would have believed she'd see the damned day?

"Dorinda, if you'll excuse Miss Killoran and I?" the viscountess asked, sweeping over.

"As you wish, my lady." The girl dipped a curtsy and made to place the jewels about Cleopatra's neck. Panic choked her.

"I'll take that," Lady Chatham said with a wide smile. Intercepting the maid's efforts, she relieved them from her hold.

With another curtsy, Dorinda took her leave.

Another time, Cleopatra would have been affronted by anyone entering her chambers without even the benefit of a knock. A knock would have been appropriate, even as the viscountess certainly reserved rights and decisions over every room in this townhouse. Her shoulders sagged.

Penelope eyed the extravagant piece in her hands. "It is lovely," she said, all the while assessing it. Those two-quarter-inch teardrops glimmered in the light.

"It is large," Cleopatra muttered, glowering at them. As though covering her in diamonds could somehow make her different from what she was—who she was: a girl from the streets.

Lady Chatham glanced up, and a rush of heat flooded Cleopatra's cheeks at the probing glimmer there.

She'd underestimated the always smiling woman . . . she was far more perceptive than Cleopatra had credited. She braced for those equally searching questions. Instead, the viscountess redeposited the necklace in the velvet case and snapped it closed.

Cleopatra studied those careful movements, not at all deceived by the casualness of them. Setting aside the jewels, Lady Chatham switched her attention to Cleopatra's gown. "You look lovely, Cleopatra."

Cleopatra stared incredulously at the pair of them in the mirror. Draped in sapphire silk, with understated butterfly combs in her black curls, Black's wife epitomized wealth, rank, and power. Whereas, Cleopatra? A great deal less. "You're a liar on that score," she charged without inflection.

"No. You *are* lovely. As is your gown," she added, as more of an afterthought.

It was a lie, and given her experience with falsehoods, they were invariably offered for one of two reasons: for the liar to obtain something he or she craved or to gain an upper hand on one's enemy. Now, by Lady Chatham's wide smile—a smile that very much reached her eyes—Cleopatra learned there was, in fact, another reason for those fabrications: to simply be nice.

Lady Chatham returned her attention to Cleopatra's necklace. "May I?" she demurred, lifting the case.

Watching her closely, Cleopatra slowly nodded. Did the other woman intend to get her to wear them, too? This dog whistle meant to call out to eligible bachelors in need of a fortune that one was theirs for the taking as long as they suffered through a connection to the Killoran family.

The viscountess popped the velvet-lined case open and reexamined the fortune in jewels resting there. "White ruffles," she said softly, a woman lost in thought who, during her reflection, had forgotten Cleopatra stood beside her.

Curiosity pulled. What was she on about? "My lady?" she asked reluctantly.

Black's wife gave her head a clearing shake. "It was my family's version of your diamond necklace," she explained, lifting the object up. "I come from a scandalous lot, and my brother and mother were of the opinion that if they"—she scrunched her skirts—"covered us in frilly white lace, it would highlight our innocence and somehow lessen the wickedness attached to our name."

Just like Broderick had believed about the jewels and fabrics he'd insisted his sisters wear, around a damned gaming hell, no less. Cleopatra's lips tugged in a wry grin. "I'd venture not a single one of your family members could be more outrageous than a brother who owns a gaming hell, and siblings who were born bastards and lived on the streets?" Another time she would have thrown out the crimes she'd committed as a way to shock. For some reason, she didn't.

To the lady's credit, she didn't so much as bat an eye at the accounting of the Killoran family.

Instead, she returned an answering smile. "Our scandals were different," she acknowledged. "But they were"—she wrinkled her nose—"*are* scandals by society's determination."

The woman rose in Cleopatra's estimation for her bluntness. She didn't try to draw like comparisons between their scandals, and Cleopatra appreciated her for it.

The viscountess proceeded to check off on her fingers. "I'd one sister who was part of a failed elopement, and then my brother married my governess. My elder sister wed a man who'd only waltzed with her on a wager." A twinkle lit her eyes as she paused on her fourth finger. "And I, of course, married a gaming hell owner, who'd been a stranger, only after we were discovered in a compromising position."

Absently, Cleopatra dropped her stare to the *D* etched upon her skin. For every scandal Lady Chatham had weathered, she still remained a lady born to their ranks. Whereas Cleopatra Killoran wore the societal differences between her and the *ton* like the actual mark made by Diggory's knife.

She stiffened as Black's wife took her hand in hers, forcing Cleopatra's gaze up. "Regardless of station or birthright or background, all are met with unkindness. I was no exception, nor will you be," she concluded softly, with no malice or delight, and only real truth. "Are you ready?"

Am I ready? I'd rather parade naked and unarmed through the streets of St. Giles, with only my fists for protection.

Lady Chatham held her elbow out, that gesture of support as much a challenge to Cleopatra as anything. It was time. The beginning of the rest of her life . . . here . . . in the fancy end of London.

Sucking in a slow breath through clenched teeth, she took the viscountess's arm.

"You know, I really would have you call me Penelope," she began as they started from the room.

Cleopatra did a quick sweep of the halls, and her gaze lingered on Adair's doorway. How to account for the disappointment in finding him gone? Because he might be one of the Blacks, but she also had more in common with that mistrustful blighter than she did the whole of the guests on Penelope's guest list.

"Are you all right?" Penelope quizzed.

"Fine. I was looking for—" She clamped her mouth tight, cursing her uncharacteristically loose lips, blaming both Adair and this damned night in equal measure.

Eyes alert, Penelope leaned her whole body close.

"For the direction of the ballroom, my lady," she finished lamely.

"This way, then," she said with her usual smile, leading Cleopatra on through the halls. "As I was saying earlier, I would that you call me

Penelope. I can ask that you use my given name, and advise it . . . but I won't compel you to do so." Black's wife brought them to a stop at the end of the hallway. "Having only friends in those I call family, and never having known that gift among the *ton*, I've come to appreciate how very lonely this world is, and would extend an offer of friendship to you."

Extend an offer of friendship. Friendship was earned, not a gift given. And it certainly didn't come after but a handful of days of knowing another person. Still, since she'd lost Reggie, Broderick, Ophelia, Gertrude, and Stephen, there had been an aching loneliness inside. "Foine," she said gruffly, and she may as well have replied with a proper tone and a curtsy for the smile she earned from Penelope.

"Splendid!" Lightly squeezing Cleopatra's arm, the other woman urged them along. "And please know that as long as you are here, and even after you . . ."

Marry—oh, God, I'm going to toss the contents of my stomach.

". . . go," Penelope blessedly settled for, so that Cleopatra was able to freely breathe again, ". . . you will always have a friend in me and my family."

A friend in the Blacks? That would be the damned day.

Adair Thorne's reaction after he'd sent her from his makeshift office and then discovered her inside the nursery was proof that such a relationship could never be reached. Not truly. No matter how much this bubbly woman might wish it.

Penelope looked as though she wished to say more, but they had reached the top of the stairwell. "Here we are."

Cleopatra stared down the thirty steps she'd counted on her first day inside this townhouse. Her gut churned as she took in the gathering below: Black, Calum Dabney, Niall Marksman and his wife, Diana, the duke's daughter whom Cleopatra had saved, and through that rescue had brought about the temporary truce. And for all her claims of confidence and self-control and indifference, in this moment, she was not the composed, fearless figure she presented to the world. She was out of her bloody mind with terror, not necessarily about the lords and ladies she'd face—they could all go hang—but for the fate awaiting her. *You are Cleopatra Killoran, Queen of the Dials, as Broderick named you. Undaunted by any. Breathe.*

Her bid for calm failed.

"Cleopatra?"

Through the buzzing in Cleopatra's ears, Penelope's concerned query came muffled, and she struggled to hear it over her own breath.

Then her gaze collided with the tall, negligent figure off to the side, removed from the group of Blacks—*Adair.*

For the immaculate cut of his expensive black garments, and the stark white of his cravat, he by all appearances may as well have been a lord born to the ranks of the guests who'd be in attendance. The hint of the streets lingered in the form of faint scars that nicked his chiseled features. His arms folded, he leaned against a marble pillar, and the sight of him so coolly unaffected, but for the ghost of a smile dimpling his left cheek, brought her back from the abyss of panic.

Despite his lack of faith and hurtful accusations from the days prior, a matching grin pulled at her lips. "I'm ready," she finally said, never taking her eyes from Adair.

As she and Black's wife made a slow descent, Penelope prattled on at her side, and Cleopatra, who'd always abhorred inane rambling, was now grateful for it. With every step that brought her closer to the marble foyer, the dread eased, and in its place was a restoration of her self-confidence.

An assurance that had nothing to do with Adair's hooded gaze . . . or the sparkle of amusement in his green eyes as he took in her yellow gown. *Liar.*

"Go to hell," she mouthed.

And just as he'd done at their meeting a week earlier, he touched his fingers to an imagined brim. Only where that act had once been filled with derision, now there was a gentle teasing.

Cleopatra and Penelope reached the bottom step, and the icy coolness of Black and his men sent reality crashing back.

Black and his brothers parted, giving her a wide berth. The only smiles from the group belonged to Diana Marskman and Penelope.

"Shall we?" Black asked in gravelly tones. He held out a stiff elbow, and resisting the urge to glance back at Adair, she placed her scarred fingers upon the sleeve of the enemy, braced to face down a sea of them.

Chapter 13

Adair had found himself with a fist to the solar plexus too many times. A man never forgot the feel of having the breath sucked from his body.

The moment Cleopatra Killoran had appeared at the top of the stairs would forever be a like moment in his life.

It was a horrifying truth he'd fought back the moment it slid forward. But nearly an hour into the ball, hovering on the side of the floor, a guard watching over the young woman, he accepted the truth of it.

From where he stood in the corner, Adair used his cover and overall invisibility to the crowd to study her.

Be it the *ton*, or the underworld, Cleopatra Killoran would never be a beauty by any standards, and the silly yellow gown she donned could never be considered anything but hideous. But as she'd come toward him, her expressive eyes glittering through her always smudged lenses, her effervescent spirit had shone brighter than her dress, and he'd been trying to muddle through ever since. She was . . . she was . . .

He silently cursed.

Where in blazes was she? Springing forward on the balls of his feet, he did a quick sweep over the heads of the shorter guests, searching for

a glittering tiara he would have mocked a week ago. Where was she . . .
? Where was she . . . ?

A small figure stepped into his direct line of vision.

"She's being introduced to Diana's family," Penelope drawled, taking up a place beside him.

Adair searched and at last found Cleopatra, conversing with the duke. Shoulders back, her delicate features an expressionless mask, she'd a bearing the queen herself would admire. Then Penelope's earlier words registered . . .

Had he been that obvious? He shifted his attention back from the minx who commanded his notice, over to his sister-in-law.

"Yes, you were," Penelope answered his silent question. "That obvious," she elucidated on a whisper. "Here." She proffered one of the two glasses in her hand.

Reluctantly, he accepted the fragile cup. He eyed it dubiously and then took a sip. Adair immediately choked on his swallow. "What is that?"

"Lemonade. My mother would argue that tepid lemonade makes any ball complete."

The *ton* would all be better off sipping from flasks of whiskey and snifters of brandy before drinking this rotted stuff. With a grimace, he downed the contents in a long swallow. "And you're suddenly one who does as Society expects," he drawled. That certainly went against everything he knew of the lady who'd maneuvered Ryker into marriage and then single-handedly converted the rooms and roles inside the Hell and Sin. The only woman he knew to rival her in spirit and spunk was Cleopatra.

"Hardly," she assured.

Unbidden, Adair's gaze went back to the ballroom floor where Cleopatra remained conversing with the sad-eyed duke.

"You don't have to watch her as though she intends to make off with the silver," Penelope said in a hushed whisper.

He whipped his head sideways.

"Despite her rough exterior, Cleopatra really is quite lovely and I'm certain incapable of cruelty."

So that is what his sister-in-law believed. That he'd been watching over the young woman the same way a constable would track a street urchin. Content to leave her to her opinion, Adair remained stoically silent. Nor would he point out that it was, in fact, the lady's husband who'd asked Adair to watch after Cleopatra.

"I know my husband expects you to dog her steps." Goodness, the woman had an uncanny ability to follow a person's unspoken thoughts. "But I'm telling you that she doesn't mean us harm."

"No," he concurred, ignoring the surprise in her eyes. Originally, he'd believed Cleopatra could have very well been the one who'd issued the orders to burn his club down. No longer. Capable of subterfuge as she clearly was, he'd gathered in the handful of days he'd known her that she would have proudly taunted him for her role in it, before she denied taking part.

"I rather think she is lonely," Penelope said softly, those quietly spoken words nearly lost to the hum of the orchestra and the ballroom revelry. But they weren't, and Adair heard them. "It is hard to leave behind one's family and make a new life with strangers."

Having joined their ranks not very long ago, after her hasty marriage, Penelope spoke as one who knew.

Staring out at Cleopatra still in discussion with Diana and her father, Adair clenched his fingers so tightly he nearly snapped the handle of his silly glass. The same way he didn't want to find her clever with a keen wit, was the same way he didn't want to contemplate Cleopatra as a forlorn, dejected woman alone in an unfamiliar world. It was far safer when she'd only been an amorphous enemy of the Killoran gang that he'd no dealings with.

The orchestra's lively reel came to a halt, and Penelope handed over her untouched glass, filling both his hands. "If you'll excuse me? I would see to Cleopatra. I . . ." She went up on tiptoe. "I . . ." Her brow wrinkled. "Drat. Where is she?"

The previously occupied duke and his daughter had been joined by Niall, but sometime after the point at which Adair had blinked, his quarry had gone. He silently cursed, looking about. "I thought you trusted her," he muttered drily.

Penelope shoved an elbow into his side. He grunted. The unexpectedness of her jab sent liquid sloshing over the sides of Penelope's glass, now in his hand, so that his fingers were coated with the sticky beverage. "Hush," his sister-in-law chided unapologetically. "I'm not watching after her. Well, I am. In a way," she prattled.

"Penelope," he said exasperatedly.

"Right. Right. I promised to introduce her to several . . . people." In short, suitors. It was the ideal plan carried out by Penelope. The sooner Cleopatra was wed, the sooner Adair—and all of his family—would be done with her and the whole of the Killoran gang.

Cursing, Penelope sank back on her heels, and without a backward glance, she started forward. Adair stared after her as her smaller form was swallowed by the crush of guests. He followed her movements, searching all the while for Cleopatra. For his assurances about Cleopatra Killoran and his own gut feeling about the young woman, all the age-old reservations trickled forward. After all, he'd known her but a handful of days. What if she even now waited for his family to be occupied and—

"Drinking lemonade, Thorne?" Cleopatra's droll whisper sounded from over his shoulder. "If anyone on the street saw you, you'd be finished."

He whipped his head about, looking for the owner of that husky contralto. Bloody hell. Where in blazes was . . . ?

A long, beleaguered sigh cut across his thoughts. "Oy, getting snuck up on and not being able to find the person?" Cleopatra stepped out of the shadows, a small grin on her face. That unjaded, real expression did funny things to his chest. "You certain you were born to the streets?"

Actually, he hadn't been. He'd been born to a baker, but when one was orphaned and lived alone in St. Giles, one didn't counter the idea that one had sprung from those dangerous cobbles. "Go to hell," he said without inflection, holding out the untouched glass of lemonade Penelope had saddled him with.

Cleopatra snorted. "You think to fob that off on me?"

"I think if you don't want me to steer you directly back to Lady Chatham, then I'd begin drinking."

She scowled and, with a go-to-hell look in her eyes, took the cup. Quickly finishing the lemonade, Cleopatra set the glass down on the floor beside the pillar and brushed the back of her hand over her mouth. "Stuff is rot," she muttered.

He grinned. Having spent the better part of the evening in the corners of the stuffy ballroom, alongside the equally stuffy lords and ladies present, he found Cleopatra's reaction very refreshing.

"Not enjoying yourself, I take it?"

"Enjoying myself?" she whispered from beside the pillar. "Do I look like I'm enjoying myself?"

That demand invited him to look. Several strands had fallen free of her chignon and hung over her modest décolletage. Unbidden, he lingered his gaze upon the soft cream swells of her breasts. He'd always preferred the women he took to his bed bountiful, with curves that overflowed in his hands. Now he had to admit there was a dangerous appeal to Cleopatra's lithe frame.

"No, I'm not enjoying myself," she muttered under her breath, blessedly unaware that he even now took time to appreciate her form. Having kissed her senseless once was enough, a damning weakness he'd be wise not show again toward this woman. "And what are you doing here in the corner?"

His neck went hot.

"Guarding me?" She narrowed her eyes. "Still don't trust me?"

Do not be fooled by the faint wounded undertone there.

"But for our first meeting last year, I've known you less than a week," he said from the side of his mouth. "Am I to expect that if I took up with your family that I should forget a lifetime feud between us?"

She flattened her lips into a mutinous line.

"And there's still the matter of your brother burning down my bloody club," he said tightly. It might not have been Cleopatra herself, but it was still people she called family and blindly defended, and gave her loyalty to. And he'd be wise to remind himself of that—and often.

It was a sad day indeed when Cleopatra sought out the company of Adair Thorne.

It was one thing to have hungered for his kiss days earlier. After all, that had been merely her body's response, something that could be explained without feelings or emotions involved. Actually, enjoying a person's presence was altogether different—and a Black, no less.

Yet, she continued to seek him out, even though he believed her family the devils responsible for his misfortune.

"My family did not set your club ablaze," she gritted out. For him to suggest that would mean the Killorans reneged on truces.

A muscle ticked at the corner of his mouth. "I didn't say *you* did," he said flatly, not removing his focus from the ballroom floor.

"You're calling me a liar and arsonist."

And say what one would of the evil acts they'd committed, neither Broderick nor Cleopatra nor any of her siblings and staff would ever dare play with fire, as Diggory had.

"You come from a family of one," he said simply.

Cleopatra recoiled, grateful that his attention was trained elsewhere so he couldn't see that his words had struck like a well-placed barb.

When he'd been living, Diggory's love of fire had been a popular tool of torture. He'd burned countless boys and girls to instill fear, and he had set conflagrations that had destroyed establishments and businesses . . . and lives. "Fire is not a trick of my brother's," she said quietly, needing him to understand that about Broderick, the boy who'd saved her and named her.

At last, Adair looked over. "It was one of Diggory's," he returned. "One of his favorite ones. And Killoran learned at that Devil's feet."

"As did you," she accurately pointed out. "As did all your siblings."

Diggory had managed countless hovels, filling them with children. His reach had extended far throughout London. Only a handful had escaped his hold . . . Adair and his siblings had been some of the fortunate souls.

He searched her face, and she hungered for the fight to defend her kin.

Adair sighed. "Don't you have gentlemen to dance with?" he asked, holding his glass up.

A nearby servant rushed over and claimed the delicate cup, then rushed off.

She searched Adair for a hint of mockery. "Not much of a dancer," she said carefully. She'd sooner cut herself than admit that even with the fortune she brought to the proverbial table, she'd not a single interested gentleman.

"Silly activity, isn't it?" he asked companionably.

"Suppose so," she settled for, wading through this unfamiliar ground. She'd not point out that she'd always enjoyed the lessons she'd received in those fancy steps. It went against everything she was to find pleasure in any ladylike pursuit . . . but something in dancing had been like gliding through the air on a wood swing her brother had set out back of the Devil's Den.

"You suppose so? And here I thought you'd be one cursing those fancy steps," he said, far too clever for his own damned good.

What were she and Adair Thorne? Mortal enemies or uneasy friends? *Friends? Pfft, we'd never be that.* They were just people with shared backgrounds, who were both uneasy with the arrangements that saw her living here. But in this new solitary world, she'd take whatever she could, where she could. "You ever take part in that?" she countered, tipping her head toward the waltzing partners.

By the horror in his eyes, she may as well have asked him to turn over the keys to his club. "Dancing?" He snorted. "No. Nor will I ever."

She secretly mourned the idea of a man who moved with his stealth and elegance, in possession of a tall, muscled frame to rival some of the finest fighters she'd ever witnessed in back-alley battles, never gracing a dance floor. "I hated it, too. Hated anything to do with the peerage. Seemed like a waste of good energy and steps."

"But then?" he asked, with a genuine curiosity there to his query.

"Then I tried it."

He chuckled. "Why do I find it hard to imagine you agreeing to any lessons on *any* ladylike activity?"

It was an accurate read on who she was as a person—and after just a short time together. As such, one would have expected Adair was right on that score.

Broderick had insisted she and her sisters all know those intricate steps. As a girl, she'd just been so damned happy whenever she'd escaped Diggory's attentions that she would have walked a tightwire across London if that was the only way. "Sometimes dancing was safer," she settled for.

A dark somberness fell across his face.

Not wanting his pity, she hurried to speak. "Oi was so certain it was a waste of valuable time. It was a frivolous activity that served no purpose." She drifted closer. "But do ya know what, Adair?"

He gave his head a slight, nearly imperceptible shake that urged her on.

"Gambling is, as well, and we built a life on that. And when ya try something else . . . like dancing," she said, discreetly motioning to the partners on the floor, "ya find for yourself what it's really like."

Adair's gaze remained fixed on her face. "And what is it like?" he asked hoarsely.

She tilted her head back and met his eyes. "Loike floating," she whispered. "When it's with the roight partner."

A charged heat passed between them as their chests moved quickly in a like rhythm, and he shifted his gaze ever so slightly, before ultimately settling on her mouth.

The column of his throat moved, and through the din of the crowded ballroom, she detected that audible swallow.

And shapeless, bespectacled Cleopatra, who'd never been looked upon as a person of beauty, in this instance, with Adair Thorne, felt . . . beautiful. Butterflies danced in her belly, and she fought to retain control of her thoughts.

"There you are."

They jerked apart and looked to Penelope. The viscountess alternated a smile between them. "You should have indicated you'd found Cleopatra," she gently chided. "I've several gentle"—Cleopatra's stomach knotted—"guests," Penelope substituted, "for you to meet."

Gentlemen. Would-be suitors, who were no doubt fortune hunters, eager to meet the Queen of the Dials, for no other purpose than the wealth she brought to their empty coffers.

"Shall we?" Penelope took Cleopatra's hand and tucked it in her elbow, forcing her to abandon her place beside Adair.

And there was surely something wrong with her that as she let herself be pulled away, without even a parting greeting exchanged between her and Adair, she wanted to remain with him. *It's only a matter of him being from your world . . . and comfortable for it.* He doesn't care that you have a Cockney accent or treat you with disdain for having deposited a glass upon the floor. Cleopatra worried at her lip. He did, however, treat her as a Killoran to be wary of. *What would he say if he knew you're not just another woman who'd survived within Diggory's gang . . . ?*

With Penelope filling the silence, as she'd already revealed a tendency to do, they made their way through the ballroom. Even over the din of the crowd, the hushed whispers trailing after them punctuated the noise. Ladies yanked their skirts back and retreated, making a path.

"Smile. It confuses them," Penelope advised through one of those patently false expressions.

"Oi don't care wot they have to say about me." Nor were her words for a brave show. It was hard to be anything but self-assured when presented with the gentlemen who tossed away family fortunes at Cleopatra's family's tables.

"There are some good gentlemen," Penelope persisted.

She stopped, forcing her hostess to either continue on and drag her down or join her on the edge of the floor. "How long have you"—she paused, remembering the greatest source of contention between her and Adair—"*did you*, live inside the Hell and Sin? Nearly a year," she accurately supplied before the other woman could. It had been her business for the past twenty years to know everything she could about her enemies, and this woman had been among them. "Oi moved into the Devil's Den when Diggory took it over."

An uncharacteristic ice frosted Penelope's features. Black had shared some of Diggory's evil with his wife, then. It was written in the hatred there.

"And I've been living in it ever since," she said in hushed tones. "The men here—the young ones, the old ones, their reprobate sons and brothers who aren't in attendance—they've all entered my club. I know how much they drink, how loose they are with their lips and their fortunes. Oi'd be hard-pressed to find a single fancy toff on your guest list who hasn't at some time or another stepped inside my hell. So, please," she urged, "do not sell me on imagined qualities of any of them. My brother wants me to make a match, and some gentleman surely needs a fortune."

Penelope opened and closed her mouth several times. "What do you want?" she asked softly, that deeply intimate question, on the side of the ballroom, with a sea of guests intently scrutinizing their exchange.

Cleopatra gave her head a terse shake. "It doesn't matter what I want." It had never been about her. It had always been about the good of the group . . . specifically, Ophelia, Gertrude, and Stephen.

"Siblings?" Penelope said with that unerring accuracy.

Ophelia, Gertrude, and Stephen. Pain filled her at the mere thought of them. They'd been all she'd known since birth. They'd looked after one another, helped one another survive; now it was far easier to not think of them at all. Cleopatra looked away. She'd become a master of self-control, and as such, hadn't truly dwelt on thoughts of them. Now Black's wife here would drag forward their images. Mayhap the fancy lady was one of those cruel sorts.

The viscountess lightly squeezed her hand. "I married my husband in a bid to save my sister so she might make a future match. I recognize that level of sacrifice."

"A person 'as to do what they ought," she said gruffly. And for her that was saving her sisters.

"Yes," Penelope agreed, a wistfulness to that one syllable. "But sometimes," she went on, her eyes going soft, "you find love where you least expect it."

Cleopatra followed her stare to where Ryker Black stood. Even across the ballroom, a powerful look passed between the couple. Feeling like an interloper, Cleopatra swiftly averted her gaze. Black's wife spoke about Cleopatra forming a *love* match? The lady was either ten times a fool or cracked in the brain if she believed Cleopatra was going to end up in a love match with a fancy toff . . . or in love with any man.

"Come along," Penelope coaxed. "Let me at least introduce you to some of the prospective gentlemen."

Cleopatra's gut clenched. Was this how the whores inside the Devil's Den felt every night? Cleopatra formed a newfound appreciation for their sentiments and a regret for having failed to consider as much before now.

"That is Lord Darby," Black's wife whispered, discreetly pointing to a golden-haired gentleman sipping from a glass of champagne. "He has two sisters he's rumored to care an inordinate amount for, refusing to force either of them into a match."

An inelegant snort escaped Cleopatra. "And why should he? He's the one who wagered away ten thousand pounds of his family's fortune," she said bluntly. Her family was the fortunate recipient of all those funds.

Mouth agape, Penelope shifted her attention elsewhere. "Very well, then mayhap Lord Corbett. He's a young widower."

"And rough with the whores he takes to his bed."

Color suffused Penelope's cheeks, and she pursed her mouth. "Certainly *not* Lord Corbett, then." Chewing at the tip of her gloved finger, the hostess continued to survey the crowd. "I wager that you may, in fact, know more than I about the gentlemen present."

That was a wager Cleopatra would readily accept and win. She, however, didn't require information about the gentlemen present. She required introductions. So that she could pledge herself forevermore to a man. In her mind, she heard Diggory's oft-repeated shout: *You don't 'ave any rights . . . you answer to me.* While Penelope considered the other gentlemen present, Cleopatra's eyes slid involuntarily closed. A cold sweat broke out on her skin. *I will be turning myself over to a man.* It was a reality made all the more real standing on the fringe of Polite Society with the viscountess playing matchmaker. As a part of Diggory's family, she'd been beaten, tortured, and mocked with words that were often crueler than his meaty fists. Despite the silent vow she'd made with herself, after being saved by Broderick, to never find herself at the mercy of a man, she now found herself in that exact place she'd never intended to be—searching for a husband.

"What do you know of Lord—"

And with Penelope putting forward another possible candidate, Cleopatra did what she'd always done best when presented with danger—she fled.

". . . Cleopatra?" Penelope's concerned voice grew more distant as the other woman searched for her.

She could search and never find. Cleopatra had perfected the art of hiding as a mere babe toddling around one of Diggory's hovels, and Black's fancy-born wife would never be a match for her. She moved speedily through the ballroom, ducking around the helpful pillars and syncing her steps with liveried servants bearing trays. The laughter and discourse blended together in her ears, a cacophony of sound that fueled her panic.

Bypassing the main entrance to the ballroom, she found her way through a side door. As soon as she stepped out, Cleopatra broke out into a full sprint to rival her thievery days in the rookeries. Her hair tumbled free of the artful arrangement her lady's maid had managed, leaving her drab brown strands falling about her shoulders. Breathless from her exertions, she brushed the hair back from her eyes and made for the servants' staircase. Cleopatra skidded to a stop, damning the slippers that sent her sliding into the wall. She caught herself hard with a grunt and pushed her spectacles back into place. Then, taking the stairs two at a time, she climbed the dark, narrow stairwell higher and higher into the peak of Black's townhouse, all the way to the servants' quarters. The dark space was quiet, with all the staff otherwise attending the evening's festivities, and provided a solemn calm.

Cleopatra crept along the wall and made for the window. Placing her palms on either side, she shoved it up slowly. The cool night air spilled into the room, and closing her eyes, she let the familiar London air fill her lungs.

Except this wasn't the familiar London, as she knew it. This was a strange place, where she'd been taken in by the enemy, who'd come to treat her as an object of pity more than anything. People for whom there was really no loyalty or affection toward her, but rather a sense of obligation.

Cleopatra opened her eyes and stared out at the tops of fancy roofs of these Mayfair townhouses. *Nor are these familiar roofs,* she thought blankly. These were ones she'd climbed upon as a child and then as a girl on the cusp of womanhood. She eyed the ledge, and then, angling her head out the window, measured the distance and windows between her spot and the top. The roof had always beckoned. It had been the one place Diggory had never been able to reach her. As such, she'd reveled in the assignments that sent her high above the London homes. For risking capture and hanging for stealing from a nob was far preferable to the terror Diggory had inflicted with a routine frequency.

Cleopatra lifted her skirts and shucked her slippers off. She tossed them under the nearest bed, where they landed with a soft thump. Her stockings followed suit. Straightening, she let her dress fall back into place and settle around her ankles with a shimmery rustle. She perched her left foot atop the sill and slowly pulled herself upright. Cleopatra stole a peek at the grounds below.

Of course, roof climbing had always been vastly easier when she'd donned boy's breeches and a tight-fitting shirt. One slight misstep, one foot snagging the hem of her gown, would see her crashing to the cobblestones as nothing more than a fond memory for her small family. The pull of the roof had always been greater, though.

Propelling herself up on her tiptoes, she reached for the sill directly overhead. Cleopatra's fingers connected with the cool stone, and curling her fingers around it, she dragged herself slowly up to the next narrow ledge. Her spectacles slipped, and she froze. Damning her dratted vision, and her desperate need of those lenses, she paused to push them back into place and then resumed her climb. With every step that carried her farther and farther away, the terror receded, and it was replaced with a solitary quiet that she'd come to crave through the years.

She continued her slow, purposeful ascent until she'd reached the sloped metal roof. The jagged slats provided an easy foothold as she made for the chimney.

Borrowing support from the cold bricks, she looked out over London. Through the faint fog of night, stars peaked out, twinkling in their distant glory. This moment belonged to Cleopatra, not Broderick or Lady Chatham and her family, and up here, for a brief time, she was beholden to none. She smiled, accepting that triumph no matter how small it was.

For now—she was free.

Chapter 14

"She's gone missing."

Adair's hearing was off. It was surely why, through the clamor of the inane festivities arranged by his sister-in-law, he'd misheard Niall.

"What?" he blurted, having no doubt about the identity of the *she* in question.

A vein bulged in Niall's street-hardened eyes. "Not 'ere," he muttered in his coarse Cockney. "Ryker wants us in his office."

They immediately fell into side-by-side step. The dandy-clad gents and satin-skirt-wearing ladies hurried to step out of their path. But then, that had been the horrified reaction they'd been met with since they'd been forced to suffer through their first *ton* event. It wasn't a response reserved for the *ton*. Men, women, and children in the streets of St. Giles also looked upon them with the same horror and awe. Only Cleopatra had been fearless around him, talking freely . . . *but sharing little*, a voice needled at the back of his brain.

His brothers were being overly suspicious . . . nay, cautious of Cleopatra. *Or mayhap you're not being sufficiently wary of the spirited woman.*

Bloody hell.

Quickening his stride, Adair reached Ryker's office first. Not bothering with the expected knock, he let himself in. Niall trailed a step behind.

Ryker stood behind his desk, barking out orders to the four Hell and Sin guards who'd taken on the role of undercover servants while Cleopatra was living here.

". . . already searched the nursery, and I have two men stationed outside, another inside at the connecting door," Flannagan was saying. "One at the window . . ."

Ears trained on that terse cataloging, Adair came forward, joining the younger guard at the desk.

"You think she'd harm the babe?" he interrupted, not certain how to explain his annoyance with Ryker. It was wrong to expect his brother to trust that a Killoran wouldn't inflict harm upon a babe of his . . . and yet . . . the gut instinct that had gotten him to see thirty years on this miserable earth had never proven faulty before.

Ryker issued a low directive to the other man, who nodded and rushed off.

"She's gone missing," Ryker said curtly, now attending Adair.

Guarding me? . . . Still don't trust me . . . ?

Her faintly hurt accusation whispered forward.

"My lord?" Covington, one of the two remaining guards, asked at Adair's side, slashing across his musings. Attired in crimson uniform, their garments were the only thing that lent their heavily muscled frames a hint of liveried footmen.

"Do another sweep of the ballroom. You and Kipling both," Ryker ordered.

As both men hustled past Niall, who served as a sentry at the doorway, Adair stared after them. *Where in blazes is she?*

"Don't you believe this is a bit of an overreaction? Mayhap the lady wanted some air or . . . ?" At the incredulous looks boring into his skin from both directions, he flushed.

"I want you to do a sweep of the main living quarters," Ryker replied, with his directives providing an answer of just what he believed about Cleopatra's disappearance. "And Niall, you—"

The door flew open, and Penelope stormed in. "What is the meaning of this?" she demanded, closing the door softly behind her. That quiet action at odds with the urgently spoken question. "There are guards running all over this house, Ryker."

"You reported her missing," he gritted out.

Penelope planted her hands on her hips. "I mentioned that she'd rushed off, and I was looking for her."

"Because you were worried," her husband said, motioning for Niall to leave.

The young viscountess tossed her arms up. "About the young woman," she said, exasperation rich in her tone. "I am worried about the young woman." With a sound of disgust, she turned to Adair, effectively dismissing her husband. "When you were speaking alone with Cleo, did she give you any indication that she was upset? After we left you, she was . . . somber."

He ran through their exchange. They'd been teasing and talkative, and other than a slight darkening of her eyes at the mention of Diggory, there'd been nothing else. "What were you speaking with her about after?" he countered.

"Her . . . marital prospects."

In short, they'd been discussing the sole reason for Cleopatra's placement here. A stinging, bitter taste filled his mouth . . . an unpleasant one that felt very much like . . . jealousy.

"Regardless of what you were discussing, I want her found," Ryker said tightly. "Adair?"

With a brusque nod, Adair quit Ryker's offices. As soon as he'd closed the door and stepped into the hall, Penelope's rapid-fire defense of Cleopatra pierced the wood panel. That muffled argument trailing in his wake, Adair hurried along the corridor.

Where is she . . . ? Where is she . . . ?

Despite his brothers' reservations, Adair didn't believe Cleopatra had come here to harm anyone. What reason would she have to deepen the feud between their families?

"You've been away from the likes of Diggory too long," he muttered under his breath, climbing the stairs to the main living quarters. He reached the landing and paused. His brother was so convinced that Cleopatra would so boldly and blatantly seek out those rooms. In this short time, knowing Cleopatra as he did, she'd never do what was expected of her, or go where one might find her.

Pressing his palm over his mouth, he tapped his index finger against his cheek. *Think. Think.* The night she'd sneaked from her rooms, how had she gotten out? Not through a door, but through the—

He immediately ceased his distracted beat.

"The window," he breathed.

He sprang into movement, knowing instinctually where he'd find her. Unheeding Ryker's orders, Adair raced up the next stairwell to where he kept rooms alongside Cleopatra's. Shoving open her chamber doors, he did a sweep of the rooms. *Empty.* Nor had he expected her to be here. Squinting in the dark, he sharpened his gaze on the window—the closed one. She'd not made use of that one. Why should she? If there was one higher . . . closer to the roof . . .

Praying he was wrong, and still knowing he was right, Adair rushed to the servants' stairway and climbed to the small, now crowded quarters. The club having been burned, and their staff without a place to reside until the repairs were complete, Ryker and Penelope, Niall and Diana, and Robert and Helena had filled every available space with the displaced staff. He pushed the door open, and a wave of cool night air filtered out into the hall.

Fear held him momentarily suspended, and then he lurched forward. A faint scrap of white fabric peeked out from under a nearby cot. Bending down, he swept up the fabric . . . and the pair of slippers haphazardly hidden. "Damn you, Cleopatra Killoran," he whispered. Letting them go, he quickly divested himself of his boots and stockings. His jacket was next. And a moment later, Adair Thorne—who'd vowed at the age of fifteen that he'd climbed his last roof—found himself scaling the narrow window ledges to the top of his brother's Mayfair townhouse.

Fifteen years out of practice, the skills and steps he'd mastered as a boy remained as strong as they'd been. Yet, height and muscle made his climb slow. Concentrating on each hand and foot placement, he pulled himself higher and higher. He stopped at the top windowsill and stole a glance down the more than one hundred feet between him and a swift plunge to the cobblestones below. His stomach lurched, and he swiftly closed his eyes. God, he forgot just how much he'd despised this task Diggory had given him years earlier. *Never look down . . .* It was a damned lesson he'd inconveniently forgotten.

Always concentrate on the path above . . .

Waiting until his heart had resumed a normal cadence, he gripped the edge of the roof. His breath coming fast, a product of fear and his exertions, Adair dragged himself atop the flat surface . . . and instantly found Cleopatra.

Their eyes collided.

Of course she'd be at the highest point, that slightly sloped portion alongside the chimney. And the damned organ in his chest resumed a wild hammering rhythm as he was filled with something he'd never believed he could feel for a Killoran—fear. He tried to make his tongue move to form words.

"You climb roofs," she said.

She'd gone missing and risked breaking her damned, beautifully long neck, and *that* is what she'd say? He counted to ten, and when he still wanted to shout down the bloody slats they now occupied, he counted to another ten.

"Pretty, isn't it?" she asked, a softness in her eyes as she stared out across the streets of Mayfair. That tenderness killed the stinging diatribe he'd intended to unleash upon her ears.

Adair liked her this way. Real and open and . . . honest. He turned out, seeing what she saw.

"I always loved it up here," she went on in wistful tones.

He clasped his hands behind him. "I never saw anything past what sent me up here," he said quietly. To steal, to escape capture, there'd never been any beauty or peace in those actions.

Cleopatra stood, and he took a quick step toward her, but she'd already hiked her skirts up and leapt from her perch. "I disagree."

"As you are wont to do," he drawled with a wink to dull the seriousness of that charge.

"When you're up here, no one can reach you. No one, unless they climb after you themselves, can come after you and force you down or hurt—"

Hurt you. His insides spasmed. She'd lived her entire life with Diggory, whereas Adair had always believed that death was preferable to serving that dark Devil.

She sucked in a deep breath. "Up here, a person is free. You're in control. There's no angry shopkeepers or fast-moving carriages or constables about. There's just you"—Cleopatra tipped her head back toward the dark night sky—"and the stars and moon."

His breath lodged in his chest, and with Cleopatra distracted, he took in the sight of her. The diamonds in her tiara shimmered with a light to match the one in her eyes. Her hair hung in loose waves about her narrow shoulders, and God help him, in the madness of this stolen interlude, he was completely and thoroughly bewitched by her. The need to brush those strands back and expose the delicate length of her neck was like a physical hungering. "I never noticed before," he said quietly. *Her. I never noticed her outside her name and my own hatred for her family.*

"A shame not to," she said with her usual matter-of-fact admonishment, bringing him to. She glanced over suddenly, and he was grateful for the cover of darkness that hid his blush.

By God, blushing. What in hell had happened to him?

She eyed him peculiarly, and to stave off any questions about his earlier study of her, he jerked his chin. "There aren't many stars in London." He chuckled. "As a boy, I didn't even believe we *had* a moon."

"But *there's* the wonder in it." With her youthful exuberance, she showed glimpses of the young woman she might have been had she been born to a fancy lord and lady. She slid her gloved palm into his and tugged him down until they lay on their backs, so close their shoulders met. "Look."

"It's a night sky," he said, angling his head to see her.

Cleopatra pointed a finger overhead. "I said, look."

He grinned. She'd the ability to lead and command better suited to the head of the King's Army. "What am I looking for?"

"There," she murmured, pointing her white-gloved fingertip to a grayish-white cloud moving across the sky. "One learns to follow the clouds." They shifted, revealing a handful of lone stars, twinkling overhead. A moment later, another drifted, concealing those flecks of light. "It was always like opening a gift," she said softly, letting her arm fall to her side. Her fingers covered his, and out of the corner of his eye, he looked at their connected digits. "Far more special than if they'd always been there," she went on, seemingly unaffected.

"Hmm," he murmured, reexamining the night sky. "I never thought about it that way." Just as he'd never considered Cleopatra to be anything different from who or what she was.

"If I stared up at the sky long enough, I forgot it all." She stretched her palms up overhead. "This got me through those darkest days."

They'd all had their dark days. Every person born to the streets was indelibly marked by the struggle of it. Adair, Calum, Niall, Ryker, and Helena had all been tortured by Diggory in their own ways. What suffering had belonged to this woman? Suddenly, he who'd always hated her for her connection to that man wanted to remain thinking of her as one who'd not known cruelty and suffering at his hands.

"He hurt you," he forced himself to say into the nighttime quiet. That truth redefined the whole way he'd allowed himself to look at her and her family.

With her elbow, she nudged him lightly in the side. "Did you think you were the only one to know hurt at his hands?"

He wasn't fooled by the lightness in her husky voice. As one who'd become a master of schooling his own emotions and feelings, he recognized that skill all too easily in another. He'd painted her as one of them . . . when in truth, Cleopatra had been more like Adair and his siblings than the monster Diggory.

"He was a monster," Adair said somberly. When she said nothing, his frustration mounted. "You won't confirm or deny that?" Again, did that speak to her loyalty to him?

"What is there to confirm or deny? Everyone knew and now remembers Diggory for precisely what he was."

"Then why did you remain with him?" It came out as a plea, for her answer mattered too damned much.

Cleopatra flipped onto her side and propped her head on her elbow, so she faced him. "Should I have fled? As you, Black, Marksman, and Dabney did with your sister?"

Why did that feel more an indictment than anything?

She turned another question on him. "You've lived on the streets. Tell me what options there were for me and my sisters, one who is partially blind?"

He started. He'd not known that about her. But then, these past days had revealed how little he truly knew about the Killorans.

"Your sister had you, and you looked after her. Well, we had Broderick."

"He could have taken you all and fled." Just as Adair and his siblings had.

A cynical laugh spilled past her lips. "You don't know anything about my brother." Nor did her tightly pressed lips indicate she intended to share anything further about Broderick Killoran.

It occurred to him how little he truly knew about Cleopatra or any members of her family. She was one of three sisters. The options and futures were dark and limited for all of their station, but even darker for women. Most found themselves whoring on the streets, others inside brothels, a handful married, and the remaining unfortunate souls—dead.

"They're the reasons you're here."

She nodded once.

She'd make a match with one of the nobs when her antipathy for those men fairly seeped from her person.

He turned onto his side, mimicking her body's position so their gazes were in direct line. "Then why did you leave the ballroom"—full of potential suitors—"and come here?" With her peculiar flight and disappearance, she'd set the household into an uproar.

"They're looking for me," she guessed. "Is that why you're here? Searching for the Killoran who's surely come to kill and steal while you're all otherwise distracted?" Under the disgust-laden deliverance, there were also undercurrents of hurt. With a sound of annoyance, she made to stand.

Adair swiftly levered himself upright and, catching her by the forearm, prevented her flight. "My brothers worried about foul play," he admitted. "My sister-in-law is worried about you."

She lifted her chin mutinously. "And what about you?"

What about him? "I was more curious what had sent you fleeing the ballroom." How had he gone from jeering and taunting the woman before him to simply trusting there was nothing underhanded about her presence here? It was the height of foolishness. By God, she was on Ryker's bloody roof. And yet . . . he just knew.

Through her smudged lenses, she peered at him.

"Here," he murmured, plucking them free of her nose. He tugged out his shirt and wiped her spectacles with the fabric. "You would be able to do far less squinting if you cleaned your lenses on occasion."

Her even, pearl-white teeth flashed bright in the dark. "Oi was searching you for a lie."

He paused in his efforts. "I know," he said on an exaggerated whisper. "I was merely jesting."

She whistled. "Didn't think you were capable of it."

Adair handed her glasses back over. "Well, it would seem we both know far less about one another than we previously believed, doesn't it?"

Hesitantly, Cleopatra accepted the delicate wire-rims and put them back on. "It does," she said gruffly.

He glanced out at the night sky. "His name was Oswyn."

Confused eyes lifted to meet his.

"You asked who betrayed me. His name was Oswyn, a man who'd been with us since we broke free from Diggory, and the first person we ever hired for our club. He turned Diana over to Diggory."

She searched his face, silent for a long while.

"Ya offering me friendship, Thorne?"

Friendship. He silently tested that word both on his tongue and in his mind. Friendship implied trust and emotions. It entailed caring after another person and trusting oneself over to them in return. Could one be friends with a person he'd been trained to hate? Or with a woman he ached to kiss, who was destined for a fancy lord who'd one day no doubt grace the seats inside Adair's club? It had been wrong to shut her out.

Her brow creased.

"Friendship," he repeated back, stretching his fingers out in the first true offering of peace between them.

Cleopatra grinned . . . and took his hand.

Chapter 15

Over the next fortnight, there were several certainties for Cleopatra.

One: for all the wealth she could bring to a marriage, the money itself was not enough to tempt lords in desperate need of funds.

Two: she still truly, and of course only secretly, yearned to dance during every ball she'd been forced to suffer through as an oddity to Polite Society.

Three: she could always count on Adair Thorne being near.

And four: despite the fact that a still-dubious-of-her Ryker Black had assigned Adair to watch after her, Cleopatra was incredibly glad for his presence and even sought him out. Daily.

It's only because you enjoy the discussion on his building plans for the Hell and Sin . . .

"That is it," she muttered, stepping out of her room. She paused.

She saw an unfamiliar *servant* staring at her through street-hardened eyes. He raked a disdainful glance up and down her person. By his scarred visage and inability to dissemble as a proper servant, he was anything but liveried staff. Another guard assigned her by Black, then. Cleopatra drew the door shut with a decisive click. Not that she blamed him for his wariness, but still, there was something annoying in having one's footsteps watched as closely as they'd been in the streets of St. Giles.

"Where ya think you're going?" the guard snarled from behind her.

Cleopatra stiffened. His coarse Cockney confirmed everything she'd already gathered about his origins and role here. Angling her head, she favored him with a condescending sneer. "I don't answer to you," she said in flawless tones her brother had insisted she perfect, and in this, she reveled in the power they gave her over this man. "A mere . . . footman," she taunted.

Hatred circled in the depths of his blue eyes. "Whore," he spat.

She'd been called so much worse in the course of her existence that insults had ceased to matter to her, and yet the vitriol in his utterance had ice skittering up her spinal column. She flattened her lips into a coolly mocking grin. "Born the son of one, I expect you *think* you might have experience in recognizing one."

He went still; then his eyebrows shot to his hairline.

Claiming victory, she yanked her skirts away and started forward.

"You bitch," he hissed in her wake.

Dismissing the guard outright, she reached Adair's door, and even though every morning they went through the formalities of her lightly rapping, this time, eager to be free of the nameless street thug, she let herself in.

Seated behind his mahogany desk, with a pencil in his hand, Adair looked briefly up from his design plans. "You're late," he observed with a grin that eased some of the tension from her previous exchange.

"I didn't realize you'd hired me to work for you." Closing the door behind her, she hurried to join him at his desk, where a familiar seat that had come to be hers was already positioned. "If so, we failed to negotiate the terms of my payment," she drawled, settling into the oak Carver chair.

He rolled his shoulders. "And here I thought you were just eager to have anything to do with a gaming hell," he said, reminding her of her own words.

Carefully studying the changes he'd made that morning, she avoided his eyes. Afraid he'd see too much. Afraid he'd know that she enjoyed his company and wanted to be here. Adair resumed making notes on his pages, and she studied him in silence for a long while. "Your brothers don't take up much time with the new plans," she observed. She'd only ever seen Adair in this room overseeing the details regarding the Hell and Sin.

Weeks earlier, he would have no doubt told her to go to hell with her questioning; now he drummed the tip of his pencil in a distracted staccato. "The role of head has . . . fallen to me." His words and eyes revealed nothing but for an infinitesimal pause. Her interest stirred.

Ryker Black, one of the most feared men in the streets of St. Giles, had ceded control of his club . . . to Adair? For the easy relationship she'd struck with him, she didn't expect he'd give her the answers to all those questions. He'd take it as probing, on her part, for Broderick. "I never thought I'd witness the day Black turned control over to anybody," she ventured, curiosity making her throw her hesitation to the wind.

Adair grunted noncommittally.

He trusted less than anyone she'd ever known in the whole of her life, which given the people she'd either dwelled with or called family, was saying a good deal, indeed.

Letting go of her curiosity, she devoted her focus to the sheets before them. "You took my advice, then," she observed, pointing to the private-quarters gaming rooms he intended to set up inside the redesigned Hell and Sin.

"You were correct." Adair tossed his pencil down and cracked his knuckles. "It was a waste of valuable space to not add tables. Lost revenue that we hadn't been able to recoup."

Cleopatra leaned forward, intently studying it. She'd spent her whole life hating Adair Thorne and his family. And yet, when presented with the opportunity to grow his fortunes on the backs of desperate women or take a loss in profit, he'd opted for the latter. Those weren't the actions of an enemy; they were the mark of a good man.

"You're quiet." He spoke with the familiarity of one who'd come to know her over these past three weeks.

"I'm always quiet," she said, fiddling with the edge of the desk. Catching that nervous movement, she swiftly lowered her hands to her lap.

"More so than usual. Do you disapprove?"

"And would it matter if I did?" she returned.

He flashed his even teeth in a heart-stopping grin. "Three weeks ago, I would have said no." How much had changed in three weeks.

"And now?"

Stretching his legs out, he crossed them at the ankles in a negligent pose. "Now I see how clever you are in matters of gaming and business, and I'd be a fool to not take your suggestions under consideration."

He'd not only contemplated her ideas, but he'd acted on them, making design changes to his club. Her heart instantly sang. In a world where women's opinions went unsolicited and unwelcomed, Adair appreciated her mind and insight. And it was heady stuff, indeed.

He stared contemplatively over the top of her head. "Certainly more intelligent than I'd ever credited a Killoran with being."

He hated you for sharing Broderick's blood. But you're not a Killoran, that taunting voice in her mind reminded her, shattering the moment.

She was grateful when Adair shifted their discourse back to the Hell and Sin. "What are your thoughts on the space I've designated for the additional gaming tables?" Straightening, he shoved aside the pages they'd been looking over and grabbed the one underneath. He laid it out before her.

Cleopatra shifted her gaze about the page and, with the tip of her index finger, counted off the marked whist, hazard, and faro tables. The transformed suites previously used for the prostitutes and their clients had been converted. "What of the women who used to . . . sleep there? I trust you've had to turn many of them out." How many women had Diggory once deemed too old to serve in their original capacity, and then simply shown them the door to the alley?

Adair shook his head. "We've turned no one out." He fished a cheroot from his jacket. "May I?"

He was asking her? Not a single man in her brother's employ or patron to their hell had ever hesitated to drink, wager, or smoke in her presence. Speechless, she waved her hand, following his languid movements as he rose and lit the small white wrapper at a nearby sconce. "We didn't turn out any of the women once the changes were made," he clarified, coming forward. He paused and drew an inhalation from the cheroot. "They served as dealers, serving girls, servants," he said after he'd exhaled a small white cloud.

"That didn't help your bottom number."

Adair blew smoke out from the corner of his mouth. "It didn't."

While he continued smoking, Cleopatra looked at the page. "Why did you do it?" she blurted, the question spilling from her lips. At his creased brow, she continued hurriedly. "You know you cannot compete with the Devil's Den as long as we offer prostitution to our members and you don't. Even with the decline in your business and the rise of our club, you still chose to do away with it. Why?" she asked, needing to understand.

Adair flicked his ashes into a small crystal dish. "My brother . . . Ryker," he elucidated, "made the overall decision after being so persuaded by his wife." Any other day the fact that Black had been cowed by a young lady would have commanded Cleopatra's amusement. Not now. "Given how our numbers have declined"—his mouth tightened—"*changed*, I doubted how wise the decision was for the hell."

Abandoning the sheet in her hands, she waved her palm, wafting about the smoke so she might better see him. "You doubted it, and saw the decline in profits, and yet you've been"—by his own words—"placed in charge of the club. You could have reinstated the club's previous policy and offered whores for your patrons. You chose not to. Why?"

Because, ultimately, her own brother cared about nothing more than the money coming into the Devil's Den. Everyone and everything could be sacrificed, as Cleopatra's presence in Black's household was proof of.

Adair took another pull from his cheroot. "I thought about it," he admitted somberly. "I've even debated my brothers in the past about the changes Ryker and his wife enacted."

One move or word from Cleopatra, and he'd say not another word. She'd come to know him that well. Cleopatra waited.

"In the end," he began quietly as he stubbed the remaining embers out in the crystal dish, "I thought of when I was a boy just orphaned." She froze, afraid to move and stymie the flow of his words. "I was a boy on my own. Diggory"—her insides twisted at the hated name—"made me one of his gang. Fed me." He grimaced. "The food we were given was barely edible."

"Rot," she said more to herself. "It was only ever a step above mud, and not much else."

He nodded, and another connection between them was forged.

"And all rations, meals, and favors were doled out according to importance served to the group."

"So, you stole," she predicted, as one who knew. As one who'd been as desperate.

He inclined his head. "And so, I stole." His hushed voice barely reached her ears. "I hated it," he went on, a man lost in his own tortured musings. "Every time, I thought of the items I was lifting. I imagined them to be cherished pieces that meant something to the person I stole from, and I hated myself for those acts."

He drew in a shuddery breath. "In providing prostitution, I'd told myself that women had a safe place to sleep. They had food and shelter." His face spasmed. "With those self-assurances I made to myself, I became everything I hated. I became"—*Diggory*—"Diggory." Adair coughed into his hand, offering her a sheepish look. "And so one day, I just . . . realized that I didn't want to be that man," he finished matter-of-factly.

How very wrong he was. With the way he spoke to Cleopatra, his valuing her opinion, and his care for his family, Adair Thorne could never be Diggory.

Whereas Cleopatra? She'd been born with evil in her veins.

Knuckles brushed along her jaw, and she looked back as Adair forced her chin up so their gazes met.

"It was wrong of me holding your connection to Diggory against you," he said quietly.

Her entire body jerked whipcord straight.

"You being part of his gang was no different than me or my brothers."

Only . . . it was altogether different.

She made to move out of his reach, but he retained his hold. His touch, a blend of tenderness and strength, brought her eyes sliding briefly closed. She'd been punched, slapped, and pinched with regular frequency by brutes in the street whom she'd tangled with over scraps. But those cruel thugs—none had ever dared put their hands upon her . . . and the ones who had when Broderick rose to power had lost fingers for it.

Never had she known a man's touch could feel like this—a gentle, fleeting caress that made her long to turn herself over to the power of his embrace once more.

Their breaths mingled—his with the acrid hint of cheroot and coffee, so very masculine and enticing. He dipped his head lower, and Cleopatra lifted hers to take his kiss.

The door flew open with a rapidity that brought both of their heads up.

Sidestepping Adair's attempts to shove her behind him, Cleopatra unsheathed the dagger in her boot and pointed it at a glowering Ryker Black. And as little as the world knew of the ruthless gaming hell owner, Cleopatra knew enough to gather from his seething silence that he was furious.

The nameless guard who'd stood sentry outside her room stared back with a derisively triumphant grin on his lips.

Adair took in the pair in the doorway: Ryker and the guard, Wilson, who'd been in their employ for more than ten years.

His brother was furious.

As long as Adair had known Ryker, the other man had been a master of dissembling. Where most couldn't gather what he was thinking and when, there were certain tells.

The vein bulging in the corner of his eye was the mark of his outrage.

Ryker moved his piercing stare from Cleopatra to Adair . . . and then settled for a lingering moment . . . a damning one . . . on the building plans for the Hell and Sin Club.

Silently cursing, Adair tucked his pistol back into the waistband of his breeches. "Usually a knock will suffice," he drawled.

That telltale vein throbbed all the more. "Miss Killoran," Ryker commanded in even tones. "If you'll excuse us?"

And Cleopatra, who'd earned his admiration for her cleverness and pride, now with her fearlessness in the face of Ryker's wrath moved up in his estimation all the more. "We were in the middle of something here, Black."

Through the years, their sister, Helena, hadn't even met Ryker's simmering rages with a challenge. Cleopatra was a fool . . . but a brave one.

Ryker's irises disappeared behind thin slits of barely suppressed rage.

She hitched her left foot up onto her seat and resheathed her weapon.

Wilson, once a young man who'd come to their employ after escaping Diggory, glared with a searing loathing at her.

At the other man's focus on her exposed limb, fury thrummed to life, and Adair hurriedly stepped between Cleopatra and Wilson's line of vision.

"Oi'm not asking you, Miss Killoran," Ryker growled, slipping into his Cockney.

Cleopatra opened her mouth to no doubt protest, but then Penelope entered the room.

It is to be a bloody gathering, then, Adair thought.

"Cleopatra," she eagerly greeted. Rocking Paisley, she tipped her chin awkwardly. "I've been searching for you. Would you join me and Paisley this morning in the nursery?"

His sister-in-law had proven herself mad on numerous scores. Anyone who believed this was anything other than a well-timed rescue on Cleopatra's behalf didn't have a brain between their ears. As proud as the young woman had proven herself to be, Adair braced for her to continue going toe-to-toe with Ryker when she stepped out from behind him.

A soft, wistful expression stole over her features as she stared at the small babe. From the gentleness in her eyes and tender smile on her lips, there was a maternal softness to Cleopatra. An odd tightening squeezed at his chest.

Adjusting Paisley, Penelope held out her fingers, and Cleopatra immediately joined her. She paused in the doorway, casting a last, lingering glance at Adair before taking her leave.

"Outside the nursery." Ryker gritted out the command for the other man, and Wilson immediately scrambled into action.

Adair watched his retreat, wanting to bloody his brother's nose for sending a guard after her like she was . . . Like she was what? A Killoran? It was precisely what she was . . . and yet, she'd also become so much more.

Disquieted, Adair curled his hands into tight balls and used the time as his brother closed the door to compose himself.

"Wot in 'ell are you doing?" Ryker might have been speaking about the weather for as casual the delivery of that query.

Adair made a dismissive sound. "She had . . . ideas for the Hell and Sin."

Ryker sprang into movement. Storming across the room, he took up position on the opposite side of Adair's desk. "You gave her the plans for the club," he boomed, slamming a fist down on the surface with such vigor, the ledgers leapt and then promptly settled into place.

He folded his arms. "I understand why you might have reservations."

"Is that what you think I have?" he asked on a dangerous whisper that would have terrified a lesser man. Adair, however, had battled Ryker numerous times as a boy and knew he bled the same crimson drops. "You believe I have reservations? She is a damned Killoran, connected forever to Diggory."

God, how he despised the reminder. For she was more than one of the men, women, and children to spring from Diggory's gang. "We are all forever connected to Diggory," he said quietly. It had just taken Adair longer to realize that in their earliest beginnings, he was more like Cleopatra Killoran than he'd ever credited.

Ryker shook his head. "It's entirely different. We left that bastard."

"She, as a woman, had fewer options than we ever did," he snapped, impatient with his brother's habitual obstinacy. *But then, weren't you of the same exact mind-set where Cleopatra was concerned?* Yet, in sharing as she had, in challenging him, she'd forced him to see life in ways that he previously hadn't.

His brother flared his nostrils. "She's lived all these years under Diggory and Killoran. She and her family have infiltrated our gaming hell, stolen our patrons, attempted to sow the seeds of mistrust between my wife and I, and undermined us at every turn, and you'd trust her? After three weeks?" The shock and condescension blended there scoured Adair.

He dragged a hand through his hair. Mayhap he had gone more than half-mad for trusting her as he did, and yet with their every exchange, the connection between them had deepened. "She saved Paisley from a drunken nursemaid." How easily his brother dismissed that.

"And I am grateful for that," Ryker said instantly. "But neither does it erase a feud that's existed so long between our families." There was an air of finality there, one that indicated Ryker didn't intend to debate Cleopatra Killoran's trustworthiness or the accuracy of his opinions. "What did you show her?" his brother asked, diverting the topic to the sheets laid out.

All of it. He'd revealed the preliminary plans and finalized ones, and then made changes based on suggestions Cleopatra had put forth. He let his silence serve as his answer.

Ryker unleashed a string of black curses. "You showed her everything? Where the men, women, and children inside the club will sleep? And eat? Where we monitor patrons?"

Adair's patience snapped. "You turned the responsibility over to me." He jabbed a finger across the table at his brother. "You and Niall and Calum all decided the paths you intend to chart, and left the Hell and Sin to my care."

Ryker leaned across the tables. "It is *all* ours. Every last damned business venture we've agreed to undertake, we agreed together."

Tugging the pages out from under his brother's hands, Adair fumed. "I haven't questioned your new role. I'd expect the same damned courtesy." Attending his efforts, he reorganized his work into piles.

"I also didn't entrust our family and those in our employ's safety to the enemy," Ryker said with an infuriating calm.

Adair tightened his hold on the design plans and concentrated on his breathing. His brother would question his ability to care for those in his employ? It was the ultimate slight a man could be dealt, particularly those who'd spent their lives on the street. "Go to hell," he ground out. For his indignation, however, doubts swirled. *What if you are making a misstep where Cleopatra is concerned . . . ? What if you already did, and you've placed your family and those at the Hell and Sin in peril . . . ?*

Pushing back those familiar doubts, he buried them. She'd shared pieces of her past and ideas for his club. He wasn't so clouded by his own hatred as Ryker was that he'd judge Cleopatra simply because of the gang she'd had the misfortune of aligning herself with. "There is no point in continuing this discussion," he said dismissively. "Despite both my and Penelope's confidence in Cleopatra"—his brother stitched his eyebrows into a knowing line—"Miss Killoran," he belatedly corrected, "you're determined to not trust the lady's word."

Ryker folded his arms. "You were going to kiss her."

The pages slipped from Adair's fingers. Had Ryker hurled a dagger at him, Adair couldn't have been any more shocked. His brother knew. Had come in and seen at just one glance the battle Adair lost every time Cleopatra was near.

"I saw you when I entered," Ryker persisted, unrelenting. "That closeness is dangerous," he said with his usual bluntness and calm. "It makes a person careless."

"One's hatred also impairs one's judgment." As his brother's was. "Here," he said, cutting Ryker off when he began to speak, "look at this." Adair tossed the folded plans over to his brother.

Instantly catching it, Ryker frowned.

"I said *look* at the damned pages," he barked.

With stiff, precise movements, his brother laid out the plans Cleopatra had offered valuable input on. Ryker studied them in silence, trailing a callused fingertip over the converted space and additional gaming tables. His brother paused.

"She was right," Adair said flatly when Ryker still wouldn't pick his head up.

Reluctantly, his brother looked at him. "They were wise revisions." The concession may as well have been pulled from him. "But it still is the height of foolishness to give a Killoran an inside look at every damned nook, cranny, and table at our club."

"If she were bent on hurting us or our club, she would have let me continue on as I was."

"If she were attempting to bring harm to any of us or our hell, she would have proceeded exactly as she has, as well," Ryker said, and there was a foreign gentleness that only made his counterargument all the more frustrating. "I'm simply asking you to use greater discretion where she is concerned. She'll be here until the end of the Season at the latest, and married hopefully sooner, and when that happens, she'll have no reason for any loyalty or obligation to our family."

The weight of a boulder crushing down on Adair's chest restricted his airflow. Given that three weeks had passed and there'd never been a suitor, or even a waltz or walk in the park, it had been all too easy to forget the purpose that brought her here—that she was only here to marry a nob, and then . . . and then, what? Then she'd just go? And there would be no more discussions about the Hell and Sin or the London night sky or—

"Adair?" his brother urged with a concern in those two syllables that brought Adair's head shooting up. "Are you all right?"

"Fine," he said quickly. "I'll have a care." Impatient to have his brother gone so he could be alone with the upheaval of his thoughts, he motioned to his desk. "I've matters to see to before my appointment with Phippen today." That, at least, was the truth.

Grateful that Ryker had always steered away from discourse that was too personal, he stared after him until he'd gone. And even as the panel clicked shut, Adair remained staring at it. Sucking in a breath through his teeth, he covered his face with his hands.

His brother was both correct and incorrect where Cleopatra was concerned. Adair would wager the future of the Hell and Sin that the young woman didn't intend any ill will on his establishment. And yet, of all the charges leveled, there was only one that held him motionless, and his stomach churning—she would marry.

Her union with a nob was the only possible conclusion to her brother's . . . and her . . . plans. It marked a ruthlessness to all the Killorans that should only further deepen his antipathy for that family, and his mistrust of her.

Yet, God help him, with his usual logic and Ryker's reminders, he fought the urge to remain here when all he wanted to do was go off and find her.

Chapter 16

Later that night, Cleopatra knelt at the edge of the cradle, contemplating the sleeping bundle resting there.

Even with the presence of the snarling Wilson, whom she'd the misfortune of being saddled with by Black, and a new, cheerful nursemaid happily bustling about the room, organizing the linens, Paisley Black's nursery was the last place Cleopatra should wish to be.

The babe blinked her impossibly large blue eyes several times, and that cloudy gaze moved over Cleopatra's face. Alas, there had always been something calming in being around babes. They represented the most unsullied part of a person's soul. At this age and size, defenseless as one was, the evil one might carry hadn't yet come out. There was nothing but an inherent need and willingness to trust.

Only this time, being here with this babe was not solely about lingering around innocence. It was about him.

Adair Thorne, whom she'd been moments away from kissing when Ryker Black interrupted. Given that untimely appearance and Adair's absence for the remainder of the day, there was no doubt he'd been raked over the proverbial coals for his dealings with her.

She scrunched her mouth up. Of course, her own brother would have been as vigilant if one of Adair's kin was forced into the Devil's Den. It was not, however, Black's wariness that grated—it was Adair's. She smiled sadly at the dark-haired babe.

Penelope's daughter let out a loud whine, and Cleopatra instantly slipped her finger into the tiny palm, which curled reflexively around it. She closed her eyes, finding and selfishly taking the solace offered by the small child. For if she was being truthful with herself, at least in this instance, she'd admit that she was terrified out of her bloody mind.

"I don't trust for a moment that you wouldn't snuff the life out of that babe," Wilson called out from where he stood at the window. Arms folded, his left heel propped against the wall, his was nothing more than a feigned insouciance.

The nursemaid, Beth, faltered. Stifling a gasp behind her fingertips, she looked between Cleopatra and Wilson.

Where Adair's doubts had oddly cut like a knife, this man's rolled as easily off her back as every other insult he periodically hurled her way.

"With your lousy judgments, it's a fortunate thing for you that you'll never be more than a second-shift guard," she said, directing that insult to the babe.

Wilson's leg slid back to the floor, the plush carpet muting the thump of his heel. "Ain't you have a fancy nob to try and catch," he jeered. "Ah, that's right. You might have a queen's fortune, but not a respectable lord would ever marry a guttersnipe such as you."

Having been brutalized and bullied by Diggory, Cleopatra knew that to engage was to feed and perpetuate the viciousness. She sang a slightly off-key tavern song that had always soothed her sisters.

As I was a walking down Paradise Street
A pretty young damsel I chanced for to meet.

She was round in the counter and bluff in the bow,
So I took in all sail and cried, "Way enough now."

I hailed her in English, she answered me clear,
"I'm from the Black Arrow bound to the
     Shakespeare."

So I tailed her my flipper and took her in tow
And yardarm to yardarm away we did go.

But as we were going she said unto me
There's a spanking full-rigger just ready for sea.

"You need to be gone now," the nursemaid chided, clapping her hands once. That slight sound brought the slumbering babe's eyes open.

"You heard the maid," Wilson called over. "Get out of the room and away from the babe."

Beth dropped her hands on her hips. "Not her. You."

"I've been instructed that this one"—he angled his head toward Cleopatra—"isn't ever to be alone with the babe."

"I've"—the young woman colored—"nursemaid business to be seeing to."

"Then you can see to it after she's gone."

"Mr. Wilson, the business I have to see to requires assistance, and given as I've no intention of asking for your help with this, I'd advise you to go. Now."

No more than an inch taller than Cleopatra, and nearly as slender, she'd the look of a waif. Cleopatra, however, had learned long ago that courage and strength came in all shapes and forms. She suppressed a smile as the nursemaid sent the muttering guard packing.

"Well, he's a miserable blighter," the young woman muttered as soon as she'd closed the door. "Making all that noise about a babe, and insulting you, no less."

"You didn't have anything you required assistance with, did you?" Cleopatra asked the nursemaid with a dawning understanding.

"That's not entirely true." Beth offered a devious grin. "I have been trying to determine just how to be rid of that nasty brute since the moment he followed you in here."

Stunned silent by that gesture of kindness, she stared on as Beth gathered Penelope's babe in her arms. Cleopatra had always believed one could learn much about another person by how one treated a babe. Diggory and his men had often railed at and insulted those tender souls. Most of their drunken wives had worried more about obtaining another pint than nursing their offspring. This unexpected champion handled the babe the way one might care for the king's crown. The fussing child instantly quieted. Rocking her in silence for another moment, Beth returned her to the cradle.

A faint click echoed around the room, and Cleopatra looked to the entrance.

Her heart flipped around as Adair stepped inside the nursery. With his dark-green Rannoch tweed waistcoat, black jacket, and the absence of a cravat, none at the evening's festivities would mistake him for one of the noblemen in attendance. And yet—she raked her gaze over his lightly scarred face—how very much more she preferred Adair Thorne's ruggedness to the pompous lords of the *ton* who couldn't be bothered with so much as a dance. Realizing too late that she remained kneeling beside Paisley's crib, ogling Adair, she burned hot.

He favored the nursemaid with a single glance that instantly sent the bold woman scurrying from the room.

Adair made his way to the side of Paisley's crib, and Cleopatra immediately restored all her attentions to the babe.

"You're late," he said in hushed tones, wholly considerate ones of a man mindful of a slumbering babe.

Cleopatra bit the inside of her lower lip. Damn him. Must he even be thoughtful in this regard, too? Couldn't he be obnoxious and loud as the latest guard he and Black had sicced on her? *Because Adair didn't want to be with you . . .* that taunting voice reminded at the back of her mind. To him, she'd always be linked to the thankfully dead Diggory and his former gang.

Ignoring his outstretched hand, Cleopatra shoved to her feet. "Been sent for me?" she asked quietly so as not to wake the babe. "Your turn now that Wilson's been relieved for the night?"

Adair homed his keen gaze on her face. "Did he offend you?" he demanded.

She immediately masked her features, going tight-lipped.

In a touch that was an unlikely blend of tenderness and strength, Adair collected her chin between his thumb and forefinger. "What did he say?"

Was this another damned test of her character? Cleopatra edged away from his hold. "Oi ain't a snitch."

Silent for a long moment, Adair swept his probing stare over her. "He insulted you, and yet you'd say nothing?"

She lifted her shoulders in a defiant shrug. "'e's no different than you and your kind. Thinks Oi'll kill the babe while ya all sleep."

Adair snapped his eyebrows together in a tense, angry line. "He said that?"

Cleopatra let her silence stand for her answer.

Adair unleashed a black curse. "I am sorry he treated you that way. I will speak to him."

Damn him for caring, and damn her for the warmth that his defense roused within her. She'd not allow herself any further weakening where Adair Thorne was concerned. "You'll speak to him?" She scoffed. "You've already doubted me ten times to Sunday."

A dull flush stained his cheeks.

"And you'll continue to do so." *And he'd no doubt toss you out on your arse if he discovered the truth.* "So, feel free to go back to avoiding me." Cleopatra took a step to get past him, desperately needing space between them. But he matched her movements. She made another move, and he swiftly placed himself in her path, blocking her retreat.

A frown formed on his hard lips. "Is that what you believe, Cleopatra Killoran? That I spent the day avoiding you?"

"No."

Some of the tension left his shoulders.

"That is precisely what I know you've been doing. You had your meeting with Black, and that was the end of ours."

His back immediately went up. "I had an appointment with my builder."

Cleopatra pursed her lips. "It ain't my business." She again made to leave, and he gripped her by the upper arm, staying her.

"Would you have the truth?"

"Are you capable of it?" she sneered, spoiling for a fight with this man. Wanting the safe, familiar comfort of the antipathy that had always existed between them. Hating him for not even relenting in this.

"Ryker still doesn't trust you," he said candidly. "He believes you wouldn't hesitate to betray our family to benefit your own."

And she wouldn't. Would she? Only everything had become so very blurred these past three weeks. She itched to dig her fingertips into her temples and drive the confusion from her muddled mind.

"You didn't ask me what I believe."

"It doesn't matter," she said tiredly, her voice heavy to her own ears.

He dropped his hip against a brocade armchair. "It doesn't?" A frosty glint iced his eyes.

Moving closer, she spoke quietly, mindful of the sleeping child. "You might speak freely about your damned club and your plans, but ultimately, you can't see past the fact that I'm . . . Killoran's sister."

She gasped as he shot a hand out, and capturing hers, began to divest her of one of her gloves. Cleopatra briefly froze and then began to wrestle her arm back. "What are you doing, Thorne?" she demanded, her heart pounding hard against her rib cage as Adair stripped away the satin fabric. A heavy pall descended over the nursery, broken only by the faint snore that periodically escaped the babe.

Cleopatra stared dumbly at the *D* seared into her flesh, a brand that marked her origins.

Soundlessly, he trailed an index finger over it.

Oh, God, does he know the significance of it? It was an inventorying process that, given his abuse, she'd never wholly understood. Why mark a person when one couldn't be bothered to so much as assign them a name?

"My brother doubted . . . doubts you," he corrected. He continued to run his finger over her palm, sending delicious shivers from that distracted caress. "Given our families' history over the years, I should also have those same reservations, Cleopatra. I continually remind myself of that." He paused his tender ministrations. "And yet, I don't. I don't believe you'll use the information I've shared against me or my club or my family. Nor do I believe you're capable of hurting"—Adair trailed his gaze over to the cradle—"anyone."

At that affirmation of his trust, her heart sang. It was a gift given in the streets, more valuable than the fleeting coin one pilfered for the permanency of it. He lightly squeezed her hand, and drawing it close to his mouth, he brushed a kiss over the inside of her palm.

A vise squeezed her chest at the intimacy of that kiss. It defied the emotionless, driven-by-need-only exchanges she'd witnessed whores and patrons at her club turn themselves over to. And the tenderness of it threatened to shatter her.

This is too much . . .

Clearing her throat, Cleopatra neatly disentangled her fingers and made a show of pushing her spectacles back into place. "Oi—I'm still not going," she said, hurriedly shifting the discourse back to what had brought him here in the first place.

Before he'd been forthright with her, and he continued working a dangerous hold inside her heart. With every day, she found herself one day further away from freedom. There would be no husband to speak freely with about the plans and ideas of a gaming hell. Given all she'd gleaned about the nobility over the years, they wouldn't even allow a wife an opinion. And she would be crushed by that in ways that Diggory had never managed to defeat her.

Adair shook his head slowly. "I don't understand."

"Not that difficult to follow. Lady B-Beaufort's ball," she expounded. "This evening," she said lamely, promptly curling her toes into the soles of her boots. As though there was, in fact, another Beaufort ball they'd been expected to attend. "I'm not going."

Adair scratched at his creased brow. "Isn't that the sole reason you're here, to attend Society events?"

No. The sole reason she was here was to make a match with a fancy nob. It was an altogether vital distinction that sent desolation sweeping through her. "I said I'm not going." She swept away in a whir of satin skirts. "Wot's the point of it?" she demanded on a loud whisper. "Oi go and sit through ball after ball, and the end is always the same." Such a realization should have her sick with the implications of what her failure would mean for her sisters. She briefly closed her eyes. *I am a selfish bastard. I don't want to make a damned match with a bloody stranger. Least of all, a nob* . . . She sprang forward on the balls of her feet to take flight.

Adair settled his palms on her shoulders, grounding her, bringing her sinking back to her heels. His touch was both calming and strengthening all at once, and she who'd forever scoffed at needing another, leaned back against his chest, taking the support he offered. "I still say you're better off without all that silly dancing nonsense," he whispered against her ear. Delicious shivers raced from the sensitive skin on her nape, down to her back. An involuntary laugh escaped her—that husky, breathless sound she'd heard from too many of the prostitutes inside the Devil's Den.

So, he thought her desire to escape the festivities had to do with her frustration at her wallflower status. Content to let him keep to that erroneous belief, preferring it to the more dangerous truth that she, who'd prided herself on her strength, was terrified at the prospect of making a match. She angled her head, looking up at him. "One of these days, Adair Thorne, I'm going to prove how wrong you are about a waltz."

He offered his usual cocksure half grin. "I'm not even sure you'd be able to convince me of that, love," he said with a wink.

He stepped away, and she mourned the loss of his nearness, and just like that, reality intruded once more.

This time, however, there were no urgings or questions about her reservations. Rather, a companionable silence, a patience, and his meaning was clear. He'd wait until she was ready. And where his presence at those staid affairs had always been reassuring, now it only served to highlight the misery of her circumstances.

For she, who'd sworn to never turn her fate and future over to a husband, could see herself with a man like Adair Thorne.

Chapter 17

Having had most of the Marquess and Marchioness of Beaufort's male guests as patrons at his club through the years, Adair knew firsthand with their vices and pomposity, the lot of them were fools.

Never before had he appreciated just how much, until this night. With Cleopatra seated on the fringe of yet another ballroom, and gentlemen stepping past her like she carried the damned plague, those noblemen proved the depth of their vanity.

Was it a wonder she hadn't wanted to suffer through another infernal affair? Or . . . waltz with a single gent here.

Shuddering in horror, he eyed Lady Beaufort's guests as they completed the intricate steps of some dance or another. His brother Niall and sister-in-law shifted into his line of vision, momentarily diverting his attention.

Well, I'll be the Devil in church on Sunday . . .

He didn't know whether to laugh, cry, or compose a list of insults to eventually heap upon his brother's head. For Niall Marksman, one of the most ruthless kingpins of London's underbelly, a man who as a child had killed at command, now performed those mincing steps. Where the other guests, Niall's wife, Diana, included, moved with an effortless grace, the partial owner of the Hell and Sin's dancing was at best lively, and at worst, horrifyingly awkward.

Only . . . as Adair studied the pairing, he saw how the two were lost in only each other; there may as well not have been another soul present. With his flushed cheeks and the smile on his scarred visage, Niall exuded a softness Adair had believed him incapable of. He'd never been a man to waste time with inane pursuits, and yet, here he stood . . . dancing with his wife.

Adair himself had never given much thought to marriage. Since he'd contributed all his stolen and then saved coins for the purchase of a share in the Hell and Sin, that club had been his everything. It had represented security and safety, and the time that went into the running of it hadn't allowed for a wife. But for the first time, he allowed himself for a brief instance the possibility of what that would be if he were married to a woman who was a partner in life.

Unbidden, his gaze traveled to the bespectacled miss glowering about the crowded ballroom. He'd never known a woman like her. Her clever mind and endless skill set in the overall running of a club had held him enthralled these past weeks . . . and God help him, if he didn't hunger for her still.

He froze as the full ramifications of his ponderings gripped him.

A servant sailed past with a tray in hand, and Adair instantly plucked a desperately needed flute of champagne from the unsuspecting footman. *Nay, I need something far stronger. Mooning over Killoran's sister.* He finished the drink in several long gulps.

Over the rim of the delicate glass, his gaze collided with Cleopatra's.

She tipped her head in the direction of the dance floor and pointed her eyes skyward. He'd come to know her well . . . too well. So much so that he could identify when she was putting on a false show about *ton* functions. He also knew her enough to have found she was even more proud than any of the people Adair called family.

"Bored?" he mouthed.

Cleopatra feigned a wide yawn, patting her lips with her palm.

That public display earned several censorious looks from ladies seated nearby. Again, Adair was reminded of just how different Cleopatra was from all the women he'd witnessed, known, or been forced to brush shoulders with because of his siblings' spouses. Raw in her every reaction and response, she earned the condemnation of the same people whose approval she sought, but he appreciated her all the more for it.

Adair shook his head. "Don't believe you," he slowly mouthed.

Cleopatra flared her eyes through the crystal lenses of her spectacles to reveal a look of mock outrage, and with a furtive movement, she lifted a finger in a crude gesture that would have escaped most of the fancy toffs present.

A sharp bark of laughter escaped him.

"Never thought I'd see the day you were enjoying yourself at an event thrown by a peer."

Adair cursed, and he spun about. Bloody hell. Caught unawares not for the first time since she'd entered his household.

Calum stared, triumphantly grinning. "And I especially never expected you'd find such pleasure at one of them that you'd fail to hear a person's approach," his brother goaded.

"Go to hell," he groused, reluctantly shifting his attention away from Cleopatra. Damn. Couldn't it have been Niall or Ryker to stumble upon him? Always laconic, they, too, never spoke about personal matters . . . unless it related to the Hell and Sin. Calum, on the other hand . . .

"Well? What held you so engrossed?"

"No one," Adair said quickly.

Calum arched a dark brow. "I didn't say *who*."

He creased his brow. What in hell was he talking about?

"I asked *what*, not *who*."

Bloody, bloody hell. Damning himself for that telling slip, Adair made a show of motioning over a servant, taking a diversionary tactic where he could. "No one, and nothing, has distracted me," he said after he'd collected another glass and the servant had gone off. *Liar.*

"Ryker mentioned there was a . . . disagreement this afternoon between you."

Adair continued to underestimate the changes that had overtaken Ryker—nay, all of his brothers, since their marriage. Gossiping had never been part of his way. *Except where the Hell and Sin had been concerned, everything had always gone . . .* "Oh?" he asked vaguely, swirling the contents of his drink. He'd called it a disagreement, had he? Neatly sidestepping what it, in fact, had been—a bloody fight, with everything except fists exchanged. "What did he say precisely?" That Adair was captivated by Cleopatra Killoran? He curled his fingers tight around his champagne glass with a force to snap the stem.

"You showed the gaming hell plans to Killoran."

Cleopatra. I showed them to Cleopatra. "Miss Killoran isn't her brother," he said, finishing off his drink.

"You didn't trust her a few weeks ago," Calum accurately pointed out. "Now you do?" he asked with his usual Calum calm and stoicism.

Adair looked him squarely in the eyes. "Despite Ryker's doubts, I do." He anticipated a like battle from Calum. "Nothing to say?" he asked gruffly when Calum remained silent. After all, hadn't he wanted to turn out the other man's wife because of her birthright?

Calum did a sweep of the ballroom, always alert, as he'd always been. "The young woman helped Paisley and made some wise recommendations for the club. Given all that *and* the fact that she single-handedly saw Diana rescued from Diggory's wife's clutches, I venture she's proven herself enough."

Both humbled and ashamed by that magnanimity, when he'd been anything but supportive of the union between Calum and his wife, Adair stared blankly into his empty glass. The lone drop clinging to the side spiraled down and hit the bottom of the crystal. By God, what a small-minded bastard he'd been.

Calum slapped him on the back. "Trust your instincts where the young woman is concerned."

It had been the rule Calum had set forth in the guidelines they'd all crafted in their bid to survive: trust your instincts.

"If you'll excuse me?" Giving him another pat, his brother took his leave.

Trust his instincts. What Calum couldn't see, didn't know, was that Adair's conflict didn't stem from Cleopatra's connection to Broderick Killoran. Rather it was her hold over Adair.

"You look as miserable as I feel," Cleopatra observed on a hushed whisper.

He whipped his head about, searching for the diminutive but strong owner of that droll pronouncement.

"It's a wonder you survived a day in the streets, Adair Thorne," she said without inflection. "I'm here."

He instantly located her behind a nearby pillar.

The bespectacled spitfire gave a jaunty wave but remained in her hiding place, out of view.

Adair folded his arms at his chest, letting the glass dangle from between his fingers.

"Are you also upset about the whole dancing business?" she teased.

The earlier restlessness his brother had left him with lifted. He fought back a grin. "I assure you not."

"Boredom?"

Ennui was safer. "Need you ask?"

"Do you want to escape?"

Escape. With her . . . ? It was a dangerously tantalizing prospect suggested.

"What do you have in mind?" he asked from the corner of his mouth.

"Lord Beaufort's office."

He'd been part of any number of underhanded acts in the whole of his life. The moment he'd established a foothold in the world and secured his future, he'd reshaped himself from a common thief . . . into a man of honor. As such—"I don't invade other men's business space," he said in hushed tones.

She let out an exasperated sigh. "You're disappointingly staid. The roof."

"No." The last roof he'd climbed would remain his brother's when he'd gone after this woman. "Lord Beaufort's billiards room?"

"The billiards room," she echoed on a husky whisper that stirred the wicked hungering she'd roused in him since their first meeting.

"Fine. First one to find it is most resourceful in St. Giles. Last one there . . . You all right, Thorne? You look queer."

"I'm fine," he said hoarsely.

"'ow's about a competition, then? Between you and I."

Did the young woman work at piquing a person's curiosity? Or was it a skill that came natural to her?

"What manner of competition?" he asked with far too much enthusiasm. He, along with his siblings, had always been practical. Jests, joking, and games had been an even greater rarity than finding food for their bellies. Despite her jaded exterior, Cleopatra had retained a light-heartedness that was infectious.

"Oi find the billiard's room, you let me teach you the steps of a waltz."

Adair covered a laugh behind his hand. "And what do I get when I win?"

She snorted. "You need me to make all decisions for you, Thorne?" She paused. "And it's *if* you win."

"We shall certainly . . ." He glanced over to the spot she'd occupied moments ago.

Gone.

And with far more enthusiasm than he'd felt the whole damned evening, Adair grinned and started for Lord Beaufort's billiards room.

Cleopatra stole through the halls of Lord Beaufort's sprawling town-house. The winding halls, covered in plush carpets, were a house thief's greatest dream. No loose floorboards or uneven slates to give a person's movements away. It made her task of locating the marquess's billiards room all the easier.

Cleopatra had been determined to never be dependent upon any man . . . in any way. As such, it was so very odd to find one's happiness so closely linked with one.

Not just any one—Adair Thorne, Black's brother. Though, in the time she'd lived among family, she'd been reared to hate, their names had mattered far less. Rather, they'd not mattered very much at all.

If your brother could hear you, he'd strip you of a say in all business dealings at the Devil's Den.

Cleopatra reached the end of the corridor and stopped. She considered each direction and then continued along the intersecting hall until she'd reached the last door. Briefly pausing, she stole a glance about and then let herself inside her host's billiards room.

The moon filtered through a crack in the brocade curtains, that faint shaft the only light to break the darkness. She blinked several times to adjust her eyes.

A soft whistle pierced the quiet. "When will I learn it's folly to doubt you, Cleopatra Killoran?" Adair drawled from his position at the velvet billiards table. "But how in hell did you find Beaufort's billiards room?"

Another time, she wagered he would have made some insulting crack about her having no doubt committed a theft in this very home. No longer. "Fancy toffs like to keep their gaming rooms farthest from all the respectable ones." With a laugh, she drifted over to the opposite end of the billiards table. "They're all the same." *And I'll be married to one.* Fighting back that depressing thought, she lifted her chin. "And what about you, Thorne? How'd you know about Beaufort's layout? Rubbing elbows with the nobs now?"

"In a way," he demurred.

Cleopatra tipped her head.

"Lady Beaufort is, in fact, Penelope's sister."

With a snort, she hitched herself up onto the edge of the table. "You already knew your way about. Oi'd say that's cheating."

He rolled a black ball back and forth between his hands. "You set the terms," he reminded her.

There'd be no dancing, then. It was silly to feel a keen disappointment, but as she'd put forward the competition, there had been a thrill of excitement at teaching Adair those sweeping movements . . . and of being in his arms. He rolled the ball toward her, and she put her palm up, preventing it from colliding with the edge of the table. "What do you want, then?" she asked, shoving the ball back.

He grinned. "I haven't decided."

Her belly fluttered wildly. She followed his languid movements as he quit his spot and fetched two sticks from the wall. "Here," he called, lightly tossing one at her.

Squinting in the dark, Cleopatra caught it to her chest.

Adair gathered the balls into the proper place at the center of the table. "The best two out of three competitions, wins?"

Her lips twitched. "You're assuming I play."

He glanced up from his task, and that slight movement sent a dark lock tumbling over his brow, lending him a boyish look. "Cleopatra Killoran, I'd wager there isn't a thing you don't know how to do."

And just like that, Cleopatra fell in love. Hopelessly, helplessly, she lost her heart to Adair Thorne.

She froze, and his gentle teasing came as muffled as the time she'd dived into the Thames to escape capture by the constable. *But God help her, this was all the worse. I love him. I've gone and fallen in love with him.* When the last possibility of a match could be with this man. Her breath came in quick, shallow spurts, and the cue slipped from her fingers, clattering to the table.

". . . and . . . Cleopatra?" Adair's easy smile slipped as concern wreathed his features.

"Two out of three," she said sharply, quickly retrieving her cue. "I cut." Through the panic swamping her senses, she bent over and launched her stick at her cue ball. It jumped and sailed past her intended mark.

"Now, that I did not expect," he murmured to himself as he attended his shot.

She pressed her eyes closed. No, it wasn't what she'd expected, either.

He valued her opinion and saw her worth, but what was more, he treated her as an equal. And beautiful. *Even with your scars and spectacles and figureless form, he'd also made you feel in ways you never believed possible.* And there could never, ever be anything more with him. Not if she were to care for her sisters so that they didn't have to marry pompous peers.

Numb, she stared emptily on as he made quick work of the billiards table.

Adair paused, his cue properly positioned. "Nervous yet?"

Terrified out of my bloody everlasting mind. "Of you? Hardly." Did he hear the faint, threadbare quality of her voice?

He deepened his smile and let his stick fly . . . at last missing a shot.

"Moi turn," she said sharply. It was vastly easier focusing on the red velvet table and her intended cue ball than the danger in loving Adair Thorne. Taking support from the familiar weight of the stick, she concentrated her energies on the white cue ball. She released her shot, and the loud *thwack* echoed around the room.

"It appears we are tied," he observed after she'd connected with her sixth and final shot. He strolled around the table, taking up position beside her. They stood, their bodies so close the heat of him scorched her arms. "Were you swindling me?"

"Wouldn't be hard to do." Clearing her throat, she fiddled with her cue. "What's the third competition to be, then?" she asked quietly, needing a diversion from the madness of her own yearnings.

Adair slipped the stick from her fingers and set it aside. "We could always split, and each claim a victory and expect a payment," he whispered, lowering his head. "I'll give you your London waltz."

The lingering hint of champagne on his breath, more intoxicating than the bubbling brew itself, brought her lashes fluttering closed. "Wot koind of payment are ya thinking in return?" she rejoined, tilting her neck so she could meet his stare squarely.

Hooding his thick lashes, he moved his heat-filled gaze from her lips, back to her eyes, and then back again. With a groan, he cupped her about the nape and devoured her mouth.

Desire exploded within as she parted her lips, tangling her tongue with his in a violent, primitive mating. Adair sank his fingertips into her hips and guided her up onto the table, and then his questing hands continued their search from her buttocks to the curve of her breasts, leaving no part of her untouched. Under the fabric of her gown, her nipples sprang hard from his attentions. She moaned and parted her legs in invitation.

He stepped between them and, breaking contact with her mouth, dragged a trail of kisses down her neck. Then, lowering her décolletage and shift, he exposed her breasts. The cool night air combined with the conflagration burning through her and tore a keening moan from her. Bending his head, he captured the peak of one breast between his lips.

Cleopatra hissed. "Adair." She arched her back, opening herself to his attentions as a throbbing ache settled at her center.

"What hold do you have over me?" he breathed against her skin, his hoarse words an echo of her very thoughts.

She tangled her fingers in his hair and dragged his mouth close for another violent kiss.

Suddenly, he stiffened. His breath coming hard and fast, he straightened.

Cleopatra collapsed on the edge of the table as he swiftly drew her gown back into place.

"I don't . . ."

He touched a silencing finger to her lips and jerked his head toward the door.

A faint muttering, followed by the periodic open and closing of doors, pierced the dense wood. Taking her by the hand, Adair all but dragged her to the window and tossed it open.

"You'll be ruined if we're caught here."

"I was ruined before I ever came," she said softly.

He tightened his jaw, glancing once again to the commotion growing closer in the halls outside. "Not like this," he muttered. "This would see that you never . . . marry a fancy toff." Did she imagine the spasm that contorted his features? Surely that paroxysm of grief was no more than a play of the shadows upon his rugged features?

He cared about her reputation. How was it possible for his hushed words to both touch her heart and wrench like a knife?

Another click of a closing door brought her back from her melancholy. She glanced between the door and the mews below. For a long, dangerous moment, she contemplated remaining precisely where she was, at Adair Thorne's side . . . and shredding her reputation and all hopes for a match. Because then there could be a *them*, together.

You fool . . . there could never be that. Not when your father tortured him and his brothers.

"I'll catch you," he whispered against her mouth.

"You think I need rescuing, Adair?"

Hefting himself over the ledge, he lowered himself by the arms until his feet dangled the ten feet below. "Everyone needs rescuing," he mouthed.

She leaned out. "Even you?"

He winked and then let go. Her heart pounded painfully against her ribs and then resumed a normal cadence as his boots hit with a solid thump. She'd jumped from higher heights scores of times, and yet the endless moment of his fall had torn a year off her life.

Silently, Adair stretched his arms up, urging her to jump.

Cleopatra lifted herself onto the ledge.

The door flew open, freezing her.

Oh, bloody hell. Her heart sank a slow, agonizing path to her soles.

Lord Landon, one of the Devil's Den's best patrons, stared back with shock stamped on his features.

A slow grin curled his lips in a roguish grin he'd worn too many times inside her club. "Miss Killoran?" he greeted, dropping a deep, formal bow.

She briefly contemplated the grounds below, finding Adair. Even with the distance separating them, worry flickered in his eyes.

Cleopatra was giving her head an imperceptible shake when the faint click of the door closing registered. She spun about.

"I must confess," Lord Landon murmured, "this is all rather unexpected."

She stiffened as he strolled over, but he avoided her altogether and cut a path over to the well-stocked sideboard. "And what is that?" she asked, the blade strapped against her lower left leg reassuring in its weight and presence. Though they'd never exchanged so much as a passing word at the Devil's Den, they'd both moved around the gaming hell floors at the same time. Lord Landon had never put a hand upon the whores and was oftentimes sought out by the women inside the Devil's Den, but she knew better than to trust a lord.

The young marquess glanced briefly away from his task of drink selection. "Why, it is not every day a young lady considers jumping from a townhouse window to escape my company."

Despite herself, a wry smile pulled at her lips. "You're a pompous one, then." Then, was there another sort?

He flashed another wolfish smile, displaying perfect pearl-white teeth. "With good reason."

A woman learned to survive in the streets by paying attention to every last detail about a man. The way a man carried oneself, the type of grin he affected, and the words he used and how he used them, told one all one needed to know.

This golden-haired nob, with his wiry frame accentuated perfectly by finely tailored dark garments, whose careless grin marked him a careless rogue to be avoided at all costs. *That's the precise type of gent Broderick would see you marry . . . and likely the only one who'd give a match with you any real thought.* "I'm not a lady," she said tightly, annoyed that she'd conceded so much as a smile for the arrogant lord. Hating Broderick all over again.

"No," he said easily, not taking his gaze from the brandy he now poured. "Had you been, it would have been *me* contemplating a jump from the windows." Setting the pilfered decanter down, he looked up, his enigmatic gaze searching.

Cleopatra shuttered her features.

"I've insulted you," he said matter-of-factly, absent of an apology.

"I'd have to give a rat's arse about you and what you said to be insulted," she said evenly.

The marquess choked on his swallow, and those gulping gasps of air bore the traces of laughter. "Brava, Miss Killoran," he managed to strangle out after he'd regained control of his breathing. He lifted his glass in salute.

Presenting him her back, Cleopatra made a show of closing the crystal windows and searched for Adair's familiar form in the shadows. Gone. She turned her attention to the stranger sipping his host's brandy at the same table Adair had her upon a short while ago. Through the reflection in the glass, she studied Lord Landon's every movement.

"You know, I really didn't mean it as an insult," the marquess went on, erasing the long stretch of silence. "I truly prefer the company of someone who has something to say about topics other than the weather."

Abandoning her post at the window, she let the curtain flutter back into place and moved cautiously about the room. "You don't know what topics I talk about," she said derisively.

The marquess winged a golden eyebrow up. "Would you make mention of our fine London weather?"

She met his question with silence.

"I did not believe so." He tossed back another long swallow. "Nor would you be in here even now with one slipper up on a windowsill if you were the same as the ladies inside that"—he pointed his glass to the doorway—"ballroom."

Cleopatra slowed her steps, halting her exit. "And you find your worth greater than those women you disparage?"

"My worth greater?" he echoed. A mirthless chuckle left his hard lips. "Miss Killoran, I know precisely what I am, and it's certainly not one who sees my worth greater than those around me." There was an unexpected somberness underlying his melodious baritone that belied the affected air of rogue he'd mastered. "I'm merely a man as bored here as you yourself."

"If you'll excuse me," she said tightly, "I should go." As it was, in being discovered by this gentleman, she'd already been ruined, and that realization only proved her selfishness. For, help her, she couldn't muster a single regret that she'd be ruined.

I'll be free . . . and one of my sisters will make the ultimate sacrifice in my stead.

207

Feeling Lord Landon's stare on her, she flattened her lips. "Do you intend to say anything?"

"About our being alone here together?" he countered, not even pretending to misunderstand. He finished his drink and discarded it on the side of the billiards table. Hitching his hip onto the edge, he swung his leg in a lazy back-and-forth rhythm. "That would depend, Miss Killoran."

The blighter would bribe her. Cleopatra's fingers twitched with the need to form a fist that she could bury in his face. "Oh?" She lifted her skirts slightly, exposing the vicious dagger strapped against her leg. "On what, my lord?"

For her wariness of the cocksure lord, it was hard to not approve of a fancy gent who merely eyed that jewel-crusted dagger with amusement. He swept his lashes lower, in a rakish leer that she'd wager he'd practiced since his university days. "A dance, Miss Killoran. I'd like a dance."

She let her skirts fall back into place. "A dance?" she blurted. That is what he'd request.

"A waltz," he clarified. "And then your secret is your own."

Cleopatra scanned his sharp-planed features for a hint of mockery. "Foine," she said finally. "One waltz." Uneasy with the gent's urbane charm, Cleopatra took a wide berth around him, making for the door. All the while she kept sight of him from the corner of her eye.

"Oh, and Miss Killoran?" he called out, as soon as her fingertips were on the handle. "Just to clarify, that set will be tonight. The next waltz."

He'd gathered she intended to sneak off, then. So, he was more clever than she'd credited. "Why do you want to dance with me?" she put to him, curiosity making her bold. Was it on a wager, similar to the kind Penelope had spoken of? Did he revel in flouting society's conventions?

"Truthfully?"

She nodded. "If you're capable of it."

"On occasion, I am." Where they'd had desperate gents inside the Devil's Den who stole or attempted to cheat, Lord Landon had never been that man. "I find you refreshing," he confessed.

Cleopatra snorted. "Oi wasn't born yesterday."

He quirked his lips at the corner. "And that is why I do. It is just a waltz, no more, and your secret meeting with me here—"

"You invaded my space first."

"—shall remain your secret still," he said over her.

A dance was all he wanted. Lord Landon, though arrogant with a rogue's smile and a rake's eye, was offering her nothing more than what she'd wanted for the past three weeks. And yet, as she nodded and fled back to the ballroom, she found it hadn't been just a waltz she'd wanted after all.

She'd wanted a set with Adair.

Chapter 18

She'd had her dance.

A waltz, to be precise, with the Marquess of Landon, and Adair on the sidelines.

He should be relieved. After all, the roguish lord had spared Adair from suffering through a lesson and then those awkward movements.

So why did he sit in his office, three hours after their return, unable to sleep . . . or even focus on his work for the Hell and Sin?

Because you wanted to be the one to take her in your arms. You wanted to curl a hand about her waist and feel her fingers upon you . . . and instead some other man had claimed that right. Just as some other man would eventually claim Cleopatra as his bride. With a curse, Adair hurled the small stub of his charcoal pencil across the room. It hit the wall with a ping and then clattered unsatisfyingly quiet to the floor.

Nor, if he were being truthful with himself in the dead of night, had it solely been about Cleopatra dancing with another man.

This frustration and annoyance came from within . . . with himself and his own damned inability to dance.

A sharp, painful laugh tore from his lungs. Oh, the bloody irony of it. He'd scorned men who'd wasted their time and energies on such inane activities as dancing, just as he'd made light of Niall and Ryker both learning the rudimentary steps. And now, here he stood, feeling wholly inadequate. For even if his role as proprietor hadn't kept him motionless, more guard than guest at Lady Beaufort's affair this evening, his inability to dance would have. He, Adair Thorne, who'd long prided himself on being a master of anything he wished to do, had wanted nothing more in his life than to take Cleopatra in his arms.

Instead, he'd stood as a seething observer.

A light knock sounded at the door. Adair swung his gaze over to the door. It was her. Somehow in the time she'd been here, he'd come to feel her presence. He swiped a frustrated hand over his face. *I'm either bloody exhausted or out of my eternal mind . . .*

He considered ignoring that rapping. Considered letting Cleopatra believe he was otherwise somewhere else.

The door opened, and Cleopatra ducked her head inside. "I don't believe for a moment that you didn't hear me," she nagged.

Adair sighed. Of course, he should have known better where this spitfire was concerned. She'd take command of any situation and space . . . including his office.

She folded her arms. "Did you just sigh because I'd come here?"

"I yawned," he mumbled, going to fetch his pencil. He stooped and, picking it up, studied it. His broken pencil. Adair scowled at the tip.

"I know the difference between a yawn and a sigh," she carried on with her usual temerity. Shoving the door closed with the heel of her foot, Cleopatra wandered over to his desk—just as she'd done so many times since she'd arrived here.

Only these late-night and early-morn exchanges were fleeting. Tonight's waltz shared between her and Lord Landon was testament to that. He gnashed his teeth, his frustration intensifying as she climbed into his usual seat, her small frame nearly swallowed by the large leather chair.

The sight of her there was deeply intimate, and yet a reminder that they'd only been playing make-believe where their relationship was concerned. Ultimately, she'd belong to another. Mayhap, Lord Landon: too handsome for his own damned good, unscarred, once fought over by the prostitutes inside Adair's club, and now by Cleopatra's easy smile that night during their set, charmer of the wary Cleopatra Killoran. A red haze of rage descended over his vision, blinding, and with it spread an insidious jealousy throughout.

Humming a tavern ditty, Cleopatra dragged her knees up to her chest and focused on the notes Phippen had sent earlier that afternoon . . . otherwise neglected by Adair.

"I haven't seen this yet," she correctly noted.

He clenched and unclenched his jaw. How damned casual she was. *When I'm a bloody mess inside.*

"Shouldn't you be asleep?" he asked, the question coming out harshly. Stalking over, he plucked the sheets from her hands and tossed them to the corner of the desk, out of her reach.

Cleopatra dropped her chin atop her knees. "We never worked out the final terms of our agreement."

It was official, with her ability to torture him, she was very much a Killoran. Only this form of cruelty was all the worse for the unintentional delivery of it. "You had your first waltz. No need for one from me," he clipped out as he gathered his papers together and proceeded to set his desk to rights.

Frowning at him, Cleopatra spoke slowly. "You never said what prize you intended to claim."

It did not escape his notice that she didn't refute his words. All she'd sought was a dance, and Lord Landon had provided her precisely what she wished, and far better than a street tough like Adair ever could . . . or would. "No, I didn't," he acknowledged, not lifting his head from his task. "I've business to see to, Cleopatra. I lost most of the evening to Beaufort's damned ball and don't have time to speak about a damned pretend wager."

Another woman would have been sent fleeing at his sharp tone.

"You're angry," she observed. Slowly lowering her legs to the floor, she stood.

From the corner of his eye, he caught a flash of creamy white skin before her modest night skirts hid that delectable flesh. Damning her for this quixotic spell she cast, and damning himself all the more for wanting her as he did, he paused in his task and released an exaggerated sigh. "Why would I be angry?"

Cleopatra lifted her shoulders in an uneven shrug. "I don't know." She lifted an index finger. "But I do know you grit your teeth loud enough when you are, and this vein . . ." Leaning up on tiptoe, she touched the corner of his right eye. "It pulses when you do. As it is now."

She knew those details about him. Adair briefly closed his eyes. For all he'd survived, he'd always believed himself above cowardice. Only to find with his inability to mention Lord Landon's name, and the searing jealousy gripping Adair even now, just how little strength he, in fact, had. He took several steps back, putting desperately needed distance between them. "I was going to require you accompany me to the Hell and Sin."

Cleopatra opened and closed her mouth several times. "What?"

She was the only woman in the whole of the kingdom who would have been diverted at the mention of taking part in the business end of discussions about his hell. "That was to be the deal," he clarified. "I'd give you your first waltz." Which Lord Landon had instead seen to. "In turn, you were to accompany me and assess Phippen's work thus far."

A little gasp burst from Cleopatra, and she moved with such alacrity, her wire-rimmed spectacles tumbled from her nose. "When?"

Not even a month ago, he'd have taken that eagerness as a sign that Killoran's sister wanted nothing more than a glimpse of the inner workings of the Hell and Sin. How odd to find this woman had been so much safer then, than she was now to him.

"Adair?" she prodded, tugging at his shirtsleeve.

"When, what?" he blurted, hurrying to retrieve her glasses. He held them over.

Cleopatra jammed the wire-rims back on. "When are we going to your club?" She chewed at the tip of her finger. "Of course, it cannot be during the day, because we'd be seen." She jabbed that same long digit up, and he grunted as it hit his nose. "Unless we go early in the morning before the *ton* awakes and—"

"We are not going anywhere during the day," he said, cutting her off abruptly. Collecting her hand, he lowered it back to her side.

She was already nodding. "Very well, the early-morn hours when the staff is sleeping and the lords and ladies have returned from their night's pleasures makes far more—"

"We're not going at night, either."

She knitted her eyebrows into a single, befuddled line.

"We're not going at all," he clarified, and resumed straightening his desk.

Silence met his pronouncement, broken only by the noisy shuffle of parchment and vellum as he organized his documents into tidy piles.

"Very well." Cleopatra moved to the opposite end of the desk.

Perplexed, he glanced up . . . and froze.

The bespectacled miss who'd wholly captivated him stood with her arms bent and stretched out before her.

What in blazes . . . ?

"You owe me a dance—"

"That you already had," he said as much for himself as for her.

"And I join you at the Hell and Sin."

He gritted his teeth. "I'm not dancing with you, Cleopatra." Because every time he took her in his arms, he became more and more lost. He needed distance from her. Space that was safe so he could see a restoration of logic and order.

"You're angry again."

God, she was relentless. "I'm not . . ."

Clearing her throat, she pointedly tapped at her closed lips. "Angry," she mouthed, and then she lifted her arms into position.

Adair searched about, feeling more cornered now than he had as a boy trapped against a back alley with the constables close. She was unrelenting. She'd not quit until he conceded to the set and a visit to his club.

As if she'd followed his thoughts, Cleopatra waggled her arms.

"Foine," he snapped. All he'd end up with by the time this lesson was through was a lesson in humiliation. Particularly as she'd so elegantly glided about Lord and Lady Beaufort's ballroom with the rakish Lord Landon. Fury whipped through Adair, and he took a lurching step toward her . . . and then stopped.

He eyed the graceful arc of her arms, lost, when as a rule a man in St. Giles didn't ever ask the way.

"Here," Cleopatra murmured. Stretching a hand out, she gathered his left one in her delicate but firm grip and guided it to her waist. His fingers tightened reflexively upon her. The warmth of her skin penetrated the thin scrap of fabric between them, searing his hand. His mouth went dry as lust bolted through him. "Put your other hand in mine," she said softly, and of its own volition, his arm came up and he found her fingers with his in a grip that felt so very right.

"Now what?" Was that question for himself . . . or for her?

"All the steps are: one, two, three. One, two three. Even," she added, as a seeming afterthought. "You'll step forward with the heel and backward with the toe to the foot." She squeezed his hand slightly, urging him through the box movements. "And count: one, two, three. One, two, three."

His pacing off, Adair stepped on her right foot. He cursed. Lord Landon hadn't missed a single bloody step. His movements had been as smooth as his rakish smile.

"*Shh.* Close your eyes, Adair."

"A man who closes his eyes is asking to be stabbed in the belly," he muttered.

"Hush," she scolded. "If you overthink the movements, they'll never come natural. Your eyes," she again instructed.

Adair hesitated and then complied. It was surely a mark of her hold over him that she managed to make him abandon so many of the rules of the streets that had guided his existence.

Cleopatra led him through the movements, neatly sidestepping the handful of furniture pieces in the otherwise empty space he'd converted into an office. Adair held himself stiffly erect, training all his efforts on the soft instructions she offered up. Her husky voice washed over him, chasing off some of the tension in his frame. Mayhap he'd been wrong about this dancing business, after all, and the fancy toffs had been correct. For there was something so damned appealing in having a woman in one's arms like this. *Nay, you wouldn't feel that way about any woman. It's this one.*

He immediately stomped her left foot.

His eyes shot open in time for him to detect Cleopatra's wince.

"Oi'm rubbish at this," he rasped, slipping into his Cockney.

Cleopatra squeezed his hands. "Eyes *closed.*"

Then she began to sing. Hers was never a voice that would be considered flawless by society's standards. It was slightly too low, and even more discordant. But there was a sultry realness to her contralto, and it only pulled him deeper and deeper into her hold.

As I was a walking down Paradise Street
A pretty young damsel I chanced for to meet.

She was round in the counter and bluff in the bow,
So I took in all sail and cried, "Way enough now."

I hailed her in English, she answered me clear,
"I'm from the Black Arrow bound to the
Shakespeare."

So I tailed her my flipper and took her in tow
And yardarm to yardarm away we did go.

But as we were going she said unto me
There's a spanking full-rigger just ready for sea.

"You sing that one often," he observed.

This time, Cleopatra faltered, missing a step. Adair quickly caught her against him. Righting her, he brought them gliding back into steps of the waltz.

"*That* has nothing to do with your waltz lesson," she said gruffly, fixing all her attentions on his shirtfront.

He caught her foot again under his, but instead of drawing back in humiliation and ending the set as he'd attempted to earlier, he continued waltzing her sloppily about his makeshift office. "No," he acknowledged. "It has to do with you." And he wanted to know because of it.

"Not much to say." The pain in her tone said enough for her. "Diggory had one of his wives"—it was what he'd called the women he bedded and gotten his brats on—"care for me and my sisters. She used to sing it." There was an air of finality that discouraged further probing.

And a little more than three weeks ago, he would have contentedly left her to her secrets and her past. A person didn't ask those personal questions, but she'd cracked the door open, and he *wanted* to walk through.

"What happened to her?"

Cleopatra abruptly stopped. "Doesn't matter," she said impatiently, taking a step out of his arms.

Settling his hands about her shoulders, Adair brought her back around. "I don't believe that." He passed somber eyes over her face.

Her skin white and her eyes ravaged, she wore her pain like a physical mark. "Oi don't talk about it."

"And I don't waltz."

Cleopatra chewed at her plump lower lip. "Fair enough." And yet, still, she said nothing.

Adair didn't press her; he allowed her the time she needed, more than half-afraid that should she not speak on her own terms, she wouldn't speak at all. "She cared for us, but not the way Diggory's other women did. Joan cleaned our scrapes when we fell, or sang us songs when we had night terrors."

What hellish dreams must have come to her as a child. Himself having survived Diggory's cruelty and having also witnessed firsthand the suffering his siblings endured, he had an idea of what her childhood must have been like. His heart ached.

Absently, Cleopatra skimmed her fingertips over the top of his recent notes from Phippen. The tension in her slender frame, however, countered all show of calm. "Then Joan made an unforgivable mistake."

Do not ask . . . Having found himself on the edge of death too many times because of cruelty exacted by Mac Diggory, he didn't want to know that unforgivable mistake. "What was it?" he asked, his voice hoarse.

"She wanted to name us. Fought Diggory on it. Said we deserved names. Said she was giving them to us whether he liked it or not." Cleopatra glanced up from his desk and offered him a chillingly empty smile. One that had no place on her lips. One that he wanted to erase from her face and instead fill her life with laughter that dulled all the darkest memories she carried.

Then her words registered. He shook his head. What . . . ?

"For many years of my life, I was simply *Girl*." Cleopatra traced the *D* upon her palm. "My sister Ophelia was *Stupid*, and Gertrude was *Twit*." A mirthless laugh bubbled in her throat but never made it past her lips. "I went through those years of my life believing my name was Girl."

Oh, God. Her profession briefly weighted his eyes closed. Dead. He wanted to kill Mac Diggory all over again, only this time with his bare hands, and not the mercifully quick bullet his sister, Helena, had put in the bastard's belly. "What did Diggory do to Joan?" he asked quietly. "After she'd wanted to give you a name?" The most basic gift passed down to a babe to begin their place in the world, and she'd been robbed of it until a stranger to whom Diggory had turned her care over stood up to fight for her.

Cleopatra drew in a slow, noisy breath through her teeth, then let it out. "'e set fire to our apartments. Diggory told me to choose."

Horror turned his blood to ice in his veins.

"Someone always pays the price for lines being crossed," she said in an eerie echo of orders that had been hurled at Adair himself by that same monster. "Oi 'ad to choose my sisters' burning room . . . or Joan's." She took her skirts in a deathlike grip, draining all the blood from her knuckles. "Oi chose my sisters."

"Oh, Cleopatra," he said on an agonized whisper. He wanted to take her pain, make it his own, and fill her life with the happiness she deserved. He'd spent years hating her, but she, in having no choice but to remain under Diggory's control, had endured far more than Adair or his siblings.

She waved her scarred palm about in a stiff gesture. "Oi did what I had to do."

"I know that." He paused. "Do you?"

Growling, she jerked her chin up. "Didn't I just say I did," she barked, sounding like a wounded pup he'd come upon outside the Hell and Sin once.

"No. You said you chose your sisters." He continued with the same calm he'd affected for that fractious dog. Had she ever made peace with the sacrifice she'd been forced to make? But then, did any of them?

A sheen of tears filled her brown eyes, those crystalline drops made all the brighter by her lenses. It was the first time he'd ever seen her cry. With an agonized groan, he pulled her into his arms.

She held herself with such tautness, a sharp wind could have snapped her slender frame. Tightening his hold upon her, Adair lowered his cheek atop the crown of her head.

When she spoke, her words emerged muffled against his chest. "She told me Oi needed to save them. *She* made the choice."

And yet, Cleopatra had claimed ownership of a decision that hadn't really been a decision, taking on the guilt of it. "Oi wish we'd been kept together," he said roughly. "Oi wish that Oi'd been part of the same end of London as you and your sisters." For how her life would have turned out differently. She and her sisters would have become part of his family, and she'd not have relied upon a merciless monster.

Cleopatra stepped out of his arms, and he fought the need to draw her back, close. "That could 'ave never been, and it could 'ave never worked," she said in deadened tones. She blinked in rapid succession and then looked up, her thick brown lashes shielding her thoughts from him . . . but not before he caught the flash of regret. As soon as that emotion flickered to life, however, it was gone. She jutted her jaw out. "After she . . . was gone, *I* took over caring for me and my family—until Broderick."

"And you've been taking care of them ever since." Did she realize she'd taken on the mantle of responsibility to assuage a guilt that would always be with her?

"I haven't done it alone," she said defensively.

Reality intruded. "Killoran." How easy it was whenever she was near to forget who her brother, in fact, was. To set aside all the enmity between their families and just . . . be two people who enjoyed being together.

"My brother," she corrected. God, how he abhorred her connection to that vile bastard, and how he resented her injecting him here. "He's a good man."

He met that with a mutinous silence. Adair knew precisely who Broderick Killoran was.

Cleopatra carried on in more wistful tones than he ever remembered her using. "He joined Diggory's gang when he was orphaned. He was educated, a scholar who knew books. Knew math and poetry and Greek mythology and how to dance and . . ." She scrunched her mouth up. "He knew a lot." She grinned wryly. "Growing up on the streets, he knows even more now."

Surprise filled him. Her revelation was the most he or his siblings had ever gleaned about the enigmatic proprietor. And the puzzle that had eluded him all these years now slid into place. Why, it all made sense. Broderick Killoran had offered Diggory the one thing none of his lesser-born street thugs could—a bookish mind.

"So that is how Diggory managed to keep books and handle a business," he said to himself.

Cleopatra nodded once. "Broderick had power over Diggory. My brother demanded he have the right to keep us safe. After Diggory realized how powerful my brother in fact was, he never laid hands on me or my sisters ever again."

How was it possible to find himself so very indebted to Broderick Killoran? His gaze slid to the scarred flesh—that letter *D* left upon her palm by a monster. A cinch squeezed off airflow to his lungs. She'd known so much suffering. Feeling her stare on him, he forced himself to say something. Cleopatra would interpret any admiration or warmth as pitying. "It's why neither me nor Ryker nor Calum had ever been of true value to him." And Diggory had been too small a man to see Helena's skill with numbers.

"Diggory's bounties all went to the Devil's Den, but it was Broderick who built it into what it is and allowed me to become who I did inside our world."

A woman of courage, strength, and influence, who with her business acumen where gaming hell business was concerned, could rival Adair and his brothers. He brushed his knuckles over her cheek. "No one made you into the woman you are. You did that all yourself." Her and the experiences that she'd suffered through and emerged triumphant, despite.

She shook her head. "You're wrong there. You see me as Oi am now. Oi wasn't always fearless. Oi didn't speak my mind to Diggory. Oi found my voice when Broderick came 'round."

Adair palmed her cheek. "Oh, Cleopatra. You've never been anything less than a warrior."

Her lips parted, and a whispery sigh wafted out.

Wanting to ease the heartache he saw there and drive back talks of Diggory and Killoran and right or wrong and good or bad, he drew her fingertips to his lips. "My turn, then."

She looked at him quizzically.

"Visit the Hell and Sin with me," he clarified.

It was an act his brother would have his head for if the truth were discovered, but for the first time since his siblings had each wed their respective spouses, Adair understood what it was to want to bring a woman nothing but laughter and happiness.

Her eyes went soft. "When?"

He grinned. "Now."

Chapter 19

There had once been a time when the sole reason Cleopatra would have cared to visit the Hell and Sin Club was to learn its inner workings so she could plot its demise and bring it down.

Forty minutes later, after a carriage ride through the empty London streets, Cleopatra made her way through the dark lanes of St. Giles, filled with an altogether different kind of eagerness to visit the hell. One that stemmed from a desire to step inside Adair's club. That was a world she was wholly comfortable within.

Nay. You want to know everything about Adair Thorne and his world for reasons that have nothing to do with the long-standing rivalry between your clubs.

Adair slipped his hand into hers, and she automatically folded her fingers around his. She stole a sideways glance at him, this man who'd come to mean so very much.

He was the first person whom she'd shared secret parts of herself with, agonizing memories she'd not even revealed to her siblings. *And what will happen when you have to leave him . . . ?*

A dull, knifelike pain stabbed at her chest, but Cleopatra pushed back the grief that came in thoughts of their parting. She would steal whatever time she had left with him.

They reached the end of the street, and he drew his hand back. "Here," he murmured, adjusting the cap he'd given her before they'd left Black's townhouse. He briefly inspected the boy's breeches and dark jacket she'd donned.

"'ow's Oi look, guv'nor?" she teased, dropping a jaunty bow.

Adair lingered his gaze on her hips, and her earlier levity faded. When he lifted his eyes to hers, the heat within their green depths scorched her. "Perfect," he said hoarsely. "You look perfect."

And Cleopatra, who'd never been made to feel anything but the boylike, bespectacled sister of Broderick Killoran, felt beautiful.

"Come," he murmured, setting a slow path along the pavement. They stepped around several drunken sailors snoring in the way. "I've guards stationed at each entrance," he explained.

"If they're worth their weight as guards, they'll wonder why you're here at this hour . . . with a young *boy*, no less."

He scowled, but he was prevented from saying anything more as they reached the steps of the club.

To the two burly guards' credit, they gave no outward reaction to Adair's late-night visit. They did each, however, linger a curious stare on Cleopatra. "Mr. Thorne," they both said in unison.

Adair inclined his head and reached past them to unlock the door. "Anything suspicious?"

"No, Mr. Thorne," the crimson-haired guard supplied. He stole another peek in Cleopatra's direction.

Adair motioned her forward.

As he closed the door behind them, she did a sweep of the spacious, open floors under construction. So this was the Hell and Sin.

Wordlessly, she moved deeper into the establishment, past beams of wood and tables littered with building supplies and materials, taking in the hell. She took every last corner in with her eyes.

Since she'd been a girl she'd heard tales of the rival club. There had been men, desperate lords and underhanded thugs of Diggory's—and her brother's—who'd infiltrated the walls of this once great place and brought back details. Cleopatra had taken in every detail of that hated family, secretly longing for a glimpse herself of how they ran their establishment. Her intrigue had only doubled upon learning of the changes Black, Thorne, and their other brothers had put into place: ending prostitution, hiring women in valuable roles throughout the club.

She picked her way over the charred carpet. All the gaming tables had since been removed, and but for several stubborn pieces of satin wallpaper that hadn't burned or been pulled off in the aftermath, there was little trace of the club she'd heard spoken of.

Sadness filled her breast for all that had been lost . . . for all Adair, who loved this world, had lost. She knew what it was to lose her home to fire, but the place that had burned down about her ears had been dank apartments filled with vermin and lice. She also knew what it was to have found security and shelter inside the Devil's Den and what it would be to lose all of that and begin from scratch.

In an effort to comfort her, Adair took her by the hand and proceeded to guide her about the club, speaking animatedly. "This is where the additional seating you suggested goes," he said, gesturing to the area. "We'll blend whist, faro, and hazard tables on this side." He pointed across the cluttered but open space. "The roulette tables and vingt-et-un will have their own places over there."

"We have a similar layout," she acknowledged. Who would have ever believed she'd be sharing details about her family's establishment with this man before her . . . and what was more, offering guidance to help improve his business. It would only represent greater competition.

Why did none of that seem to matter any longer?

Because you love him . . . and that is so much greater than the profits earned or the patrons fought over.

Adair continued speaking with a boyish enthusiasm that only made her feel all the more miserable. *I want him to be the bearish, angry man who confiscated my blade.*

She allowed him to tug her to the back of the hell. "These are the private game rooms you suggested," he said as she stepped inside.

This space, largely complete, bore no hint of the chaos of the previous part of the establishment. Sapphire-blue satin wallpaper had been affixed to the walls. Rich mahogany gaming tables were set a distance apart, allowing for privacy. With the matching mahogany bar and crystal chandelier, the elegant rooms were befitting a White's or Brooke's, and not the seedy establishments owned by their respective families.

"Well?"

She turned back, and at the bright grin on his face, she hesitated. "It is lovely."

His smile slipped. "You disapprove." How much he'd come to know her that he'd sensed that reluctance on her part.

Cleopatra clasped her hands before her. "It's not that I *disapprove.*"

Adair looked pointedly at her hands.

Damning that telling gesture, she let her arms drop. "You need to figure out what you want," she said bluntly, giving him the truth he sought. "I already told you before, Adair," she went on before he could speak. "You don't know what it is you want. You don't know if you want to be a seedy hell or a fancy club in the posh ends of London."

Splotches of red suffused his cheeks. "The 'ell and Sin *is* a seedy hell."

"Why?" she shot back. "Because you were born in the streets? You rose up." They both had. "And yet, you're now stranded between two worlds." Cleopatra caught his hands in hers and gave a light, reassuring squeeze. "It's time to pick one."

Horror rounded out his eyes. "What are you suggesting?" he demanded, his voice graveled like an old Roman road.

She retained his hands when he made to pull them back, tightening her grip. "You've spent weeks on the rebuild and redesign. You're constantly revising ideas—"

"Because you made suggestions that I hadn't considered," he bit out.

"Because you don't want to make this the place where your club is forever established," she predicted. "You, just like your brothers and sister, want out of St. Giles."

Adair ripped his arms back and held them up as if he'd been burned.

"There's nothing wrong with that," she said gently, drifting closer. "You spent your life believing certain things to be fact: your place was in St. Giles, my family is evil, you could only run a scandalous club." She tilted her head back so she could meet his gaze. "Not everything is as it always seems. It—"

Adair swallowed her words with his lips.

She stilled, and then she wrapped her arms about his neck and drew herself closer to the hard wall of his chest.

His tongue stroked between her lips over and over until she melted against him, a molten puddle of uselessness. "Are you . . . doing this to silence me?" she managed to gasp out between his bold, erotic kisses.

"Would you care if I did?" he breathed against the place where her pulse throbbed at her neck. He nipped and sucked at that sensitive flesh.

Moaning, she arched her head so he could better avail himself of her flesh. "I w-wouldn't b-be pleased . . ." She struggled to get the words out, clutching her fingers in his lush brown hair and holding him close. "I d-don't like to be—" He slipped free the laces at the top of her chest, and the fabric fell open, exposing her skin to the cool night air. Lowering his head, he caught a nipple between his lips. She hissed out a breath as he laved the tender bud, suckling it. "I—I confess," she cried out softly, dropping her head back. "I—I've quite f-forgotten what I was . . ." He flicked his tongue back and forth over the swollen tip and then turned his attentions over to her other, neglected breast. "Adair," she pleaded.

He caught her up, and then scooping her in his arms, he carried her over to the leather button sofa at the center of the room. Pausing, he stooped over her, his hands on the edges of his shirt. His chest moved with the force of one who'd raced across London and back. She dipped her eyes lower, to the muscular expanse of his oaklike thighs . . . and at the apex where his shaft tented the fabric of those dark garments.

"Look at me, Cleopatra."

All the air left her.

He stared at her, his eyes hot with hungering. *For me . . . he desires me.* And she marveled that a man such as Adair Thorne, a model of male perfection, wanted her.

"I want to make love to you," he said. His voice was husky and low, and it heightened the growing need to have him back in her arms.

She smiled slowly, and then never taking her gaze from his, with steady fingers Cleopatra lifted the shirt over her head and tossed it to the wood floor. The white lawn fabric landed in a noiseless heap.

Adair's Adam's apple worked up and down, and he stretched out a reverent hand, palming her left breast. He tweaked the sensitive tip, bringing her eyes briefly closed. She bit the inside of her cheek when he again stopped. But then, he began working her breeches down over her waist, sliding them past her hips.

Unabashed, she kicked them away and stood before him naked.

"You are so beautiful," he breathed hoarsely.

His compliment fueled her, and going up on tiptoe, she pressed herself against his chest. Gripping his nape, she forced his head down for her kiss, mating her mouth with his. All these years she'd scoffed at the women inside the Devil's Den who'd excitedly whispered about sex. Only now, with Adair's strong, callused palms roving a path along her buttocks and cupping that supple flesh, did she understand what compelled so many of those women. There was no shame or regret. There was just a burning heat that seared her from the inside. Guiding her down onto the sofa, Adair came over her and laid claim to her mouth once more. They dueled with their tongues, thrusting and parrying. Their breath came melded as one in a ragged, desperate rhythm.

He slipped a hand between her legs, finding the thatch of curls there. She went taut at the intimacy of his touch, and then a shuddery gasp burst from her lips as he parted her folds to caress the slick nub there. Of their own volition, Cleopatra's hips lifted, arching higher as yearning drove back all reservations, and she was capable of nothing else but feeling. She clamped down hard on her lower lip as he slid a finger inside and began to stroke her. In and out. Over and over until Cleopatra was reduced to incoherency. "Adair," she keened his name, and it became a litany. A pressure continued to build at her aching center, and he slipped another long digit inside. She increased the frantic gyrating of her hips.

And then he stopped.

She cried out and stretched her arms up to drag him back to her.

But he only stood, and with stiff, frantic movements, stripped his shirt overhead, then tossed it aside. Her mouth went dry, and she roved her gaze over his heavily muscled chest, lightly matted with tight coils of dark curls and marked with jagged scars. He epitomized a warrior's beauty.

Adair tugged free first one boot, then the other, letting them fall beside him. He moved his hands to his waist and then slowly shoved the dark breeches off.

Her whispery gasp was lost in the noisy rustle of the garment hitting the floor. She stared on in wonder. His thick, tall manhood jutted proudly toward his flat belly. It throbbed under her scrutiny. Wordlessly, she reached her hand out and lightly folded him in her fingers.

A sound better suited a wounded bear ripped from Adair's throat, and she paused, looking up. "Oi'm sorry," she said, instantly lightening her grip. She'd kneed, kicked, punched, and grabbed enough assailants in that very region over the years to know it was given to pain.

"No," he rasped, guiding her back to his length.

She hesitated. "Oi didn't hurt you?"

"Only in the best possible way," he squeezed out between clenched teeth.

Cleopatra explored him tentatively at first, and emboldened by his groan, she deepened her strokes. He was like heated steel in her hand.

"Stop," he entreated, staying her movements.

She looked questioningly up at him, but he immediately shifted over her, taking her mouth again in a kiss. They tangled with their tongues in a primitive dance that increased the sharp ache at her core until incoherent pleas were falling from her lips.

She dimly registered Adair settling between her thighs, and she let her legs fall wider. His shaft pressed hard and thick against her damp curls.

"Please," she begged, not knowing what she pleaded for, only knowing he could assuage the ache at her center.

He responded by palming her there. Biting her lower lip as the desperate hunger built, she looked at him wildly. All these years, she'd believed this act was a dirty one that stripped a woman of pride and strength. Only to be set gloriously free, under the power of his touch. "I need . . . more," she breathed, reveling in that new freedom, abandoning everything she'd erroneously believed as a woman. There was no shame in this. Only wonder.

He slipped two fingers inside her sopping channel, slowly torturing her with his ministrations.

An incoherent plea spilled past her lips. "Please," she moaned. She had no pride where this man was concerned. He entered her slowly, inch by agonizing inch, stretching the tight virginal walls.

The chiseled planes of his features tightened, and a sheen of sweat formed on his brow. "I've never felt anything like this," he rasped, stopping when his manhood reached the thin flesh she'd preserved in the streets of St. Giles.

For him. I saved myself for this man and only him . . .

"Oi don't want to hurt you," he said in low, guttural tones.

Cleopatra held him close. "I want this," she panted. Before she left him, she needed to know him in this way. Wanted to take every memory of Adair Thorne she could.

He clenched his eyes and pressed forward.

A scream tore from her lips, and Adair instantly covered her mouth with his, swallowing the sound of her pain.

He stilled inside her, going absolutely motionless.

Breaking his kiss, Cleopatra tightened her arms about him. As one who'd been punched, kicked, and burned, she'd thought herself largely immune to pain, only to find she was still human, after all. "That 'urt," she acknowledged in ragged tones.

Adair touched his lips to the corner of her mouth, then trailed a tender path of butterfly-soft kisses to her brow. "Oi'd rather cut myself with my own knife than cause you pain."

She didn't want to think of his suffering. Cleopatra focused on evening her breaths. "Oi'm fine," she finally said.

The ghost of a smile dimpled his cheek, and Adair gently shoved her spectacles back into their proper place. "Cleopatra, are you trying to reassure *me*?"

"Ya look loike you're going to toss the contents of your belly, Thorne. Green like you just—" He reclaimed her lips in a tender joining that rekindled the fluttering inside her belly.

And then he began to move. She held herself stiffly at the slow drag of him. The dull throbbing of pain receded, and in its place was the familiar ache of desire. Their chests moved together with the force of their breaths.

Cleopatra laid her palms on the side of Adair's neck so she could retain his gaze, wanting to see him as he made love to her. He leaned down and caught her mouth. Then the slide of his tongue between her lips matched the pace he'd set for them.

She gasped and lifted her hips, meeting his movements as he filled her again and again. "Yes," she rasped as he dragged her back up to that precipice where she'd hovered before. The pulsing between her legs intensified, so she could focus on nothing but the feel of their bodies joining together.

Adair gripped her hips and stroked her harder. Faster. "Come for me," he urged.

"Yes," she whimpered. "I want . . . I want . . ." Cleopatra went taut, and then he pulled free and thrust home once more. She softly screamed, exploding in a blur of white light.

With a hoarse shout, he came inside her in long, rippling waves. Rapturous shudders racked her body as she took all of him. His chest heaving, Adair collapsed. He caught his weight with his elbows, anchoring them on either side of her head.

Tears pricked behind her lashes as their ragged breaths filtered around the quiet of the room. She tried to speak. "I never felt . . . I didn't know . . . I . . ." Cleopatra struggled to find adequate words to capture what she was feeling—and failed.

Adair kissed the tip of her nose, that gesture so achingly tender, her heart filled all the more with her love for him. "This isn't why I brought you here," he said, a smile in his voice.

In one fluid movement, he rolled her from under him. She gasped as he reversed their bodies' positions and brought her atop him. The crisp curls matting his chest tickled her cheek. Cleopatra struggled herself into a semiupright position and propped her chin on him. "I would not mind if you did," she teased.

He gave her a teasing swat on her backside, eliciting a sharp laugh. "Minx." Adair opened his eyes, and her own dazed, silly smile reflected back in his eyes.

When have I ever been this happy? This trusting? With anyone? Having kept even her own sisters out, she'd believed herself incapable of this closeness with another person.

And he'd despise you if he knew who you really are.

It was the ultimate secret she'd convinced herself Adair didn't need to know because she was only a fleeting presence in his life.

"Why so somber all of a sudden?" he murmured. He stroked a palm over her back in smooth, calming circles that only made her want to cry.

And she didn't cry. I'm not Cleopatra Killoran. I'm . . .

Tears blurred her vision, and she swung herself upright. Reluctantly, she shifted onto the tiny sliver of space at the corner of the sofa, needing some distance between her and Adair . . . and her inherent weakness for him.

From the corner of her eye, she watched him.

He stood, beautiful in his naked splendor, and gathered his garments. Grateful for his diversion, she sought to put together a shattered heart. *Futile. It is futile.* She wanted what she could never have—him. Too much divided them. It had divided them from the moment she'd come squalling into the miserable world that was St. Giles, and it had only grown in time.

Her relief was short-lived. Adair fished a white kerchief out of his jacket and returned to her side. He dropped to his haunches beside her and proceeded to wipe the remnants of his seed and her blood from between her thighs.

Averting her gaze . . . praying he believed it was false modesty, she took the cloth from him and finished the task. She set it down on the floor and jumped up. She winced at the soreness there. Ignoring the discomfort, she scrambled into her garments. At her back, the rustle of clothing indicated Adair went through those same rituals.

After she'd finished, Cleopatra glanced at the opposite wall.

"I'm sorry."

She blinked slowly. Had she uttered that aloud?

"I should not have touched you," Adair said hollowly.

Let him believe that is what compels your silence. Then, there would be no questions. There'd be nothing more than his own guilt. And she'd certainly caused others enough pain and suffering in her existence where a misunderstanding on Adair Thorne's part was the least of her crimes. She pressed her hands to her face. Who would believe she, Cleopatra Killoran, was incapable of that lie?

"I wanted this, Adair," she insisted, turning about to face him.

"You have regrets."

Not for the reasons he believed. Not even about *what* he believed. *Don't be a coward. Tell him.* Mayhap it wouldn't matter.

You're a fool if you believe that.

She needed to tell him. Needed to have it out between them—who she, in fact, was. Cleopatra strolled over to the doorway and looked out at the mess that was the main rooms of his gaming floor. Given their connection to Diggory, Adair was certainly right to have his reservations where she and her family were concerned. She rested her cheek against the smooth doorjamb. "I'm *so sorry.*"

Feeling him beside her, she looked up. He held himself whipcord straight, but revealed nothing.

"About your club." She searched for evidence of the same fury that came with any reminder of the blaze. "We did not do this." She needed him to know that—more . . . to believe it. Just as she needed one thing to not matter to him.

A grimness settled over his features. "That's not why I've brought you here," he murmured, and regret pulled inside that he should still doubt her word and whom her family were as people.

She planted her feet, digging in. "Mayhap it's not. But we'll have the discussion. You don't know the manner of man my brother is."

"I know precisely the type he is," he said flatly, pulling his jacket on. "I've dealt with him and men of his ilk since I was a boy of seven."

The idea that the two men she loved most in this world hated one another as they did gutted her.

"Ya can woipe those thoughts from your head," Cleopatra said tightly. "'e was . . . is the best brother."

"You'd defend a man who'd sell you at the marital altar."

She recoiled. "That is . . . was . . . will be my decision," she said quickly, her words rolling together, as just the mention of marriage sent fear surging through her.

Cleopatra rushed forward, until just a foot of space divided them. "You think he's selling me for a title—"

"I know that's what he's doing."

"But he looked after me. He stood up to Diggory when no one else did to protect my siblings and I." She paused. "He gave me a name and lived to see another day for it."

That revelation brought him up short. "He named you." She didn't know what to make of that halting statement.

Cleopatra nodded. "And he fought Diggory when most others who'd tried, failed," she added as an afterthought. "He called me Cleopatra"—she dared him with her eyes to make light of her name—"and told me I didn't have royal blood in my veins, but I was as fierce and as clever as that queen herself." An Egyptian woman Cleopatra had never even heard of until her brother entered her life with his fancy words and love of books.

"It is a name befitting queens and warriors," he said, almost as if to himself. "It suits you."

Unnerved by that husky acknowledgment, she doffed her spectacles and cleaned the lenses. "He swore that someday we would have connections to kings and lords." She'd laughed at him then. The sheer lunacy to believe street brats like Cleopatra and her sisters would ever be looked at as anything more than women those toffs might one day want to take up against an alley wall.

"And that's so important to him . . . and you?" Heavy recrimination coated that query.

"Security is important," she countered. "After . . ." *Say it. Say her name.* Adair, in opening the window into Cleopatra's past, had given her the strength to do so. "After Joan was killed, Broderick came along," she shared, putting her spectacles back in place. She'd not allowed herself to think of that woman who, when she'd burned to death in that hovel, hadn't been many years older than Cleopatra was now herself.

She walked on wooden legs over to a nearby worktable and stared beyond it. The back of her nape pricked with the feel of Adair's stare upon her. What was it about Adair that made her able to speak about those darkest times in her life? About Joan and her sister being beat into blindness and the agony of fear and . . . She pressed her eyes closed, fighting for a semblance of control. Cleopatra concentrated on drawing in slow, even breaths.

"What happened to Joan," Adair said quietly from just over her shoulder, "was not your fault."

Her breath came all the faster. *Stop talking. Please, stop talking.* She was going to splinter apart with the pain of that past.

Adair rested a strong, reassuring palm upon her right shoulder. "It was an evil that belonged only to Diggory. You're incapable of the evil he forced upon you."

I'm not. Because I have evil pumping in my veins . . . Her throat thickened, and she couldn't get out that truth.

"You've taken over the care of your sisters," Adair continued, "looking after everyone else . . . and never yourself."

The unexpectedness of his words held her frozen. "I want to take care of them," she said belatedly, curling her fingers until the nails dug sharply against the branded *D* on her left palm. She did. Ophelia, Gertrude, and Stephen were her everything. And now, Adair is, too . . . Oh, God.

"You feel you have to take care of them," he challenged, bringing her about to face him. "Because of Joan."

She wrenched away, her heart knocking loudly in her ears. She wanted to stick her fingers in her ears until his words were nothing more than muffled silence. Because he only spoke the truth . . . *You've spent your life after Joan trying to be everything and everyone to your siblings* . . . "You know nothing about it," she rasped.

"I know everything about it," he said bluntly. "We all live with the guilt of what we've done in the streets." He took a step toward her. "But marrying a fancy gent"—*a man you don't love*—"will not ease the pain of what you and Joan lost that night."

Cleopatra skittered a panicky gaze about, but he persisted.

"It will only result in you sacrificing your own happiness for your sisters."

"But that is what you do when you love someone," she cried out. She tossed her hands high. "I had to sacrifice Joan—"

"And now you're sacrificing yourself," he said quietly.

"Why are you doing this?" she implored.

"Because I love you."

The shock of his graveled pronouncement ushered in a blanket of silence. Cleopatra fluttered a hand to her chest. "You . . ."

Adair opened and closed his mouth. He gave his head a slow, befuddled shake. "I love you," he repeated, making that profession all the more real.

He loves you on a lie. That taunting voice whispered around the chambers of her mind. She closed her eyes tight, and Diggory's face was there. His evil smile, pockmarked visage . . .

Cleopatra whirled away from him. "Ya love me," she spat. "Ya don't know anything about me . . ." Whereas Cleopatra knew everything about who this man was. Knew he was good and honorable and that he put thoughts of the women inside his club above profit, sparing them from a life of prostitution.

"I know so much."

She could hear the gentle smile in his voice.

But not the most important part.

"You're fearless and clever and strong and—"

"Diggory was my father."

Adair froze midsentence, his rugged features forming a frozen mask. Was it shock? Horror? Disbelief? Mayhap it was all three etched there?

"What?" he asked, taking a step back.

She followed that slight, but telling, movement, and her heart shattered, falling into a million useless pieces at his feet. *Damn you for loving him. And damn you for caring that it matters to him.* An agonized laugh bubbled in her chest, and she forcibly fought it back. After the terror Diggory had inflicted upon Adair's family, how had she been naive enough to believe it might not matter to Adair? "Diggory was my father," she repeated, watching his features closely. "'e sired me. Gave me life." How many ways could she say it that it might sink into his confused state?

Horror flashed to life in his green eyes. "Your father," he echoed dumbly.

And it was then she had confirmation of what she'd always known. There could never, ever be anything more with Adair. It wouldn't have mattered if there was no need for a nobleman for her. For a great chasm had always and would always exist between them. Her hatred for Mac Diggory burned through her like a cancer, vicious and biting. That mark of hate in itself was testament to her late sire.

And with Adair standing there ashen-faced and silent, Cleopatra did what she'd always done—she fled.

"Cleopatra!" His startled shout stretched across the quiet.

Heart pumping, she flew through the decrepit club, bolting for that doorway.

"Stop," he called out, his voice closer. Then a loud crash, and a thunder of curses.

Not sparing a glance, she raced out the front of the Hell and Sin, past the startled guards, and into the familiar streets of St. Giles—free.

Chapter 20

He'd lost her.

After five hours of searching the streets of St. Giles with the hastily assembled search team at the Hell and Sin, Cleopatra remained gone.

Given her ability to scale a roof and drift through shadows, she could be anywhere.

His stomach turned over itself as his carriage rolled through the fashionable end of London, onward to Ryker and Penelope's residence. At one time, the idea of Cleopatra Killoran out on her own would not have roused even a hint of unease. After all, the whole of London knew the ruthlessness that family was capable of.

Everything had changed. Terror held him firm in its manaclelike grip. And all the worst possibilities of what could happen to her in the dangerous streets of St. Giles wreaked havoc on his mind. Evil men who'd force themselves upon her. Thieves who'd fight her for whatever she carried on her person. His breath rasped loudly in his ears.

Or mayhap she simply returned to her family.

That thought should be the reassuring one that relieved the pressure in his chest.

So, why didn't it? Why did it feel the instant she returned to Killoran was the last he'd ever see her? And then his life would be empty again, when he'd not realized how very lonely it was.

"Because you handled her confession like a bloody arse," he muttered into the carriage. Adair dragged his hands through his hair. He'd said nothing. He'd merely repeated back her words like some bloody lackwit. Shock had held him numb and kept him stupidly silent, keeping him from giving her that which she'd deserved to hear: that her blood did not define her. That the fact that Diggory had sired her did not make her lesser or evil. That in giving her life, she stood as evidence that Diggory had done at least one thing right in his horrid existence.

But I said nothing . . .

Restless, he ripped back the red velvet curtain just as Ryker's residence pulled into focus. Not even waiting for it to rock to a full stop, Adair tossed the door open and leapt out. He shot his arms out to steady himself and then, sprinting past a handsomely dressed couple, took the steps two at a time.

The butler immediately drew the door open.

Not breaking stride, Adair continued abovestairs. He needed a bath, a shave, a change of garments. All of it had to wait. It was secondary compared to her. Everything was. First, he had to find his damned brother, who usually was in the nursery at this—

"Adair!"

That chipper greeting halted his retreat. Reluctantly, he paused halfway up to the main living quarters and glanced back.

His sister-in-law Penelope gathered her skirts and hurried up to meet him. "There you are," she said. "I've been . . ." She sniffed the air. "I've been . . ." She wrinkled her nose. "I've been looking for you." Penelope pressed a hand to her nose. "You need a bath," she blurted.

His neck went hot. "Yes." Running around the streets of St. Giles and through puddles filled with horse shite and the Devil knew what else, would do that to a person's stench.

Penelope motioned for him to continue, and he gave thanks for being spared any company. He needed coffee. Something to clear his head. His relief was short-lived. Penelope hurried to match his stride. "Wilson," his sister-in-law said to the stone-faced footman stationed at the end of the hall.

Nay, he was not truly a footman. He was a guard ordered there by Ryker. A man who now studiously avoided Adair's eyes.

"Yes, my lady?" Wilson trotted over and dropped an ugly bow.

"See a bath is readied for Mr. Thorne."

The younger man rushed to do his mistress's bidding.

"Wilson?" Adair called out, staying his movements. He wanted to settle his rage somewhere, and he had found a perfect target in the man who'd callously insulted Cleopatra.

"Yes, Mr. Thorne?"

"You insulted Miss Killoran." How was Adair's voice this even? How, when panic choked his senses at her absence?

Wilson swallowed loudly. "S-sir?"

"If you so much as utter her name incorrectly, you'll not find employment in a single hell in the whole of London," he said on a steely whisper. "Are we clear?"

An uncharacteristically silent Penelope alternated a wide-eyed stare between them.

The younger man gave a jerky nod. "W-we are, Mr. Thorne."

"Now get out."

Snapping back into movement, Wilson rushed off.

Adair found an unholy delight in the other man's unease. Wilson still didn't know that when the Hell and Sin was rebuilt, he answered only to Adair.

You don't know what it is you want. You don't know if you want to be a seedy hell or a fancy club in the posh ends of London.

Cleopatra's words floated forward, renewing his panic. Politeness be damned, he lengthened his stride, heading toward the nursery.

"You are visiting the nursery," his sister-in-law panted, her smaller legs keeping up. "Quite devoted of you. A wonderful uncle . . ."

He'd hand it to Ryker's wife. The lady was tenacious.

"But before you do," Penelope said, staying him as he reached for the handle of the nursery door, "it is about Cleopatra."

His heart knocked to a painful stop in his chest.

A gasp ripped from Penelope's lips as he took her by the shoulders.

"What is it? Do you know where she is? Has Killoran sent word?" For the first time, he gave thanks for her ruthless brother's quest for a connection to the nobility. The bounder wouldn't quit until she was paired up with a fancy nob.

"Have I seen her?" Penelope repeated back. "She's in the White Parlor."

He immediately snatched his hands from his sister-in-law. "What?" he rasped, relief filling him. "You've seen her?" Relief and annoyance blended together, and he gnashed his teeth. All this time he'd been gripped with fear for her safety, and she'd come . . . here. It had been the last place he'd thought to look for her. "You're certain you've seen her . . . today," he elucidated.

"Seen her? Of course, I've seen her. We had breakfast together and . . ."

While she prattled on, relief weighted his eyes shut.

". . . but I'm not altogether certain about Lord Landon."

That brought Adair snapping back to. "What?"

His sister scrunched her brow. "Are you certain you're all right?" she countered, pressing the back of her hand to his head. "I assumed you were perspiring, but mayhap you're not feeling well?"

Since he'd blurted out his love for Cleopatra Killoran, it certainly felt that way. It left a man unsure of which way was up, down, sideways, or in between. "I'm fine," he said, ducking away from her hand.

"Yes, well. I was seeking you out because . . ." Penelope paused and stole a glance about. Adair bit the inside of his cheek to keep from demanding she spit out whatever she intended to say about Cleopatra. "She has a suitor."

Except that.

He'd rather she not blurt *that* out. He opened his mouth, attempting to form words.

A suitor?

"I know what you are thinking," Penelope whispered.

No, I'll wager what is left of my soul that you have no bloody idea.

"It's incredibly early for a fashionable visit. Quite unfashionable, really."

"Penelope," he said impatiently.

"Oh, yes. Right. Right." His sister-in-law wrung her hands together. "It is Lord Landon."

The expert dancer who'd given Cleopatra her first waltz. A bloody rogue whose smile only hinted at the wicked deeds Adair, as the proprietor of the Hell and Sin, very well knew the man was responsible for. "What about Lord Landon?" he snapped.

"He is . . . the suitor."

The suitor. They were two words that hinted at a distinction of something more . . . between Cleopatra and . . . another man that wasn't Adair. And it didn't matter if it was Lord Landon or the Lord God himself, the seething white-hot jealousy would fill him all the same. A memory trickled in of that elegant bastard as he'd put his hand upon Cleopatra's waist, entirely too damned low, as he'd twirled her about—

He growled.

"That was my fear," Penelope said, misunderstanding the reason for his fury. "I don't tend to accept rumors at mere face value, given my own family's experience with them. But I thought you would have firsthand evidence of whether or not the rumors about the gentleman are, in fact, true."

They were true. The titled lord was in debt, frequented the wicked hells in London, and tossed down the few coins he did have to grow his fortunes. Such a detail had only been viewed as beneficial for how it could increase Adair's own coffers. Now he saw how it made Landon a match for Killoran's intentions.

"Adair?" his sister-in-law asked haltingly.

He gave his head a shake to clear the haze. "What are you telling me this for?" he asked curtly.

Penelope's mouth fell agape. "I . . ." She frowned. "I simply thought after all the time you've spent looking after the young woman that you should have an interest to see that she doesn't end up with a rake. I also thought you should perhaps be the guard stationed outside the room."

Had Ryker's wife hefted a blade from her boot and tossed it at his chest, she could not have cut him more. "Is that wot Oi am? A damned guard to oversee Cleopatra Killoran. 'ave someone else do it."

"Adair?" his sister-in-law called after him.

Ignoring her, knowing he was a bastard for unleashing his temper unfairly on her, he sought out his rooms. He slammed the door hard behind him and then turned the lock with a satisfying click. He shucked his wrinkled and sweaty garments and took a step inside the steaming bath that had been readied. The heat stung his flesh, and he hissed out through his teeth but welcomed the pain because pain posed a distraction from every bloody revelation made by Ryker's wife.

Except . . . what if she *did* desire a man like Landon? Adair froze, one leg partially in the bath. He dragged his hands over his face as he confronted the depth with which she'd come to matter to him. And selfish bastard that he was, born to only care about his own needs and desires, Adair hated the idea of some fancy lord winning her heart—or any man.

A month ago, the only detail of this day that would have commanded his focus and vitriol was the truth of Cleopatra's identity.

I simply thought after all the time you've spent looking after the young woman that you should have an interest to see that she doesn't end up with a rake.

End up with a rake . . . which conjured images of Cleopatra at the end of a church altar with another bloody man who wasn't Adair . . .

Cursing roundly, he slid under the surface of the water, dunking his head. The water muffled his hearing, blotting out sound.

And the bloody rub of it was, despite his wish to forget about Cleopatra—and damn Penelope's request of him to hell—he wanted to be outside that parlor. Needed to be there.

Adair broke the surface and gasped for breath. He shoved his long, sopping strands obscuring his vision back behind his ears. *Fucking Mayfair. Goddamned Ryker for insisting I watch over her.* It was a task that had become a study in self-torture. He hurried to scrub the scent of the London streets from his skin . . . before he took up a post outside the White Parlor where Cleopatra even now was courted by that damned rake, Lord Landon.

Given Broderick's expectations for her, and the need to spare her sisters from sacrificing themselves for the good of the family, Cleopatra should be elated at Lord Landon's visit.

She should be.

And yet, he'd been here in Penelope's parlor for the better part of thirty minutes, and she couldn't manage to drum up a jot of eagerness . . . not even the feigned, pretend sort.

To do so would require her to set aside a lifetime of loathing for people such as the marquess. She might need a fancy toff for a husband, but it didn't mean it erased a history of hatred. As the flash of horror in Adair's eyes had stood testament to.

But then . . . you also hated Adair Thorne and his family. Now you've fallen in love with him, come to call his sister-in-law friend, and learned to respect Adair's siblings.

"You're far quieter than I recall you at the club," Lord Landon murmured. "In fact, I'd always taken you as one to speak freely." He stretched his long legs out before him and hooked them at the ankles. It was a lazy, languid pose that would have shocked a lady. If he sought to elicit a reaction, he'd have to do far better than that.

"Oi speak freely," she said, deliberately adopting her familiar Cockney, "that is, when Oi 'ave something to say and the person merits talking to." *Why do you want to horrify him? Because you don't truly want to marry him . . . or anyone. Other than Adair Thorne.* Her heart spasmed violently.

Lord Landon only grinned. Laying his arms along the sides of his chair, he tapped a distracted beat. "You don't like me very much, do you?" he asked with a bluntness she could appreciate.

Cleopatra lifted one shoulder in a half shrug. "I don't know you."

He scoffed. "Come. I'd wager you know how much I'm in debt for, my drink preferences, the hours I keep, the wom—"

Apparently, for all his rakishness, he'd retained enough of society's expected decorum that he'd let that go unfinished. She shot an eyebrow up. "The women you bed?"

Crimson color splashed upon the marquess's cheeks, and he immediately jerked upright in his chair. Fancy toffs. The rogues, rakes, and scoundrels thought they were so much more dangerous than they were, failing to realize they could never reach the shade of darkness fitting a person born to the streets.

"You're right," she at last said. "I know those details about you. However, that doesn't mean I know anything about you." Not truly. At one time, she'd have believed the size of his purse and the vices he was slave to were all that defined him—or any person. Until Adair.

"And is that important to you?" He clasped his hands at his flat stomach. "Knowing . . . a suitor."

With tousled golden curls, unmarred cheeks, and sapphire eyes, he'd a beauty that any lady would be enthralled by. How much more

Cleopatra preferred Adair's scarred features. "Is that what you are?" she asked instead, with a candidness that earned another grin. Only this smile he donned dimpled his cheek and met his eyes, showing hints of a man, and not an affected rake.

"That is what I am." Lord Landon inclined his head. "I'm in need of a bride."

"Because you're in deep to my brother." Adair would never be a man to sell himself for a fortune. *Unlike you* . . . The truth of that slammed into her. She sat here in blatant condemnation of the marquess for his willingness to do something Cleopatra herself intended.

He abandoned his casual pose. "Because I inherited a bankrupt marquessate."

Another nob would likely have sputtered and quit the room at her insolence. Lord Landon's speaking to her on an equal level raised her opinion of him mightily.

"The gaming tables did not prove the way to reverse your fortune."

His mouth tightened. "They did not. Though I'm generally luckier than I've been this past year."

Cleopatra dropped her elbows upon her knees and leaned closer. "Lord Landon, do you forget I've lived in a gaming hell? One that you frequent nearly nightly."

"Indeed, not." He either failed to note, hear, or care about her sarcastic statement more than anything. "It is, in fact, why I'm here."

"To court me." She forced herself to say those three words as a reminder that there was no certainty or permanency to a mere courtship.

"To marry you." He grinned. "Or rather, to ask you to marry me."

Through her smudged lenses, Cleopatra blinked once. Twice. And then a third time. Surely she'd misheard him. For Cleopatra knew next to nothing about the ways of Polite Society—at least where propriety and decorum were concerned—but she knew enough to know they certainly didn't go about offering marriage after just two meetings.

A twinkle danced in his blue eyes. "I see I've shocked you." His tone hinted at an inordinate delight in that fact.

And for the first time in her existence on this earth, she was remarkably without a cheeky retort. He wanted to . . . marry her. Her toes curled into the soles of her slippers. Nay, not her. He didn't even know her. Mayhap he was merely a bored nobleman, making light of an interloper to the *haute ton*. "*You* want to marry *me*?" she asked warily, studying him closely for hint of teasing.

"I need a bride," he said frankly. He paused. "A wealthy one. And you, by rumors and whispers, are in search of a titled husband."

Her brother's intentions had been that transparent, then. Not for the first time since the plan had been cooked up and Cleopatra thrust into an unfamiliar world, she felt a dangerously building resentment for her brother.

The marquess removed his gloves and beat them together. *Why . . . why . . . he has the look of a bored gent?* "Are the rumors . . . true?" he ventured.

She met that next bold query with silence.

He sighed. "You disapprove of rumors," he went on, stuffing the immaculate white gloves inside his sapphire jacket.

"I disapprove of a bloody nob who'd make light of me." Normally she did. Now she prayed that he was, in fact, just a pompous bored lord, merely toying with her.

"This isn't making fun," he said, his voice carried a new gravity that only increased the terror clamoring in her breast. "What I propose is a . . ." He tapped a finger against his lips. "A . . . business arrangement. If the rumors are in fact true, and you are in need of a titled husband, I am offering myself for that role."

How coldly methodical he made it all sound. It was an arrangement she'd considered and resolved herself to prior to coming to Black's household. Yet to have them laid out so . . . by this man, a stranger she'd only observed at the Devil's Den and who'd met with her only once prior to this, turned her stomach. *I am no different than him* . . . And whether or not she'd agreed to Broderick's plan to help the family, she'd become a whore in her own right.

A floorboard groaned from somewhere in the corridor, and she briefly glanced at the doorway. *Adair.*

He's there. She knew it the way she knew where to put her foot when climbing to keep from plunging to her death. It was an instinctiveness that could not be explained or understood.

"Why would I marry you?" She finally got words out, a question. "Oi don't know you at all."

Lord Landon gave a small shrug. "Ours would be no different than so many other *ton* marriages. You would have your connections to the nobility; I would have the necessary funds to . . ."

Her ears pricked up—but ultimately, when he spoke, he withheld that single revealing detail about his circumstances.

"I would have my finances set to right. I'd, of course, require an heir and the necessary spare."

"Of course," she said drily. Here, all these years she'd believed ruthlessness a trait reserved for the bastards of St. Giles.

"I'd agree to set aside a portion of your dowry so that it remains in your hands forever."

That in itself was a generous offer that said something about the marquess and proved he was not necessarily the heart-hardened nobleman his marriage offer painted him to be, but a man who was desperate, and desperation was something Cleopatra understood. It was an abhorrent emotion she was all too familiar with.

Lord Landon withdrew a watch fob. The gold gleamed brightly in the early-morn sun as he consulted the piece. "I ask that you consider it, Miss Killoran. You'll find I'm not cruel." He may as well have just declared his preference for taking tea. Coming to his feet, he tucked away the watch.

Cleopatra abruptly stood, eager for him to take his leave. "Oi . . . I don't know what to say," she said. That raw honesty would have earned her a beating from Diggory and a lecture from Broderick.

Reaching inside his jacket, the marquess drew his gloves on one at a time. "It is my hope that you'll say yes . . . and relatively soon. I'd hope to have an answer on your decision by the end of the week."

By the end of the week? With his request and the terms he'd laid out, he was precisely what she'd come to Mayfair for—a titled husband, a quick marriage, and then a secure future for her siblings. *It's too quick . . . I don't know him . . . he's a stranger . . .*

But as he'd said, what did it truly matter if her ultimate purpose was a business arrangement? There would never be more between her and any man. Not now when she'd fallen so helplessly and hopelessly in love with Adair.

Her heart buckled. "I . . . I will think on it," she promised.

"Splendid," he said with his roguish charm. It didn't escape her notice that he didn't so much as lift his attention from the gloves he now jammed his long, uncallused fingers into.

"Why me?" she called when he'd taken three steps. "Surely there are ladies of your own station who are wanting of a title and fat in the pockets." *That you needn't come here and put an offer to me.* Cleopatra clamped her lips tight to keep from blurting out those unspoken words.

The marquess wheeled back, that enigmatic grin affixed to his lips. "*That* is why, Miss Killoran. I might be a rake, battling back creditors and fast approaching dun territory, but I'm also a man who appreciates directness and honesty. You're wise with your brother's business and unafraid to go toe-to-toe with some men that even I would be wary of."

He'd been watching her that closely, then, at the Devil's Den. Cleopatra frowned, unsure what to make of that revelation.

"Nor do you cower. As such, I'd take marriage to you over any simpering debutante who converses about the weather and her needlepoint."

Dropping a quick bow that ended all questions, the marquess turned on his heel and left.

Cleopatra stood there after he'd gone. The longcase clock's ticking was inordinately loud in the parlor, and she focused on that overwhelming beat. Never before had she been more relieved with a person's abrupt departure, which given the hell she'd endured in St. Giles and the monsters whose company she'd suffered through in Diggory's gang, was saying a good deal, indeed. He wanted to marry her.

It could be done . . . *would* be done, if she simply agreed to the cool, businesslike terms laid forth by Lord Landon. Marriage had never been anything she'd aspired to. Quite the opposite. She'd learned early on, after Diggory's earliest wives had married him, and then promptly taken their own lives rather than suffer his abuse, that she wanted no part of marriage.

Everything's changed.

Cleopatra's legs weakened, and she sank onto the edge of Penelope's sofa.

"Ya going to pretend ya aren't out there?" she asked into the quiet.

"Depends." Adair's muffled voice came from outside the door Lord Landon had closed on his way out.

She dug her fingertips into her temples and rubbed. "On what?"

"You looking for company?"

Her lower lip quivered, and she blasted herself for that weakness, but Lord help her, she could not stop it. After all he'd learned about her parentage early this morn, she'd simply expected he'd want nothing more to do with her. Instead, he'd stood outside the closed parlor door listening. To what end? Because he'd been instructed to be there? Or because he wanted to be there? "I might be," she said when she trusted herself to speak.

Adair pushed the door open and stepped inside. He did a quick sweep of the room before settling his focus on her.

Cleopatra stood and moved behind the sofa, needing space, fearing what he'd say. In this instance, it was far safer to attend the dreadful offer Lord Landon had made her than the final words she'd offered to Adair earlier today.

He pushed the heavy panel closed and leaned against it, studying her through his thick lashes.

At an impasse, Cleopatra plucked at the satin brocade upholstery. "'e offered me marriage."

"Oi know. Oi 'eard it."

There should be outrage over his listening in on her conversation with the marquess. Instead, she was simply grateful she didn't have to recount the exchange. She tried to make sense of his emotionless tones.

Adair pushed away from the door and strolled over. She silently damned him for being so coolly unaffected. So calm when her nerves were stretched so tight. She was one wrong word from losing control.

He stopped before her and brushed his knuckles over her jaw in a caress so fleeting she might have imagined it were it not for the heat left by his touch. "Wot are ya going to do?"

She jerked her chin up. "Does it matter? Oi marry 'im then my time 'ere is done. The agreement between our families is met and ya don't 'ave to 'ave one of Diggory's whelps underfoot." Her lower lip quivered, and she quickly caught it between her teeth.

Adair's gaze, however, fell to her mouth, taking in that sign of her weakness. Why must he look so closely? "Oi should have said something," he said quietly. "Oi didn't know wot to say because Oi didn't expect it . . ." He grimaced. "About your . . . your . . ."

"Father," she said bluntly, not allowing him to dance around the truth of her origins.

Loathing so strong flashed in his eyes that she took a step back, ravaged by it, hating herself for having come to care so very much about this man's opinion of her. "Diggory was never your father," he said in graveled tones. "'e gave you life, and that was likely the only good thing he ever did in his sorry existence." Adair held her gaze. "An Oi'll always 'ate him for wot he did to me and mine . . ."

Tears clouded her vision. How could she truly expect him to forgive her connection to the beast who'd tortured him? She glanced away, but Adair, with his tender touch, forced her eyes back to his.

"But Cleopatra, Oi hate him as much for what he did to you. You aren't responsible for his crimes. You aren't him."

This from the man who'd been unable to divorce her connection to Broderick Killoran? "But you said . . ."

He made a low sound of protest. "I know what I said," he hastily cut in. "Oi said ya weren't to be trusted. Oi doubted you at every turn. But I was wrong. You've more honor and strength and courage than most people Oi know."

A tear slipped down her cheek. "Why are ya doing this?" she begged, tears hoarsening her voice. "You're supposed to hate me. Tell Black who Oi am and turn me out. End the arrangement between our families."

"Oh, Cleopatra." A heart-wrenching smile curved those hard lips that had explored hers so passionately just hours before. "You still don't know."

She shook her head. "Know what?"

"Oi love ya too damned much to do any of that." His smile died, and with it went all the light in the room. "Don't do it."

Tension coursed through her and jerked her spine erect. "Oi don't—"

"Oi'm being honest with you," he said sharply, capturing her by the shoulders. "Don't you dare pretend ya don't know what Oi'm speaking about." The way he slipped in and out of his Cockney and cultured tones spoke to the thin grasp he had on his composure. "Don't marry him. Ya deserve more, Cleopatra."

She wetted her lips. Did he believe himself to be that more? For he was. And yet in marrying him, she'd be forsaking her siblings. *But if I*

do not take the gift of love for myself, I'm forsaking myself . . . and Adair.
"What are you saying?" she asked softly, needing clarity of what he truly sought.

Adair dropped his brow to hers. "Marry me."

There it was. Her heart tripped several beats. Who knew two words could cause this giddy lightness inside one's soul? She briefly closed her eyes. Taking the gift he held out would mean putting her happiness above her siblings, when the whole of her life, Ophelia, Gertrude, and more recently, Stephen, had been put first. But if she did not do this, she would be forever empty and broken in ways she'd never recover. They would be all right. Each of them. They were strong. Strong enough to set their own course and defy Broderick, just as Cleopatra had. "I—"

Frantic footsteps pounded in the corridor, and then the door crashed open.

Adair instantly shoved her behind him, drawing his weapon.

Ryker Black stood framed in the entrance, his nostrils flared, his cheeks flushed, and fury in his eyes. A moment later he was joined by his brothers Calum and Niall. Their stony-faced expressions stirred unease in even her breast. "The deal," Black said on a steely whisper, "is off."

Adrenaline pumping through his veins at the unexpected intrusion from his brothers, Adair looked at the trio in the doorway.

"What in blazes are you talking about?" he snapped.

A leather folder in hand, Ryker strode forward. "It was her family," he said flatly, jabbing the folio in Cleopatra's direction.

Again demonstrating the braveness that had snagged his heart, Cleopatra moved out from behind him to glower at his brother. "Oi don't know how many times—"

"I've had Bow Street Runners investigating your family and watching my club."

A gasp hissed past Cleopatra's lips.

Fury coursed through him. "Ya 'ad her family investigated and you didn't think to tell me?" This omission was no different from the vital information they'd withheld from him about the future of the Hell and Sin . . . and their family.

"We thought given 'ow . . . close you've become to her that it moight be best to otherwise say nothing," Niall answered with his usual bluntness.

Adair took a lunging step forward, his fingers twitching with the need to bury themselves in the face of Niall . . . and all of them.

Ever the peacemaker, Calum swiftly inserted himself between them. "Enough," he boomed. "The decision about whether or not to include you in discussions on the Killorans matters less than the findings revealed."

Four pairs of eyes went to Cleopatra.

Even with her slight stature, she stood proudly, a veritable soldier capable of defeating one of those great Spartan warriors. "Oi don't know how many times Oi'll have to defend my family against your charges." She jammed her hands on her hips and glowered at Adair's brothers. "We aren't arsonists, and Oi'm not a liar."

It didn't escape Adair's notice that she'd only included herself in that latter statement. It was a detail Ryker wouldn't miss, either. His brother thinned his eyes into narrow slits.

"We found one of your men sneaking around the Hell and Sin."

"*Pfft,*" Cleopatra scoffed. "Doesn't mean anything. Could have been any reason he was there. And you didn't even say who—"

"Brewster," Niall spat.

Killoran's head guard.

Cleopatra faltered. "Oi don't believe it."

"He somehow sneaked past our guards and was discovered inside, Miss Killoran," Calum said gently.

"I still don't believe you. There was another reason he was there." Cleopatra paused, looking to Adair. "Brewster wouldn't. He's too honorable. Tell them my family wouldn't do that."

Except . . . Adair couldn't do that. Because he didn't know them. He looked away, but not before he saw the flash of hurt in her eyes.

"We found a ruby-studded dagger stuck in the wall of the recently completed rooms. You can read it all here, yourself, Miss Killoran," Ryker snapped, hurling the folder at her.

Cleopatra instantly shot her hands out, but it sailed to the hardwood floor with a noisy thwack. The bespectacled spitfire immediately sank to her haunches and recovered the folder. Adair took a step closer to read those damning pages, but she snapped them close, glaring at him like he was the grime under the heel of her boot.

A pang struck sharp in his chest, and he cursed his brothers to hell for springing this upon them. For not allowing him any time to think it through, to read the file . . . to interview Brewster.

Her head bent over the top sheet, Cleopatra's spectacles slid forward, and she angrily shoved them back into place, reading frantically through . . . and then she stopped. It was an imperceptible pause that most would miss, but studying her as closely as he did, he saw it. She knew the truth from whatever was written there. Cleopatra briefly caught his gaze, and a flash of worry turned her brown eyes a shade darker.

Then she looked away, effectively shutting him out.

Her fingers shook slightly as she shut the folder. "It wasn't Brewster," she said in her usual defiance, erecting a barrier between them.

"He's being brought in for an interview now."

All the color bled from Cleopatra's cheeks, leaving her an ashen shade of gray.

"Your belongings are being packed as we speak," Ryker went on with his usual ruthlessness.

"Ya cannot send her away," Adair gritted out, and a sickening dread twisted in his belly.

"I am sending her away," Ryker said tightly. "The terms of our arrangement only existed as long as there was a truce. The truce was off the minute the fire was set." His face set into a hard mask that sent shivers of apprehension skittering along Adair's spine. "I'm having charges brought against Killoran for organizing the plot."

Cleopatra cried out and surged forward. "Ya bastard!" Adair caught her in his arms. She thrashed and flailed wildly. "Ya'd see to put my brother in Newgate? He didn't burn down your damned club."

"His head guard did," Niall called over the fray. "Do ya expect us to believe 'e acted on his own without any interference from his employer?"

"Oi don't care what ya believe, ya miserable rotted cur," she spat.

Out of breath from his attempts to restrain her, Adair adjusted his hold, and all the while his panic spiraled. His brothers would never trust Cleopatra. They'd never see her or know her the way Adair did. What kind of future could they have together with this enmity between their families?

"Let me go," she hissed, and wiggled herself free. Cleopatra bolted to the corner of the room, and his heart lurched painfully. She'd the look of a wounded, fearful animal braced for battle.

"Have you spoken to Killoran?" Adair demanded.

Varying degrees of shock and pity filled the three pairs of accusatory eyes now on him.

Ryker rolled his shoulders. "I'm going shortly. The constable has orders not to make any formal arrests until we speak."

"Bastard," Cleopatra spat again.

Adair held a palm up, silencing her. "I'll not let you turn Cleopatra away without confirmation of an investigation."

"Oi don't want to stay here," Cleopatra said quietly, with a restoration of her usual calm that increased the dread knocking around his insides. There was a resignation there that hinted at her double meaning. She didn't want to be here with him.

Presenting his back to his brothers, Adair strode over to where Cleopatra had taken up position. Careful to angle his body in a way to conceal their exchange, he lowered his brow close to hers. "Don't you dare quit on me because this is hard," he demanded in hushed tones. "Our families hate one another, but in time—"

"Stop."

He'd expected to see rage reflected behind her round wire-rimmed spectacles. The grief there hit him like a kick to the gut.

"You need to stop them. You need to go protect my brother." Tears shimmered in her eyes. "It wasn't Broderick."

And mayhap it spoke to just how much he'd been ensnared by this woman before him . . . but he believed her.

"You're not leaving." He turned back to his brothers and glared them all into silence, dared them to deny him. "She's not leaving. She'll remain . . . until I return." And then he'd take her from here, a place where she was constantly doubted and questioned . . . and marry her. *That is, if she's willing to take you with all the tumult that comes because of your family . . .* His hands formed reflexive fists.

"I don't see the point in her staying," Niall said, resisting. "Even if it wasn't Killoran, it was Brewster, or"—he glared at Cleopatra—"another in their club. The end result is the same."

"She. Is. Staying," he barked. Dismissing his family once more, he whipped about, prepared to convince her to remain.

"Don't let them take him to Newgate," she pleaded.

The evidence of her suffering, begging like one stripped of her pride, ran ragged across his heart. "I won't," he vowed. "I'll return." And when he did, he'd convince her that their love was enough to overcome even the age-old feud between their families. He lingered, wanting to have that talk now. "I love you," he mouthed.

Her throat moved spasmodically. "I know," she whispered.

He gave her a pointed look, and a half sob burst from her lips. She touched her fingers in a quick, bold caress over his scarred cheek. "I love you, too."

My God. My family is guilty.

Just not in the way Adair's family believed.

Having suffered through the eternal stretch of time since Adair and his brothers took themselves off to meet Broderick, Cleopatra had changed her attire and bided her time.

Now, cap low on her head and with garments pilfered from one of the servants, Cleopatra wound her way through the Mayfair alleys, keeping close to the servants' entrances and away from the now busy streets.

With every step, the nausea churned all the more in her belly. *I'm going to vomit . . .*

Mayhap she was wrong. Mayhap she'd merely read the file incorrectly, or mayhap the erroneous information had been reported. Or mayhap she was the naive one . . . and Adair and his brothers had been proven the correct ones, after all.

Her throat constricted, and she rasped for breath around that tightening. Stepping out at the end of Haymarket Street, she hailed a hack. The driver, in tattered garments, eyed her.

She hurled a sovereign at him. "There'll be more," she said in the low, gravelly tones she'd learned to use early on.

Pocketing the coin, the young man scrambled back into his seat.

Cleopatra climbed inside and pulled the door closed quickly.

And as the carriage rattled onward to the seedy streets of St. Giles, Cleopatra Killoran, who'd believed God had quit the likes of her long, long ago . . . prayed.

Please, let me be wrong. Please, let me be in time. Please, just please, let it all go back to the easy, happy times I've known these past weeks with Adair.

But the same way intuition had saved her and her siblings more times than a person ought to be saved, she knew. Whereas Adair—he'd still retained enough goodness in him that he'd trusted what was before his eyes. She'd asked him to go to Broderick, and he'd never given a thought as to why she'd not join him. And for that, she was grateful.

Cleopatra peeked out the faded velvet curtain, watching, waiting, waiting—

She shot a hand up and rapped hard on the ceiling.

The carriage came to a jarring halt. With a grunt, Cleopatra caught herself hard against the side; her cheek slammed against the window. Hurriedly righting her cap and spectacles, she pushed the door open. "Wait," she ordered, tossing back another coin.

The streets of St. Giles never slept. They were bustling during the day and noisy at night. If one wanted to escape notice, there was always a crush of bodies or constant activity to provide cover. Still, Cleopatra wished it were nightfall. Hunching her shoulders, Cleopatra darted around passing carriages. She reached the edge of the pavement and ducked down the alley between a vacant building . . . and the Hell and Sin.

Construction workers rushed back and forth with enormous beams of wood. The echo of a hammer's rhythmic bang hinted at the important work being done inside.

Cleopatra squinted, measuring the slight distance between the roofs of the bakery, the building owned by Adair and his family . . . and the Hell and Sin. Unleashing a stream of inventive curses in her mind, she darted down the dank, dark thoroughfare until she'd reached the back door of the bakery. Silently, letting herself in through a crack in the door, she slipped inside. Using the boisterous shouts of the proprietor from deep within the shop and the giggles and loud discourse of the staff, busy at work, to her benefit, Cleopatra crept through the room. A short while later, having taken the stairs quickly and quietly, she found herself at the top of the roof.

She briefly eyed the distance between her and the ground, and her heart dropped. Had she truly once found this thrilling? *I never saw anything past what sent me up here.* How right he'd been.

She'd ascribed beauty to her rooftop climbs. Yet, when she'd been above the London streets, she'd been . . . alone, stealing solitary moments in a dark world. It was a testament to how empty her life had been before Adair. He'd filled her days with more happiness than she'd known in the whole of her existence. And after all her family had done, there could never be anything more between them. Her throat convulsed. But she could still save his club, and perhaps that would be gift enough that he might remember her fondly after she'd gone.

Reminded of her purpose, Cleopatra took a small running start and then leapt across the three-foot gap between the buildings. Her heart sped up and climbed into her throat all at the same time, as it always did when she went jumping between roofs. Her feet danced wildly in the air in a stretch of time that was surely only a handful of seconds but always felt eternal.

She landed on her feet in a crouching position. Panting from her efforts, Cleopatra got onto all fours and crawled over to the edge of the stucco establishment. A sea of workers oversaw their tasks below. Only a bloody fool out of his damned head would ever declare open war with a potential sea of witnesses about.

A fool . . . or a lackwit . . . or . . . a child.

She bit down hard on her lower lip.

Recalled to her purpose, Cleopatra took her next jump across without hesitation. Windows ajar and the building still structurally damaged, there were plenty of entryways for Cleopatra to make her way through. She quickly lowered herself down the edge of the building and swung her legs into the nearest open window.

As soon as her feet collided with the floor, she froze. Her heart pounded as she waited for someone to storm the room and cart her off to Newgate for being found lurking here.

However, the cacophony of noise from within muted even the sounds of her heavy breathing. Cleopatra did a quick sweep of the servants' quarters. Stained with soot and still stinking of smoke, these rooms had been largely untouched. And yet . . . they, too, would need to be fully gutted and restored.

You don't know if it was him . . . you're going on nothing more than a report obtained by Ryker Black and his family. Such a detail would have blinded her to all logic before. No more. Although Adair's brother had proven mistrustful of her and her kin at every turn, he'd still never revealed himself to be anything but honorable . . . and thorough. Whereas Cleopatra had blindly believed and trusted that her kin were incapable of true evil . . . that her family was good. She'd wrongly lectured Adair, and now she would be made a liar in the worst possible way.

She firmed her mouth and hurried from the servants' quarters. Slinking about the Hell and Sin like the common street thief she'd once been, Cleopatra did a swift inventory of the rooms on the highest floor, then paused. Rubbing her mouth, she looked about. "Black's office," she whispered. Of course.

Springing into movement, Cleopatra found the servants' stairways and descended to the next floor. But for some soot, the satin wallpaper was largely untouched. And though the acrid odor of smoke lingered in the air, the floor might as well have been otherwise unaffected. Still, all of it would need to be replaced. She pressed a hand against her mouth. So much senseless damage. So much loss.

Systematically, she went door by door, passing bedroom after bedroom after parlor, and then a library.

A library. Adair and his family kept a library for their family. Drawn to the room, Cleopatra moved deeper inside to where a walnut console table sat. Atop the marble surface rested a thick leather book. *You have more pressing details to attend to than snooping inside Adair's life here . . .*

And yet . . .

Cleopatra opened the volume filled with rows upon neat rows of names and book titles. She skimmed page after page. "It is a library," she whispered, once again staggered by the depth of the generosity in this family when her own had been so singularly focused on their own wealth and power.

Yes, the Devil's Den had risen, and the Hell and Sin had begun a gradual fall, but how much more good they'd accomplished than Cleopatra's family.

Numb, she set the book down.

Squaring her jaw, she set out to find Ryker Black's office, winding her way through the building.

A muffled crash sounded from the path she'd just taken. A moment later, the pungent aroma of smoke filtered around her senses, holding her frozen, transporting her back to another fire. One that had ended lives and destroyed a home.

I'll not let Adair lose another part of this club. Familial relationship be damned, she'd not let her brother destroy this hell or perpetuate a feud. Fighting back the fear that gripped her, she raced toward the noise and burning smell. *Where is he . . . ? Where is he . . . ?* Cleopatra skidded to a stop outside—the library. *No.*

With all the papers and pages, it was the perfect room to set ablaze if one wanted to destroy a home by fire. Cleopatra pushed the door open, and a wave of heat hit her, sucking the breath from her lungs. Crimson flames already licked at the edges of leather volumes, and hissing and popping embers were spreading quickly along the shelving.

What have you done?

Coughing, Cleopatra frantically eyed the beloved space. There was no way she could stop this. She waved her hand, warding off the thick smoke billowing about . . .

Another loud thump echoed behind her.

She looked back, and her heart crumpled to her toes as fire engulfed the room.

Heat scorching her skin, Cleopatra did a frantic sweep of the brilliant conflagration set.

Terror licking at the corners of her mind and spiraling through her, Cleopatra buried her face in her elbow. She squinted, struggling to see past the thick haze of smoke blanketing the room. Gasping for proper breath, she frantically searched around. Weren't there any bloody windows in this place? Rushing back into the smoke-clogged hall, she did another sweep. Flames had already consumed the opposite end of the corridor. Fear mobilizing her, she rushed down the lone corridor not yet consumed.

A blast of cool, clean air slapped her face, and she sucked in great, heaving breaths full. Cleopatra struggled toward that blessed window, giving thanks. And her heart promptly fell.

The tiny sill was designed at best for a child pickpocket, and not much more. Hanging out the window, she peered up past the flames spilling from the window below, just as a small body hefted himself up onto the roof. "Stephen," she cried hoarsely. *Damn you. Damn you for doing this.*

A moment later, a familiar head of tousled golden hair appeared. Her brother shook his head, befuddlement stamped on his child's features . . . and then terror. "C-Cleopatra? Why . . . why . . . ?"

She closed her eyes.

I'm trapped . . .

Chapter 21

They'd come full circle.

It was another meeting between two embittered, long-fighting gangs whose history of hatred for one another went back to their tender years. For all intents and purposes, the tense silence hovering in the air may as well have been a re-creation of the meeting four weeks earlier—when Cleopatra had first entered his life.

And nothing had been the same since.

Nor do I want to go back to the bitter, angry person I'd been.

Cleopatra had changed him. Adair, who'd been wary of all, wanted her in his life, as his partner. He, who'd thought himself so very content with his purposeful existence.

He slid his gaze around Broderick Killoran's office: pistols brandished and bodies tense, his family still remained as jaded as they'd always been. Blinded by their hatred and resentment, they would hold Cleopatra responsible for the crimes of her father.

I have to make this right . . . There has to be a mistake . . .

He froze. "It doesn't make sense, Ryker," Adair said from the corner of his mouth, in barely audible tones. With her emphatic defense,

Cleopatra had surely realized as much. It had been why she'd sent him here.

Calum, with his long-heightened sense of hearing, gave him a dark, silencing look.

Ignoring it, Adair moved closer to Ryker.

One of the burly guards behind Killoran's desk alternated his pistol between them. "Not another step," the man barked.

In reply, Niall brought his pistol up, leveling it at the guard nearest him.

"Think about it," Adair whispered, unfazed by the weapon pointed at his chest. "Killoran would have to be a bloody fool to not at the very least wait until the terms of the truce were met." Cleopatra's marriage. "Why would he act now?" he continued through flat lips.

Ryker flexed his jaw. "I don't know," he said grudgingly. "Perhaps it's a mark of his arrogance."

Adair shook his head. "He values his power and prestige above all. He'd not jeopardize that by harming either our club or family—"

"He's already harmed our club," Ryker put in.

"—before Cleopatra marries."

His brother frowned.

"You know I'm right," Adair pressed.

"You two over there. Quiet," the taller guard in the corner of the room barked.

The door opened, and Killoran swept inside. "Black," he called out. "Thorne, Dabney, Marksman. Always a *pleasure*." He moved the way a king might at court, among his lesser subjects. Not breaking stride, he lifted his right hand up. His three guards, without hesitation, sheathed their weapons and filed to the corner of the room.

Adair followed their practiced movements better suited to soldiers and found a grudging respect for that complete control of his men and their routine.

Cleopatra's brother perched his hip on the corner of his desk. "Black. I trust all is well with my sister?"

It was the first question put to them . . . not about their arrangement or business or any of the thousand other contentions between them . . . but his sister, Cleopatra.

Ryker grinned a coldly dark grin, devoid of humor and full of threat.

Adair took a step forward. "Cleopatra is fine," he said quietly.

Killoran swung his focus over to him, his keen gaze saying he'd seen more than Adair intended with that assurance. Straightening, Cleopatra's brother strolled to the sideboard and poured himself a tall snifter of brandy. "You had better hope she is, Thorne." He paused, setting the decanter down. "For if she's not," he went on when he'd turned back, "I'll off you all." He followed that threat with a toast.

"Another threat," Niall snarled, taking a lunging step forward. "After what you've done, Oi expect nothing more from the likes of you and your people."

One of Killoran's men matched his steps, but the head proprietor lifted another hand, gesturing his guard back into place.

"Oh?" Killoran grinned over the rim of his glass. "And what am I have rumored to have done—"

Ryker tossed the leather folio into the center of the room. It landed with a soft *thwack* on the Aubusson carpet.

His earlier bravado flagged, and Killoran hesitated.

"We know everything," his brother growled. "We found your man lurking at the club. Next time, you'd be wise not to leave a Diggory calling card."

Adair studied Cleopatra's brother closely. One could always tell much about a person's guilt by their reaction . . . or nonreaction . . . to a heated charge. Confusion darkened the rival proprietor's eyes. He glanced over to Adair and quickly concealed that show. "Rather cryptic of you," Cleopatra's brother drawled. "I wouldn't have taken you or your brothers as ones given to theatrics." Glass in hand, Broderick strolled over and retrieved the folder. Returning to his desk, he offered his back to the assembled guests.

It was just another telltale indication of the other man's origins—ones that Cleopatra had revealed. The rustle of page after page being turned crowded out the silence of the room. Killoran's shoulders went taut, and his upper arm muscles strained the fabric of his jacket.

"Brewster was discovered inside the club."

"I see that," Killoran said evenly as he closed up the folder and turned it over.

"He's going to Newgate," Niall called out. "For arson and attempted murder, Killoran."

The color bled from his face.

"And we're having you investigated for plotting the fire," Calum murmured, his calming soberness a marked juxtaposition of Niall's hardheadedness.

"You're making a mistake." To Killoran's credit, he responded dismissively to threats against himself. He set the folder down on the edge of his desk. "Brewster had no part in anything."

"Then you—"

"If I wanted to destroy your club, Black, it would have been in ashes long before now," Cleopatra's brother impatiently cut in, his words an echo of her protestations.

In the first crack of his remarkable composure, Killoran dusted a hand over his face. "Outside."

His guards hesitated, then filed from the room. When they'd gone, he leveled his stare on Ryker. "I give you my word that Brewster is not responsible."

"He took the blame for it," Niall retorted.

Stepping past his brother, Adair hung on to the unspoken admission his brother was too blinded by hatred to hear. Words that suggested Killoran knew. "Who is responsible, then?"

Killoran's features screwed up in a pained mask.

"Who is the owner of the dagger?" Adair prodded, and Niall removed the blade in question from his boot, brandishing it for Killoran's inspection. "Who—" He stared unblinking at the glittering tear-shaped stones. His heart beat to a slow halt, then picked up a frantic rhythm.

"Adair?"

Ignoring the worry in Calum's voice, he stalked over to his brother and grabbed the dagger. He turned it over, inspecting the familiar symbol upon that hilt. His stomach dipped. The blade was a replication done in different stones of Cleopatra's. "Whose is this?" he demanded, hoarsely, not truly wanting an answer. For it could only be someone who mattered to Cleopatra.

After she . . . was gone, I took over caring for me and my family . . . And you've been taking care of them ever since.

He briefly closed his eyes. And she'd of course known as soon as she'd read the file. Her quaking fingers and ashen skin had revealed as much. "Whose is it?" he asked thickly.

Killoran gave his head a slight shake, a pleading one.

The door flew open, and a golden-haired child stumbled inside. Unmindful of the pistols turned on him, he tripped over himself in his haste to reach Killoran. "Oi did something bad," he rasped, falling into him.

Killoran caught the boy as he collapsed against him. "Stephen—"

Stephen. Cleopatra's youngest sibling, a brother of nine.

"Not now," he said quietly, with more tenderness than Adair had believed him capable of.

"Y-you d-don't understand," the boy cried as Killoran all but dragged him to the door. "Oi set a fire at the Hell and Sin." Cleopatra's brother stopped in his tracks.

That admission sucked the life from the room.

Stephen yanked his arm from his brother's. "And Cleopatra is inside."

Silence met that pronouncement, and then the room exploded in an incoherent cacophony of noise and sound. Adair stood numb; the boy's frantic admission plunged him into hell. With jerky movements, he rushed over and grabbed the soot-stained child by the shoulders, bringing him up on his tiptoes.

Stephen squeaked.

"Where is she?"

"An office above the mews."

"Calum's office," Ryker said quietly.

Adair quickly released Cleopatra's brother and dragged shaking fingers through his hair. Turning on his heel, he staggered away and then raced from the room.

Cleopatra.

"Adair, wait."

He ignored Calum's shouts and raced through the corridors, past confused guards, and out into the busy gaming hell.

A sob caught in his throat. How damned important it had all seemed. He and his brothers had carried on as though nothing mattered more in the whole bloody world than the rivalry between their club and the Devil's Den. What had any of it mattered? He shoved past the guards at the front and spilled out into the street.

Quickly locating the street lad holding his horse, he bolted over and ripped the reins from his hands. With calls for another promised purse trailing behind, he kicked his mount into a hard gallop.

She'd known.

She'd known it was her youngest brother, and knowing her as Adair did, she'd intended to stop the boy from doing any more damage.

None of it matters, Cleopatra. None of it . . . It could all burn.

All of it could be replaced, rebuilt, and restored . . . but not her— the only person who mattered. The only woman he loved or would ever love.

Time continued in a peculiar pace where it alternated between rolling together in rapidly passing moments and dragging at a never-ending pace. With every cobblestone that brought him closer to his club, the burning sting of smoke grew, until it permeated the air, thick as death. It was the same demon that had destroyed his parents and sister and then crippled his club.

His pulse pounding loud in his ears, he urged Hercules on. The mount whinnied nervously, but the loyal creature galloped ahead.

Adair brought him to a stop three buildings away. Hercules pawed and scratched at the air before settling his feet upon the earth. Adair jumped down, dimly registering one of the builders coming forward to gather the reins.

Oh, God.

Panic clogging his brain, Adair did a circle, scanning the crowds of people lining the streets of St. Giles for just one. One bespectacled spitfire whose life had come to mean more than his own. "Cleopatra," he shouted hoarsely, the conflagration that ravaged the entire front facade of the club muffling that plea. *Good God, where is she . . . ?*

Phippen rushed over. ". . . it's spread to all floors, Mr. Thorne. The fire brigade's been unable to . . ."

Half-mad, Adair stared at the other man's mouth as it moved, unable to put together those words. For one endless moment, he was plunged back into the hell of his past. The scorching heat of the flames destroying his family's bakery, consuming his parents and sister. A tortured moan spilled from his lips as he was reduced to the boy he'd been: helpless, frozen in fear and horror.

". . . no one inside will have ever survived that . . ."

The world whirred back to the present. He gave his head a hard shake. *She is in there.* Adair took several lurching steps toward the burning buildings. He'd not lose her as he'd lost his family.

Two pairs of strong arms immediately dragged him back.

"Let me go, ya rotted bastards," he thundered, wrestling against their hold.

"Ya cannot go in there," Ryker's graveled voice shouted into his ear.

His brothers had arrived.

"If she's in there, she didn't—"

Adair wrenched free and, whipping around, punched his brother in the chin; the force of that blow sent his brother's head whipping back.

"Don't you say it," he rasped. "She is not dead." He'd know it. For if she'd been killed by those flames, his heart would have died along with her. He shoved his way through the throng of builders and onlookers, past the fire brigade—

When a shout went up.

Several strangers pointed.

Adair followed the frantic gesturing to the small figure at the top of the burning hell.

"Cleopatra," he breathed.

Flames licked at the corners of the building, slowly eating away the edges of the roof. Adair tossed his jacket off and, breaking through the crowd, raced to the bakery, as of yet untouched by the conflagration. Blood roared through his veins, fueling him. She'd not perish as his parents had. Not even God himself could take her from him.

She is alive. She is alive. It was a litany inside his mind that drove his every step, until he'd reached the top of bakery. Dragging himself out the window, the thick heat dampened his skin. He cursed, wishing for the first time in the whole of his life that he wore gloves. Swiftly dusting his palms along the sides of his pants, he pulled himself up and onto the rooftop. As soon as his feet found purchase, he went racing. Adair leapt the three feet and came down hard on the next roof. He was up again and running, his heart knocking around his rib cage and his breath coming hard and fast.

Adair skidded to a stop. "Cleopatra," he thundered over the din of the blaze.

Searching the grounds below, she pitched forward slightly.

His heart jumped into his throat.

Cleopatra shot her arms out, steadying herself, and then searched about—ultimately finding him. At the sight of her—cheeks covered in ash, her garments singed, and her brown hair hanging haphazardly about her small shoulders—relief coursed through him.

He cupped his hands around his mouth and shouted. "Come to me." Holding his arms open, Adair urged her on.

Cleopatra limped around the perimeter of the building, stopping only when she was directly across from him. "The f-fire has weakened the roof," she cried, her voice cracking and rough from the smoke.

As if the blaze sought to demonstrate her point, the far-left corner crumpled, and crimson flames jumped high to consume the remnants.

Cleopatra closed her eyes.

"Don't you dare go weak on me now, Cleopatra Killoran," he thundered. Her ghosts were his. He'd not allow either of them to be defeated by fire.

Her throat moved. "I can't," she shouted into the noise.

"You can do—"

Cleopatra angled her body, displaying her leg.

His muscles knotted. *No.*

The large angry-red burn at the juncture where her ankle met her foot would make any movements difficult. *Christ.*

A tear slid down her cheek, and that single expression of her grief and regret ravaged him worse than the fire raging below.

Cursing, Adair charged forward and jumped over the three-foot space dividing them, to Cleopatra's protestations. He caught himself, landing on his haunches, and then straightened. Cleopatra stumbled forward and launched herself into his arms. "You foolish, foolish, man. Why would you do that?" she cried, grabbing his face between her hands. "Why?"

He gathered her soot-stained digits, raising her knuckles to his mouth one at a time. "Do you trust me?" Not awaiting an answer, he scooped her into his arms and, sucking in a fortifying breath, raced forward.

He gasped as his heels collided with the satisfying feel of purchase. The weight of her in his arms sent him pitching forward, and he came down hard on his knees. Adair swiftly rolled onto his back, so Cleopatra lay sprawled over him.

He tightened his hold on Cleopatra, absorbing the slight, reassuring feel of her against him. *Alive. She is alive.*

"You c-came," she whispered, her voice ragged against his ear.

Had she truly believed he wouldn't? That he wouldn't scale whatever building, regardless of height, to have her in his arms?

"Adair!" The frantic shouting from below brought him to.

"Come." He stood, sweeping her into his arms. "This is truly the last roof either of us will ever climb," he vowed.

At his back, the roof of the Hell and Sin dissolved, swallowing the building in a fiery conflagration, and with the only dream he'd allowed himself from the earliest years of his life gone, and the only hope he had for the future in his arms, he made for the edge and the path to safety.

Chapter 22

"You were saved by one of Black's men."

Sprawled in her bed, with her burned leg now treated, bandaged, and propped up, Cleopatra stared at the trio of young women at her bedside.

Reggie jammed an elbow into Ophelia's side.

"*Oomph.* What?" her sister groused. "We were *all* thinking it, and someone really should have said it . . . long before now."

"I believe Cleopatra knows very well who saved her," Gertrude said with her usual pragmatism. "She wasn't unconscious, just . . ." Burned and weak from the smoke inhalation. But she'd always known who'd braved a burning building and saved her. Not one of Black's men. Not a rival, nor a member of Black's gang. Not even her brother, who'd come to the base of the burning Hell and Sin. Rather, Adair Thorne, who'd lost his family to fire and risked that same torturous fate—for her.

And it had been her youngest brother who'd destroyed everything Adair had loved.

Tears filled her eyes. Only it was Stephen, not the brother everyone had believed was guilty.

Ophelia patted her hand. "There is no shame in being saved by a Black. We're just happy you are alive."

Cleopatra blinked slowly. Is that what her sisters believed accounted for her misery? That Cleopatra's hatred was so great that she lay here— *ashamed* for having been rescued by Adair?

As her sisters spoke over one another, she stared blankly back, feeling like an outsider in a foreign world. *That is who I was, too.* Judgmental and guided so much by hatred that she couldn't see they were all defined not by their kin . . . but by who they were on the inside.

Adair had shown her that. That she was so very much more than Diggory.

Cleopatra turned her face away.

And my family repaid that gift by torching that which he loved most.

Removing the spare pair of spectacles she'd donned since hers had been lost, Cleopatra brushed back the tears streaking down her cheeks.

Clearing her throat, Ophelia quietly spoke. "I trust it will not leave too bad a scar."

"Do you know me so little you believe I care about the scars?" Cleopatra cried, that hoarse shout ushering in another wave of thick silence. The puckered, blistered flesh just above her ankle was excruciating by its own right, and stung with the same vicious pain as when Diggory had branded her. And yet . . . her heart crumpled. "There are altogether different types of suffering," she said tiredly.

"Oh, dear. You are. . . *crying.*"

And if she weren't so bloody miserable and hurting inside, she'd have found amusement at the horror wrapped in Ophelia's tone, and the scolding administered once again by Reggie.

"She is entitled to a good cry," Reggie said softly. "She's endured more than most these four weeks."

They of course assumed she'd been silently suffering in Black's residence, and her near death atop a burning building was the cause of her moroseness.

"Oi can't do it." The admission ripped from her still raw throat, and the three women looked at her like she'd descended into the final depth of madness. "Oi can't marry a nob to make Broderick his connections." Odd that it should be easier to speak about her decision than the uncertain fate of her brother. The crime of burning down a nobleman's club would only be met with a fate of Newgate. Of course, given Stephen's treachery against him and his family, there could never, ever be anything more with Adair . . . she still couldn't sell herself in marriage. Not when her heart would only belong to him.

Cleopatra sucked in a shuddery breath through her teeth, grateful that they'd never been a family to pry and probe. Their silence allowed her to gather her thoughts. She lifted her gaze from the floral coverlet and met her sisters' gazes. "Oi thought I could . . ." And then for the first time in the whole of her existence, she uttered words she never before had . . . and certainly never thought to give to her sisters. "But I can't. I cannot marry a nob." Not any gentleman. Not even to save her siblings.

Silence enveloped the room.

"I love him."

Ophelia cocked her head and did a search of the room with her gaze. "Love who?" she blurted, startling a painful laugh from Cleopatra.

She buried her face in her palms. "Adair Thorne."

"*Thorne?* You love one of Black's . . . *oomph.*" Ophelia cursed. "Would you stop hitting me, Reggie?"

"Let your sister talk," Reggie chided.

Biting her lower lip, Cleopatra managed a shaky nod. "I love him." She breathed that aloud inside the Devil's Den, in this room she'd slept in since she'd been a girl, schooled on all the reasons to hate Adair Thorne and his family. "He's a good man. He became my friend." Once she would have cringed at uttering that admission aloud, feeling weak for it. "We talked about everything, and he never sought to change me but solicited my opinion and teased with me and didn't think me silly for wanting to dance—"

"*You* . . . want to dance?" Ophelia squawked. "You, who mocked me for enjoying Monsieur La Frange's lessons, all of a sudden like *oomph* . . . by God, if you jab me one more time, Reggie—"

"And he danced with me," Cleopatra whispered. And he'd made love to her. "And . . ." *I want it all with him. I want to be his wife and partner in every way.* Unable to share those intimate truths with even her sisters, she fell silent. "And it cannot be, any longer."

"Because of Stephen," Gertrude supplied.

She nodded once. Because despite all her assurances to the contrary, her family was responsible for the very crime she'd so adamantly insisted against from the very start. Reggie stuck a kerchief under her nose, and Cleopatra took it and blew her nose noisily into the fabric. "I cannot marry a lord," she looked to her sisters. "Not even for you."

"Is that what you believe?" Gertrude demanded, hurt lending a tremor to her voice. "That we'd ever expect you to sacrifice your happiness . . . for *us*?"

"Happiness," she echoed, a tear escaping from behind her lashes. She furiously swatted at it. There can be no future with Adair in it, and as such, there could be none of the happiness her sister spoke of.

When Gertrude made to speak, Reggie held a hand up. "May I speak to Cleo, alone?"

Gertrude and Ophelia hesitated, then reluctantly made their leave.

"They're listening at the door," Cleopatra whispered as soon as they'd gone.

Reggie settled into the chair beside Cleopatra's bed. "Then we'll have to speak more quietly." She gathered Cleopatra's hands and gave them a firm squeeze. "Your brother, as long as I have known him, has been relentless in whatever goal he's set." A wistful smile hovered on the crimson-haired woman's lips. "If he wanted noblemen as patrons inside of the most dangerous hell in London, he merely decided on a number and that happened." A little laugh bubbled past her lips, clear and bell-like. "I often said he could convince rain to cede control of the English sun over the sky." Her smile dipped as a melancholy darkened her blue-green gaze. "I never knew there was a man such as him."

Frowning, Cleopatra studied the other woman's reaction, truly listening to Reggie. *My God* . . . "You care for him," she blurted.

Crimson color chased away every last freckle on Reggie's face. "What . . . ?" she squawked, slapping a hand to her chest. "No. I . . . you don't . . ." She stammered. "You misunderstand what I was . . . am trying to say. Your brother . . ." Reggie scrunched her mouth up.

Her brother, whom Reggie very clearly had feelings for. Mayhap Cleopatra saw it now because her own heart had been so opened.

"Your brother cannot be deterred in any of his goals," the other woman finally settled for. "He can convince a person to do anything and even get that person to believe they, in fact, were the owner of the decision." She held her gaze. "But he cannot control Gertrude and he cannot control Ophelia." She paused. "And he cannot control you. They will be all right. They'll find love." *Just as I did* . . .

"There cannot be love. Not with . . ." Her lower lip quivered, and she bit it to hide that tremble. "Not with everything that's come."

Reggie smoothed her palm over the top of Cleopatra's head. "There'll always be love. That won't go away simply because of anything that's come to pass or won't or will. You love him," she said simply. "And if he's truly a man who's deserving of your love, he'll not hold you to blame for your brother's crimes."

The chamber door opened, and Broderick stepped inside.

Reggie instantly hopped up. "I'll leave you to speak with your brother," she said quietly.

Cleopatra carefully studied the other woman's retreating back. She lingered, her gaze touching briefly on Broderick. Wordlessly, he stepped aside, allowing Reggie to take her leave. Her fool brother's focus, however, remained fixed on Cleopatra.

Reggie shut the door, leaving them alone.

"How are you feeling?" he asked, coming over.

Like my heart is breaking and I'll never be happy again. Was I truly happy before Adair? "How is Stephen?" she countered. Since she'd returned home, and the truth of his actions these past months had come to light, he'd carefully avoided Cleopatra. Instead, by her sisters' accounts, he remained largely confined to his rooms, with a guard assigned him.

Broderick lingered at the doorway. "He's afraid to see you."

Conflict raged within. Had Stephen been born to a different station and a different lot, he *would* have been a child. But he'd been shaped by the ugliness of life, like all of them. "I'm his sister," she finally said. Of all the people to fear, Cleopatra should be the last of them.

Silently, Broderick reached behind him, pressing the handle.

Shuffling back and forth on his feet, Stephen directed his gaze to the floor. And in this instance, he'd the look of the child he, in fact, was.

"Stephen," she greeted in steady tones, wanting to rail at him, knowing it would accomplish nothing. No diatribe she rained down on him could ever restore all Adair had lost. *And all I lost, as well . . .*

Her youngest sibling reluctantly picked his head up.

Broderick motioned him forward, that single, wordless command as masterful on the always recalcitrant child as it was on all the most hardened thugs in the streets. Stephen came to a stop beside him.

"Why?" she implored. "Why would you do this?"

"I—I did not think you would b-be angry if you found out." He spoke so faintly, Cleopatra leaned forward in a bid to hear. "They are the enemy."

They are the enemy.

Cleopatra sank back.

Four words Diggory had uttered countless times to all of them, passing down the torch of his hatred, keeping that flame burning strong. Cleopatra herself had been as guilty of hating sight unseen, knowing nothing really about Adair or his brothers. She looked hope-lessly at her brother.

"We are not arsonists or murderers, Stephen." Broderick's harsh chastisement set the boy's lips to trembling.

"I didn't want anyone to die."

Which by the miracle of God himself, no one had. But others had been burned in the first blaze set by him, and cherished businesses had been lost.

Cleopatra turned her palms up. "Then tell me why. Make me understand—"

"Because I didn't want you to go there," Stephen cried out. "I wanted you to stay here with me . . . with us."

Her heart cracked.

"And you knew if the truce were broken, that Ryker Black would force me to return," she breathed.

Her youngest brother nodded once.

Over the top of his bent head, Cleopatra and Broderick exchanged looks.

"It's all your fault," Stephen snarled at Broderick, and then favoring him with a dark glare, he raced from the room, slamming the door in his wake.

Broderick dusted a tired hand over his face. "Black and his brothers came by a short while ago."

She froze. His brothers. Adair. Adair had come. Did he wonder after her? Wish to see her? Or had it all been about exacting payment? "Wh-what will happen to him?"

Her brother grabbed the chair vacated a short while ago by Reggie and pulled it closer to the bed. "Black asked if I was capable of watch-ing after him to see that he doesn't carry out the same acts." Again. "I assured him I would," he said, after he'd sat.

Her heart thudded wildly as she silently screamed for him to continue.

"They promised not to pursue criminal charges."

"What?" she whispered.

Stretching his legs out before him, Broderick shrugged. "It would seem Adair Thorne convinced them that the child should not be punished, but mentored."

If it was possible, her heart filled to overflowing with her love for him.

"I'm not marrying a lord," she said without preamble, wanting her piece said. He froze. She loved her brother, would always love him, and understood the hunger for security, but she now knew it could not come at the cost of her, or any of her siblings', happiness. "I don't want to marry anyone."

Broderick lowered his eyebrows. "You don't want to marry anyone?"

No, that wasn't altogether accurate, either. "I love him. I love Adair Thorne, and I don't care about the security, wealth, or connections that would come in marrying a lord." When at one time nothing had seemed more vital. "I'll not wed when my heart belongs to another."

Her profession was met with a blanket of silence. Broderick drummed his fingertips on the scalloped arms of his seat. "Adair Thorne of the Hell and Sin?"

She nodded. "I don't believe there is another Adair Thorne, is there?" she asked in a bid for levity.

He abruptly stopped his incessant tapping. "He's not who I imagined as a husband for you," he said drily.

No, with his lack of noble connections, Adair wouldn't have been, but she loved him for who he was. "He is a good man, Broderick."

"We may beg to differ there," he muttered under his breath.

"Our brother burned his club down, and he forgave him. Convinced his brothers to do the same," she said directly. "I don't know a better man."

Broderick sighed. "I only wanted you with the best."

And to him, a link to the peerage defined that. "I'm tired, Broderick," she said wearily, lying back down.

"Of course." He shoved to his feet, pausing when he reached the doorway. "You're certain you love him?" he tried again. "Because I believe—"

"I love him, Broderick."

Mumbling, he gave his head a shake.

"And Broderick," she called, when he'd opened the heavy panel.

He glanced back.

"Someday you'll understand something of it, too."

Broderick snorted. "I assure you that will certainly never be a concern there. You're certain about—"

"I said, I'm certain." Cleopatra pointed to the doorway.

Sighing, he let himself out.

Cleopatra lay there, grateful for the click of the door signaling the parade of visitors was at an end. She didn't want any more questions about her time with Adair or discussions about the fire that had ruined his club. And her heart. She didn't want to talk about how her heart was aching anymore.

A firm knock on the door ended the all-too-brief solitude.

Damning her brother's tenacity, she shouted. "I said I'm . . . certain, Broderick. I—" Her words died quickly as the door opened and a tall, beloved silhouette filled the entrance. "Adair," she whispered, blinking slowly, certain she'd conjured him of her own greatest desires.

"Cleopatra," he returned in his low, mellifluous baritone.

She drank in the sight of him as he came over. Immaculately clad in a midnight jacket and breeches, he exuded power and beauty. How was it possible to so miss a person after just a single day apart? "How did you get in here?" She glanced to the window.

He chuckled. "No scaling involved. Your brother allowed me to see you."

Broderick had? Trying to make sense of that incongruity, Cleopatra struggled up onto her elbows. "Why are you here?" she asked quietly.

Quirking his lips in the corner, he perched himself at the edge of her mattress. "And where should I be, Miss Killoran?" He brushed his knuckles over her cheek in that familiar, tender caress.

Then the horror of the past twenty-four hours slashed into the stolen moment of joy in seeing him again. "Your club." As soon as the words slipped out, she flinched. "I didn't mean . . . what I'd intended to say . . ." She looked at him squarely. "I am so sorry about your club, Adair." How inadequate that apology was when he'd lost what mattered most. "All the hours you toiled over that building, and my b-brother destroyed it a-all." Her voice cracked again.

Adair let his hand fall to the bed. "Do you know the interesting thing about my club, Cleopatra?"

His ruined club. She shook her head.

"All these years, my siblings and I placed the Hell and Sin above all else. Nothing and no one superseded the club in importance." He smiled wryly. "Then my sister married, and then Ryker, and Niall, and eventually Calum. I resented them," he admitted. His gaze traveled over to the wide windows across the room. "I could not understand how they could forget all the effort and struggle and strife that went into building it . . . for a person."

Cleopatra bit down hard on her lower lip. Unable to meet his eyes, she studied her coverlet.

"Until you."

That husky murmur brought her head shooting up. She touched a hand to her chest.

He nodded. "The Hell and Sin can be replaced." Adair shifted closer until their thighs brushed. He paused, lingering his stare on her bandaged lower leg. His face contorted in a paroxysm of agony. "But you, Cleopatra, cannot." Emotion hoarsened his voice. "When I learned you were there, in that building, I didn't think about the money I'd stolen as a boy to purchase it. I didn't think about the first patrons who'd stepped through the doors or the money lost." He cupped her face in his hands, and she struggled to see him through the tears clouding her vision. Those drops fell fast and furiously down her cheeks, and he brushed each drop away. Another only replaced it. "I thought about you. I thought about marrying you, and having children with you. I love you, Cleopatra."

She ached to take the gift he stretched out before her. It was all she'd never known she wanted, and now the only thing she desperately needed. Still, reality held her back. "What will you do now—"

"What will we do now?" he amended, and her heart quickened.

We. A marriage where he'd never seek to change her into someone she was not, or would ever be. A union that was a true partnership.

Adair drew himself closer and dropped his brow against hers. "You were correct. I've been straddling two worlds, committing to neither . . . and part of that has been fear to leave the only streets I've ever known." He spoke with an animation that stirred an equal excitement within her. "I thought of a club, the way you described, in the fashionable end of London, safe streets where our children will know greater security than either of us did."

A tantalizing image stirred—of a future with him . . . and babes: a gift she'd not allowed herself even to dream of. Now she let the possibilities sweep through her, filling every corner of her being with a healing warmth. "Babies," she repeated, her voice hoarse. Not children forced to murder, steal, and beg, but cherished ones who'd be nurtured and loved by her and Adair.

He caressed her cheek. "Brave, clever, beautiful girls like their mama."

Tears pricked behind her lashes. At one time, she would have viewed those as tokens of weakness. No more. Adair had shown her there was no shame to be found in feeling. "And boys. Honorable, good, and handsome like their da."

"A compromise?" Adair pressed his brow to hers, an easy smile on his lips. "We'll have both."

A half laugh, half sob escaped her. "Agreed."

He caught a lone teardrop with the pad of his thumb.

His grin dipped as a somberness settled within his rugged features.

"What is it?" she asked hesitantly, not wanting anything to intrude on the future he'd so beautifully painted of their lives together.

"I'll not have them live as we did. Not in St. Giles or the Dials, but a place where we might have apartments within or a townhouse nearby if you want that, because whatever you want is yours."

Cleopatra cupped him about his nape and angled her lips up toward his. "You still don't know?" she whispered against his mouth. How could he *not* know?

He shook his head once.

"I love you, Adair Thorne. *You* are all I ever want, Adair Thorne. You are all I want."

And as he kissed her, Cleopatra smiled, eager for their future—together.

Acknowledgments

Writing a book is just the first part of the publishing journey. There is so, so much more that goes into a story, from its inception to the final product that lands in readers' hands. From the multiple rounds of developmental edits and then copyedits to the cover creation and marketing plan, it requires a team.

I'm so very fortunate to, in Montlake Romance, have the most amazing one an author could have ever hoped for.

About the Author

Photo © 2016 Kimberly Rocha

USA Today bestselling author Christi Caldwell blames novelist Judith McNaught for luring her into the world of historical romance. When Christi was at the University of Connecticut, she began writing her own tales of love—ones where even the most perfect heroes and heroines had imperfections. She learned to enjoy torturing her couples before they earned their well-deserved happily ever after.

Christi lives in Southern Connecticut, where she spends her time writing, chasing after her son, and taking care of her twin princesses-in-training. Fans who want to keep up with the latest news and information can sign up for Christi's newsletter at www.ChristiCaldwell.com or follow her on Facebook (AuthorChristiCaldwell) or Twitter (@ChristiCaldwell).